SHE HALTED A FEW PACES OFF

—*Maruja*

DRIFT FROM TWO SHORES
MARUJA
BY SHORE AND SEDGE
THANKFUL BLOSSOM

BY

BRET HARTE

ILLUSTRATED

VIGILANS ET AUDAX

P. F. COLLIER & SON
NEW YORK

CONTENTS

1

MARUJA

CHAPTER I

MORNING was breaking on the high road to San José. The long lines of dusty, level track were beginning to extend their vanishing point in the growing light; on either side the awakening fields of wheat and oats were stretching out and broadening to the sky. In the east and south the stars were receding before the coming day; in the west a few still glimmered, caught among the bosky hills of the cañada del Raimundo, where night seemed to linger. Thither some obscure, low-flying birds were slowly winging; thither a gray coyote, overtaken by the morning, was awkwardly limping. And thither a tramping wayfarer turned, plowing through the dust of the highway still unslaked by the dewless night, to climb the fence and likewise seek the distant cover.

For some moments man and beast kept an equal pace and gait with a strange similarity of appearance and expression; the coyote bearing that resemblance to his more civilized and harmless congener, the dog, which the tramp bore to the ordinary pedestrians, but both exhibiting the same characteristics of lazy vagabondage and semi-lawlessness; the coyote's slouching amble and uneasy stealthiness being repeated in the tramp's shuffling step and sidelong glances. Both were young, and physically vigorous, but both displayed the same vacillating and awkward disinclination to direct effort. They continued thus half a mile apart unconscious of each other, until the superior faculties of the brute warned him of the contiguity of aggressive civilization, and he cantered off suddenly to the right, fully five minutes before the barking of dogs caused the man to make a detour to the left to avoid entrance upon a cultivated domain that lay before him.

The trail he took led to one of the scant water-courses that issued, half spent, from the cañada, to fade out utterly on the hot June plain. It was thickly bordered with willows and alders, that made an arbored and feasible path through the dense woods and undergrowth. He continued along it as if aimlessly; stopping from time to time to look at different objects in a dull mechanical fashion, as if rather to prolong his useless hours, than from any curious instinct, and to occasionally dip in the unfrequent pools of water the few crusts of bread he had taken from his pocket. Even this appeared to be suggested more by coincidence of material in the bread and water, than from the promptings of hunger. At last he reached a cup-like hollow in the hills lined with wild clover and thick with resinous odors. Here he crept under a manzanita-bush and disposed himself to sleep. The act showed he was already familiar with the local habits of his class, who used the unfailing dry starlit nights for their wanderings, and spent the hours of glaring sunshine asleep or resting in some wayside shadow.

Meanwhile the light quickened, and gradually disclosed the form and outline of the adjacent domain. An avenue cut through a park-like wood, carefully cleared of the undergrowth of gigantic ferns peculiar to the locality, led to the entrance of the cañada. Here began a vast terrace of lawn, broken up by enormous bouquets of flower-beds bewildering in color and profusion, from which again rose the flowering vines and trailing shrubs that hid pillars, veranda, and even the long façade of a great and dominant mansion. But the delicacy of floral outlines running to the capitals of columns and at times mounting to the pediment of the roof, the opulence of flashing color or the massing of tropical foliage, could not deprive it of the imperious dignity of size and space. Much of this was due to the fact that the original casa—an adobe house of no mean pretensions, dating back to the early Spanish occupation—had been kept intact, sheathed in a shell of dark-red wood, and still retaining its patio, or inner court-yard, surrounded by low galleries, while additions, greater in extent than the main building, had been erected—not as wings and projections, but massed upon it on either side, changing its rigid square outlines to a vague parallelogram. While the patio retained the Spanish conception of al fresco seclusion, a vast colonnade of veranda on the southern side was a concession to American taste, and its breadth gave that depth of shadow to the inner rooms which had been lost in the thinner shell of the new erection. Its cloistered gloom was lightened by the red fires of cardinal flowers dropping from the roof, by the yellow sunshine of the jessamine creeping up the columns, by billows of heliotropes breaking over its base as a purple sea. Nowhere else did the opulence of this climate of blossoms show itself as vividly. Even the Castilian roses, that grew as vines along the east front, the fuchsias, that attained the dignity of trees, in the patio, or the four or five monster passion-vines that bestarred the low western wall, and told over and over again their mystic story—paled before the sensuous glory of the south veranda.

As the sun arose, that part of the quiet house first touched by its light seemed to waken. A few lounging peons and servants made their appearance at the entrance of the patio, occasionally reinforced by an earlier life from the gardens and stables. But the south façade of the building had not apparently gone to bed at all: lights were still burning dimly in the large ball-room; a tray with glasses stood upon the veranda near one of the open French windows, and further on, a half-shut yellow fan lay like a fallen leaf. The sound of carriage-wheels on the gravel terrace brought with it voices and laughter and the swiftly passing vision of a char-à-bancs filled with muffled figures bending low to avoid the direct advances of the sun.

As the carriage rolled away, four men lounged out of a window on the veranda, shading their eyes against the level beams. One was still in evening dress, and one in the uniform of a captain of artillery; the others had already changed their gala attire, the elder of the party having assumed those extravagant tweeds which the tourist from Great Britain usually offers as a gentle concession to inferior yet more florid civilization. Nevertheless, he beamed back heartily on the sun, and remarked, in a pleasant

Scotch accent, that: Did they know it was very extraordinary how clear the morning was, so free from clouds and
mist and fog? The young man in evening dress fluently
agreed to the facts, and suggested, in idiomatic French-
English, that one comprehended that the bed was an insult
to one's higher nature and an ingratitude to their gracious
hostess, who had spread out this lovely garden and walks
for their pleasure; that nothing was more beautiful than
the dew sparkling on the rose, or the matin song of the
little birds.

The other young man here felt called upon to point out
the fact that there was no dew in California, and that the
birds did not sing in that part of the country. The foreign young gentleman received this statement with pain
and astonishment as to the fact, with passionate remorse as
to his own ignorance. But still, as it was a charming day,
would not his gallant friend, the Captain here, accept the
challenge of the brave Englishman, and "walk him" for
the glory of his flag and a thousand pounds?

The gallant Captain, unfortunately, believed that if he
walked out in his uniform he would suffer some delay from
being interrogated by wayfarers as to the locality of the
circus he would be pleasantly supposed to represent, even
if he escaped being shot as a rare California bird by the
foreign sporting contingent. In these circumstances, he
would simply lounge around the house until his carriage
was ready.

Much as it pained him to withdraw from such amusing
companions, the foreign young gentleman here felt that he,
too, would retire for the present to change his garments,
and glided back through the window at the same moment
that the young officer carelessly stepped from the veranda
and lounged towards the shrubbery.

"They've been watching each other for the last hour. I
wonder what's up?" said the young man who remained.

The remark, without being confidential, was so clearly
the first sentence of natural conversation that the Scotchman, although relieved, said, "Eh, man?" a little
cautiously.

"It's as clear as this sunshine that Captain Carroll and

Garnier are each particularly anxious to know what the other is doing or intends to do this morning."

"Why did they separate, then?" asked the other.

"That's a mere blind. Garnier's looking through his window now at Carroll, and Carroll is aware of it."

"Eh!" said the Scotchman, with good-humored curiosity. "Is it a quarrel? Nothing serious, I hope. No revolvers and bowie-knives, man, before breakfast, eh?"

"No," laughed the younger man. "No! To do Maruja justice, she generally makes a fellow too preposterous to fight. I see you don't understand. You're a stranger; I'm an old habitué of the house—let me explain. Both of these men are in love with Maruja; or, worse than that, they firmly believe her to be in love with *them*."

"But Miss Maruja is the eldest daughter of our hostess, is she not?" said the Scotchman; "and I understood from one of the young ladies that the Captain had come down from the Fort particularly to pay court to Miss Amita, the beauty."

"Possibly. But that wouldn't prevent Maruja from flirting with him."

"Eh! but are you not mistaken, Mr. Raymond? Certainly a more quiet, modest, and demure young lassie I never met."

"That's because she sat out two waltzes with you, and let you do the talking, while she simply listened."

The elder man's fresh color for an instant heightened, but he recovered himself with a good-humored laugh. "Likely—likely. She's a capital good listener."

"You're not the first man that found her eloquent. Stanton, your banking friend, who never talks of anything but mines and stocks, says she's the only woman who has any conversation; and we can all swear that she never said two words to him the whole time she sat next to him at dinner. But she *looked* at him as if she had. Why, man, woman, and child all give her credit for any grace that pleases themselves. And why? Because she's clever enough not to practice any one of them—as graces. I don't know the girl that claims less and gets more. For instance, you don't call her pretty?" ․ ․ ․

"Wait a bit. Ye'll not get on so fast, my young friend; I'm not prepared to say that she's not," returned the Scotchman, with good-humored yet serious caution.

"But you would have been prepared yesterday, and have said it. She can produce the effect of the prettiest girl here, and without challenging comparison. Nobody thinks of her—everybody experiences her."

"You're an enthusiast, Mr. Raymond. As an habitué of the house, of course, you—"

"Oh, my time came with the rest," laughed the young man, with unaffected frankness. "It's about two years ago now."

"I see—you were not a marrying man."

"Pardon me—it was because I was."

The Scotchman looked at him curiously.

"Maruja is an heiress. I am a mining engineer."

"But, my dear fellow, I thought that in your country—"

"In *my* country, yes. But we are standing on a bit of old Spain. This land was given to Doña Maria Saltonstall's ancestors by Charles V. Look around you. This veranda, this larger shell of the ancient casa, is the work of the old Salem whaling captain that she married, and is all that is American here. But the heart of the house, as well as the life that circles around the old patio, is Spanish. The Doña's family, the Estudillos and Guitierrez, always looked down upon this alliance with the Yankee captain, though it brought improvement to the land, and increased its value forty-fold, and since his death ever opposed any further foreign intervention. Not that that would weigh much with Maruja if she took a fancy to any one; Spanish as she is throughout, in thought and grace and feature, there is enough of the old Salem witches' blood in her to defy law and authority in following an unhallowed worship. There are no sons; she is the sole heiress of the house and estate—though, according to the native custom, her sisters will be separately portioned from the other property, which is very large."

"Then the Captain might still make a pretty penny on Amita," said the Scotchman."

"If he did not risk and lose it all on Maruja. There is

enough of the old Spanish jealousy in the blood to make even the gentle Amita never forgive his momentary defection."

Something in his manner made the Scotchman think that Raymond spoke from baleful experience. How else could this attractive young fellow, educated abroad and a rising man in his profession, have failed to profit by his contiguity to such advantages, and the fact of his being an evident favorite?

"But with this opposition on the part of the relatives to any further alliances with your countrymen, why does our hostess expose her daughters to their fascinating influence?" said the elder man, glancing at his companion. "The girls seem to have the usual American freedom."

"Perhaps they are therefore the less likely to give it up to the first man who asks them. But the Spanish duenna still survives in the family—the more awful because invisible. It's a mysterious fact that as soon as a fellow becomes particularly attached to any one—except Maruja—he receives some intimation from Pereo."

"What! the butler? That Indian-looking fellow? A servant?"

"Pardon me—the mayordomo. The old confidential servitor who stands in *loco parentis*. No one knows what he says. If the victim appeals to the mistress, she is indisposed; you know she has such bad health. If in his madness he makes a confidante of Maruja, that finishes him."

"How?"

"Why, he ends by transferring his young affections to her—with the usual result."

"Then you don't think our friend the Captain has had this confidential butler ask his intentions yet?"

"I don't think it will be necessary," said the other, dryly.

"Umph! Meantime, the Captain has just vanished through yon shrubbery. I suppose that's the end of the mysterious espionage you have discovered. No! De'il take it! but there's that Frenchman popping out of the myrtle-bush. How did the fellow get there? And, bless me! here's our lassie, too!"

"Yes!" said Raymond, in a changed voice, "It's Maruja!"

She had approached so noiselessly along the bank that bordered the veranda, gliding from pillar to pillar as she paused before each to search for some particular flower, that both men felt an uneasy consciousness. But she betrayed no indication of their presence by look or gesture. So absorbed and abstracted she seemed that, by a common instinct, they both drew nearer the window, and silently waited for her to pass or recognize them.

She halted a few paces off to fasten a flower in her girdle. A small youthful figure, in a pale yellow dress, lacking even the maturity of womanly outline. The full oval of her face, the straight line of her back, a slight boyishness in the contour of her hips, the infantine smallness of her sandaled feet and narrow hands, were all suggestive of fresh, innocent, amiable youth—and nothing more.

Forgetting himself, the elder man mischievously crushed his companion against the wall in mock virtuous indignation. "Eh, sir," he whispered, with an accent that broadened with his feelings. "Eh, but look at the puir wee lassie! Will ye no be ashamed o' yerself for putting the tricks of a Circe on sic a honest gentle bairn? Why, man, you'll be seein' the sign of a limb of Satan in a bit thing with the mother's milk not yet out of her! She a flirt, speerin' at men, with that modest downcast air? I'm ashamed of ye, Mister Raymond. She's only thinking of her breakfast, puir thing, and not of yon callant. Another sacrilegious word and I'll expose you to her. Have ye no pity on youth and innocence?"

"Let me up," groaned Raymond, feebly, "and I'll tell you how old she is. Hush—she's looking."

The two men straightened themselves. She had, indeed, lifted her eyes towards the window. They were beautiful eyes, and charged with something more than their own beauty. With a deep brunette setting even to the darkened cornea, the pupils were blue as the sky above them. But they were lit with another intelligence. The soul of the Salem whaler looked out of the passion-darkened orbits of the mother, and was resistless.

She smiled recognition of the two men with sedate girl-ishness and a foreign inclination of the head over the flowers she was holding. Her straight, curveless mouth became suddenly charming with the parting of her lips over her white teeth, and left the impress of the smile in a lighting of the whole face even after it had passed. Then she moved away. At the same moment Garnier approached her.

"Come away, man, and have our walk," said the Scotch-man, seizing Raymond's arm. "We'll not spoil that fellow's sport."

"No; but she will, I fear. Look, Mr. Buchanan, if she hasn't given him her flowers to carry to the house while she waits here for the Captain!"

"Come away, scoffer!" said Buchanan, good-humoredly, locking his arm in the young man's and dragging him from the veranda towards the avenue, "and keep your observations for breakfast."

CHAPTER II

IN the mean time, the young officer, who had disappeared in the shrubbery, whether he had or had not been a spectator of the scene, exhibited some signs of agitation. He walked rapidly on, occasionally switching the air with a wand of willow, from which he had impatiently plucked the leaves, through an alley of ceanothus, until he reached a little thicket of evergreens, which seemed to oppose his further progress. Turning to one side, however, he quickly found an entrance to a labyrinthine walk, which led him at last to an open space and a rustic summer-house that stood beneath a gnarled and venerable pear-tree. The summer-house was a quaint stockade of dark madroño boughs thatched with red-wood bark, strongly suggestive of deeper woodland shadow. But in strange contrast, the floor, table, and benches were thickly strewn with faded rose-leaves, scattered as if in some riotous play of children. Captain Carroll brushed them aside hurriedly with his impatient foot, glanced around hastily, then threw himself on the rustic bench at full length and twisted his mustache be-

tween his nervous fingers. Then he rose as suddenly, with
a few white petals impaled on his gilded spurs and stepped
quickly into the open sunlight.

He must have been mistaken! Everything was quiet
around him, the far-off sound of wheels in the avenue came
faintly, but nothing more.

His eye fell upon the pear-tree, and even in his preoccupation he was struck with the signs of its extraordinary
age. Twisted out of all proportion, and knotted with excrescences, it was supported by iron bands and heavy stakes,
as if to prop up its senile decay. He tried to interest himself in the various initials and symbols deeply carved in
bark, now swollen and half obliterated. As he turned back
to the summer-house, he for the first time noticed that the
ground rose behind it into a long undulation, on the crest
of which the same singular profusion of rose-leaves were
scattered. It struck him as being strangely like a gigantic
grave, and that the same idea had occurred to the fantastic
dispenser of the withered flowers. He was still looking at
it, when a rustle in the undergrowth made his heart beat
expectantly. A slinking gray shadow crossed the undulation and disappeared in the thicket. It was a coyote. At
any other time the extraordinary appearance of this vivid
impersonation of the wilderness, so near a centre of human
civilization and habitation, would have filled him with wonder. But he had room for only a single thought now.
Would *she* come?

Five minutes passed. He no longer waited in the summer-house, but paced impatiently before the entrance to the
labyrinth. Another five minutes. He was deceived, undoubtedly. She and her sisters were probably waiting for
him and laughing at him on the lawn. He ground his heel
into the clover, and threw his switch into the thicket. Yet
he would give her *one*—only one moment more.

"Captain Carroll!"

The voice had been and was to *him* the sweetest in the
world; but even a stranger could not have resisted the spell
of its musical inflection. He turned quickly. She was advancing towards him from the summer-house.

"Did you think I was coming that way—where everybody

could follow me?" she laughed, softly. "No; I came through the thicket over there," indicating the direction with her flexible shoulder, "and nearly lost my slipper and my eyes—look!" She threw back the inseparable lace shawl from her blond head, and showed a spray of myrtle clinging like a broken wreath to her forehead. The young officer remained gazing at her silently.

"I like to hear you speak my name," he said, with a slight hesitation in his breath. "Say it again."

"Car-roll, Car-roll, Car-roll," she murmured gently to herself two or three times, as if enjoying her own native trilling of the r's. "It's a pretty name. It sounds like a song. Don Carroll, eh! El Capitan Don Carroll."

"But my first name is Henry," he said, faintly

"'Enry—that's not so good. Don Enrico will do. But El Capitan Carroll is best of all. I must have it always: El Capitan Carroll!"

"Always?" He colored like a boy.

"Why not?" He was confusedly trying to look through her brown lashes; she was parrying him with the steel of her father's glance. "Come! Well! Captain Carroll! It was not to tell me your name—that I knew already was pretty—Car-roll!" she murmured again, caressing him with her lashes; "it was not for this that you asked me to meet you face to face in this—cold"—she made a movement of drawing her lace over her shoulders—"cold daylight. That belonged to the lights and the dance and the music of last night. It is not for this you expect me to leave my guests, to run away from Monsieur Garnier, who pays compliments, but whose name is not pretty—from Mr. Raymond, who talks *of* me when he can't talk *to* me. They will say, This Captain Carroll could say all that before them."

"But if they knew," said the young officer, drawing closer to her with a paling face but brightening eyes, "if they knew I had anything else to say, Miss Saltonstall—something—pardon me—did I hurt your hand?—something for *her* alone—is there one of them that would have the right to object? Do not think me foolish, Miss Saltonstall—but—I beg—I implore you to tell me before I say more."

"Who would have a right?" said Maruja, withdrawing

her hand but not her dangerous eyes. "Who would dare forbid you talking to me of my sister? I have told you that Amita is free—as we all are."

Captain Carroll fell back a few steps and gazed at her with a troubled face. "It is possible that you have misunderstood, Miss Saltonstall?" he faltered. "Do you still think it is Amita that I"—he stopped and added passionately, "Do you remember what I told you?—have you forgotten last night?"

"Last night was—last night!" said Maruja, slightly lifting her shoulders. "One makes love at night—one marries in daylight. In the music, in the flowers, in the moonlight, one says everything; in the morning one has breakfast—when one is not asked to have councils of war with captains and commandantes. You would speak of my sister, Captain Car-roll—go on. Doña Amita Carroll sounds very, very pretty. I shall not object." She held out both her hands to him, threw her head back, and smiled.

He seized her hands passionately. "No, no! you shall hear me—you shall understand me. I love *you*, Maruja—you, and you alone. God knows I can not help it—God knows I would not help it if I could. Hear me. I will be calm. No one can hear us where we stand. I am not mad. I am not a traitor! I frankly admired your sister. I came here to see her. Beyond that, I swear to you, I am guiltless to her—to you. Even she knows no more of me than that. I saw you, Maruja. From that moment I have thought of nothing—dreamed of nothing else."

"That is—three, four, five days and one afternoon ago! You see, I remember. And now you want—what?"

"To let me love you, and you only. To let me be with you. To let me win you in time, as you should be won. I am not mad, though I am desperate. I know what is due to your station and mine—even while I dare to say I love you. Let me hope, Maruja, I only ask to hope."

She looked at him until she had absorbed all the burning fever of his eyes, until her ears tingled with his passionate voice, and then—she shook her head.

"It can not be, Carroll—no! never!"

He drew himself up under the blow with such simple and

manly dignity that her eyes dropped for the moment. "There is another, then?" he said, sadly.

"There is no one I care for better than you. No! Do not be foolish. Let me go. I tell you that because you can be nothing to me—you understand, to *me*. To my sister Amita, yes."

The young soldier raised his head coldly. "I have pressed you hard, Miss Saltonstall—too hard, I know, for a man who has already had his answer; but I did not deserve this. Good-by."

"Stop," she said, gently. "I meant not to hurt you, Captain Carroll. If I had, it is not thus I would have done. I need not have met you here. Would you have loved me the less if I had avoided this meeting?"

He could not reply. In the depths of his miserable heart, he knew that he would have loved her the same.

"Come," she said, laying her hand softly on his arm, "do not be angry with me for putting you back only five days to where you were when you first entered our house. Five days is not much of happiness or sorrow to forget, is it, Carroll—Captain Carroll?" Her voice died away in a faint sigh. "Do not be angry with me, if—knowing you could be nothing more—I wanted you to love my sister, and my sister to love you. We should have been good friends—such good friends."

"Why do you say, 'Knowing it could be nothing more'?" said Carroll, grasping her hand suddenly. "In the name of Heaven, tell me what you mean!"

"I mean I can not marry unless I marry one of my mother's race. That is my mother's wish, and the will of her relations. You are an American, not of Spanish blood."

"But surely this is not your determination?"

She shrugged her shoulders. "What would you? It is the determination of my people."

"But knowing this"—he stopped; the quick blood rose to his face.

"Go on, Captain Carroll. You would say, Knowing this, why did I not warn you? Why did I not say to you when we first met 'You have come to address my sister; do not fall in love with me—I can not marry a foreigner.'"

"You are cruel, Maruja. But, if that is all, surely this prejudice can be removed? Why, your mother married a foreigner—an American."

"Perhaps that is why," said the girl, quietly. She cast down her long lashes, and with the point of her satin slipper smoothed out the soft leaves of the clover at her feet. "Listen; shall I tell you the story of our house? Stop! some one is coming. Don't move; remain as you are. If you care for me, Carroll, collect yourself, and don't let that man think he has found *us* ridiculous." Her voice changed from its tone of slight caressing pleading to one of suppressed pride. *"He* will not laugh much, Captain Carroll; truly, no."

The figure of Garnier, bright, self-possessed, courteous, appeared at the opening of the labyrinth. Too well-bred to suggest, even in complimentary raillery, a possible sentimental situation, his politeness went further. It was so kind in them to guide an awkward stranger by their voices to the places where he could not stupidly intrude!

"You are just in time to interrupt or to hear a story that I have been threatening to tell," she said, composedly; "an old Spanish legend of this house. You are in the majority now, you two, and can stop me if you choose. Thank you. I warn you it is stupid; it isn't new; but it has the excuse of being suggested by this very spot." She cast a quick look of subtle meaning at Carroll, and throughout her recital appealed more directly to him, in a manner delicately yet sufficiently marked to partly soothe his troubled spirit.

"Far back, in the very old times, Caballeros," said Maruja, standing by the table in mock solemnity, and rapping upon it with her fan, "this place was the home of the coyote. Big and little, father and mother, Señor and Señora Coyotes, and the little muchacho coyotes had their home in the dark cañada, and came out over these fields, yellow with wild oats and red with poppies, to seek their prey. They were happy. For why? They were the first; they had no history, you comprehend, no tradition. They married as they liked" (with a glance at Carroll), "nobody objected; they increased and multiplied. But the plains were fertile; the game was plentiful; it was not fit that it should be for the beasts alone. And so, in the course of time, an Indian chief, a heathen, Koorotora, built his wigwam here."

"I beg your pardon," said Garnier, in apparent distress, "but I caught the gentleman's name imperfectly."

Fully aware that the questioner only wished to hear again her musical enunciation of the consonants, she repeated, "Koorotora," with an apologetic glance at Carroll, and went on. "This gentleman had no history or tradition to bother him, either; whatever Señor Coyote thought of the matter, he contented himself with robbing Señor Koorotora's wig- wam when he could, and skulking around the Indian's camp at night. The old chief prospered, and made many jour- neys round the country, but always kept his camp here. This lasted until the time when the holy Fathers came from the South, and Portala, as you have all read, uplifted the wooden Cross on the sea-coast over there, and left it for the heathens to wonder at. Koorotora saw it on one of his journeys, and came back to the cañada full of this wonder. Now, Koorotora had a wife."

"Ah, we shall commence now. We are at the beginning. This is better than Señora Coyota," said Garnier, cheerfully.

"Naturally, she was anxious to see the wonderful object. She saw it, and she saw the holy Fathers, and they con- verted her against the superstitious heathenish wishes of her husband. And more than that, they came here—"

"And converted the land also; is it not so? It was a lovely site for a mission," interpolated Garnier, politely.

"They built a mission and brought as many of Koo- rotora's people as they could into the sacred fold. They brought them in in a queer fashion sometimes, it is said; dragoons from the Presidio, Captain Carroll, lassoing them and bringing them in at the tails of their horses. All ex- cept Koorotora. He defied them; he cursed them and his wife in his wicked heathenish fashion, and said that they too should lose the mission through the treachery of some woman, and that the coyote should yet prowl through the ruined walls of the church. The holy Fathers pitied the wicked man—and built themselves a lovely garden. Look at that pear-tree! There is all that is left of it!"

She turned with a mock heroic gesture, and pointed her

fan to the pear-tree. Garnier lifted his hands in equally simulated wonder. A sudden recollection of the coyote of the morning recurred to Carroll uneasily. "And the Indians," he said, with an effort to shake off the feeling; "they, too, have vanished."

"All that remained of them is in yonder mound. It is the grave of the chief and his people. He never lived to see the fulfillment of his prophecy. For it was a year after his death that our ancestor, Manuel Guitierrez, came from old Spain to the Presidio with a grant of twenty leagues to settle where he chose. Doña Maria Guitierrez took a fancy to the cañada. But it was a site already in possession of the Holy Church. One night, through treachery, it was said, the guards were withdrawn and the Indians entered the mission, slaughtered the lay brethren, and drove away the priests. The Commandant at the Presidio retook the place from the heathens, but on representation to the Governor that it was indefensible for the peaceful Fathers without a large military guard, the official ordered the removal of the mission to Santa Cruz, and Don Manuel settled his twenty leagues grant in the cañada. Whether he or Doña Maria had anything to do with the Indian uprising, no one knows; but Father Pedro never forgave them. He is said to have declared at the foot of the altar that the curse of the Church was on the land, and that it should always pass into the hands of the stranger."

"And that was long ago, and the property is still in the family," said Carroll, hurriedly, answering Maruja's eyes.

"In the last hundred years there have been no male heirs," continued Maruja, still regarding Carroll. "When my mother, who was the eldest daughter, married Don José Saltonstall against the wishes of the family, it was said that the curse would fall. Sure enough, Caballeros, it was that year that the forged grants of Micheltorrena were discovered; and in our lawsuit your government, Captain, handed over ten leagues of the llano land to the Doctor West, our neighbor."

"Ah, the gray-headed gentleman who lunched here the other day? You are friends, then? You bear no malice?" said Garnier.

"What would you?" said Maruja, with a slight shrug of her shoulders. "He paid his money to the forger. Your corregidores upheld him, and said it was no forgery," she continued, to Carroll.

In spite of the implied reproach, Carroll felt relieved. He began to be impatient of Garnier's presence, and longed to renew his suit. Perhaps his face showed something of this, for Maruja added, with mock demureness, "It's always dreadful to be the eldest sister; but think what it is to be in the direct line of a curse! Now, there's Amita—*she's* free to do as she likes, with no family responsibility; while poor me!" She dropped her eyes, but not until they had again sought and half-reproved the brightening eyes of Carroll.

"But," said Garnier, with a sudden change from his easy security and courteous indifference to an almost harsh impatience, "you do not mean to say, Mademoiselle, that you have the least belief in this rubbish, this ridiculous canard?"

Maruja's straight mouth quickly tightened over her teeth. She shot a significant glance at Carroll, but instantly resumed her former manner.

"It matters little what a foolish girl like myself believes. The rest of the family, even the servants and children, all believe it. It is a part of their religion. Look at these flowers around the pear-tree, and scattered on that Indian mound. They regularly find their way there on saints' days and festas. *They* are not rubbish, Monsieur Garnier; they are propitiatory sacrifices. Pereo would believe that a temblor would swallow up the casa if we should ever forego these customary rites. Is it a mere absurdity that forced my father to build these modern additions around the heart of the old adobe house, leaving it untouched, so that the curse might not be fulfilled even by implication?"

She had assumed an air of such pretty earnestness and passion; her satin face was illuminated as by some softly sensuous light within more bewildering than mere color, that Garnier, all devoted eyes and courteous blandishment, broke out: "But this curse must fall harmlessly before the incarnation of blessing; Miss Saltonstall has no more to fear than the angels. She is the one predestined through her charm, through her goodness, to lift it forever."

Carroll could not have helped echoing the aspirations of his rival, had not the next words of his mistress thrilled him with superstitious terror.

"A thousand thanks, Señor. Who knows? But I shall have warning when it falls. A day or two before the awful invader arrives, a coyote suddenly appears in broad daylight, mysteriously, near the casa. This midnight marauder, now banished to the thickest cañon, comes again to prowl around the home of his ancestors. Caramba! Señor Captain, what are you staring at? You frighten me! Stop it, I say!"

She had turned upon him, stamping her little foot in quite a frightened, childlike way.

"Nothing," laughed Carroll, the quick blood returning to his cheek. "But you must not be angry with one for being quite carried away with your dramatic intensity. By Jove! I thought I could see the *whole* thing while you were speaking—the old Indian, the priest, and the coyote!" His eyes sparkled. The wild thought had occurred to him that perhaps, in spite of himself, he was the young woman's predestined fate; and in the very selfishness of his passion he smiled at the mere material loss of lands and prestige that would follow it. "Then the coyote has always preceded some change in the family fortunes?" he asked, boldly.

"On my mother's wedding-day," said Maruja, in a lower voice, "after the party had come from church to supper in the old casa, my father asked, 'What dog is that under the table?' When they lifted the cloth to look, a coyote rushed from the very midst of the guests and dashed out across the patio. No one knew how or when he entered."

"Heaven grant that we do not find he has eaten our breakfast!" said Garnier, gayly, "for I judge it is waiting us. I hear your sister's voice among the others crossing the lawn. Shall we tear ourselves away from the tombs of our ancestors, and join them?"

"Not as I am looking now, thank you," said Maruja, throwing the lace over her head. "I shall not submit myself to a comparison of their fresher faces and toilets by you two gentlemen. Go you both and join them. I shall wait and say an *Ave* for the soul of Koorotora, and slip back alone the way I came."

She had steadily evaded the pleading glance of Carroll, and though her bright face and unblemished toilet showed the inefficiency of her excuse, it was evident that her wish to be alone was genuine and without coquetry. They could only lift their hats and turn regretfully away.

As the red cap of the young officer disappeared amidst the evergreen foliage, the young woman uttered a faint sigh, which she repeated a moment after as a slight nervous yawn. Then she opened and shut her fan once or twice, striking the sticks against her little pale palm, and then, gathering the lace under her oval chin with one hand, and catching her fan and skirt with the other, bent her head and dipped into the bushes. She came out on the other side near a low fence, that separated the park from a narrow lane which communicated with the high road beyond. As she neared the fence, a slinking figure limped along the lane before her. It was the tramp of the early morning.

They raised their heads at the same moment and their eyes met. The tramp, in that clearer light, showed a spare, but bent figure, roughly clad in a miner's shirt and canvas trousers, splashed and streaked with soil, and half hidden in a ragged blue cast-off army overcoat lazily hanging from one shoulder. His thin sun-burnt face was not without a certain sullen, suspicious intelligence, and a look of half-sneering defiance. He stopped, as a startled, surly animal might have stopped at some unusual object, but did not exhibit any other discomposure. Maruja stopped at the same moment on her side of the fence.

The tramp looked at her deliberately, and then slowly lowered his eyes. "I'm looking for the San José road, hereabouts. Ye don't happen to know it?" he said, addressing himself to the top of the fence.

It had been said that it was not Maruja's way to encounter man, woman, or child, old or young, without an attempt at subjugation. Strong in her power and salient with fascination, she leaned gently over the fence, and with the fan raised to her delicate ear, made him repeat his ques-

tion under the soft fire of her fringed eyes. He did so,
but incompletely, and with querulous laziness.

"Lookin'—for—San José road—here'bouts."

"The road to San José," said Maruja, with gentle slow-
ness, as if not unwilling to protract the conversation, "is
about two miles from here. It is the high road to the left
fronting the plain. There is another way, if—"

"Don't want it! Mornin'."

He dropped his head suddenly forward, and limped away
in the sunlight.

CHAPTER III

BREAKFAST, usually a movable feast at La Mision Perdida,
had been prolonged until past midday; the last of the
dance guests had flown, and the home party—with the exception of Captain Carroll, who had returned to duty at
his distant post—were dispersing; some as riding cavalcades
to neighboring points of interest; some to visit certain
notable mansions which the wealth of a rapid civilization
had erected in that fertile valley. One of these in particular, the work of a breathless millionaire, was famous
for the spontaneity of its growth and the reckless extravagance of its appointments.

"If you go to Aladdin's Palace," said Maruja, from the
top step of the south porch, to a wagonette of guests, "after
you've seen the stables with mahogany fittings for one hundred horses, ask Aladdin to show you the enchanted chamber,
inlaid with California woods and paved with gold quartz."

"We would have a better chance if the Princess of China
would only go with us," pleaded Garnier, gallantly.

"The Princess will stay at home with her mother, like a
good girl," returned Maruja, demurely.

"A bad shot of Garnier's this time," whispered Raymond
to Buchanan, as the vehicle rolled away with them. "The
Princess is not likely to visit Aladdin again."

"Why?"

"The last time she was there, Aladdin was a little too
Persian in his extravagance: offered her his house, stables,
and himself."

"Not a bad catch—why, he's worth two millions, I hear."

"Yes; but his wife is as extravagant as himself."

"His *wife*, eh? Ah, are you serious; or must you say something derogatory of the lassie's admirers too?" said Buchanan, playfully threatening him with his cane. "Another word, and I'll throw you from the wagon."

After their departure, the outer shell of the great house fell into a profound silence, so hollow and deserted that one might have thought the curse of Koorotora had already descended upon it. Dead leaves of roses and fallen blossoms from the long line of vine-wreathed columns lay thick on the empty stretch of brown veranda, or rustled and crept against the sides of the house, where the regular breath of the afternoon "trades" began to arise. A few cardinal flowers fell like drops of blood before the open windows of the vacant ball-room, in which the step of a solitary servant echoed faintly. It was Maruja's maid, bringing a note to her young mistress, who, in a flounced morning dress, leaned against the window. Maruja took it, glanced at it quietly, folded it in a long fold, and put it openly in her belt. Captain Carroll, from whom it came, might have carried one of his despatches as methodically. The waiting-woman noticed the act, and was moved to suggest some more exciting confidences.

"The Doña Maruja has, without doubt, noticed the bouquet on her dressing-room table from the Señor Garnier?"

The Doña Maruja had. The Doña Maruja had also learned with pain that, bribed by Judas-like coin, Faquita had betrayed the secrets of her wardrobe to the extent of furnishing a ribbon from a certain yellow dress to the Señor Buchanan to match with a Chinese fan. This was intolerable!

Faquita writhed in remorse, and averred that through this solitary act she had dishonored her family.

The Doña Maruja, however, since it was so, felt that the only thing left to do was to give her the polluted dress, and trust that the Devil might not fly away with her.

Leaving the perfectly consoled Faquita, Maruja crossed the large hall, and, opening a small door, entered a dark passage through the thick adobe wall of the old casa, and ap-

parently left the present century behind her. A peaceful
atmosphere of the past surrounded her not only in the low
vaulted halls terminating in grilles or barred windows; not
only in the square chambers whose dark rich but scanty
furniture was only a foil to the central elegance of the lace-
bordered bed and pillows; but in a certain mysterious odor
of dried and desiccated religious respectability that penetrated everywhere, and made the grateful twilight redolent
of the generations of forgotten Guitierrez who had quietly
exhaled in the old house. A mist as of incense and flowers
that had lost their first bloom veiled the vista of the long
corridor, and made the staring blue sky, seen through narrow windows and loopholes, glitter like mirrors let into the
walls. The chamber assigned to the young ladies seemed half
oratory and half sleeping-room, with a strange mingling of
the convent in the bare white walls, hung only with cruci-
fixes and religious emblems, and of the seraglio in the
glimpses of lazy figures, reclining in the deshabille of short
silken saya, low camisa, and dropping slippers. In a broad
angle of the corridor giving upon the patio, its balustrade
hung with brightly colored serapes and shawls, surrounded
by voluble domestics and relations, the mistress of the casa
half reclined in a hammock and gave her noonday audience.

Maruja pushed her way through the clustered stools and
cushions to her mother's side, kissed her on the forehead,
and then lightly perched herself like a white dove on the
railing. Mrs. Saltonstall, a dark, corpulent woman, re-
deemed only from coarseness by a certain softness of expression and refinement of gesture, raised her heavy brown
eyes to her daughter's face.

"You have not been to bed, Mara?"

"No, dear. Do I look it?"

"You must lie down presently. They tell me that Captain Carroll returned suddenly this morning."

"Do you care?"

"Who knows? Amita does not seem to fancy José,
Estéban, Jorge, or any of her cousins. She won't look at
Juan Estudillo. The Captain is not bad. He is of the
government. He is—"

"Not more than ten leagues from here," said Maruja,

playing with the Captain's note in her belt. "You can send for him, dear little mother. He will be glad."

"You will ever talk lightly—like your father! She was not then grieved—our Amita—eh?"

"She and Dorotea and the two Wilsons went off with Raymond and your Scotch friend in the wagonette. She did not cry—to Raymond."

"Good," said Mrs. Saltonstall, leaning back in her hammock. "Raymond is an old friend. You had better take your siesta now, child, to be bright for dinner. I expect a visitor this afternoon—Dr. West."

"Again! What will Pereo say, little mother?"

"Pereo," said the widow, sitting up again in her hammock, with impatience, "Pereo is becoming intolerable. The man is as mad as Don Quixote; it is impossible to conceal his eccentric impertinence and interference from strangers, who can not understand his confidential position in our house or his long service. There are no more mayordomos, child. The Vallejos, the Briones, the Castros, do without them now. Dr. West says, wisely, they are ridiculous survivals of the patriarchal system."

"And can be replaced by intelligent strangers," interrupted Maruja, demurely.

"The more easily if the patriarchal system has not been able to preserve the respect due from children to parents. No, Maruja! No; I am offended. Do not touch me! And your hair is coming down, and your eyes have rings like owls. You uphold this fanatical Pereo because he leaves *you* alone and stalks your poor sisters and their escorts like the Indian, whose blood is in his veins. The saints only can tell if he did not disgust this Captain Carroll into flight. He believes himself the sole custodian of the honor of our family—that he has a sacred mission from this Don Fulano of Koorotora to avert its fate. Without doubt he keeps up his delusions with aguardiente, and passes for a prophet among the silly peons and servants. He frightens the children with his ridiculous stories, and teaches them to decorate that heathen mound as if it were a shrine of Our Lady of Sorrows. He was almost rude to Dr. West yesterday."

"But you have encouraged him in his confidential position here," said Maruja. "You forget, my mother, how you got him to 'dueña' Enriqueta with the Colonel Brown; how you let him frighten the young Englishman who was too attentive to Dorotea; how you set him even upon poor Raymond, and failed so dismally that I had to take him myself in hand."

"But if I choose to charge him with explanations that I can not make myself without derogating from the time-honored hospitality of the casa, that is another thing. It is not," said Doña Maria, with a certain massive dignity, that, inconsistent as it was with the weakness of her argument, was not without impressiveness, "it is not yet, Blessed Santa Maria, that we are obliged to take notice ourself of the pretensions of every guest beneath our roof like the match-making, daughter-selling English and Americans. And *then* Pereo had tact and discrimination. Now he is mad! There are strangers and strangers. The whole valley is full of them—one can discriminate, since the old families year by year are growing less."

"Surely not," said Maruja, innocently. "There is the excellent Ramierrez, who has lately almost taken him a wife from the singing-hall in San Francisco; he may yet be snatched from the fire. There is the youthful José Castro, the sole padroño of our national bull-fight at Soquel, the famous horse-breaker, and the winner of I know not how many races. And have we not Vincente Peralta, who will run, it is said, for the American Congress. He can read and write—truly I have a letter from him here." She turned back the folded slip of Captain Carroll's note and discovered another below.

Mrs. Saltonstall tapped her daughter's hand with her fan. "You jest at them, yet you uphold Pereo! Go, now, and sleep yourself into a better frame of mind. Stop! I hear the Doctor's horse. Run and see that Pereo receives him properly."

Maruja had barely entered the dark corridor when she came upon the visitor,—a gray, hard-featured man of sixty, —who had evidently entered without ceremony. "I see you did not wait to be announced," she said, sweetly. "My mother will be flattered by your impatience. You will find her in the patio."

"Pereo did not announce me, as he was probably still under the effect of the aguardiente he swallowed yesterday," said the Doctor, dryly. "I met him outside the tienda on the highway the other night, talking to a pair of cut-throats that I would shoot on sight."

"The mayordomo has many purchases to make, and must meet a great many people," said Maruju. "What would you? We can not select *his* acquaintances; we can hardly choose our own," she added, sweetly.

The Doctor hesitated, as if to reply, and then, with a grim "Good-morning," passed on towards the patio. Maruja did not follow him. Her attention was suddenly absorbed by a hitherto unnoticed motionless figure, that seemed to be hiding in the shadow of an angle of the passage, as if waiting for her to pass. The keen eyes of the daughter of Joseph Saltonstall were not deceived. She walked directly towards the figure, and said, sharply, "Pereo!"

The figure came hesitatingly forward into the light of the grated window. It was that of an old man, still tall and erect, though the hair had disappeared from his temples, and hung in two or three straight, long dark elf-locks on his neck. His face, over which one of the bars threw a sinister shadow, was the yellow of a dried tobacco-leaf, and veined as strongly. His garb was a strange mingling of the vaquero and the ecclesiastic—velvet trousers, open from the knee down, and fringed with bullion buttons; a broad red sash around his waist, partly hidden by a long, straight chaqueta; with a circular sacerdotal cape of black broadcloth slipped over his head through a slit-like opening braided with gold. His restless yellow eyes fell before the young girl's; and the stiff, varnished, hard-brimmed sombrero he held in his wrinkled hands trembled.

"You are spying again, Pereo," said Maruja, in another dialect than the one she had used to her mother. "It is unworthy of my father's trusted servant."

"It is that man—that coyote, Doña Maruja, that is unworthy of your father, of your mother, of *you!*" he ges-

ticulated, in a fierce whisper. "I, Pereo, do not spy. I
follow, follow the track of the prowling, stealing brute
until I run him down. Yes, it was *I*, Pereo, who warned
your father he would not be content with the half of the
land he stole! It was I, Pereo, who warned your mother
that each time he trod the soil of La Mision Perdida he
measured the land he could take away!" He stopped pant-
ingly, with the insane abstraction of a fixed idea glittering
in his eyes.

"And it was *you*, Pereo," she said, caressingly, laying her
soft hand on his heaving breast, "*you* who carried me in
your arms when I was a child. It was you, Pereo, who
took me before you on your pinto horse to the rodeo, when
no one knew it but ourselves, my Pereo, was it not?" He
nodded his head violently. "It was you who showed me the
gallant caballeros, the Pachecos, the Castros, the Alvarados,
the Estudillos, the Peraltas, the Vallejos." His head kept
time with each name as the fire dimmed in his wet eyes.
"You made me promise I would not forget them for the
Americanos who were here. Good! That was years ago!
I am older now. I have seen many Americans. Well, I
am still free!"

He caught her hand, and raised it to his lips with a
gesture almost devotional. His eyes softened; as the exaltation of passion passed, his voice dropped into the querulousness of privileged age. "Ah, yes!—you, the first-born, the
heiress—of a verity, yes! You were ever a Guitierrez.
But the others? Eh, where are they now? And it was always: 'Eh, Pereo, what shall we do to-day? Pereo, good
Pereo, we are asked to ride here and there; we are expected to visit the new people in the valley—what say you,
Pereo? Who shall we dine to-day?' Or: 'Enquire me of
this or that strange caballero—and if we may speak.' Ah,
it is but yesterday that Amita would say: 'Lend me thine
own horse, Pereo, that I may outstrip this swaggering
Americano that clings ever to my side,' ha! ha! Or the
grave Dorotea would whisper: 'Convey to this Señor Pre-
sumptuous Pomposo that the daughters of Guitierrez do
not ride alone with strangers!' Or even the little Liseta
would say, he! he! 'Why does the stranger press my foot

in his great hand when he helps me into the saddle? Tell him that is not the way, Pereo.' Ha! ha!" He laughed childishly, and stopped. "And why does Señorita Amita now—look—complain that Pereo, old Pereo, comes between her and this Señor Raymond—this maquinista? Eh, and why does *she,* the lady mother, the Castellaña, shut Pereo from her councils?" he went on, with rising excitement. "What are these secret meetings, eh?—what these appointments, alone with this Judas—without the family—without *me!*"

"Hearken, Pereo," said the young girl, again laying her hand on the old man's shoulder; "you have spoken truly—but you forget—the years pass. These are no longer strangers; old friends have gone—these have taken their place. My father forgave the Doctor—why can not you? For the rest, believe in me—me—Maruja"—she dramatically touched her heart over the international complications of the letters of Captain Carroll and Peralta. "I will see that the family honor does not suffer. And now, good Pereo, calm thyself. Not with aguardiente, but with a bottle of old wine from the Mision refectory that I will send to thee. It was given to me by thy friend, Padre Miguel, and is from the old vines that were here. Courage, Pereo! And thou sayest that Amita complains that thou comest between her and Raymond. So! What matter? Let it cheer thy heart to know that I have summoned the Peraltas, the Pachecos, the Estudillos, all thy old friends, to dine here to-day. Thou wilt hear the old names, even if the faces are young to thee. Courage! Do thy duty, old friend; let them see that the hospitality of La Mision Perdida does not grow old, if its mayordomo does. Faquita will bring thee the wine. No; not *that* way; thou needest not pass the patio, nor meet that man again. Here, give me thy hand. I will lead thee. It trembles, Pereo! These are not the sinews that only two years ago pulled down the bull at Soquel with thy single lasso! Why, look! I can drag thee; see!" and with a light laugh and a boyish gesture, she half pulled, half dragged him along, until their voices were lost in the dark corridor.

Maruja kept her word. When the sun began to cast long

shadows along the veranda, not only the outer shell of La
Mision Perdida, but the dark inner heart of the old casa,
stirred with awakened life. Single horsemen and carriages
began to arrive; and, mingled with the modern turnouts of
the home party and the neighboring Americans, were a few
of the cumbrous vehicles and chariots of fifty years ago,
drawn by gayly trapped mules with bizarre postilions, and
occasionally an outrider. Dark faces looked from the bal-
cony of the patio, a light cloud of cigarette-smoke made the
dark corridors the more obscure, and mingled with the forgotten incense. Bare-headed pretty women, with roses
starring their dark hair, wandered with childish curiosity
along the broad veranda and in and out of the French
windows that opened upon the grand saloon. Scrupulously
shaved men with olive complexion, stout men with accurately curving whiskers meeting at their dimpled chins,
lounged about with a certain unconscious dignity that made
them contentedly indifferent to any novelty of their surroundings. For a while the two races kept mechanically
apart; but, through the tactful gallantry of Garnier, the
cynical familiarity of Raymond, and the impulsive recklessness of Aladdin, who had forsaken his enchanted Palace on
the slightest of invitations, and returned with the party in
the hope of again seeing the Princess of China, an interchange of civilities, of gallantries, and even of confidences,
at last took place. Jovita Castro had heard (who had
not?) of the wonders of Aladdin's Palace, and was it of
actual truth that the ladies had a bouquet and a fan to
match their dress presented to them every morning, and that
the gentlemen had a champagne cocktail sent to their rooms
before breakfast? "Just you come, Miss, and bring your
father and your brothers, and stay a week and you'll see,"
responded Aladdin, gallantly. "Hold on! What's your
father's first name? I'll send a team over there for you
to-morrow." "And is it true that you frightened the handsome Captain Carroll away from Amita?" said Dolores
Briones, over the edge of her fan to Raymond. "Perfectly," said Raymond, with ingenuous frankness. "I made
it a matter of life or death. He was a soldier, and naturally
preferred the former as giving him a better chance for pro-

motion." "Ah! we thought it was Maruja you liked best."
"That was two years ago," said Raymond, gravely. "And
you Americanos can change in that time?" "I have just
experienced that it can be done in less," he responded, over
the fan, with bewildering significance. Nor were these confidences confined to only one nationality. "I always thought
you Spanish gentlemen were very dark, and wore long mus-
taches and a cloak," said pretty little Miss Walker, gazing
frankly into the smooth round face of the eldest Pacheco—
"why, you are as fair as I am." "Eaf I tink that, I am for
ever mizzarable," he replied, with grave melancholy. In
the dead silence that followed he was enabled to make his
decorous point. "Because I shall not ezcape ze fate of Nar-
cissus." Mr. Buchanan, with the unrestrained and irresponsible enjoyment of a traveler, entered fully into the
spirit of the scene. He even found words of praise for
Aladdin, whose extravagance had at first seemed to him
almost impious. "Eh, but I'm not prepared to say he is a
fool, either," he remarked to his friend the San Francisco
banker. "Those who try to pick him up for one," returned
the banker, "will find themselves mistaken. His is the prodi-
gality that loosens others' purse-strings besides his own.
Everybody contents himself with criticising his way of
spending money, but is ready to follow his way of making it."

The dinner was more formal, and when the mistress of
the house, massive in black silk, velvet and gold embroidery,
moved like a pageant to the head of her table, where she
remained like a sacerdotal effigy, not even the presence of
the practical Scotchman at her side could remove the prevailing sense of restraint. For a while the conversation of
the relatives might have been brought with them in their
antique vehicles of fifty years ago, so faded, so worn, and
so springless it was. General Pico related the festivities at
Monterey, on the occasion of the visit of Sir George Simpson early in the present century, of which he was an eye-
witness, with great precision of detail. Don Juan Estudillo
was comparatively frivolous, with anecdotes of Louis Phi-
lippe, whom he had seen in Paris. Far-seeing Pedro Guitierrez was gloomily impressed with a Mongolian invasion

of California by the Chinese, in which the prevailing religion would be supplanted by heathen temples, and polygamy engrafted on the Constitution. Everybody agreed however, that the vital question of the hour was the settlement of land titles—Americans who claimed under preëmption and the native holders of Spanish grants were equally of the opinion.

In the midst of this the musical voice of Maruja was heard saying, "What is a tramp?"

Raymond, on her right, was ready but not conclusive. A tramp, if he could sing, would be a troubadour; if he could pray, would be a pilgrim friar—in either case a natural object of womanly solicitude. But as he could do neither, he was simply a curse.

"And you think that is not an object of womanly solicitude? But that does not tell me *what* he is."

A dozen gentlemen, swept in the radius of those softly-inquiring eyes, here started to explain. From them it appeared that there was no such thing in California as a tramp, and there were also a dozen varieties of tramp in California.

"But is he always very uncivil?" asked Maruja.

Again there were conflicting opinions. You might have to shoot him on sight, and you might have him invariably run from you. When the question was finally settled, Maruja was found to have become absorbed in conversation with some one else.

Amita, a taller copy of Maruja, and more regularly beautiful, had built up a little pile of bread crumbs between herself and Raymond, and was listening to him with a certain shy, girlish interest that was as inconsistent with the serene regularity of her face as Maruja's self-possessed, subtle intelligence was incongruous to her youthful figure. Raymond's voice, when he addressed Amita, was low and earnest; not from any significance of matter, but from its frank confidential quality.

"They are discussing the new railroad project, and your relations are all opposed to it; to-morrow they will each apply privately to Aladdin for the privilege of subscribing."

"I have never seen a railroad," said Amita, slightly coloring;

"but you are an engineer, and I know they must be something very clever."

Notwithstanding the coolness of the night, a full moon drew the guests to the veranda, where coffee was served, and where, mysteriously muffled in cloaks and shawls, the party took upon itself the appearance of groups of dominoed masqueraders, scattered along the veranda and on the broad steps of the porch in gypsy-like encampments, from whose cloaked shadow the moonlight occasionally glittered upon a varnished boot or peeping satin slipper. Two or three of these groups had resolved themselves into detached couples, who wandered down the acacia walk to the sound of a harp in the grand saloon or the occasional uplifting of a thin Spanish tenor. Two of these couples were Maruja and Garnier, followed by Amita and Raymond.

"You are restless to-night, Maruja," said Amita, shyly endeavoring to make a show of keeping up with her sister's boyish stride, in spite of Raymond's reluctance. "You are paying for your wakefulness to-day."

The same idea passed through the minds of both men. She was missing the excitement of Captain Carroll's presence.

"The air is so refreshing away from the house," responded Maruja, with a bright energy that belied any suggestion of fatigue or moral disquietude. "I'm tired of running against those turtle-doves in the walks and bushes. Let us keep on to the lane. If you are tired, Mr. Raymond will give you his arm."

They kept on, led by the indomitable little figure, who, for once, did not seem to linger over the attentions, both piquant and tender, with which Garnier improved his opportunity. Given a shadowy lane, a lovers' moon, a pair of bright and not unkindly eyes, a charming and not distant figure—what more could he want? Yet he wished she hadn't walked so fast. One might be vivacious, audacious, brilliant, at an Indian trot; but impassioned—never! The pace increased; they were actually hurrying. More than that, Maruja had struck into a little trot; her lithe body swaying from side to side, her little feet straight as an arrow before her; accompanying herself with a quaint musical chant, which she obligingly explained had been taught her as a child by Pereo. They stopped only at the hedge, where she had that morning encountered the tramp.

There is little doubt that the rest of the party was disconcerted: Amita, whose figure was not adapted to this Camilla-like exercise; Raymond, who was annoyed at the poor girl's discomfiture; and Garnier, who had lost a golden opportunity, with the faint suspicion of having looked ridiculous. Only Maruja's eyes, or rather the eyes of her lamented father, seemed to enjoy it.

"You are too effeminate," she said, leaning against the fence, and shading her eyes with her fan, as she glanced around in the staring moonlight. "Civilization has taken away your legs. A man ought to be able to trust to his feet all day, and to nothing else."

"In fact—a tramp," suggested Raymond.

"Possibly. I think I should like to have been a gypsy, and to have wandered about, finding a new home every night."

"And a change of linen on the early morning hedges," said Raymond. "But do you think seriously that you and your sister are suitably clad to commence to-night; It is bitterly cold," he added, turning up his collar. "Could you begin by showing a pal the nearest haystack or henroost?"

"Sybarite!" She cast a long look over the fields and down the lane. Suddenly she started. "What is that?"

She pointed to a tall erect figure slowly disappearing on the other side of the hedge.

"It's Pereo, only Pereo. I knew him by his long serape," said Garnier, who was nearest the hedge, complacently. "But what is surprising, he was not there when we came, nor did he come out of that open field. He must have been walking behind us on the other side of the hedge."

The eyes of the two girls sought each other simultaneously, but not without Raymond's observant glance. Amita's brow darkened as she moved to her sister's side, and took her arm with a confidential pressure that was returned. The two men, with a vague consciousness of some *contretemps*, dropped a pace behind, and began to talk to each other, leaving the sisters to exchange a few words in a low tone as they slowly returned to the house.

Meanwhile, Pereo's tall figure had disappeared in the shrubbery, to emerge again in the open area by the summer-house and the old pear-tree. The red sparks of two or three cigarettes in the shadow of the summer-house, and the crouching forms of two shawled women came forward to greet him.

"And what hast thou heard, Pereo?" said one of the women.

"Nothing," said Pereo, impatiently. "I told thee I would answer for this little primogenita with my life. She is but leading this Frenchman a dance, as she has led the others, and the Doña Amita and her Raymond are but wax in her hands. Besides, I have spoken with the little 'Ruja to-day, and spoke my mind, Pepita, and she says there is nothing."

"And whilst thou wert speaking to her, my poor Pereo, the devil of an American Doctor was speaking to her mother, thy mistress—our mistress, Pereo! Wouldst thou know what he said? Oh, it was nothing."

"Now, the curse of Koorotora on thee, Pepita!" said Pereo, excitedly. "Speak, fool, if thou knowest anything!"

"Of a verity, no. Let Faquita, then, speak: she heard it." She reached out her hand, and dragged Maruja's maid, not unwilling, before the old man.

"Good! 'Tis Faquita, daughter of Gomez, and a child of the land. Speak, little one. What said this coyote to the mother of thy mistress?"

"Truly, good Pereo, it was but accident that befriended me."

"Truly, for thy mistress's sake, I hoped it had been more. But let that go. Come, what said he, child?"

"I was hanging up a robe behind the curtain in the oratory when Pepita ushered in the Americano. I had no time to fly."

"Why shouldst thou fly from a dog like this?" said one of the cigarette-smokers who had drawn near.

"Peace!" said the old man.

"When the Doña Maria joined him they spoke of affairs. Yes, Pereo, she, thy mistress, spoke of affairs to this man

—ay, as she might have talked to *thee*. And, could he advise this? and could he counsel that? and should the cattle be taken from the lower lands, and the fields turned to grain? and had he a purchaser for Los Osos?"

"Los Osos! It is the boundary land—the frontier—the line of the arroyo—older than the Mision," muttered Pereo.

"Ay, and he talked of the—the—I know not what it is! —the r-r-rail-r-road."

"The railroad," gasped the old man. "I will tell thee what it is! It is the cut of a burning knife through La Mision Perdida—as long as eternity, as dividing as death. On either side of that gash life is blasted; wherever that cruel steel is laid the track of it is livid and barren; it cuts down all barriers; leaps all boundaries, be they cañada or cañon; it is a torrent in the plain, a tornado in the forest; its very pathway is destruction to whoso crosses it—man or beast; it is the heathenish God of the Americanos; they build temples for it, and flock there and worship it whenever it stops, breathing fire and flame like a very Moloch."

"Eh! St. Anthony preserve us!" said Faquita, shuddering; "and yet they spoke of it as 'shares' and 'stocks,' and said it would double the price of corn."

"Now, Judas pursue thee and thy railroad, Pereo," said Pepita, impatiently. "It is not such bagatela that Faquita is here to relate. Go on, child, and tell all that happened."

"And then," continued Faquita, with a slight affectation of maiden bashfulness, in the closer-drawing circle of cigarettes, "and then they talked of other things and of themselves; and, of a verity, this gray-bearded Doctor will play the goat and utter gallant speeches, and speak of a lifelong devotion and of the time he should have a right to protect—"

"The right, girl! Didst thou say the right? No, thou didst mistake. It was not *that* he meant?"

"Thy life to a quarter peso that the little Faquita does not mistake," said the evident satirist of the household. "Trust to Gomez' muchacha to understand a proposal."

When the laugh was over, and the sparks of the cigarette, cleverly whipped out of the speaker's lips by Faquita's fan, had disappeared in the darkness, she resumed, pettishly, "I know not what you call it when he kissed her hand and held it to his heart."

"Judas!" gasped Pereo. "But," he added, feverishly, "she, the Doña Maria, thy mistress, *she* summoned thee at once to call me to cast out this dust into the open air; thou didst fly to her assistance? What! thou sawest this, and did nothing—eh?" He stopped, and tried to peer into the girl's face. "No! Ah, I see; I am an old fool. Yes; it was Maruja's own mother that stood there. He! he! he!" he laughed piteously; "and she smiled and smiled and broke the coward's heart, as Maruja might. And when he was gone, she bade thee bring her water to wash the filthy Judas stain from her hand."

"Santa Ana!" said Faquita, shrugging her shoulders. "She did what the veriest muchacha would have done. When he had gone, she sat down and cried."

The old man drew back a step, and steadied himself by the table. Then, with a certain tremulous audacity, he began: "So! that is all you have to tell—nothing! Bah! A lazy slut sleeps at her duty, and dreams behind a curtain! Yes, dreams!—you understand—*dreams!* And for this she leaves her occupations, and comes to gossip here! Come," he continued, steadily working himself into a passion, "come, enough of this! Get you gone!—you, and Pepita, and Andreas, and Victor—all of you—back to your duty. Away! Am I not master here? Off! I say!"

There was no mistaking the rising anger of his voice. The cowed group rose in a frightened way and disappeared one by one silently through the labyrinth. Pereo waited until the last had vanished, and then, cramming his stiff sombrero over his eyes with an ejaculation, brushed his way through the shrubbery in the direction of the stables.

Later, when the full glory of the midnight moon had put out every straggling light in the great house; when the long veranda slept in massive bars of shadow, and even the trade-winds were hushed to repose, Pereo silently issued from the stable-yard in vaquero's dress, mounted and caparisoned. Picking his way cautiously along the turf-bordered edge of the gravel path, he noiselessly reached a gate that led to the lane. Walking his spirited mustang with difficulty until

the house had at last disappeared in the intervening foliage,
he turned with an easy canter into a border bridle-path that
seemed to lead to the cañada. In a quarter of an hour he
had reached a low amphitheatre of meadows, shut in a half
circle of grassy treeless hills.

Here, putting spurs to his horse, he entered upon a
singular exercise. Twice he made a circuit of the meadow
at a wild gallop, with flying serape and loosened rein, and
twice returned. The third time his speed increased; the
ground seemed to stream from under him; in the distance
the limbs of his steed became invisible in their furious action, and, lying low forward on his mustang's neck, man
and horse passed like an arrowy bolt around the circle.
Then something like a light ring of smoke up-curved from
the saddle before him, and, slowly uncoiling itself in mid
air, dropped gently to the ground as he passed. Again,
and once again, the shadowy coil sped upward and onward,
slowly detaching its snaky rings with a weird deliberation
that was in strange contrast to the impetuous onset of the
rider, and yet seemed a part of his fury. And then turning,
Pereo trotted gently to the centre of the circle.

Here he divested himself of his serape, and, securing it in
a cylindrical roll, placed it upright on the ground and once
more sped away on his furious circuit. But this time he
wheeled suddenly before it was half completed and bore
down directly upon the unconscious object. Within a hundred feet he swerved slightly; the long detaching rings again
writhed in mid air and softly descended as he thundered
past. But when he had reached the line of circuit again, he
turned and made directly for the road he had entered.
Fifty feet behind his horse's heels, at the end of a shadowy
cord, the luckless serape was dragging and bounding after
him!"

"The old man is quiet enough this morning," said Andreas, as he groomed the sweat-dried skin of the mustang
the next day. "It is easy to see, friend Pinto, that he has
worked off his madness on thee."

CHAPTER IV

THE Rancho of San Antonio might have been a characteristic asylum for its blessed patron, offering as it did a secure retreat from temptations for the carnal eye, and affording every facility for uninterrupted contemplation of the sky above, unbroken by tree or elevation. Unlike La Mision Perdida, of which it had been part, it was a level plain of rich adobe, half the year presenting a billowy sea of tossing verdure breaking on the far-off horizon line, half the year presenting a dry and dusty shore, from which the vernal sea had ebbed, to the low sky that seemed to mock it with a visionary sea beyond. A row of rough, irregular, and severely practical sheds and buildings housed the machinery and the fifty or sixty men employed in the cultivation of the soil, but neither residential mansion nor farmhouse offered any nucleus of rural comfort or civilization in the midst of this wild expanse of earth and sky. The simplest adjuncts of country life were unknown: milk and butter were brought from the nearest town; weekly supplies of fresh meat and vegetables came from the same place; in the harvest season, the laborers and harvesters lodged and boarded in the adjacent settlement and walked to their work. No cultivated flower bloomed beside the unpainted tenement, though the fields were starred in early spring with poppies and daisies; the humblest garden plant or herb had no place in that prolific soil. The serried ranks of wheat pressed closely round the straggling sheds and barns and hid the lower windows. But the sheds were fitted with the latest agricultural machinery; a telegraphic wire connected the nearest town with an office in the wing of one of the buildings, where Dr. West sat, and in the midst of the wilderness severely checked his accounts with nature.

Whether this strict economy of domestic outlay arose from an ostentatious contempt of country life and the luxurious habits of the former landholders, or whether it was a purely business principle of Dr. West, did not appear. Those who knew him best declared that it was both. Certain it was that unqualified commercial success crowned and dignified his method. A few survivors of the old native families came to see his strange machinery, that did the work of so many idle men and horses. It is said that he offered to "run" the distant estate of Joaquin Padilla from his little office amidst the grain of San Antonio. Some shook their heads, and declared that he only sucked the juices of the land for a few brief years to throw it away again; that in his fierce haste he skimmed the fatness of ages of gentle cultivation on a soil that had been barely tickled with native oaken plowshares.

His own personal tastes and habits were as severe and practical as his business: the little wing he inhabited contained only his office, his living room or library, his bedroom, and a bath-room. This last inconsistent luxury was due to a certain cat-like cleanliness which was part of his nature. His iron-gray hair—a novelty in this country of young Americans—was always scrupulously brushed, and his linen spotless. A slightly professional and somewhat old-fashioned respectability in his black clothes was also characteristic. His one concession to the customs of his neighbors was the possession of two or three of the half-broken and spirited mustangs of the country, which he rode with the fearlessness, if not the perfect security and ease, of a native. Whether the subjection of this lawless and powerful survival of a wild and unfettered nature around him was part of his plan, or whether it was only a lingering trait of some younger prowess, no one knew; but his grim and decorous figure, contrasting with the picturesque and flowing freedom of the horse he bestrode, was a frequent spectacle in road and field.

It was the second day after his visit to La Mision Perdida. He was sitting by his desk, at sunset, in the faint afterglow of the western sky, which flooded the floor through the open door. He was writing, but presently lifted his head, with an impatient air, and called out, "Harrison!"

The shadow of Dr. West's foreman appeared at the door.

"Who's that you're talking to?"

"Tramp, sir."

"Hire him, or send him about his business. Don't stand gabbling there."

"That's just it, sir. He won't hire for a week or a day. He says he'll do an odd job for his supper and a shake-down, but no more."

"Pack him off! . . . Stay. . . . What's he like?"

"Like the rest of 'em, only a little lazier, I reckon."

"Umph! Fetch him in."

The foreman disappeared, and returned with the tramp already known to the reader. He was a little dirtier and grimier than on the morning he had addressed Maruja at La Mision Perdida; but he wore the same air of sullen indifference, occasionally broken by furtive observation. His laziness—or weariness—if the term could describe the lassitude of perfect physical condition, seemed to have increased; and he leaned against the door as the Doctor regarded him with slow contempt. The silence continuing, he deliberately allowed himself to slip down into a sitting position in the doorway, where he remained.

"You seem to have been born tired," said the Doctor, grimly.

"Yes."

"What have you got to say for yourself?"

"I told *him*," said the tramp, nodding his head towards the foreman, "what I'd do for a supper and a bed. I don't want anything but that."

"And if you don't get what you want on your own conditions, what'll you do?" asked the Doctor, dryly.

"Go."

"Where did you come from?"

"States."

"Where are you going?"

"On."

"Leave him to me," said Dr. West to his foreman. The man smiled, and withdrew.

The Doctor bent his head again over his accounts. The tramp, sitting in the doorway, reached out his hand, pulled a young wheat-stalk that had sprung up near the doorstep, and slowly nibbled it. He did not raise his eyes to the Doctor, but sat, a familiar culprit awaiting sentence, without fear, without hope, yet not without a certain philosophical endurance of the situation.

"Go into that passage," said the Doctor, lifting his head as he turned a page of his ledger, "and on the shelf you'll find some clothing stores for the men. Pick out something to fit you."

The tramp arose, moved towards the passage, and stopped. "It's for the job only, you understand?" he said.

"For the job," answered the Doctor.

The tramp returned in a few moments with overalls and woolen shirt hanging on his arm and a pair of boots and socks in his hand. The Doctor had put aside his pen. "Now go into that room and change. Stop! First wash the dust from your feet in that bath-room."

The tramp obeyed, and entered the room. The Doctor walked to the door, and looked out reflectively on the paling sky. When he turned again he noticed that the door of the bath-room was opened, and the tramp, who had changed his clothes by the fading light, was drying his feet. The Doctor approached, and stood for a moment watching him.

"What's the matter with your foot?"[1] he asked, after a pause.

"Born so."

The first and second toe were joined by a thin membrane.

"Both alike?" asked the Doctor.

"Yes," said the young man, exhibiting the other foot.

"What did you say your name was?"

"I didn't say it. It's Henry Guest, same as my father's."

"Where were you born?"

"Dentville, Pike County, Missouri."

"What was your mother's name?"

"Spalding, I reckon."

"Where are your parents now?"

"Mother got divorced from father, and married again down South, somewhere. Father left home twenty years ago. He's somewhere in California—if he ain't dead."

"He isn't dead."

"How do you know?"

---

[1] This apparent classical plagiarism is actually a fact of identification on record in the California Law Reports. It is therefore unnecessary for me to add that the attendant circumstances and characters are purely fictitious.—B. H.

"Because I am Henry Guest, of Dentville, and"—he stopped, and, shading his eyes with his hand as he deliberately examined the tramp, added coldly—"your father, I reckon."

There was a slight pause. The young man put down the boot he had taken up. "Then I'm to stay here?"

"Certainly not. Here my name is only West, and I have no son. You'll go on to San José, and stay there until I look into this thing. You haven't got any money, of course?" he asked, with a scarcely suppressed sneer.

"I've got a little," returned the young man.

"How much?"

The tramp put his hand into his breast, and drew out a piece of folded paper containing a single gold coin.

"Five dollars. I've kept it a month; it doesn't cost much to live as I do," he added, dryly.

"There's fifty more. Go to some hotel in San José, and let me know where you are. You've got to live, and you don't want to work. Well, you don't seem to be a fool; so I needn't tell you that if you expect anything from me, you must leave this matter in my hands. I have chosen to acknowledge you to-day of my own free will: I can as easily denounce you as an impostor to-morrow, if I choose. Have you told your story to any one in the valley?"

"No."

"See that you don't, then. Before you go, you must answer me a few more questions."

He drew a chair to his table, and dipped a pen in the ink, as if to take down the answers. The young man, finding the only chair thus occupied, moved the Doctor's books aside, and sat down on the table beside him.

The questions were repetitions of those already asked, but more in detail, and thoroughly practical in their nature. The answers were given straightforwardly and unconcernedly, as if the subject was not worth the trouble of invention or evasion. It was difficult to say whether questioner or answerer took least pleasure in the interrogation, which might have referred to the concerns of a third party. Both, however, spoke disrespectfully of their common family, with almost an approach to sympathetic interest.

"You might as well be going now," said the Doctor, finally rising. "You can stop at the fonda, about two miles further on, and get your supper and bed, if you like."

The young man slipped from the table, and lounged to the door. The Doctor put his hands in his pockets and followed him. The young man, as if in unconscious imitation, had put *his* hands in his pockets also, and looked at him.

"I'll hear from you, then, when you are in San José?" said Dr. West, looking past him into the grain, with a slight approach to constraint in his indifference.

"Yes—if that's agreed upon," returned the young man, pausing on the threshold. A faint sense of some purely conventional responsibility in their position affected them both. They would have shaken hands if either had offered the initiative. A sullen consciousness of gratuitous rectitude in the selfish mind of the father; an equally sullen conviction of twenty years of wrong in the son, withheld them both. Unpleasantly observant of each other's awkwardness, they parted with a feeling of relief.

Dr. West closed the door, lit his lamp, and, going to his desk, folded the paper containing the memoranda he had just written and placed it in his pocket. Then he summoned his foreman. The man entered, and glanced around the room as if expecting to see the Doctor's guest still there.

"Tell one of the men to bring round 'Buckeye.'"

The foreman hesitated. "Going to ride to-night, sir?"

"Certainly; I may go as far as Saltonstall's. If I do, you needn't expect me back till morning.

"Buckeye's mighty fresh to-night, boss. Regularly bucked his saddle clean off an hour ago, and there ain't a man dare exercise him."

"I'll bet he don't buck his saddle off with me on it," said the Doctor, grimly. "Bring him along."

The man turned to go. "You found the tramp pow'ful lazy, didn't ye?"

"I found a heap more in him than in some that call themselves smart," said Dr. West, unconsciously setting up an irritable defense of the absent one. "Hurry up that horse!"

The foreman vanished. The Doctor put on a pair of

leather leggings, large silver spurs, and a broad soft-brimmed hat, but made no other change in his usual half-professional conventional garb. He then went to the window and glanced in the direction of the highway. Now that his son was gone, he felt a faint regret that he had not prolonged the interview. Certain peculiarities in his manner, certain suggestions of expression in his face, speech, and gesture, came back to him now with unsatisfied curiosity. "No matter," he said to himself; "he'll turn up soon again—as soon as I want him, if not sooner. He thinks he's got a mighty soft thing here, and he isn't going to let it go. And there's that same d——d sullen dirty pride of his mother, for all he doesn't cotton to her. Wonder I didn't recognize it at first. And hoarding up that five dollars! That's Jane's brat, all over! And, of course," he added, bitterly, "nothing of *me* in him. No; nothing! Well, well, what's the difference?" He turned towards the door, with a certain sullen defiance in his face so like the man he believed he did not resemble, that his foreman, coming upon him suddenly, might have been startled at the likeness. Fortunately, however, Harrison was too much engrossed with the antics of the irrepressible Buckeye, which the ostler had just brought to the door, to notice anything else. The arrival of the horse changed the Doctor's expression to one of more practical and significant resistance. With the assistance of two men at the head of the restive brute, he managed to vault into the saddle. A few wild plunges only seemed to settle him the firmer in his seat—each plunge leaving its record in a thin red line on the animal's flanks, made by the cruel spurs of its rider. Any lingering desire of following his son's footsteps was quickly dissipated by Buckeye, who promptly bolted in the opposite direction, and, before Dr. West could gain active control over him, they were half a mile on their way to La Mision Perdida.

Dr. West did not regret it. Twenty years ago he had voluntarily abandoned a legal union of mutual unfaithfulness and misconduct, and allowed his wife to get the divorce he might have obtained for equal cause. He had abandoned to her the issue of that union—an infant son. Whatever he chose to do now was purely gratuitous; the only hold which this young stranger had on his respect was that *he* also recognized that fact with a cold indifference equal to his own. At present the half-savage brute he bestrode occupied all his attention. Yet he could not help feeling his advancing years tell upon him more heavily that evening; fearless as he was, his strength was no longer equal when measured with the untiring youthful malevolence of his unbroken mustang. For a moment he dwelt regretfully on the lazy half-developed sinews of his son; for a briefer instant there flashed across him the thought that those sinews ought to replace his own; ought to be *his* to lean upon—that thus, and thus only, could he achieve the old miracle of restoring his lost youth by perpetuating his own power in his own blood; and he, whose profound belief in personality had rejected all hereditary principle, felt this with a sudden exquisite pain. But his horse, perhaps recognizing a relaxing grip, took that opportunity to "buck." Curving his back like a cat, and throwing himself into the air with an unexpected bound, he came down with four stiff, inflexible legs, and a shock that might have burst the saddle-girths, had not the wily old man as quickly brought the long rowels of his spurs together and fairly locked his heels under Buckeye's collapsing barrel. It was the mustang's last rebellious struggle. The discomfited brute gave in, and darted meekly and apologetically forward, and, as it were, left all its rider's doubts and fears far behind in the vanishing distance.

CHAPTER V

MEANWHILE, the subject of Dr. West's meditations was slowly making his way along the high-road towards the fonda. He walked more erect and with less of a shuffle in his gait; but whether this was owing to his having cast the old skin of garments adapted to his slouch, and because he was more securely shod, or whether it was from the sudden straightening of some warped moral quality, it would have been difficult to say. The expression of his face certainly gave no evidence of actual and prospective good fortune;

if anything, the lines of discontent around his brow and mouth were more strongly drawn. Apparently, his interview with his father had only the effect of reviving and stirring into greater activity a certain dogged sentiment that, through long years, had become languidly mechanical. He was no longer a beaten animal, but one roused by a chance success into a dangerous knowledge of his power. In his honest workman's dress, he was infinitely more to be feared than in his rags; in the lifting of his downcast eye, there was the revelation of a baleful intelligence. In his changed condition, civilization only seemed to have armed him against itself.

The fonda, a long low building, with a red-tiled roof extending over a porch or whitewashed veranda, in which drunken vaqueros had been known to occasionally disport their mustangs, did not offer a very reputable appearance to the eye of young Guest as he approached it in the gathering shadows. One or two half-broken horses were securely fastened to the stout cross-beams of some heavy posts driven in the roadway before it, and a primitive trough of roughly excavated stone stood near it. Through a broken gate at the side there was a glimpse of a grass-grown and deserted court-yard piled with the disused packing-cases and barrels of the tienda, or general country shop, which huddled under the same roof at the other end of the building. The opened door of the fonda showed a low-studded room fitted up with a rude imitation of an American bar on one side, and containing a few small tables, at which half a dozen men were smoking, drinking, and playing cards. The faded pictorial poster of the last bull-fight at Monterey, and an American "Sheriff's notice" were hung on the wall and in the door-way. A thick yellow atmosphere of cigarette smoke, through which the inmates appeared like brown shadows, pervaded the room.

The young man hesitated before this pestilential interior, and took a seat on a bench on the veranda. After a moment's interval, the yellow landlord came to the door with a look of inquiry, which Guest answered by a demand for lodging and supper. When the landlord had vanished again in the cigarette fog, the several other guests, one after the other, appeared at the doorway, with their cigarettes in their mouths and their cards still in their hands, and gazed upon him.

There may have been some excuse for their curiosity. As before hinted, Guest's appearance in his overalls and woolen shirt was somewhat incongruous, and, for some inexplicable reason, the same face and figure which did not look inconsistent in rags and extreme poverty now at once suggested a higher social rank both of intellect and refinement than his workman's dress indicated. This, added to his surliness of manner and expression, strengthened a growing suspicion in the mind of the party that he was a fugitive from justice—a forger, a derelict banker, or possibly a murderer. It is only fair to say that the moral sense of the spectators was not shocked at the suspicion, and that a more active sympathy was only withheld by his reticence. An unfortunate incident seemed to complete the evidence against him. In impatiently responding to the landlord's curt demand for prepayment of his supper, he allowed three or four pieces of gold to escape from his pocket on the veranda. In the quick glances of the party, as he stooped to pick them up, he read the danger of his carelessness.

His sullen self-possession did not seem to be shaken. Calling to the keeper of the tienda, who had appeared at his door in time to witness the Danaë-like shower, he bade him approach, in English.

"What sort of knives have you got?"

"Knives, Señor?"

"Yes; bowie-knives or dirks. Knives like that," he said, making an imaginary downward stroke at the table before him.

The shopkeeper entered the tienda, and presently reappeared with three or four dirks in red leather sheaths. Guest selected the heaviest, and tried its point on the table.

"How much?"

"Tres pesos."

The young man threw him one of his gold pieces, and slipped the knife and its sheath in his boot. When he had received his change from the shopkeeper, he folded his arms and leaned back against the wall in quiet indifference.

The simple act seemed to check aggressive, but not insinuating, interference. In a few moments one of the men appeared at the doorway.

"It is fine weather for the road, little comrade!"

Guest did not reply.

"Ah! the night, it ess splendid," he repeated, in broken English, rubbing his hands, as if washing in the air.

Still no reply.

"You shall come from Sank Hosay?"

"I sha'ant."

The stranger muttered something in Spanish, but the landlord, who reappeared to place Guest's supper on a table on the veranda, here felt the obligation of interfering to protect a customer apparently so aggressive and so opulent. He pushed the inquisitor aside, with a few hasty words, and, after Guest had finished his meal, offered to show him his room. It was a dark vaulted closet on the ground-floor, gaining light from the stable-yard through a barred iron grating. At the first glimpse it looked like a prison cell; looking more deliberately at the black tresseled bed, and the votive images hanging on the wall, it might have been a tomb.

"It is the best," said the landlord. "The Padre Vincento will have none other on his journey."

"I suppose God protects him," said Guest; "that door don't." He pointed to the worm-eaten door, without bolt or fastening.

"Ah, what matter! Are we not all friends?"

"Certainly," responded Guest, with his surliest manner, as he returned to the veranda. Nevertheless, he resolved not to occupy the cell of the reverend Padre; not from any personal fear of his disreputable neighbors, though he was fully alive to their peculiarities, but from the nomadic instinct which was still strong in his blood. He felt he could not yet bear the confinement of a close room or the propinquity of his fellow-man. He would rest on the veranda until the moon was fairly up, and then he would again take to the road.

He was half reclining on the bench, with the slowly closing and opening lids of some tired but watchful animal, when the sound of wheels, voices, and clatter of hoofs on the highway arrested his attention, and he sat upright. The moon was slowly lifting itself over the limitless stretch of grain-fields before him on the other side of the road, and dazzling him with its level lustre. He could barely discern a cavalcade of dark figures and a large vehicle rapidly approaching, before it drew up tumultuously in front of the fonda.

It was a pleasure party of ladies and gentlemen on horseback and in a four-horsed char-à-bancs returning to La Mision Perdida. Buchanan, Raymond, and Garnier were there; Amita and Dorotea in the body of the char-à-bancs, and Maruja seated on the box. Much to his own astonishment and that of some others of the party, Captain Carroll was among the riders. Only Maruja and her mother knew that he was recalled to refute a repetition of the gossip already circulated regarding his sudden withdrawal; only Maruja alone knew the subtle words which made that call so potent yet so hopeless.

Maruja's quick eyes, observant of everything, even under the double fire of Captain Carroll and Garnier, instantly caught those of the erect figure on the bench in the veranda. Surely that was the face of the tramp she had spoken to! and yet there was a change, not only in the dress but in the general resemblance. After the first glance, Guest withdrew his eyes and gazed at the other figures in the char-à-bancs without moving a muscle.

Maruja's whims and caprices were many and original; and when, after a sudden little cry and a declaration that she could stand her cramped position no longer, she leaped from the box into the road, no one was surprised. Garnier and Captain Carroll quickly followed.

"I should like to look into the fonda while the horses are being watered," she said, laughingly, "just to see what it is that attracts Pereo there so often." Before any one could restrain this new caprice, she was already upon the veranda.

To reach the open door, she had to pass so near Guest that her soft white flounces brushed his knees, and the flowers in her girdle left their perfume in his face. But he neither moved nor raised his eyes. When she had passed, he rose quietly and stepped into the road.

On her nearer survey, Maruja was convinced it was the same man. She remained for an instant, with a little hand on the door-post. "What a horrid place, and what dreadful people!" she said in audible English as she glanced quickly after Guest. "Really, Pereo ought to be warned against keeping such company. Come, let us go."

She contrived to pass Guest again in regaining the carriage; but in the few moments' further delay he walked on down the road before them, and, by the time they were ready to start, he was slowly sauntering some hundred yards ahead. They passed him at a rapid trot, but the next moment the char-à-bancs was suddenly pulled up.

"My fan!" cried Maruja. "Blessed Santa Maria!—my fan!"

A small black object, seen distinctly in the moonlight, was lying on the road, directly in the track of the sauntering stranger. Garnier attempted to alight; Carroll reined in his horse.

"Stop, all of you!" said Maruja; "that man will bring it to me."

It seemed as if he would. He stopped and picked it up, and approached the carriage. Maruja stood up in her seat, with her veil thrown back, her graceful hand extended, her eyes and mouth tremulous with an irresistible smile. The stranger came nearer, singled out Captain Carroll, tossed the fan to him with a slight nod, and passed on the other side.

"One moment," said Maruja, almost harshly, to the driver. "One moment," she continued, drawing her purse from her pocket brusquely. "Let me reward this civil gentleman of the road! Here, sir;" but, before she could continue, Carroll wheeled to her side, and interposed. "Pray collect yourself, Miss Saltonstall," he said, hurriedly; "you can not tell who this man may be. He does not seem to be one who would insult you, or whom *you* would insult gratuitously."

"Give me the fan, Captain Carroll," she said, with a soft and caressing smile. "Thank you." She took it, and, breaking it through the middle between her gloved hands, tossed it into the highway. "You are right—it smells of the fonda—and the road. Thank you, again. You are so thoughtful for me, Captain Carroll," she murmured, raising her eyes gently to his, and then suddenly withdrawing them with a half sigh. "But I am keeping you all. Go on."

The carriage rolled away and Guest returned from the hedge to the middle of the road. San José lay in the opposite direction from the disappearing cavalcade; but, on leaving the fonda, he had determined to lead his inquisitors astray by doubling and making a circuit of the hostelry through the fields hidden in the tall grain. This he did, securely passing them within sound of their voices, and was soon well on his way again. He avoided the highway, and, striking a trail through the meadows, diverged to the right, where the low towers and brown walls of a ruined mission church rose above the plain. This would enable him to escape any direct pursuit on the high road, besides, from its slight elevation, giving him a more extended view of the plain. As he neared it, he was surprised to see that, although it was partly dismantled, and the roof had fallen in the central aisle, a part of it was still used as a chapel, and a light was burning behind a narrow opening, partly window and partly shrine. He was almost upon it, when the figure of a man who had been kneeling beneath, with his back towards him, rose, crossed himself devoutly, and stood upright. Before he could turn, Guest disappeared round the angle of the wall, and the tall erect figure of the solitary worshiper passed on without heeding him.

But if Guest had been successful in evading the observation of the man he had come so suddenly upon, he was utterly unconscious of another figure that had been tracking *him* for the last ten minutes through the tall grain, and had even succeeded in gaining the shadow of the wall behind him; and it was this figure, and not his own, that eventually attracted the attention of the tall stranger. The pursuing figure was rapidly approaching the unconscious Guest; in another moment it would have been upon him, when it was suddenly seized from behind by the tall devotee.

There was a momentary struggle, and then it freed itself, with the exclamation, "Pereo!"

"Yes—Pereo!" said the old man, panting from his exertions. "And thou art Miguel. So thou wouldst murder a man for a few pesos!" he said, pointing to the knife which the desperado had hurriedly hid in his jacket, "and callest thyself a Californian!"

"'Tis only an Americano—a runaway, with some ill-gotten gold," said Miguel, sullenly, yet with unmistakable fear of the old man. "Besides, it was only to frighten him, the braggart. But since thou fearest to touch a hair of those interlopers—"

"Fearest!" said Pereo, fiercely, clutching him by the throat, and forcing him against the wall. "Fearest! sayest thou. I, Pereo, fear? Dost thou think I would soil these hands, that might strike a higher quarry, with blood of thy game?"

"Forgive me, padroño," gasped Miguel, now thoroughly alarmed at the old man's awakened passion; "pardon; I meant that, since thou knowest him—"

"I know him?" repeated Pereo scornfully, contemptuously throwing Miguel aside, who at once took that opportunity to increase his distance from the old man's arm. "I know him? Thou shalt see. Come hither, child," he called, beckoning to Guest. "Come hither, thou hast nothing to fear now."

Guest, who had been attracted by the sound of altercation behind him, but who was utterly unconscious of its origin or his own relation to it, came forward impatiently. As he did so, Miguel took to his heels. The act did not tend to mollify Guest's surly suspicions, and, pausing a few feet from the old man, he roughly demanded his business with him.

Pereo raised his head, with the dignity of years and habits of command. The face of the young man confronting him was clearly illuminated by the moonlight. Pereo's eyes suddenly dilated, his mouth stiffened, he staggered back against the wall.

"Who are you?" he gasped, in uncertain English.

Believing himself the subject of some drunkard's pastime, Guest replied, savagely, "One who has enough of this d——d nonsense, and will stand no more of it from any one, young or old," and turned abruptly on his heel.

"Stay, one moment, Señor, for the love of God!"

Some keen accent of agony in the old man's voice touched even Guest's selfish nature. He halted.

"You are—a stranger here?"—faltered Pereo. "Yes?"

"I am."

"You do not live here?—you have no friends?"

"I told you I am a stranger. I never was here before in my life," said Guest, impatiently.

"True; I am a fool," said the old man, hurriedly, to himself. "I am mad—mad! It is not *his* voice. No! It is not *his* look, now that his face changes. I am crazy." He stopped, and passed his trembling hands across his eyes. "Pardon, Señor," he continued, recalling himself with a humility that was almost ironical in its extravagance. "Pardon, pardon! Yet, perhaps it is not too much to have wanted to know who was the man one has saved."

"Saved!" repeated Guest, with incredulous contempt.

"Ay!" said Pereo, haughtily, drawing his figure erect; "ay, saved! Señor." He stopped and shrugged his shoulders. "But let it pass—I say—let it pass. Take an old man's advice, friend: show not your gold hereafter to strangers lightly, no matter how lightly you have come by it. Good-night!"

Guest for a moment hesitated whether to resent the old man's speech, or to let it pass as the incoherent fancy of a brain maddened by drink. Then he ended the discussion by turning his back abruptly and continuing his way to the high-road.

"So!" said Pereo, looking after him with abstracted eyes, "so! it was only a fancy. And yet—even now, as he turned away, I saw the same cold insolence in his eye. Caramba! Am I mad—mad—that I must keep forever before my eyes, night and day, the image of that dog in every outcast, every ruffian, every wayside bully that I meet? No, no, good Pereo! Softly! this is mere madness, good Pereo," he murmured to himself; "thou wilt have none of it; none, good Pereo. Come, come!" He let his head fall slowly forward on his breast, and in that action, seeming to take up again the burden of a score more years upon his shoulders, he moved slowly away.

When he entered the fonda half an hour later, the awe in which he was held by the half superstitious ruffians appeared to have increased. Whatever story the fugitive Miguel had told his companions regarding Pereo's protection of the young stranger, it was certain that it had its full effect. Obsequious to the last degree, the landlord was so profoundly touched, when Pereo, not displeased with this evidence of his power over his countrymen, condescendingly offered to click glasses with him, that he endeavored to placate him still further.

"It is a pity your worship was not here earlier," he began, with a significant glance at the others, "to have seen a gallant young stranger that was here. A spice of wickedness about him, truly—a kind of Don Cæsar—but bearing himself like a very caballero always. It would have pleased your worship, who likes not those canting Puritans such as our neighbor yonder."

"Ah," said Pereo, reflectively, warming under the potent fires of flattery and aguardiente, "possibly I *have* seen him. He was like—"

"Like none of the dogs thou hast seen about San Antonio," interrupted the landlord. "Scarcely did he seem Americano, though he spoke no Spanish."

The old man chuckled to himself viciously. "And thou, thou old fool, Pereo, must needs see a likeness to thine enemy in this poor runaway child—this fugitive Don Juan! He! he!" Nevertheless, he still felt a vague terror of the condition of mind which had produced this fancy, and drank so deeply to dispel his nervousness that it was with difficulty he could mount his horse again. The exaltation of liquor, however, appeared only to intensify his characteristics: his face became more lugubrious and melancholy; his manner more ceremonious and dignified; and, erect and stiff in his saddle from the waist upwards, but leaning from side to side with the motion of his horse, like the tall mast of some laboring sloop, he "loped" away towards the House of the Lost Mission. Once or twice he broke into senti-

mental song. Strangely enough, his ditty was a popular
Spanish refrain of some matador's aristocratic inamo-
rata:—

> Do you see my black eyes?
> I am Manuel's Duchess,—

sang Pereo, with infinite gravity. His horse's hoofs seemed
to keep time with the refrain, and he occasionally waved
in the air the long leather thong of his bridle-rein.

It was quite late when he reached La Mision Perdida.
Turning into the little lane that led to the stable-yard, he
dismounted at a gate in the hedge which led to the summer-
house of the old Mision garden, and, throwing his reins on
his mustang's neck, let the animal precede him to the
stables. The moon shone full on the inclosure as he emerged
from the labyrinth. With uncovered head he approached
the Indian mound, and sank on his knees before it.

The next moment he rose, with an exclamation of terror,
and his hat dropped from his trembling hand. Directly before him, a small, gray, wolfish-looking animal had stopped
half-way down the mound on encountering his motionless
figure. Frightened by his outcry, and unable to retreat,
the shadowy depredator had fallen back on his slinking
haunches with a snarl, and bared teeth that glittered in the
moonlight.

In an instant the expression of terror on the old man's
ashen face turned into a fixed look of insane exaltation.
His white lips moved; he advanced a step further, and held
out both hands towards the crouching animal.

"So! It is thou—at last! And comest thou here thy
tardy Pereo to chide? Comest *thou*, too, to tell the poor
old man his heart is cold, his limbs are feeble, his brain
weak and dizzy? that he is no longer fit to do thy master's
work? Ay, gnash thy teeth at him! Curse him!—curse
him in thy throat! But listen!—listen, good friend—I will
tell thee a secret—ay, good gray friar, a secret—such a
secret! A plan, all mine—fresh from this old gray head;
ha! ha!—all mine! To be wrought by these poor old arms;
ha! ha! All mine! Listen!"

He stealthily made a step nearer the affrighted animal.

With a sudden sidelong snap, it swiftly bounded by his side, and vanished in the thicket; and Pereo, turning wildly, with a moan sank down helplessly on the grave of his forefathers.

CHAPTER VI

To the open chagrin of most of the gentlemen and the unexpected relief of some of her own sex, Maruja, after an evening of more than usual caprice and willfulness, retired early to her chamber. Here she beguiled Enriquita, a younger sister, to share her solitude for an hour, and with a new and charming melancholy presented her with mature counsel and some younger trinkets and adornments.

"Thou wilt find them but folly, 'Riquita; but thou art young, and wilt outgrow them as I have. I am sick of the Indian beads, everybody wears them; but they seem to suit thy complexion. Thou art not yet quite old enough for jewelry; but take thy choice of these." " 'Ruja," replied Enriquita, eagerly, "surely thou wilt not give up this necklace of carved amber, that was brought thee from Manilla —it becomes thee so! Everybody says it. All the caballeros, Raymond and Victor, swear that it sets off thy beauty like nothing else." "When thou knowest men better," responded Maruja, in a deep voice, "thou wilt care less for what they say, and despise what they do. Besides, I wore it to-day—and—I hate it." "But what fan wilt thou keep thyself? The one of sandal-wood thou hadst to-day?" continued Enriquita, timidly eying the pretty things upon the table. "None," responded Maruja, didactically, "but the simplest, which I shall buy myself. Truly, it is time to set one's self against this extravagance. Girls think nothing of spending as much upon a fan as would buy a horse and saddle for a poor man." "But why so serious tonight, my sister?" said the little Enriquita, her eyes filling with ready tears. "It grieves me," responded Maruja, promptly, "to find thee, like the rest, giving thy soul up to the mere glitter of the world. However, go, child, take the beads, but leave the amber; it would make thee yellower than thou art, which the blessed Virgin forbid! Good-night!"

She kissed her affectionately, and pushed her from the room. Nevertheless, after a moment's survey of her lonely chamber, she hastily slipped on a pale satin dressing-gown, and, darting across the passage, dashed into the bedroom of the youngest Miss Wilson, haled that sentimental brunette from her night toilet, dragged her into her own chamber, and, enwrapping her in a huge mantle of silk and gray fur, fed her with chocolates and chestnuts, and, reclining on her sympathetic shoulder, continued her arraignment of the world and its follies until nearly daybreak.

It was past noon when Maruja awoke, to find Faquita standing by her bedside with ill-concealed impatience.

"I ventured to awaken the Doña Maruja," she said, with vivacious alacrity, "for news! Terrible news! The American, Dr. West, is found dead this morning in the San José road!"

"Dr. West dead!" repeated Maruja, thoughtfully, but without emotion.

"Surely dead—very dead. He was thrown from his horse and dragged by the stirrups—how far, the Blessed Virgin only knows. But he is found dead—this Dr. West —his foot in the broken stirrup, his hand holding a piece of the bridle! I thought I would waken the Doña Maruja, that no one else should break it to the Doña Maria."

"That no one else should break it to my mother?" repeated Maruja, coldly. "What mean you, girl?"

"I mean that no stranger should tell her," stammered Faquita, lowering her bold eyes.

"You mean," said Maruja, slowly, "that no silly, staring, tongue-wagging gossip should dare to break upon the morning devotions of the lady mother with open-mouthed tales of horror! You are wise, Faquita! I will tell her myself. Help me to dress."

But the news had already touched the outer shell of the great house, and little groups of the visitors were discussing it upon the veranda. For once, the idle badinage of a pleasure-seeking existence was suspended; stupid people with facts came to the fore; practical people with inquiring minds became interesting; servants were confidentially appealed to; the local expressman became a hero, and it was even noticed that he was intelligent and good-looking.

"What makes it more distressing," said Raymond, joining one of the groups, "is, that it appears the Doctor visited Mrs. Saltonstall last evening, and left the casa at eleven. Sanchez, who was perhaps the last person who saw him alive, says that he noticed his horse was very violent, and the Doctor did not seem able to control him. The accident probably happened half an hour later, as he was picked up about three miles from here, and from appearances must have been dragged, with his foot in the stirrup, fully half a mile before the girth broke and freed the saddle and stirrup together. The mustang, with nothing on but his broken bridle, was found grazing at the rancho as early as four o'clock, an hour before the body of his master was discovered by the men sent from the rancho to look for him."

"Eh, but the man must have been clean daft to have trusted himself to one of those savage beasts of the country," said Mr. Buchanan. "And he was no so young either —about sixty, I should say. It didna look even respectable, I remember, when we met him the other day, careering over the country for all the world like one of those crazy Mexicans. And yet he seemed steady and sensible enough when he didna let his schemes of 'improvements' run away with him like yon furious beastie. Eh well, puir man—it was a sudden ending! And his family—eh?"

"I don't think he has one—at least here," said Raymond. "You can't always tell in California. I believe he was a widower."

"Ay, man, but the heirs; there must be considerable property?" said Buchanan, impatiently.

"Oh, the heirs. If he's made no will, which doesn't look like so prudent and practical a man as he was—the heirs will probably crop up some day."

"*Probably!* crop up some day," repeated Buchanan, aghast.

"Yes. You must remember that *we* don't take heirs quite as much into account as you do in the old country. The loss of the *man,* and how to replace *him,* is much more to us than the disposal of his property. Now, Doctor West was a power far beyond his actual possessions—and we will know very soon how much those were dependent upon him."

"What do you mean?" asked Buchanan, anxiously.

"I mean that five minutes after the news of the Doctor's death was confirmed, your friend Mr. Stanton sent a messenger with a despatch to the nearest telegraphic office, and that he himself drove over to catch Aladdin before the news could reach him."

Buchanan looked uneasy; so did one or two of the native Californians who composed the group, and who had been listening attentively. "And where is this same telegraphic office?" asked Buchanan, cautiously.

"I'll drive you over there presently," responded Raymond, grimly. "There'll be nothing doing here to-day. As Dr. West was a near neighbor of the family, his death suspends our pleasure-seeking until after the funeral."

Mr. Buchanan moved away. Captain Carroll and Garnier drew nearer the speaker. "I trust it will not withdraw from us the society of Miss Saltonstall," said Garnier, lightly—"at least, that she will not be inconsolable."

"She did not seem to be particularly sympathetic with Dr. West the other day," said Captain Carroll, coloring slightly with the recollection of the morning in the summer-house, yet willing, in his hopeless passion, even to share that recollection with his rival. "Did you not think so, Monsieur Garnier?"

"Very possibly; and, as Miss Saltonstall is quite artless and childlike in the expression of her likes and dislikes," said Raymond, with the faintest touch of irony, "you can judge as well as I can."

Garnier parried the thrust lightly. "You are no kinder to our follies than you are to the grand passions of these gentlemen. Confess, you frightened them horribly. You are—what is called—a bear—eh? You depreciate in the interests of business."

Raymond did not at first appear to notice the sarcasm. "I only stated," he said, gravely, "that which these gentlemen will find out for themselves before they are many hours older. Dr. West was the brain of the county, as Aladdin is its life-blood. It only remains to be seen how far the loss of that brain affects the county. The Stock Exchange market in San Francisco will indicate that to-day in the shares of the San Antonio and Soquel Railroad and the West Mills and Manufacturing Co. It is a matter that may affect even our friends here. Whatever West's social standing was in this house, lately he was in confidential business relations with Mrs. Saltonstall." He raised his eyes for the first time to Garnier as he added, slowly, "It is to be hoped that if our hostess has no social reasons to deplore the loss of Dr. West, she at least will have no other."

With a lover's instinct, conscious only of some annoyance to Maruja, in all this, Carroll anxiously looked for her appearance among the others. He was doomed to disappointment, however. His half-timid inquiries only resulted in the information that Maruja was closeted with her mother. The penetralia of the casa was only accessible to the family; yet, as he wandered uneasily about, he could not help passing once or twice before the quaint low archway, with its grated door, that opened from the central hall. His surprise may be imagined when he suddenly heard his name uttered in a low voice; and, looking up, he beheld the soft eyes of Maruja at the grating.

She held the door partly open with one little hand, and made a sign for him to enter with the other. When he had done so, she said, "Come with me," and preceded him down the dim corridor. His heart beat thickly; the incense of this sacred inner life, with its faint suggestion of dead rose-leaves, filled him with a voluptuous languor; his breath was lost, as if a soft kiss had taken it away; his senses swam in the light mist that seemed to suffuse everything. His step trembled as she suddenly turned aside, and, opening a door, ushered him into a small vaulted chamber.

In the first glance it seemed to be an oratory or chapel. A large gold and ebony crucifix hung on the wall. There was a *prie-dieu* of heavy dark mahogany in the centre of the tiled floor; there was a low ottoman or couch, covered with a mantle of dark violet velvet, like a pall; there were two quaintly carved stiff chairs; a religious, almost ascetic, air pervaded the apartment; but no dreamy eastern seraglio could have affected him with an intoxication so profoundly and mysteriously sensuous.

Maruja pointed to a chair, and then, with a peculiarly feminine movement, placed herself sideways upon the otto-man, half reclining on her elbow on a high cushion, her deep billowy flounces partly veiling the funereal velvet be-low. Her oval face was pale and melancholy, her eyes moist as if with recent tears; an expression as of troubled passion lurked in their depths and in the corners of her mouth. Scarcely knowing why, Carroll fancied that thus she might appear if she were in love; and the daring thought made him tremble.

"I wanted to speak with you alone," she said, gently, as if in explanation; "but don't look at me so. I have had a bad night, and now this calamity"—she stopped and then added, softly, "I want you to do a favor for—my mother?"

Captain Carroll, with an effort, at last found his voice. "But *you* are in trouble; *you* are suffering. I had no idea this unfortunate affair came so near to you."

"Nor did I," said Maruja, closing her fan with a slight snap. "I knew nothing of it until my mother told me this morning. To be frank with you, it now appears that Dr. West was her most intimate business adviser. All her af-fairs were in his hands. I cannot expain how, or why, or when; but it is so."

"And is that all?" said Carroll, with boyish openness of relief. "And you have no other sorrow?"

In spite of herself, a tender smile, such as she might have bestowed on an impulsive boy, broke on her lips. "And is that not enough? What would you? No—sit where you are! We are here to talk seriously. And you do not ask what is this favor my mother wishes?"

"No matter what it is, it shall be done," said Carroll, quickly. "I am your mother's slave if she will but let me serve at your side. Only," he paused, "I wish it was not business—I know nothing of business."

"If it were only business, Captain Carroll," said Maruja, slowly, "I would have spoken to Raymond or the Señor Buchanan; if it were only confidence, Pereo, our mayordomo, would have dragged himself from his sick-bed this morning to do my mother's bidding. But it is more than that—it is the functions of a gentleman—and my mother, Captain Carroll, would like to say of—a friend."

He seized her hand and covered it with kisses. She withdrew it gently.

"What have I to do?" he asked, eagerly.

She drew a note from her belt. "It is very simple. You must ride over to Aladdin with that note. You must give it to him *alone*—more than that, you must not let any one who may be there think you are making any but a social call. If he keeps you to dine—you must stay—you will bring back anything he may give you and deliver it to me secretly for her."

"Is that all?" asked Carroll, with a slight touch of disappointment in his tone.

"No," said Maruja, rising impulsively. "No, Captain Carroll—it is *not* all! And you shall know all, if only to prove to you how we confide in you—and to leave you free, after you have heard it, to do as you please." She stood before him, quite white, opening and shutting her fan quickly, and tapping the tiled floor with her little foot. "I have told you Dr. West was my mother's business adviser. She looked upon him as more—as a friend. Do you know what a dangerous thing it is for a woman who has lost one protector to begin to rely upon another? Well, my mother is not yet old. Dr. West appreciated her—Dr. West did not depreciate himself—two things that go far with a woman, Captain Carroll, and my mother is a woman." She paused, and then, with a light toss of her fan, said: "Well, to make an end, but for this excellent horse and this too ambitious rider, one knows not how far the old story of my mother's first choice would have been repeated, and the curse of Koorotora again fallen on the land."

"And you tell me this—you, Maruja—you who warned me against my hopeless passion for you?"

"Could I foresee this?" she said, passionately; "and are

you mad enough not to see that this very act would have made *your* suit intolerable to my relations?"

"Then you did think of my suit, Maruja," he said, grasping her hand.

"Or any one's suit," she continued, hurriedly, turning away with a slight increase of color in her cheeks. After a moment's pause, she added, in a gentler and half-reproachful voice, "Do you think I have confided my mother's story to you for this purpose only? Is this the help you proffer?"

"Forgive me, Maruja," said the young officer, earnestly. "I am selfish, I know—for I love you. But you have not told me yet how I could help your mother by delivering this letter, which any one could do."

"Let me finish then," said Maruja. "It is for you to judge what may be done. Letters have passed between my mother and Dr. West. My mother is imprudent; I know not what she may have written, or what she might not write, in confidence. But you understand, they are not letters to be made public nor to pass into any hands but hers. They are not to be left to be bandied about by his American friends; to be commented upon by strangers; to reach the ears of the Guitierrez. They belong to that grave which lies between the Past and my mother; they must not rise from it to haunt her."

"I understand," said the young officer, quietly. "This letter, then, is my authority to recover them?"

"Partly, though it refers to other matters. This Mr. Prince, whom you Americans call Aladdin, was a friend of Dr. West; they were associated in business, and he will probably have access to his papers. The rest we must leave to you."

"I think you may," said Carroll, simply.

Maruja stretched out her hand. The young man bent over it respectfully and moved towards the door.

She had expected him to make some protestation—perhaps even to claim some reward. But the instinct which made him forbear even in thought to take advantage of the duty laid upon him, which dominated even his miserable passion for her, and made it subservient to his exaltation

of honor; this epaulet of the officer, and blood of the gentleman, this simple possession of knighthood not laid on
by perfunctory steel, but springing from within—all this,
I grieve to say, was partly unintelligible to Maruja, and
not entirely satisfactory. Since he had entered the room
they seemed to have changed their situations; he was no
longer the pleading lover that trembled at her feet. For
one base moment she thought it was the result of his knowledge of her mother's weakness; but the next instant, meeting his clear glance, she colored with shame. Yet she
detained him vaguely a moment before the grated door in
the secure shadow of the arch. He might have kissed her
there! He did not.

In the gloomy stagnation of the great house, it was
natural that he should escape from it for a while, and the
saddling of his horse for a solitary ride attracted no attention. But it might have been noticed that his manner
had lost much of that nervous susceptibility and anxiety
which indicates a lover; and it was with a return of his
professional coolness and precision that he rode out of the
patio as if on parade. Erect, observant, and self-possessed,
he felt himself "on duty," and, putting spurs to his horse,
cantered along the high-road, finding an inexpressible relief in motion. He was doing something in the interest
of helplessness and of *her*. He had no doubt of his right
to interfere. He did not bother himself with the rights of
others. Like all self-contained men, he had no plan of
action, except what the occasion might suggest.

He was more than two miles from La Mision Perdida,
when his quick eye was attracted by a saddle-blanket lying
in the roadside ditch. A recollection of the calamity of
the previous night made him rein in his horse and examine
it. It was without doubt the saddle-blanket of Dr. West's
horse, lost when the saddle came off, after the Doctor's
body had been dragged by the runaway beast. But a second
fact forced itself equally upon the young officer. It was
lying nearly a mile from the spot where the body had been
picked up. This certainly did not agree with the accepted
theory that the accident had taken place further on, and
that the body had been dragged until the saddle came

3   v. 1

off where it was found. His professional knowledge of equitation and the technique of accoutrements exploded the idea that the saddle could have slipped here, the saddle-blanket fallen and the horse have run nearly a mile hampered by the saddle hanging under him. Consequently, the saddle, blanket, and unfortunate rider must have been precipitated together, and at the same moment, on or near this very spot. Captain Carroll was not a detective; he had no theory to establish, no motive to discover, only as an officer, he would have simply rejected any excuse offered on those terms by one of his troopers to account for a similar accident. He troubled himself with no further deduction. Without dismounting, he gave a closer attention to the marks of struggling hoofs near the edge of the ditch, which had not yet been obliterated by the daily travel. In doing so, his horse's hoof struck a small object partly hidden in the thick dust of the highway. It seemed to be a leather letter or memorandum case adapted for the breast pocket. Carroll instantly dismounted and picked it up. The name and address of Dr. West were legibly written on the inside. It contained a few papers and notes, but nothing more. The possibility that it might disclose the letters he was seeking was a hope quickly past. It was only a corroborative fact that the accident had taken place on the spot where he was standing. He was losing time; he hurriedy put the book in his pocket, and once more spurred forward on his road.

CHAPTER VII

THE exterior of Aladdin's Palace, familiar as it already was to Carroll, struck him that afternoon as looking more than usually unreal, ephemeral, and unsubstantial. The Moorish arches, of the thinnest white pine; the arabesque screens and lattices that looked as if made of pierced cardboard; the golden minarets that seemed to be glued to the shell-like towers, and the hollow battlements that visibly warped and cracked in the fierce sunlight,—all appeared more than ever like a theatrical scene that might sink through the ground, or vanish on either side to the sound of the prompter's whistle. Recalling Raymond's cynical insinuations, he could not help fancying that the house had been built by a conscientious genie with a view to the possibility of the lamp and the ring passing, with other effects, into the hands of the sheriff.

Nevertheless, the servant who took Captain Carroll's horse summoned another domestic, who preceded him into a small waiting-room off the gorgeous central hall, which looked not unlike the private bar-room of a first-class hotel, and presented him with a sherry cobbler. It was a peculiarity of Aladdin's Palace that the host seldom did the honors of his own house, but usually deputed the task to some friend, and generally the last new-comer. Carroll was consequently not surprised when he was presently joined by an utter stranger, who again pressed upon him the refreshment he had just declined. "You see," said the transitory host, "I'm a stranger myself here, and haven't got the ways of the regular customers; but call for anything you like, and I'll see it got for you. Jim" (the actual Christian name of Aladdin) "is headin' a party through the stables. Would you like to join 'em—they ain't more than half through now—or will you come right to the billiard-room—the latest thing out in stained glass and iron—ez pretty as fresh paint? or will you meander along to the bridal suite, and see the bamboo and silver dressing-room, and the white satin and crystal bed that cost fifteen thousand dollars as it stands. Or," he added, confidentially, "would you like to cut the whole cussed thing, and I'll get out Jim's 2.32 trotter and his spider-legged buggy and we'll take a spin over to the Springs afore dinner?" It was, however, more convenient to Carroll's purpose to conceal his familiarity with the Aladdin treasures, and to politely offer to follow his guide through the house. "I reckon Jim's pretty busy just now," continued the stranger; "what with old Doc West going under so suddent, just ez he'd got things boomin' with that railroad and his manufactory company. The stocks went down to nothing this morning; and, 'twixt you and me, the boys say," he added, mysteriously sinking his voice, "it was jest the tightest squeeze

there whether there wouldn't be a general burst-up all
round. But Jim was over at San Antonio afore the Doctor's body was laid out; just ran that telegraph himself
for about two hours; had a meeting of trustees and direc-
tors afore the Coroner came; had the Doctor's books and
papers brought over here in a buggy, and another meeting
before luncheon. Why, by the time the other fellows began
to drop in to know if the Doctor was really dead, Jim
Prince had discounted the whole affair two years ahead.
Why, bless you, nearly everybody is in it. That Spanish
woman over there, with the pretty daughter—that high-
toned Greaser with the big house—you know who I
mean." . . .

"I don't think I do," said Carroll, coldly. "I know a
lady named Saltonstall, with several daughters."

"That's her; thought I'd seen you there once. Well, the
Doctor's got her into it, up to the eyes. I reckon she's
mortgaged everything to him."

It required all Carroll's trained self-possession to prevent his garrulous guide from reading his emotion in his
face. This, then, was the secret of Maruja's melancholy.
Poor child! how bravely she had borne up under it; and *he*,
in his utter selfishness, had never suspected it. Perhaps
that letter was her delicate way of breaking the news to
him, for he should certainly now hear it all from Aladdin's
lips. And this man, who evidently had succeeded to the
control of Dr. West's property, doubtless had possession of
the letters too! Humph! He shut his lips firmly together,
and strode along by the side of his innocent guide, erect
and defiant.

He did not have long to wait. The sound of voices, the
opening of doors, and the trampling of feet indicated that
the other party were being "shown over" that part of the
building Carroll and his companion were approaching.
"There's Jim and his gang now," said his cicerone; "I'll
tell him you're here, and step out of this show business
myself. So long! I reckon I'll see you at dinner." At
this moment Prince and a number of ladies and gentlemen
appeared at the further end of the hall; his late guide
joined them, and apparently indicated Carroll's presence,

as, with a certain lounging, off-duty, officer-like way, the young man sauntered on.

Aladdin, like others of his class, objected to the military, theoretically and practically; but he was not above recognizing their social importance in a country of no society, and of even being fascinated by Carroll's quiet and secure self-possession and self-contentment in a community of restless ambition and aggressive assertion. He came forward to welcome him cordially; he introduced him with an air of satisfaction; he would have preferred if he had been in uniform, but he contented himself with the fact that Carroll, like all men of disciplined limbs, carried himself equally well in mufti.

"You have shown us everything," said Carroll, smiling, "except the secret chamber where you keep the magic lamp and ring. Are we not to see the spot where the incantation that produces these marvels is held, even if we are forbidden to witness the ceremony? The ladies are dying to see your sanctum—your study—your workshop—where you really live."

"You'll find it a mere den, as plain as my bed-room," said Prince, who prided himself on the Spartan simplicity of his own habits, and was not averse to the exhibition. "Come this way." He crossed the hall, and entered a small, plainly furnished room, containing a table piled with papers, some of which were dusty and worn-looking. Carroll instantly conceived the idea that these were Dr. West's property. He took his letter quietly from his pocket; and, when the attention of the others was diverted, laid it on the table, with the remark, in an undertone, audible only to Prince, "From Mrs. Saltonstall."

Aladdin had that sublime audacity which so often fills the place of tact. Casting a rapid glance at Carroll, he cried, "Hallo!" and, wheeling suddenly round on his following guests, with a bewildering extravagance of playful brusqueness, actually bundled them from the room. "The incantation is on!" he cried, waving his arms in the air; "the genie is at work. No admittance except on business! Follow Miss Wilson," he added, clapping both hands on the shoulders of the prettiest and shyest young lady of the party, with an irresistible paternal familiarity. "She's your hostess. I'll honor her drafts to any amount;" and before they were aware of his purpose or that Carroll was no longer among them, Aladdin had closed the door, that shut with a spring lock, and was alone with the young man. He walked quickly to his desk, took up the letter, and opened it.

His face of dominant, self-satisfied good-humor became set and stern. Without taking the least notice of Carroll, he rose, and, stepping to a telegraph instrument at a side table, manipulated half a dozen ivory knobs with a sudden energy. Then he returned to the table, and began hurriedly to glance over the memoranda and indorsements of the files of papers piled upon it. Carroll's quick eye caught sight of a small packet of letters in a writing of unmistakable feminine delicacy, and made certain they were the ones he was in quest of. Without raising his eyes, Mr. Prince asked, almost rudely,—

"Who else has she told this to?"

"If you refer to the contents of that letter, it was written and handed to me about three hours ago. It has not been out of my possession since then."

"Humph! Who's at the casa? There's Buchanan, and Raymond, and Victor Guitierrez, eh?"

"I think I can say almost positively that Mrs. Saltonstall has seen no one but her daughter since the news reached her, if that is what you wish to know," said Carroll, still following the particular package of letters with his eyes, as Mr. Prince continued his examination. Prince stopped.

"Are you sure?"

"Almost sure."

Prince rose, this time with a greater ease of manner, and, going to the table, ran his fingers over the knobs, as if mechanically. "One would like to know at once all there is to know about a transaction that changes the front of four millions of capital in about four hours, eh, Captain?" he said, for the first time really regarding his guest. "Just four hours ago, in this very room, we found out that the widow Saltonstall owed Dr. West about a million, tied up in investments, and we calculated to pull her through with perhaps the loss of half. If she's got this assignment of the Doctor's property that she speaks of in her letter, as collateral security, and it's all regular, and she—so to speak —steps into Dr. West's place, by G—d, sir, we owe *him* about three millions, and we've got to settle with *her*—and that's all about it. You've dropped a little bomb-shell in here, Captain, and the splinters are flying around as far as San Francisco, now. I confess it beats me regularly. I always thought the old man was a little keen over there at the casa—but she was a woman, and he was a man for all his sixty years, and *that* combination I never thought of. I only wonder she hadn't gobbled him up before."

Captain Carroll's face betrayed no trace of the bewilderment and satisfaction at this news of which he had been the unconscious bearer, nor of resentment at the coarseness of its translation.

"There does not seem to be any memorandum of this assignment," continued Prince, turning over the papers.

"Have you looked here?" said Carroll, taking up the packet of letters.

"No—they seem to me some private letters she refers to in this letter, and that she wants back again."

"Let us see," said Carroll, untying the packet. There were three or four closely written notes in Spanish and English.

"Love-letters, I reckon," said Prince—"that's why the old girl wants 'em back. She don't care to have the wheedling that fetched the Doctor trotted out to the public."

"Let us look more carefully," said Carroll, pleasantly, opening each letter before Prince, yet so skillfully as to frustrate any attempt of the latter to read them. "There does not seem to be any memorandum here. They are evidently only private letters."

"Quite so," said Prince.

Captain Carroll retied the packet and put it in his pocket. "Then I'll return them to her," he said, quietly.

"Hullo!—here—I say," said Prince, starting to his feet.

"I said I would return them to her," repeated Carroll, calmly.

"But I never gave them to you! I never consented to their withdrawal from the papers."

"I'm sorry you did not," said Carroll, coldly; "it would have been more polite."

"Polite! D—n it, sir! I call this stealing."

"Stealing, Mr. Prince, is a word that might be used by the person who claims these letters to describe the act of any one who would keep them from *her*. It really can not apply to you or me."

"Once for all, do you refuse to return them to me?" said Prince, pale with anger.

"Decidedly."

"Very well, sir! We shall see." He stepped to the corner and rang a bell. "I have summoned my manager, and will charge you with the theft in his presence."

"I think not."

"And why, sir?"

"Because the presence of a third party would enable me to throw this glove in your face, which, as a gentleman, I couldn't do without witnesses." Steps were heard along the passage; Prince was no coward in a certain way; neither was he a fool. He knew that Carroll would keep his word; he knew that he should have to fight him; that, whatever the issue of the duel was, the cause of the quarrel would be known, and scarcely redound to his credit. At present there were no witnesses to the offered insult, and none would be wiser. The letters were not worth it. He stepped to the door, opened it, said, "No matter," and closed it again.

He returned with an affectation of carelessness. "You are right. I don't know that I'm called upon to make a scene here which the *law* can do for me as well elsewhere. It will settle pretty quick whether you've got the right to those letters, and whether you've taken the right way to get them, sir."

"I have no desire to evade any responsibility in this matter, legal or otherwise," said Carroll, coldly, rising to his feet.

"Look here," said Prince, suddenly, with a return of his brusque frankness; "you might have *asked* me for those letters, you know."

"And you wouldn't have given them to me," said Carroll.

Prince laughed. "That's so! I say, Captain. Did they teach you this sort of strategy at West Point?"

"They taught me that I could neither receive nor give an insult under a white flag," said Carroll, pleasantly. "And they allowed me to make exchanges under the same rule. I picked up this pocket-book on the spot where the accident occurred to Dr. West. It is evidently his. I leave it with you, who are his executor."

The instinct of reticence before a man with whom he could never be confidential kept him from alluding to his other discovery.

Prince took the pocket-book, and opened it mechanically. After a moment's scrutiny of the memoranda it contained, his face assumed something of the same concentrated attention it wore at the beginning of the interview. Raising his eyes suddenly to Carroll, he said, quickly,—

"You have examined it?"

"Only so far as to see that it contained nothing of importance to the person I represent," returned Carroll, simply.

The capitalist looked at the young officer's clear eyes. Something of embarrassment came into his own as he turned them away.

"Certainly. Only memoranda of the Doctor's business. Quite important to us, you know. But nothing referring to *your* principal." He laughed. "Thank you for the exchange. I say—take a drink!"

"Thank you—no!" returned Carroll, going to the door. "Well, good-by."

He held out his hand. Carroll, with his clear eyes still regarding him, passed quietly by the outstretched hand, opened the door, bowed, and made his exit.

A slight flush came into Prince's cheek. Then, as the door closed, he burst into a half-laugh. Had he been a dramatic villain, he would have added to it several lines of soliloquy, in which he would have rehearsed the fact that the opportunity for revenge had "come at last"; that the "haughty victor who had just left with his ill-gotten spoil

had put into his hands the weapon of his friend's destruction"; that the "hour had come"; and, possibly he might
have said, "Ha! ha!" But, being a practical, good-natured,
selfish rascal, not much better or worse than his neighbors,
he sat himself down at his desk and began to carefully consider how *he* could best make use of the memoranda jotted
down by Dr. West of the proofs of the existence of his son,
and the consequent discovery of a legal heir to his property.

CHAPTER VIII

WHEN Faquita had made sure that her young mistress
was so securely closeted with Doña Maria that morning as
to be inaccessible to curious eyes and ears, she saw fit to
bewail to her fellow-servants this further evidence of the
decay of the old feudal and patriarchal mutual family confidences. "Time was, thou rememberest, Pepita, when an
affair of this kind was openly discussed at chocolate with
everybody present, and before us all. When Joaquin Padilla was shot at Monterey, it was the Doña herself who
told us, who read aloud the letters describing it and the
bullet-holes in his clothes, and made it quite a gala-day—
and he was a first-cousin of Guitierrez. And now, when
this American goat of a doctor is kicked to death by a
mule, the family must shut themselves up, that never a question is asked or answered." "Ay," responded Pepita; "and
as regards that, Sanchez there knows as much as they do,
for it was he that almost saw the whole affair."

"How?—sawest it?" inquired Faquita, eagerly.

"Why, was it not he that was bringing home Pereo, who
had been lying in one of his trances or visions—blessed St.
Antonio preserve us!" said Pepita, hastily crossing herself
—"on Kooratora's grave, when the Doctor's mustang
charged down upon them like a wild bull, and the Doctor's
foot half out of the stirrups, and he not yet fast in his
seat? And Pereo laughs a wild laugh and says: 'Watch
if the coyote does not drag yet at his mustang's heels;'
and Sanchez ran and watched the Doctor out of sight,
careering and galloping to his death!—ay, as Pereo prophe-

sied. For it was only half an hour afterward that Sanchez again heard the tramp of his hoofs—as if it were here—and knowing it two miles away—thou understandest, he said to himself: 'It is over.'"

The two women shuddered and crossed themselves.

"And what says Pereo of the fulfillment of his prophecy?" asked Faquita, hugging herself in her shawl with a certain titillating shrug of fascinating horror.

"It is even possible he understands it not. Thou knowest how dazed and dumb he ever is after these visions—that he comes from them as one from the grave, remembering nothing. He has lain like a log all the morning."

"Ay; but this news should awaken him, if aught can. He loved not this sneaking Doctor. Let us seek him; mayhap, Sanchez may be there. Come! The mistress lacks us not just now; the guests are provided for. Come!"

She led the way to the eastern angle of the casa communicating by a low corridor with the corral and stables. This was the old "gate-keep" or quarters of the mayordomo, who, among his functions, was supposed to exercise a supervision over the exits and entrances of the house. A large steward's room or office, beyond it a room of general assembly, half guard-room, half servants' hall, and Pereo's sleeping-room, constituted his domain. A few peons were gathered in the hall near the open door of the apartment where Pereo lay.

Stretched on a low pallet, his face yellow as wax, a light burning under a crucifix near his head, and a spray of blessed palm, popularly supposed to avert the attempts of evil spirits to gain possession of his suspended faculties, Pereo looked not unlike a corpse. Two muffled and shawled domestics, who sat by his side, might have been mourners, but for their voluble and incessant chattering.

"So thou art here, Faquita," said a stout virago. "It is a wonder thou couldst spare time from prayers for the repose of the American Doctor's soul to look after the health of thy superior, poor Pereo! Is it, then, true that Doña Maria said she would have naught more to do with the drunken brute of her mayordomo?"

The awful fascination of Pereo's upturned face did not

prevent Faquita from tossing her head as she replied, pertly, that she was not there to defend her mistress from lazy gossip. "Nay, but *what* said she?" asked the other attendant.

"She said Pereo was to want for nothing; but at present she could not see him."

A murmur of indignation and sympathy passed through the company. It was followed by a long sigh from the insensible man. "His lips move," said Faquita, still fascinated by curiosity. "Hush! he would speak."

"His lips move, but his soul is still asleep," said Sanchez, oracularly. "Thus they have moved since early morning, when I came to speak with him, and found him lying here in a fit upon the floor. He was half dressed, thou seest, as if he had risen to go forth, and had been struck down so—"

"Hush! I tell thee he speaks," said Faquita.

The sick man was faintly articulating through a few tiny bubbles that broke upon his rigid lips. "He—dared —me! He—said—I was old—too old."

"Who dared thee? Who said thou wast too old?" asked the eager Faquita, bending over him.

"He, Koorotora himself! in the shape of a coyote."

Faquita fell back with a little giggle, half of shame, half of awe.

"It is ever thus," said Sanchez, sententiously; "it is what he said last night, when I picked him up on the mound. He will sleep now—thou shalt see. He will get no further than Koorotora and the coyote—and then he will sleep."

And to the awe of the group, and the increased respect for Sanchez's wisdom, Pereo seemed to fall again into a lethargic slumber. It was late in the evening when he appeared to regain perfect consciousness. "Ah—what is this?" he said, roughly, sitting up in bed, and eying the watchers around him, some of whom had succumbed to sleep, and others were engaged in playing cards. "Caramba! are ye mad? Thou, Sanchez, here; who shouldst be at thy work in the stables! Thou, Pepita, is thy mistress asleep or dead, that thou sittest here? Blessed San Antonio! would ye drive me mad?" He lifted his hand to his head, with a dull movement of pain, and attempted to rise from the bed.

"Softly, good Pereo; lie still," said Sanchez, approaching him. "Thou hast been ill—so ill. These, thy friends, have been waiting only for this moment to be assured that thou art better. For this idleness there is no blame—truly none. The Doña Maria has said that thou shouldst lack no care; and, truly, since the terrible news there has been little to do."

"The terrible news?" repeated Pereo.

Sanchez cast a meaning glance upon the others, as if to indicate this confirmation of his diagnosis.

"Ay, terrible news! The Doctor West was found this morning dead two miles from the casa."

"Dr. West dead!" repeated Pereo, slowly, as if endeavoring to master the real meaning of the words. Then, seeing the vacuity of his question reflected on the faces of those around him, he added, hurriedly, with a feeble smile, "O—ay—dead! Yes! I remember. And he has been ill—very ill, eh?"

"It was an accident. He was thrown from his horse, and so killed," returned Sanchez, gravely.

"Killed—by his horse! sayest thou?" said Pereo, with a sudden fixed look in his eye.

"Ay, good Pereo. Dost thou not remember when the mustang bolted with him down upon us in the lane, and then thou didst say he would come to evil with the brute? He did—blessed San Antonio!—within half an hour!"

"How—thou sawest it?"

"Nay; for the mustang was running away and I did not follow. Bueno! it happened all the same. The Alcalde, Coroner, who knows all about it, has said so an hour ago! Juan brought the news from the rancho where the inquest was. There will be a funeral the day after to-morrow! and so it is that some of the family will go. Fancy, Pereo, a Guitierrez at the funeral of the Americano Doctor! Nay, I doubt not that the Doña Maria will ask thee to say a prayer over his bier."

"Peace, fool! and speak not of thy lady mistress,"

thundered the old man, sitting upright. "Begone to the stables. Dost thou hear me? Go!"

"Now, by the Mother of Miracles," said Sanchez, hastening from the room as the gaunt figure of the old man rose, like a sheeted spectre, from the bed, "that was his old self again! Blessed San Antonio! Pereo had recovered."

The next day he was at his usual duties, with perhaps a slight increase of sternness in his manner. The fulfillment of his prophecy related by Sanchez added to the superstitious reputation in which he was held, although Faquita voiced the opinions of a growing skeptical party in the statement that it was easy to prophesy the Doctor's accident, with the spectacle of the horse actually running away before the prophet's eyes. It was even said that Doña Maria's aversion to Pereo since the accident arose from a belief that some assistance might have been rendered by him. But it was pointed out by Sanchez that Pereo had, a few moments before, fallen under one of those singular, epileptic-like strokes to which he was subject, and not only was unfit, but even required the entire care of Sanchez at the time. He did not attend the funeral, nor did Mrs. Saltonstall; but the family was represented by Maruja and Amita, accompanied by one or two dark-faced cousins, Captain Carroll, and Raymond. A number of friends and business associates from the neighboring towns, Aladdin and a party from his house, the farm laborers, and a crowd of working men from his mills in the foot-hills, swelled the assemblage that met in and around the rude agricultural sheds and outhouses which formed the only pastoral habitation of the Rancho of San Antonio. It had been a characteristic injunction of the deceased that he should be buried in the midst of one of his most prolific grain fields, as a grim return to that nature he was impoverishing, with neither mark nor monument to indicate the spot; and that even the temporary mound above him should, at the fitting season of the year, be leveled with the rest of the field by the obliterating plowshares. A grave was accordingly dug about a quarter of a mile from his office amidst a "volunteer" crop so dense that the large space mown around the narrow opening, to admit of the presence of the multitude, seemed like a golden amphitheatre.

A distinguished clergyman from San Francisco officiated.

A man of tact and politic adaptation, he dwelt upon the blameless life of the deceased, on his practical benefit for civilization in the county, and even treated his grim Pantheism in the selection of his grave as a formal recognition of the text, "dust to dust." He paid a not ungrateful compliment to the business associates of the deceased, and, without actually claiming in the usual terms "a continuance of past favors" for their successors, managed to interpolate so strong a recommendation of the late Doctor's commercial projects as to elicit from Aladdin the expressive commendation that his sermon was "as good as five per cent. in the stock."

Maruja, who had been standing near the carriage, languidly silent and abstracted even under the tender attentions of Carroll, suddenly felt the consciousness of another pair of eyes fixed upon her. Looking up, she was surprised to find herself regarded by the man she had twice met, once as a tramp and once as a wayfarer at the fonda, who had quietly joined a group not far from her. At once impressed by the idea that this was the first time that he had really looked at her, she felt a singular shyness creeping over her, until, to her own astonishment and indignation, she was obliged to lower her eyes before his gaze. In vain she tried to lift them, with her old supreme power of fascination. If she had ever blushed, she felt she would have done so now. She knew that her face must betray her consciousness; and at last she—Maruja, the self-poised and all-sufficient goddess—actually turned, in half-hysterical and girlish bashfulness, to Carroll for relief in an affected and exaggerated absorption of his attentions. She scarcely knew that the clergyman had finished speaking, when Raymond approached them softly from behind. "Pray don't believe," he said, appealingly, "that all the human virtues are about to be buried—I should say sown—in that wheat-field. A few will still survive, and creep about above the Doctor's grave. Listen to a story just told me, and dis-

believe—if you dare—in human gratitude. Do you see that
picturesque young ruffian over there?"

Maruja did not lift her eyes. She felt herself breathlessly hanging on the speaker's next words.

"Why, that's the young man of the fonda, who picked up
your fan," said Carroll, "isn't it?"

"Perhaps," said Maruja, indifferently. She would have
given worlds to have been able to turn coldly and stare at
him at that moment with the others, but she dared not.
She contented herself with softly brushing some dust from
Captain Carroll's arm with her fan and a feminine suggestion of tender care which thrilled that gentleman.

"Well," continued Raymond, "that Robert Macaire over
yonder came here some three or four days ago as a tramp,
in want of everything but honest labor. Our lamented
friend consented to parley with him, which was something
remarkable in the Doctor; still more remarkable, he gave
him a suit of clothes, and, it is said, some money, and sent
him on his way. Now, more remarkable than all, our
friend, on hearing of his benefactor's death, actually tramps
back here to attend his funeral. The Doctor being dead,
his executors not of a kind to emulate the Doctor's spas-
modic generosity, and there being no chance of future
favors, the act must be recorded as purely and simply
gratitude. By Jove! I don't know but that he is the only
one here who can be called a real mourner. I'm here because your sister is here; Carroll comes because *you* do,
and you come because your mother can not."

"And who tells you these pretty stories?" asked Maruja,
with her face still turned towards Carroll.

"The foreman, Harrison, who, with an extensive practical
experience of tramps, was struck with this exception to the
general rule."

"Poor man; one ought to do something for him," said
Amita, compassionately.

"What!" said Raymond, with affected terror, "and spoil
this perfect story? Never! If I should offer him ten
dollars, I'd expect him to kick me; if he took it, I'd expect
to kick *him*."

"He is not so bad-looking, is he, Maruja?" asked Amita

of her sister. But Maruja had already moved a few paces off with Carroll, and seemed to be listening to him only. Raymond smiled at the pretty perplexity of Amita's eyebrows over this pronounced indiscretion.

"Don't mind them," he whispered; "you really cannot expect to dueña your elder sister. Tell me, would you actually like me to see if I could assist the virtuous tramp? You have only to speak." But Amita's interest appeared to be so completely appeased with Raymond's simple offer that she only smiled, blushed, and said "No."

Maruja's quick ears had taken in every word of these asides, and for an instant she hated her sister for her aimless declination of Raymond's proposal. But becoming conscious—under her eyelids—that the stranger was moving away with the dispersing crowd, she rejoined Amita with her usual manner. The others had reëntered the carriage, but Maruja took it into her head to proceed on foot to the rude building whence the mourners had issued. The foreman, Harrison, flushed and startled by this apparition of inaccessible beauty at his threshold, came eagerly forward. "I shall not trouble you now, Mr. Har-r-r-rison," she said, with a polite exaggeration of the consonants; "but some day I shall ride over here, and ask you to show me your wonderful machines."

She smiled, and turned back to seek her carriage. But before she had gone many yards she found that she had completely lost it in the intervening billows of grain. She stopped, with an impatient little Spanish ejaculation. The next moment the stalks of wheat parted before her and a figure emerged. It was the stranger.

She fell back a step in utter helplessness.

He, on his side, retreated again into the wheat, holding it back with extended arms to let her pass. As she moved forward mechanically, without a word he moved backward, making a path for her until she was able to discern the coachman's whip above the bending heads of the grain just beyond her. He stopped here and drew to one side, his arms still extended, to give her free passage. She tried to speak, but could only bow her head, and slipped by him with a strange feeling—suggested by his attitude—that she was evading his embrace. But the next moment his arms were lowered, the grain closed around him, and he was lost to her view. She reached the carriage almost unperceived by the inmates, and pounced upon her sister with a laugh.

"Blessed Virgin!" said Amita, "where did you come from?"

"From there!" said Maruja, with a slight nervous shiver, pointing to the clustering grain.

"We were afraid you were lost."

"So was I," said Maruja, raising her pretty lashes heavenwards, as she drew a shawl tightly round her shoulders.

"Has anything happened? You look strange," said Carroll, drawing closer to her.

Here eyes were sparkling, but she was very pale.

"Nothing, nothing!" she said, hastily, glancing at the grain again.

"If it were not that the haste would have been absolutely indecent, I should say that the late Doctor had made you a ghostly visit," said Raymond, looking at her curiously.

"He would have been polite enough not to have commented on my looks," said Maruja. "Am I really such a fright?"

Carroll thought he had never seen her so beautiful. Her eyelids were quivering over their fires as if they had been brushed by the passing wing of a strong passion.

"What are you thinking of?" said Carroll, as they drove on.

She was thinking that the stranger had looked at her admiringly, and that his eyes were blue. But she looked quietly into her lover's face, and said, sweetly, "Nothing, I fear, that would interest you!"

CHAPTER IX

THE news of the assignment of Dr. West's property to Mrs. Saltonstall was followed by the still more astonishing discovery that the Doctor's will further bequeathed to her his entire property, after payment of his debts and liabilities. It was given in recognition of her talents and business integrity during their late association, and as an evidence of the confidence and "undying affection" of the testator. Nevertheless, after the first surprise, the fact was accepted by the community as both natural and proper under that singular instinct of humanity which acquiesces without scruple in the union of two large fortunes, but sharply questions the conjunction of poverty and affluence, and looks only for interested motives where there is disparity of wealth. Had Mrs. Saltonstall been a poor widow instead of a rich one; had she been the Doctor's housekeeper instead of his business friend, the bequest would have been strongly criticised—if not legally tested. But this combination, which placed the entire valley of San Antonio in the control of a single individual, appeared to be perfectly legitimate. More than that, some vague rumor of the Doctor's past and his early entanglements only seemed to make this eminently practical disposition of his property the more respectable, and condoned for any moral irregularities of his youth.

The effect upon the collateral branches of the Guitierrez family and the servants and retainers was even more impressive. For once, it seemed that the fortunes and traditions of the family were changed; the female Guitierrez, instead of impoverishing the property, had augmented it; the foreigner and intruder had been despoiled; the fate of La Mision Perdida had been changed; the curse of Koorotora had proved a blessing; his prophet and descendant, Pereo, the mayordomo, moved in an atmosphere of superstitious adulation and respect among the domestics and common people. This recognition of his power he received at times with a certain exaltation of grandiloquent pride beyond the conception of any but a Spanish servant, and at times with a certain dull, pained vacancy of perception and an expression of frightened bewilderment which also went far to establish his reputation as an unconscious seer and thaumaturgist. "Thou seest," said Sanchez to the partly skeptical Faquita, "he does not know more than an infant what is his power. That is the proof of it." The Doña Maria alone did not participate in this appreciation of Pereo, and when it was proposed that a feast or celebra-

tion of rejoicing should be given under the old pear-tree
by the Indian's mound, her indignation was long remembered by those that witnessed it. "It is not enough that
we have been made ridiculous in the past," she said to Maruja, "by the interference of this solemn fool, but that the
memory of our friend is to be insulted by his generosity
being made into a triumph of Pereo's idiotic ancestor.
One would have thought those coyotes and Koorotora's bones
had been buried with the cruel gossip of your relations"—
(it had been the recent habit of Doña Maria to allude to
"the family" as being particularly related to Maruja alone)
—"over my poor friend. Let him beware that his ancestor's mound is not uprooted with the pear-tree, and his
heathenish temple destroyed. If, as the engineer says, a
branch of the new railroad can be established for La Mision
Perdida, I agree with him that it can better pass at that
point with less sacrifice to the domain. It is the one uncultivated part of the park, and lies at the proper angle."

"You surely would not consent to this, my mother?" said
Maruja, with a sudden impression of a newly found force
in her mother's character.

"Why not, child?" said the relict of Mr. Saltonstall and
the mourner of Dr. West, coldly. "I admit it was discreet
of thee in old times to have thy sentimental passages there
with caballeros who, like the guests of the hidalgo that kept
a skeleton at his feast, were reminded of the mutability of
their hopes by Koorotora's bones and the legend. But with
the explosion of this idea of a primal curse, like Eve's, on
the property," added the Doña Maria, with a slight bitterness, "thou mayest have thy *citas*—elsewhere. Thou canst
scarcely keep this Captain Carroll any longer at a distance
by rattling those bones of Koorotora in his face. And of a
truth, child, since the affair of the letters, and his discreet
and honorable conduct since, I see not why thou shouldst.
He has thy mother's reputation in his hands."

"He is a gentleman, my mother," said Maruja, quietly.

"And they are scarce, child, and should be rewarded and
preserved. That is what I meant, silly one; this Captain
is not rich—but then, thou hast enough for both."

"But it was Amita that first brought him here," said Maruja, looking down with an air of embarrassed thoughtfulness, which Doña Maria chose to instantly accept as exaggerated coyness.

"Do not think to deceive me or thyself, child, with this folly. Thou art old enough to know a man's mind, if not thine own. Besides, I do not know that I shall object to her liking for Raymond. He is very clever, and would be a relief to some of thy relatives. He would be invaluable to us in the emergencies that may grow out of these mechanical affairs that I do not understand—such as the mill and the railroad."

"And you propose to take a few husbands as partners in the business?" said Maruja, who had recovered her spirits. "I warn you that Captain Carroll is as stupid as a gentleman could be. I wonder that he has not blundered in other things as badly as he has in preferring me to Amita. He confided to me only last night, that he had picked up a pocket-book belonging to the Doctor and given it to Aladdin, without a witness or receipt, and evidently of his own accord."

"A pocket-book of the Doctor's?" repeated Doña Maria.

"Ay; but it contained nothing of thine," said Maruja. "The poor child had sense enough to think of that. But I am in no hurry to ask your consent and your blessing yet, little mother. I could even bear that Amita should precede me to the altar, if the exigencies of thy 'business' require it. It might also secure Captain Carroll for me. Nay, look not at me in that cheapening, commercial way—with compound interest in thine eyes. I am not so poor an investment, truly, of thy original capital."

"Thou art thy father's child," said her mother, suddenly kissing her; "and that is saying enough, the Blessed Virgin knows. Go now," she continued, gently pushing her from the room, "and send Amita hither." She watched the disappearance of Maruja's slightly rebellious shoulders, and added to herself, "And this is the child that Amita really believes is pining with lovesickness for Carroll, so that she can neither sleep nor eat. This is the girl that Faquita would have me think hath no longer any heart in her dress or in her finery! Soul of Joseph Saltonstall!" ejaculated the widow, lifting her shoulders and her eyes together, "thou hast much to account for."

Two weeks later she again astonished her daughter. "Why dost thou not join the party that drives over to see the wonders of Aladdin's Palace to-day? It would seem more proper that thou shouldst accompany thy guests than Raymond and Amita."

"I have never entered his doors since the day he was disrespectful to my mother's daughter," said Maruja, in surprise.

"Disrespectful!" repeated Doña Maria, impatiently. "Thy father's daughter ought to know that such as he may be ignorant and vulgar, but can not be disrespectful to her. And there are offenses, child, it is much more crushing to forget than to remember. As long as he has not the presumption to *apologize*, I see no reason why thou mayst not go. He has not been here since that affair of the letters. I shall not permit him to be uncivil over *that*— dost thou understand? He is of use to me in business. Thou mayst take Carroll with thee; he will understand that."

"But Carroll will not go," said Maruja. "He will not say what passed between them, but I suspect they quarreled."

"All the better, then, that thou goest alone. He need not be reminded of it. Fear not but that he will be only too proud of thy visit to think of aught else."

Maruja, who seemed relieved at this prospect of being unaccompanied by Captain Carroll, shrugged her shoulders and assented.

When the party that afternoon drove into the courtyard of Aladdin's Palace, the announcement that its hospitable proprietor was absent, and would not return until dinner, did not abate either their pleasure or their curiosity. As already intimated to the reader, Mr. Prince's functions as host were characteristically irregular; and the servant's suggestion, that Mr. Prince's private secretary would attend to do the honors, created little interest, and was laughingly waived by Maruja. "There really is not the slightest necessity to trouble the gentleman," she said, politely. "I know the house thoroughly, and I think I have shown it once or twice before for your master. Indeed," she added, turning to her party, "I have been already complimented on my skill as a cicerone." After a pause, she continued, with a slight exaggeration of action and in her deepest contralto, "Ahem, ladies and gentlemen, the hall and court in which we are now standing is a perfect copy of the Court of Lions at the Alhambra, and was finished in fourteen days in white pine, gold, and plaster, at a cost of ten thousand dollars. A photograph of the original structure hangs on the wall: you will observe, ladies and gentlemen, that the reproduction is perfect. The Alhambra is in Granada, a province of Spain, which it is said in some respects to resemble California, where you have probably observed the Spanish language is still spoken by the old settlers. We now cross the stable-yard on a bridge which is a fac-simile in appearance and dimensions of the Bridge of Sighs at Venice, connecting the Doge's Palace with the State Prison. Here, on the contrary, instead of being ushered into a dreary dungeon, as in the great original, a fresh surprise awaits us. Allow me, ladies and gentlemen, to precede you for the surprise. We open a door thus—and—presto!"—

She stopped, speechless, on the threshold; the fan fell from her gesticulating hand.

In the centre of a brilliantly-lit conservatory, with golden columns, a young man was standing. As her fan dropped on the tessellated pavement, he came forward, picked it up, and put it in her rigid and mechanical fingers. The party, who had applauded her apparently artistic climax, laughingly pushed by her into the conservatory, without noticing her agitation.

It was the same face and figure she remembered as last standing before her, holding back the crowding grain in the San Antonio field. But here he was appareled and appointed like a gentleman, and even seemed to be superior to the garish glitter of his new surroundings.

"I believe I have the pleasure of speaking to Miss Saltonstall," he said, with the faintest suggestion of his former manner in his half-resentful sidelong glance. "I hear that you offered to dispense with my services, but I knew that Mr. Prince would scarcely be satisfied if I did not urge it once more upon you in person. I am his private secretary."

At the same moment, Amita and Raymond, attracted by the conversation, turned towards him. Their recognition of the man they had seen at Dr. West's was equally distinct. The silence became embarrassing. Two pretty girls of the party pressed to Amita's side, with half-audible whispers. "What is it?" "Who's your handsome and wicked-looking friend?" "Is this the surprise?"

At the sound of their voices, Maruja recovered herself coldly. "Ladies," she said, with a slight wave of her fan, "this is Mr. Prince's private secretary. I believe it is hardly fair to take up his valuable time. Allow me to thank you, sir, FOR PICKING UP MY FAN."

With a single subtle flash of the eye she swept by him, taking her companions to the other end of the conservatory. When she turned, he was gone.

"This was certainly an unexpected climax," said Raymond, mischievously. "Did you really arrange it beforehand? We leave a picturesque tramp at the edge of a grave; we pass over six weeks and a Bridge of Sighs, and hey, presto! we find a private secretary in a conservatory! This is quite the regular Aladdin business."

"You may laugh," said Maruja, who had recovered her spirits, "but if you were really clever you'd find out what it all means. Don't you see that Amita is dying of curiosity?"

"Let us fly at once and discover the secret, then," said Raymond, slipping Amita's arm through his. "We will consult the oracle in the stables. Come."

The others followed, leaving Maruja for an instant alone. She was about to rejoin them when she heard footsteps in the passage they had just crossed, and then perceived that the young stranger had merely withdrawn to allow the party to precede him before he returned to the other building through the conservatory, which he was just entering. In turning quickly to escape, the black lace of her over-skirt caught in the spines of a snaky-looking cactus. She stopped to disengage herself with feverish haste in vain. She was about to sacrifice the delicate material, in her impatience, when the young man stepped quietly to her side.

"Allow me. Perhaps I have more patience, even if I have less time," he said, stooping down. Their ungloved hands touched. Maruja stopped in her efforts and stood up. He continued until he had freed the luckless flounce, conscious of the soft fire of her eyes on his head and neck.

"There," he said, rising, and encountering her glance. As she did not speak, he continued: "You are thinking, Miss Saltonstall, that you have seen me before, are you not? Well—you *have;* I asked you the road to San José one morning when I was tramping by your hedge."

"And as you probably were looking for something better —which you seem to have found—you didn't care to listen to *my* directions," said Maruja, quickly.

"I found a man—almost the only one who ever offered me a gratuitous kindness—at whose grave I afterwards met you. I found another man who befriended me here—where I meet you again."

She was beginning to be hysterically nervous lest any one should return and find them together. She was conscious of a tingling of vague shame. Yet she lingered. The strange fascination of his half-savage melancholy, and a reproachfulness that seemed to arraign her, with the rest of the world, at the bar of his vague resentment, held the delicate fibres of her sensitive being as cruelly and relentlessly as the thorns of the cactus had gripped her silken lace. Without knowing what she was saying, she stammered that she "was glad he connected her with his better fortune," and began to move away. He noticed it with his sidelong lids, and added, with a slight bitterness:—

"I don't think I should have intruded here again, but I thought you had gone. But I—I—am afraid you have not seen the last of me. It was the intention of my employer, Mr. Prince, to introduce me to you and your mother. I suppose he considers it part of my duties here. I must warn you that, if you are here when he returns, he will insist upon it, and upon your meeting me with these ladies at dinner."

"Perhaps so—he is my mother's friend," said Maruja; "but you have the advantage of us—you can always take to the road, you know."

The smile with which she had intended to accompany this speech did not come as readily in execution as it had in conception, and she would have given worlds to have recalled her words. But he said, "That's so," quietly, and turned away, as if to give her an opportunity to escape. She moved hesitatingly towards the passage and stopped. The sound of the returning voices gave her a sudden courage.

"Mr.—"

"Guest," said the young man.

"If we do conclude to stay to dinner as Mr. Prince has said nothing of introducing you to my sister, you must let *me* have that pleasure."

He lifted his eyes to hers with a sudden flush. But she had fled.

She reached her party, displaying her torn flounce as the cause of her delay, and there was a slight quickness in her breathing and her speech which was attributed to the same grave reason. "But, only listen," said Amita, "we've got it all out of the butler and the grooms. It's such a romantic story!"

"What is?" said Maruja, suddenly.

"Why, the private tramp's."

"The peripatetic secretary," suggested Raymond.

"Yes," continued Amita, "Mr. Prince was so struck with his gratitude to the old Doctor that he hunted him up in San José, and brought him here. Since then Prince has been so interested in him—it appears he was somebody in the States, or has rich relations—that he has been telegraphing and making all sorts of inquiries about him, and has even sent out his own lawyer to hunt up everything about him. Are you listening?"

"Yes."

"You seem abstracted."

"I am hungry."

"Why not dine here; it's an hour earlier than at home. Aladdin would fall at your feet for the honor. Do!"

Maruja looked at them with innocent vagueness, as if the possibility were just beginning to dawn upon her.

"And Clara Wilson is just dying to see the mysterious unknown again. Say yes, little Maruja."

Little Maruja glanced at them with a large maternal compassion. "We shall see."

Mr. Prince, on his return an hour later, was unexpectedly delighted with Maruja's gracious acceptance of his invitation to dinner. He was thoroughly sensible of the significance which his neighbors had attached to the avoidance by the Saltonstall heiress of his various parties and gorgeous festivities ever since a certain act of indiscretion—now alleged to have been produced by the exaltation of wine—had placed him under ban. Whatever his feelings were towards her mother, he could not fail to appreciate fully this act of the daughter, which rehabilitated him. It was with more than his usual extravagance—shown even in a certain exaggeration of respect towards Maruja—that he welcomed the party, and made preparations for the dinner. The telegraph and mounted messengers were put into rapid requisition. The bridal suite was placed at the disposal of the young ladies for a dressing-room. The attendant genii surpassed themselves. The evening dresses of Maruja, Amita, and the Misses Wilson, summoned by electricity from La Mision Perdida, and dispatched by the fleetest conveyances, were placed in the arms of their maids, smothered with bouquets, an hour before dinner. An operatic concert troupe, passing through the nearest town, were diverted from their course by the slaves of the ring to discourse hidden music in the music-room during dinner. "Bite my finger, Sweetlips," said Miss Clara Wilson, who had a neat taste for apt quotation, to Maruja, "that I may see if I am awake. It's the Arabian Nights all over again!"

The dinner was a marvel, even in a land of gastronomic marvels; the dessert a miracle of fruits, even in a climate that bore the products of two zones. Maruja, from her seat beside her satisfied host, looked across a bank of yellow roses at her sister and Raymond, and was timidly conscious of the eyes of young Guest, who was seated at the other

end of the table, between the two Misses Wilson. With a
strange haunting of his appearance on the day she first
met him, she stole glances of half-frightened curiosity at
him while he was eating, and was relieved to find that he
used his knife and fork like the others, and that his appetite
was far from voracious. It was his employer who was the
first to recall the experiences of his past life, with a certain
enthusiasm and the air of a host anxious to contribute to
the entertainment of his guests. "You'd hardly believe,
Miss Saltonstall, that that young gentleman over there
walked across the Continent—and two thousand odd miles,
wasn't it?—all alone, and with not much more in the way
of traps than he's got on now. Tell 'em, Harry, how the
Apaches nearly gobbled you up, and then let you go because they thought you as good an Injun as any one of
them, and how you lived a week in the desert on two biscuits
as big as that." A chorus of entreaty and delighted anticipation followed the suggestion. The old expression of
being at bay returned for an instant to Guest's face, but,
lifting his eyes, he caught a look of almost sympathetic
anxiety from Maruja's, who had not spoken.

"It became necessary for me, some time ago," said Guest,
half explanatorily, to Maruja, "to be rather explicit in the
details of my journey here, and I told Mr. Prince some
things which he seems to think interesting to others. That
is all. To save my life on one occasion, I was obliged to
show myself as good as an Indian, in his own way, and I
lived among them and traveled with them for two weeks.
I have been hungry, as I suppose others have on like oc-
casions, but nothing more."

Nevertheless, in spite of his evident reticence, he was
obliged to give way to their entreaties, and, with a certain
grim and uncompromising truthfulness of statement, recounted some episodes of his journey. It was none the less
thrilling that he did it reluctantly, and in much the same
manner as he had answered his father's questions, and as
he had probably responded to the later cross-examination
of Mr. Prince. He did not tell it emotionally, but rather
with the dogged air of one who had been subjected to a
personal grievance for which he neither asked nor expected

sympathy. When he did not raise his eyes to Maruja's, he kept them fixed on his plate.

"Well," said Prince, when a long-drawn sigh of suspended emotion among the guests testified to his powers as a caterer to their amusement, "what do you say to some music with our coffee to follow the story?"

"It's more like a play," said Amita to Raymond. "What a pity Captain Carroll, who knows all about Indians, isn't here to have enjoyed it. But I suppose Maruja, who hasn't lost a word, will tell it to him."

"I don't think she will," said Raymond, dryly, glancing at Maruja, who, lost in some intricate pattern of her Chinese plate, was apparently unconscious that her host was waiting her signal to withdraw.

At last she raised her head, and said, gently but audibly, to the waiting Prince,—

"It is positively a newer pattern; the old one had not that delicate straw line in the arabesque. You must have had it made for you."

"I did," said the gratified Prince, taking up the plate. "What eyes you have, Miss Saltonstall. They see everything."

"Except that I'm keeping you all waiting," she returned, with a smile, letting the eyes in question fall with a half-parting salutation on Guest as she rose. It was the first exchange of a common instinct between them, and left them as conscious as if they had pressed hands.

The music gave an opportunity for some desultory conversation, in which Mr. Prince and his young friend received an invitation from Maruja to visit La Mision, and the party, by common consent, turned into the conservatory, where the genial host begged them each to select a flower from a few especially rare exotics. When Maruja received hers, she said, laughingly, to Prince, "Will you think me very importunate if I ask for another?" "Take what you like—you have only to name it," he replied, gallantly. "But that's just what I can't do," responded the young girl, "unless," she added, turning to Guest, "unless you can assist me. It was the plant I was examining to-day." "I think I can show it to you," said Guest, with a slight increase of

color, as he preceded her towards the memorable cactus near
the door, "but I doubt if it has any flower."

Nevertheless, it had. A bright red blossom, like a spot of
blood drawn by one of its thorns. He plucked it for her,
and she placed it in her belt.

"You are forgiving," he said, admiringly.

"*You* ought to know that," she returned, looking down.

"*I?*—why?"

"You were rude to me twice."

"Twice!"

"Yes—once at the Mision of La Perdida; once in the road
at San Antonio."

His eyes became downcast and gloomy. "At the Mision
that morning, I, a wretched outcast, only saw in you a
beautiful girl intent on overriding me with her merciless
beauty. At San Antonio I handed the fan I picked up to
the man whose eyes told me he loved you."

She started impatiently. "You might have been more gallant, and found more difficulty in the selection," she said,
pertly. "But since when have you gentlemen become so
observant and so punctilious? Would you expect him to be
as considerate of others?"

"I have few claims that any one seems bound to respect," he returned, brusquely. Then, in a softer voice, he
added, looking at her, gently,—

"You were in mourning when you came here this afternoon, Miss Saltonstall."

"Was I? It was for Dr. West—my mother's friend."

"It was very becoming to you."

"You are complimenting me. But I warn you that
Captain Carroll said something better than that; he said
mourning was not necessary for me. I had only to
'put my eye-lashes at half-mast.' He is a soldier you
know."

"He seems to be as witty as he is fortunate," said Guest,
bitterly.

"Do you think he is fortunate?" said Maruja, raising her
eyes to his. There was so much in this apparently simple
question that Guest looked in her eyes for a suggestion.
What he saw there for an instant made his heart stop beat-

ing. She apparently did not know it, for she began to tremble too.

"Is he not?" said Guest, in a low voice.

"Do you think he ought to be?" she found herself whispering.

A sudden silence fell upon them. The voices of their companions seemed very far in the distance; the warm breath of the flowers appeared to be drowning their senses; they tried to speak, but could not; they were so near to each other that the two long blades of a palm served to hide them. In the midst of this profound silence a voice that was like and yet unlike Maruja's said twice, "Go! go!" but each time seemed hushed in the stifling silence. The next moment the palms were pushed aside, the dark figure of a young man slipped like some lithe animal through the shrubbery, and Maruja found herself standing, pale and rigid, in the middle of the walk, in the full glare of the light, and looking down the corridor toward her approaching companions. She was furious and frightened; she was triumphant and trembling; without thought, sense, or reason, she had been kissed by Henry Guest, and—had returned it.

The fleetest horses of Aladdin's stud that night could not carry her far enough or fast enough to take her away from that moment, that scene, and that sensation. Wise and experienced, confident in her beauty, secure in her selfishness, strong over others' weaknesses, weighing accurately the deeds and words of men and women, recognizing all there was in position and tradition, seeing with her father's clear eyes the practical meaning of any divergence from that conventionality which as a woman of the world she valued, she returned again and again to the trembling joy of that intoxicating moment. She though of her mother and sisters, of Raymond and Garnier, of Aladdin—she even forced herself to think of Carroll—only to shut her eyes, with a faint smile, and dream again the brief but thrilling dream of Guest that began and ended in their joined and parted lips. Small wonder that, hidden and silent in her enwrappings, as she lay back in the carriage, with her pale face against the cold starry sky, two other stars came out and glistened and trembled on her passion-fringed lashes.

CHAPTER X

THE rainy season had set in early. The last three weeks
of summer drought had drained the great valley of its life-
blood; the dead stalks of grain rustled like dry bones over
Dr. West's grave. The desiccating wind and sun had
wrought some disenchanting cracks and fissures in Aladdin's Palace, and otherwise disjoined it, so that it not only
looked as if it were ready to be packed away, but had become finally untenable in the furious onset of the southwesterly rains. The gorgeous furniture of the reception-
rooms was wrapped in mackintoshes, the conservatory was
changed into an aquarium, the Bridge of Sighs crossed an
actual canal in the stable-yard. Only the billiard-room and
Mr. Prince's bed-room and office remained intact, and
in the latter, one stormy afternoon, Mr. Prince himself
sat busy over his books and papers. His station-
wagon, splashed and streaked with mud, stood in the
court-yard, just as it had been driven from the station,
and the smell of the smoke of newly-lit fires showed that
the house had been opened only for this hurried visit of
its owner.

The tramping of horse hoofs in the court-yard was soon
followed by steps along the corridor, and the servant ushered
Captain Carroll into the presence of his master. The Captain did not remove his military overcoat, but remained
standing erect in the centre of the room, with his forage
cap in his hand.

"I could have given you a lift from the station," said
Prince, "if you had come that way. I've only just got in
myself."

"I preferred to ride," said Carroll, dryly.

"Sit down by the fire," said Prince, motioning to a chair,
"and dry yourself."

"I must ask you first the purport of this interview," said
Carroll, curtly, "before I prolong it further. You have
asked me to come here in reference to certain letters I returned to their rightful owner some months ago. If you

seek to reclaim them again, or to refer to a subject which must remain forgotten, I decline to proceed further."

"It *does* refer to the letters, and it rests with you whether they shall be forgotten or not. It is not my fault if the subject has been dropped. You must remember that until yesterday you have been absent on a tour of inspection and could not be applied to before."

Carroll cast a cold glance at Prince, and then threw himself into a chair, with his overcoat still on and his long military boots crossed before the fire. Sitting there in profile Prince could not but notice that he looked older and sterner than at their last interview, and his cheeks were thinned as if by something more than active service.

"When you were here last summer," began Prince, leaning forward over his desk, "you brought me a piece of news that astounded me, as it did many others. It was the assignment of Dr. West's property to Mrs. Saltonstall. That was something there was no gainsaying; it was a purely business affair, and involved nobody's rights but the assignor. But this was followed, a day or two after, by the announcement of the Doctor's will, making the same lady the absolute and sole inheritor of the same property. That seemed all right too; for there were, apparently, no legal heirs. Since then, however, it has been discovered that there is a legal heir—none other than the Doctor's only son. Now, as no allusion to the son's existence was made in that will —which was a great oversight of the Doctor's—it is a fiction of the law that such an omission is an act of forgetfulness, and therefore leaves the son the same rights as if there had been no will at all. In other words, if the Doctor had seen fit to throw his scapegrace son a hundred dollar bill, it would have been legal evidence that he remembered him. As he did not, it's a fair legal presumption that he forgot him, or that the will is incomplete."

"This seems to be a question for Mrs. Saltonstall's lawyers—not for her friends," said Carroll, coldly.

"Excuse me; that remains for you to decide—when you hear all. You understand at present, then, that Dr. West's property, both by assignment and will, was made over, in the event of his death, not to his legal heirs, but to a com-

4   v. 1

parative stranger. It looked queer to a good many people, but the only explanation was, that the Doctor had fallen very much in love with the widow—that he would have probably married her—had he lived."

With an unpleasant recollection that this was almost exactly Maruja's explanation of her mother's relations to Dr. West, Carroll returned, impatiently, "If you mean that their private relations may be made the subject of legal discussion, in the event of litigation in regard to the property, that again is a matter for Mrs. Saltonstall to decide—and not her friends. It is purely a matter of taste."

"It may be a matter of discretion, Captain Carroll."

"Of discretion!" repeated Carroll, superciliously.

"Well," said Prince, leaving his desk and coming to the fire-place, with his hands in his pockets, "what would you call it, if it could be found that Dr. West, on leaving Mrs. Saltonstall's that night, did *not* meet with an accident, was *not* thrown from his horse, but was coolly and deliberately murdered!"

Captain Carroll's swift recollection of the discovery he himself had made in the road, and its inconsistency with the accepted theory of the accident, unmistakably showed itself in his face. It was a moment before he recovered himself.

"But even if it can be proved to have been a murder and not an accident, what has that to do with Mrs. Saltonstall or her claim to the property?"

"Only that she was the one person directly benefited by his death."

Captain Carroll looked at him steadily, and then rose to his feet. "Do I understand that you have called me here to listen to this infamous aspersion of a lady?"

"I have called you here, Captain Carroll, to listen to the arguments that may be used to set aside Dr. West's will, and return the property to the legal heir. You are to listen to them or not, as you choose; but I warn you that your opportunity to hear them in confidence and convey them to your friend will end here. *I* have no opinion in the case. *I* only tell you that it will be argued that Dr. West was unduly influenced to make a will in Mrs. Saltonstall's favor; that, after having done so, it will be shown that, just before his death, he became aware of the existence of his son and heir, and actually had an interview with him; that he visited Mrs. Saltonstall that evening, with the records of his son's identity and a memorandum of his interview in his pocket-book; and that, an hour after leaving the house, he was foully murdered. That is the theory which Mrs. Saltonstall has to consider. I told you I have no opinion. I only know that there are witnesses to the inter view of the Doctor and his son; there is evidence of murder, and the murderer is suspected; there is the evidence of the pocket-book, with the memorandum picked up on the spot, which you handed me yourself."

"Do you mean to say that you will permit this pocket-book, handed you in confidence, to be used for such an infamous purpose?" said Carroll.

"I think you offered it to me in exchange for Dr. West's letters to Mrs. Saltonstall," returned Prince, dryly. "The less said about that, the less is likely to be said about compromising letters written by the widow to the Doctor, which she got you to recover—letters which they may claim had a bearing on the case, and even lured him to his fate."

For an instant Captain Carroll recoiled before the gulf which seemed to open at the feet of the unhappy family. For an instant a terrible doubt possessed him, and in that doubt he found a new reason for a certain changed and altered tone in Maruja's later correspondence with him, and the vague hints she had thrown out of the impossibility of their union. "I beg you will not press me to greater candor," she had written, "and try to forget me before you learn to hate me." For an instant he believed—and even took a miserable comfort in the belief—that it was this hideous secret, and not some coquettish caprice, to which she vaguely alluded. But it was only for a moment; the next instant the monstrous doubt passed from the mind of the simple gentleman, with only a slight flush of shame at his momentary disloyalty.

Prince, however, had noticed it, not without a faint sense of sympathy. "Look here!" he said, with a certain brusqueness, which in a man of his character was less dangerous

than his smoothness. "I know your feelings to that family
—at least to one of them—and, if I've been playing it
pretty rough on you, it's only because you played it rather
rough on *me* the last time you were here. Let's understand each other. I'll go so far as to say *I* don't believe
that Mrs. Saltonstall had anything to do with that murder,
but, as a business man, I'm bound to say that these circumstances and her own indiscretion are quite enough to bring
the biggest pressure down on her. I wouldn't want any
better 'bear' on the market value of her rights than this.
Take it at its best. Say that the Coroner's verdict is set
aside, and a charge of murder against unknown parties is
made—"

"One moment, Mr. Prince," said Carroll. "I shall be one
of the first to insist that this is done, and I have confidence
enough in Mrs. Saltonstall's honest friendship for the Doctor to know that she will lose no time in pursuing his
murderers."

Prince looked at Carroll with a feeling of half envy and
half pity. "I think not," he said, dryly; "for all suspicion
points to one man as the perpetrator, and that man was
Mrs. Saltonstall's confidential servant—the mayordomo,
Pereo." He waited for a moment for the effect of this announcement on Carroll, and then went on: "You now understand that, even if Mrs. Saltonstall is acquitted of any
connivance with or even knowledge of the deed, she will
hardly enjoy the prosecution of her confidential servant for
murder."

"But how can this be prevented? If, as you say, there are
actual proofs, why have they not been acted upon before?
What can keep them from being acted upon now?"

"The proofs have been collected by one man, have been
in possession of one man, and will only pass out of his
possession when it is for the benefit of the legal heir—who
does not yet even know of their existence."

"And who is this one man?"

"Myself."

"You?—You?" said Carroll, advancing towards him.
"Then this is *your* work!"

"Captain Carroll," said Prince, without moving, but

drawing his lips tightly together and putting his head on one side, "I don't propose to have another scene like the one we had at our last meeting. If you try on anything of that kind, I shall put the whole matter into a lawyer's hands. I don't say that you won't regret it; I don't say that I sha'nt be disappointed, too, for I have been managing this thing purely as a matter of business, with a view to profiting by it. It so happens that we can both work to the same end, even if our motives are not the same. I don't call myself an officer and a gentleman, but I reckon I've run this affair about as delicately as the best of them, and with a d——d sight more horse sense. I want this thing hushed up and compromised, to get some control of the property again, and to prevent it depreciating, as it would, in litigation; you want it hushed up for the sake of the girl and your future mother-in-law. I don't know anything about your laws of honor, but I've laid my cards on the table for you to see, without asking what you've got in your hand. You can play the game or leave the board, as you choose." He turned and walked to the window—not without leaving on Carroll's mind a certain sense of firmness, truthfulness, and sincerity which commanded his respect.

"I withdraw any remark that might have seemed to reflect on your business integrity, Mr. Prince," said Carroll, quietly. "I am willing to admit that you have managed this thing better than I could, and, if I join you in an act to suppress these revelations, I have no right to judge of your intentions. What do you propose to have me do?"

"To state the whole case to Mrs. Saltonstall, and to ask her to acknowledge the young man's legal claim without litigation."

"But how do you know that she would not do this without—excuse me—without intimidation?"

"I only reckon that a woman clever enough to get hold of a million, would be clever enough to keep it—against others."

"I hope to show you are mistaken. But where is this heir?"

"Here."

"Here?"

"Yes. For the last six months he has been my private secretary. I know what you are thinking of, Captain Carroll. You would consider it indelicate—eh? Well, that's just where we differ. By this means I have kept everything in my own hands—prevented him from getting into the hands of outsiders—and I intend to dispose of just as much of the facts to him as may be necessary for him to prove his title. What bargain I make with *him*—is my affair."

"Does he suspect the murder?"

"No. I did not think it necessary for his good or mine. He can be an ugly devil if he likes, and although there wasn't much love lost between him and the old man, it wouldn't pay to have any revenge mixed up with business. He knows nothing of it. It was only by accident that, looking after his movements while he was here, I ran across the tracks of the murderer."

"But what has kept him from making known his claim to the Saltonstalls? Are you sure he has not?" said Carroll, with a sudden thought that it might account for Maruja's strangeness.

"Positive. He's too proud to make a claim unless he could thoroughly prove it, and only a month ago he made me promise to keep it dark. He's too lazy to trouble himself about it much anyway—as far as I can see. D——d if I don't think his being a tramp has made him lose his taste for everything! Don't worry yourself about *him*. He isn't likely to make confidences with the Saltonstalls, for he don't like 'em, and never went there but once. Instinctively or not, the widow didn't cotton to him; and I fancy Miss Maruja has some old grudge against him for that fan business on the road. She isn't a girl to forgive or forget anything, as I happen to know," he added, with an uneasy laugh.

Carroll was too preoccupied with the danger that seemed to threaten his friends from this surly pretender to resent Prince's tactless allusion. He was thinking of Maruja's ominous agitation at his presence at Dr. West's grave. "Do they suspect him at all?"—he asked, hurriedly.

"How should they? He goes by the name of Guest—which was his father's real name until changed by an act of legislation when he first came here. Nobody remembers it. We only found it out from his papers. It was quite legal, as all his property was acquired under the name of West."

Carroll rose and buttoned his overcoat. "I presume you are able to offer conclusive proofs of everything you have asserted?"

"Perfectly."

"I am going to the Mision Perdida now," said Captain Carroll, quietly. "To-morrow I will bring you the answer—Peace or War." He walked to the door, lifted his hand to his cap, with a brief military salutation, and disappeared.

CHAPTER XI

As Captain Carroll urged his horse along the miry road to La Mision Perdida, he was struck with certain changes in the landscape before him other than those wrought by the winter rains. There were the usual deep gullies and trenches, half-filled with water, in the fields and along the road, but there were ominous embankments and ridges of freshly turned soil, and a scattered fringe of timbers following a cruel, undeviating furrow on the broad grazing lands of the Mission. But it was not until he had crossed the arroyo that he felt the full extent of the late improvements. A quick rumbling in the distance, a light flash of steam above the willow copse, that drifted across the field on his right, and he knew that the railroad was already in operation. Captain Carroll reined in his frightened charger, and passed his hand across his brow with a dazed sense of loss. He had been gone only four months—yet he already felt strange and forgotten.

It was with a feeling of relief that he at last turned from the high-road into the lane. Here everything was unchanged, except that the ditches were more thickly strewn with the sodden leaves of fringing oaks and sycamores. Giving his horse to a servant in the court-yard, he did not

enter the patio, but, crossing the lawn, stepped upon the
long veranda. The rain was dripping from its eaves and
striking a minute spray from the vines that clung to its
columns; his footfall awoke a hollow echo as he passed, as
if the outer shell of the house were deserted; the formal
yews and hemlocks that in summer had relieved the dazzling glare of six months' sunshine had now taken gloomy
possession of the garden, and the evening shadows, thick-
ened by rain, seemed to lie in wait at every corner. The
servant, who had, with old-fashioned courtesy, placed the
keys and the "disposition" of that wing of the house at his
service, said that Doña Maria would wait upon him in the
salon before dinner. Knowing the difficulty of breaking
the usual rigid etiquette, and trusting to the happy intervention of Maruja—though here, again, custom debarred
him from asking for her—he allowed the servant to remove
his wet overcoat, and followed him to the stately and solemn
chamber prepared for him. The silence and gloom of the
great house, so grateful and impressive in the ardent summer, began to weigh upon him under this shadow of an
overcast sky. He walked to the window and gazed out on
the cloister-like veranda. A melancholy willow at an angle
of the stables seemed to be wringing its hands in the rising wind. He turned for relief to the dim fire that flickered
like a votive taper in the vault-like hearth, and drew a chair
towards it. In spite of the impatience and preoccupation
of a lover, he found himself again and again recurring to
the story he had just heard, until the vengeful spirit of the
murdered Doctor seemed to darken and possess the house.
He was striving to shake off the feeling, when his attention
was attracted to stealthy footsteps in the passage. Could it
be Maruja? He rose to his feet, with his eye upon the
door. The footsteps ceased—it remained closed. But another door, which had escaped his attention in the darkened
corner, slowly swung on its hinges, and, with a stealthy
step, Pereo, the mayordomo, entered the room.

Courageous and self-possessed as Captain Carroll was by
nature and education, this malevolent vision, and incarnation of the thought uppermost in his mind, turned him cold.
He had half drawn a derringer from his breast, when his

eye fell on the grizzled locks and wrinkled face of the old man, and his hand dropped to his side. But Pereo, with the quick observation of insanity, had noticed the weapon, and rubbed his hands together, with a malicious laugh.

"Good! good! good!" he whispered, rapidly, in a strange bodiless voice; " 't will serve! 't will serve! And you are a soldier too—and know how to use it! Good, it is a Providence!" He lifted his hollow eyes to heaven, and then added, "Come! come!"

Carroll stepped towards him. He was alone and in the presence of an undoubted madman—one strong enough, in spite of his years, to inflict a deadly injury, and one whom he now began to realize might have done so once before. Nevertheless, he laid his hand on the old man's arm, and, looking him calmly in the eye, said, quietly, "Come? Where, Pereo? I have only just arrived."

"I know it," whispered the old man, nodding his head violently. "I was watching them, when you rode up. That is why I lost the scent; but together we can track them still —we can track them. Eh, Captain, eh! Come! Come!" and he moved slowly backward, waving his hand towards the door.

"Track whom, Pereo?" said Carroll, soothingly. "Whom do you seek?"

"Whom?" said the old man, startled for a moment and passing his hand over his wrinkled forehead. "Whom? Eh! Why, the Doña Maruja and the little black cat—her maid—Faquita!"

"Yes, but why seek them? Why track them?"

"Why?" said the old man, with a sudden burst of impotent passion. "*You* ask me why! Because they are going to the rendezvous again. They are going to seek him, Do you understand—to seek *him*—the Coyote!"

"Carroll smiled a faint smile of relief—"So—the Coyote!"

"Ay," said the old man, in a confidential whisper; "the Coyote! But not the *big* one—you understand—the little one. The big one is dead—dead—dead! But the little one lives yet. You shall do for *him* what I, Pereo—listen—" he glanced around the room furtively—"what I—the good old Pereo, did for the big one! Good, it is a Providence. Come!"

Of the terrible thoughts that crossed Carroll's mind at this unexpected climax one alone was uppermost. The trembling irresponsible wretch before him meditated some vague crime—and Maruja was in danger. He did not allow himself to dwell upon any other suspicion suggested by that speech; he quickly conceived a plan of action. To have rung the bell and given Pereo into the hands of the servants would have only exposed to them the lunatic's secret —if he had any—and he might either escape in his fury or relapse into useless imbecility. To humor him and follow him, and trust afterwards to his own quickness and courage to avert any calamity, seemed to be the only plan. Captain Carroll turned his clear glance on the restless eyes of Pereo, and said, without emotion, "Let us go, then, and quickly. You shall track them for me; but remember, good Pereo, you must leave the rest to me."

In spite of himself, some accidental significance in this ostentatious adjuration to lull Pereo's suspicions struck him with pain. But the old man's eyes glittered with gratified passion as he said, "Ay, good! I will keep my word. Thou shalt work thy will on the little one as I have said. Truly it is a Providence! Come!" Seeing Captain Carroll glance round for his overcoat, he seized a poncho from the wall, wrapped it round him, and grasped his hand. Carroll, who would have evaded this semblance of disguise, had no time to parley, and they turned together, through the door by which Pereo had entered, into a long dark passage, which seemed to be made through the outer shell of the building that flanked the park. Following his guide in the profound obscurity, perfectly conscious that any change in his madness might be followed by a struggle in the dark, where no help could reach them, they presently came to a door that opened upon the fresh smell of rain and leaves. They were standing at the bottom of a secluded alley, between two high hedges that hid it from the end of the garden. Its grass-grown walk and untrimmed hedges showed that it was seldom used. Carroll, still keeping close to Pereo's side, felt him suddenly stop and tremble.

"Look!" he said, pointing to a shadowy figure some distance before them; "look, 'tis Maruja, and alone!"

With a dexterous movement, Carroll managed to slip his arm securely through the old man's, and even to throw himself before him, as if in his eagerness to discern the figure.

"'Tis Maruja—and alone!" said Pereo, trembling. "Alone! Eh! And the Coyote is not here!" He passed his hand over his staring eyes. "So." Suddenly he turned upon Carroll. "Ah, do you not see, it is a trick! The Coyote is escaping with Faquita! Come! Nay; thou wilt not? Then will I!" With an unexpected strength born of his madness, he freed his arm from Carroll and darted down the alley. The figure of Maruja, evidently alarmed at his approach, glided into the hedge, as Pereo passed swiftly by, intent only on his one wild fancy. Without a further thought of his companion or even the luckless Faquita, Carroll also plunged through the hedge, to intercept Maruja. But by that time she was already crossing the upper end of the lawn, hurrying towards the entrance to the patio. Carroll did not hesitate to follow. Keeping in view the lithe, dark, active little figure, now hidden by an intervening cluster of bushes, now fading in the gathering evening shadows, he nevertheless did not succeed in gaining upon her until she had nearly reached the patio. Here he lost ground, as turning to the right, instead of entering the court-yard, she kept her way toward the stables. He was near enough, however, to speak. "One moment, Miss Saltonstall," he said hurriedly; "there is no danger. I am alone. But I must speak with you."

The young girl seemed only to redouble her exertions. At last she stopped before a narrow door hidden in the wall, and fumbled in her pocket for a key. That moment Carroll was upon her.

"Forgive me, Miss Saltonstall—Maruja; but you must hear me! You are safe, but I fear for your maid, Faquita!"

A little laugh followed his speech; the door yielded and opened to her vanishing figure. For an instant the lace shawl muffling her face was lifted, as the door closed and locked behind her. Carroll drew back in consternation. It was the laughing eyes and saucy face of Faquita!

CHAPTER XII

WHEN Captain Carroll turned from the high-road into the lane, an hour before, Maruja and Faquita had already left the house by the same secret passage and garden-door that opened afterwards upon himself and Pereo. The young women had evidently changed dresses: Maruja was wearing the costume of her maid; Faquita was closely veiled and habited like her mistress; but it was characteristic that, while Faquita appeared awkward and over-dressed in her borrowed plumes, Maruja's short saya and trim bodice, with the striped shawl that hid her fair head, looked infinitely more coquettish and bewitching than on its legitimate owner.

They passed hurriedly down the long alley, and at its further end turned at right angles to a small gate half hidden in the shrubbery. It opened upon a venerable vineyard, that dated back to the occupation of the padres, but was now given over to the chance cultivation of peons and domestics. Its long, broken rows of low vines, knotted and overgrown with age, reached to the thicketed hillside of buckeye that marked the beginning of the cañada. Here Maruja parted from her maid, and, muffling the shawl more closely round her head, hastily passed between the vine rows to a ruined adobe building near the hillside. It was originally part of the refectory of the old Mision, but had been more recently used as a viñadero's cottage. As she neared it, her steps grew slower, until, reaching its door, she hesitated, with her hand timidly on the latch. The next moment she opened it gently; it was closed quickly behind her, and, with a little stifled cry, she found herself in the arms of Henry Guest.

It was only for an instant; the pleading of her white hands, disengaged from his neck, where at first they had found themselves, and uplifted before her face, touched him more than the petitioning eyes or the sweet voiceless mouth, whose breath even was forgotten. Letting her sink into the chair from which he had just risen, he drew back a step, with his hands clasped before him, and his dark half-savage eyes bent earnestly upon her. Well might he have gazed. It was no longer the conscious beauty, proud and regnant, seated before him; but a timid, frightened girl, struggling with her first deep passion.

All that was wise and gentle that she had intended to say, all that her clear intellect and experience had taught her, died upon her lips with that kiss. And all that she could do of womanly dignity and high-bred decorum was to tuck her small feet under her chair, in the desperate attempt to lengthen her short skirt, and beg him not to look at her.

"I have had to change dresses with Faquita, because we were watched," she said, leaning forward in her chair and drawing the striped shawl around her shoulders. "I have had to steal out of my mother's house and through the fields, as if I was a gypsy. If I only were a gypsy, Harry, and not—"

"And not the proudest heiress in the land," he interrupted, with something of his old bitterness. "True, I had forgot."

"But I never reminded *you* of it," she said, lifting her eyes to his. "I did not remind you of it on that day—in —in—in the conservatory, nor at the time you first spoke of—of—love to me—nor from the time I first consented to meet you here. It is *you,* Harry, who have spoken of the difference of our condition, *you* who have talked of my wealth, my family, my position—until I would gladly have changed places with Faquita as I have garments, if I had thought it would make you happier."

"Forgive me, darling!" he said, dropping on one knee before her and bending over the cold little hand he had taken, until his dark head almost rested in her lap. "Forgive me! You are too proud, Maruja, to admit, even to yourself, that you have given your heart where your hand and fortune could not follow. But others may not think so. I am proud, too, and will not have it said that I have won you before I was worthy of you."

"You have no right to be more proud than I, sir," she

said, rising to her feet, with a touch of her old supreme assertion. "No—don't, Harry—please, Harry—there!" Nevertheless, she succumbed; and, when she went on, it was with her head resting on his shoulder. "It's this deceit and secrecy that is so shameful, Harry. I think I could bear everything with you, if it were all known—if you came to woo me like—like—the others. Even if they abused you—if they spoke of your doubtful origin—of your poverty—of your hardships! When they aspersed you, I could fight them; when they spoke of your having no father that you could claim, I could even lie for you, I think, Harry, and say that you had; if they spoke of your poverty, I would speak of my wealth; if they talked of your hardships, I should only be proud of your endurance—if I could only keep the tears from my eyes!" They were there now. He kissed them away.

"But if they threatened you? If they drove me from the house?"

"I should fly with you," she said, hiding her head in his breast.

"What if I were to ask you to fly with me now?" he said, gloomily.

"Now!" she repeated, lifting her frightened eyes to his. His face darkened, with its old look of savage resentment. "Hear me, Maruja," he said, taking her hands tightly in his own. "When I forgot myself—when I was mad that day in the conservatory, the only expiation I could think of was to swear in my inmost soul that I would never take advantage of your forgiveness, that I would never tempt you to forget yourself, your friends, your family, for me, an unknown outcast. When I found you pitied me, and listened to my love—I was too weak to forego the one ray of sunshine in my wretched life—and, thinking that I had a prospect before me in an idea I promised to reveal to you later, I swore never to beguile you or myself in that hope by any act that might bring you to repent it—or myself to dishonor. But I taxed myself too much, Maruja. I have asked too much of you. You are right, darling; this secrecy—this deceit—is unworthy of us! Every hour of it—blest as it has been to me—every

moment—sweet as it is—blackens the purity of our only
defense, makes you false and me a coward! It must end
here—to-day! Maruja, darling, my precious one! God
knows what may be the success of my plans. We have
but one chance now. I must leave here to-day, never to
return, or I must take you with me. Do not start, Maruja—but hear me out. Dare you risk all? Dare you fly
with me now, to-night, to the old Padre at the ruined
Mision, and let him bind us in those bonds that none dare
break? We can take Faquita with us—it is but a few
miles—and we can return and throw ourselves at your
mother's feet. She can only drive us forth together. Or
we can fly from this cursed wealth, and all the misery it has
entailed—forever."

She raised her head, and, with her two hands on his
shoulders, gazed at him with her father's searching eyes, as
if to read his very soul.

"Are you mad, Harry!—think what you propose! Is
this not tempting me? Think again, dearest," she said, half
convulsively, seizing his arm when her grasp had slipped
from his shoulder.

There was a momentary silence as she stood with her
eyes fixed almost wildly on his set face. But a sudden shock
against the bolted door and an inarticulate outcry startled
them. With an instinctive movement, Guest threw his arm
round her.

"It's Pereo," she said, in a hurried whisper, but once
more mistress of her strength and resolution. "He is seeking *you!* Fly at once. He is mad, Harry; a raving lunatic. He watched us the last time. He has tracked us here.
He suspects you. You must not meet him. You can escape through the other door, that opens upon the cañada.
If you love me—fly!"

"And leave *you* exposed to his fury—are you mad!
No. Fly yourself by the other door, lock it behind
you, and alarm the servants. I will open this door
to him, secure him here, and then be gone. Do not fear
for me. There is no danger—and if I mistake not," error
he added, with a strange significance, "he will hardly
attack me!"

"But he may have already alarmed the household. Hark!"

There was the noise of a struggle outside the door, and then the voice of Captain Carroll, calm and collected, rose clearly for an instant. "You are quite safe, Miss Saltonstall. I think I have him secure, but perhaps you had better not open the door until assistance comes."

They gazed at each other, without a word. A grim challenge played on Guest's lips. Maruja lifted her little hands deliberately, and clasped them round his defiant neck.

"Listen, darling," she said, softly and quietly, as if only the security of silence and darkness encompassed them. "You asked me just now if I would fly with you—if I would marry you, without the consent of my family—against the protest of my friends—and at once! I hesitated, Harry, for I was frightened and foolish. But I say to you now that I will marry you when and where you like—for I love you, Harry, and you alone."

"Then let us go at once," he said, passionately seizing her; "we can reach the road by the cañada before assistance comes—before we are discovered. Come!"

"And you will remember in the years to come, Harry," she said, still composedly, and with her arms still around his neck, "that I never loved any but you—that I never knew what love was before, and that since I have loved you —I have never thought of any other. Will you not?"

"I will—and now—"

"And now," she said, with a superb gesture towards the barrier which separated them from Carroll, "OPEN THE DOOR!"

CHAPTER XIII

WITH a swift glance of admiration at Maruja, Guest flung open the door. The hastily-summoned servants were already bearing away the madman, exhausted by his efforts. Captain Carroll alone remained there, erect and motionless, before the threshold.

At a sign from Maruja, he entered the room. In the

flash of light made by the opening door, he had been perfectly conscious of her companion, but not a motion of his eye or the movement of a muscle of his face betrayed it. The trained discipline of his youth stood him in good service, and for the moment left him master of the situation.

"I think no apology is needed for this intrusion," he said, with cool composure. "Pereo seemed intent on murdering somebody or something, and I followed him here. I suppose I might have got him away more quietly, but I was afraid you might have thoughtlessly opened the door." He stopped, and added, "I see now how unfounded was the supposition."

It was a fatal addition. In the next instant, the Maruja who had been standing beside Guest, conscious-stricken and remorseful in the presence of the man she had deceived, and calmly awaiting her punishment, changed at this luckless exhibition of her own peculiar womanly weapons. The old Maruja, supreme, ready, undaunted, and passionless, returned to the fray.

"You were wrong, Captain," she said, sweetly; "fortunately, Mr. Guest—whom I see you have forgotten in your absence—was with me, and I think would have felt it his duty to have protected me. But I thank you all the same, and I think even Mr. Guest will not allow his envy of your good fortune in coming so gallantly to my rescue to prevent his appreciating its full value. I am only sorry that on your return to La Mision Perdida you should have fallen into the arms of a madman before extending your hands to your friends."

Their eyes met. She saw that he hated her—and felt relieved.

"It may not have been so entirely unfortunate," he said, with a coldness strongly in contrast with his gradually blazing eyes, "for I was charged with a message to you, in which this madman is supposed by some to play an important part."

"Is it a matter of business?" said Maruja, lightly, yet with a sudden instinctive premonition of coming evil in the relentless tones of his voice.

"It is business, Miss Saltonstall—purely and simply business," said Carroll, dryly, "under whatever *other* name it may have been since presented to you."

"Perhaps you have no objection to tell it before Mr. Guest," said Maruja, with an inspiration of audacity; "it sounds so mysterious that it must be interesting. Otherwise, Captain Carroll, who abhors business, would not have undertaken it with more than his usual enthusiasm."

"As the business *does* interest Mr. Guest, or Mr. West, or whatever name he may have decided upon since I had the pleasure of meeting him," said Carroll—for the first time striking fire from the eyes of his rival—"I see no reason why I should not, even at the risk of telling you what you already know. Briefly, then, Mr. Prince charged me to advise you and your mother to avoid litigation with this gentleman, and admit his claim, as the son of Dr. West, to his share of the property."

The utter consternation and bewilderment shown in the face of Maruja convinced Carroll of his fatal error. She *had* received the addresses of this man without knowing his real position! The wild theory that had seemed to justify his resentment—that she had sold herself to Guest to possess the property—now recoiled upon him in its utter baseness. She had loved Guest for himself alone; by this base revelation he had helped to throw her into his arms.

But he did not even yet know Maruja. Turning to Guest, with flashing eyes, she said, "Is it true—are you the son of Dr. West, and"—she hesitated—"kept out of your inheritance by *us?*"

"I *am* the son of Dr. West," he said, earnestly, "though I alone had the right to tell you that at the proper time and occasion. Believe me that I have given no one the right—least of all any tool of Prince—to *trade* upon it."

"Then," said Carroll, fiercely, forgetting everything in his anger, "perhaps you will disclaim before this young lady the charge made by your employer that Pereo was instigated to Dr. West's murder by her mother?"

Again he had overshot the mark. The horror and indignation depicted in Guest's face was too plainly visible to Maruja, as well as himself, to permit a doubt that the idea was as new as the accusation. Forgetting her bewilderment at these revelations, her wounded pride, a torturing doubt suggested by Guest's want of confidence in her—indeed everything but the outraged feelings of her lover, she flew to his side. "Not a word," she said, proudly, lifting her little hand before his darkening face. "Do not insult me by replying to such an accusation in my presence. Captain Carroll," she continued, turning towards him, "I cannot forget that you were introduced into my mother's house as an officer and a gentleman. When you return to it as such, and not as a *man of business,* you will be welcome. Until then, farewell!"

She remained standing, erect and passionless, as Carroll, with a cold salutation, stepped back and disappeared in the darkness; and then she turned, and, with tottering step and a little cry, fell upon Guest's breast. "O Harry—Harry! —why have you deceived me!"

"I thought it for the best, darling," he said, lifting her face to his. "You know now the prospect I spoke of—the hope that buoyed me up! I wanted to win you myself alone, without appealing to your sense of justice or even your sympathies! I did win you. God knows, if I had not, you would never have learned through me that a son of Dr. West had ever lived. But that was not enough. When I found that I could establish my right to my father's property, I wanted you to marry me before *you* knew it; so that it never could be said that you were influenced by anything but love for me. That was why I came here to-day. That was why I pressed you to fly with me!"

He ceased. She was fumbling with the buttons of his waistcoat. "Harry," she said, softly, "did you think of the property when—when—you kissed me in the conservatory?"

"I thought of nothing but *you,*" he answered, tenderly.

Suddenly she started from his embrace. "But Pereo!— Harry—tell me quick—no one—nobody can think that this poor demented old man could—that Dr. West was—that— it's all a trick—isn't it? Harry—speak!"

He was silent for a moment, and then said, gravely, "There were strange men at the fonda that night, and—my father was supposed to carry money with him. My own life was attempted at the Mision the same evening for the sake of some paltry gold pieces that I had imprudently shown. I was saved solely by the interference of one man. That man was Pereo, your mayordomo!"

She seized his hand and raised it joyfully to her lips. "Thank you for those words! And you will come to him with me at once; and he will recognize you; and we will laugh at those lies; won't we, Harry?"

He did not reply. Perhaps he was listening to a confused sound of voices rapidly approaching the cottage. Together they stepped out into the gathering night. A number of figures were coming towards them, among them Faquita, who ran a little ahead to meet her mistress.

"Oh, Doña Maruja, he has escaped!"

"Who? Not Pereo!"

"Truly. And on his horse. It was saddled and bridled in the stable all day. One knew it not. He was walking like a cat, when suddenly he parted the peons around him, like grain before a mad bull—and behold! he was on the pinto's back and away. And, alas! there is no horse that can keep up with the pinto. God grant he may not get in the way of the r-r-railroad, that, in his very madness, he will even despise."

"My own horse is in the thicket," whispered Guest, hurriedly, in Maruja's ear. "I have measured him with the pinto before now. Give me your blessing, and I will bring him back if he be alive."

She pressed his hand and said, "Go." Before the astonished servants could identify the strange escort of their mistress, he was gone.

It was already quite dark. To any but Guest, who had made the topography of La Mision Perdida a practical study, and who had known the habitual circuit of the mayordomo in his efforts to avoid him, the search would have been hopeless. But, rightly conjecturing that he would in his demented condition follow the force of habit, he spurred his horse along the high-road until he reached the lane leading to the grassy amphitheatre already described, which was once his favorite resort. Since then it had participated in the terrible transformation already wrought in the valley by the railroad. A deep cutting through one of the grassy hills had been made for the line that now crossed the lower arc of the amphitheatre.

His conjecture was justified on entering it by the appearance of a shadowy horseman in full career round the circle, and he had no difficulty in recognizing Pereo. As there as no other exit than the one by which he came, the other being inaccessible by reason of the railroad track, he calmly watched him twice make the circuit of the arena, ready to ride towards him when he showed symptoms of slackening his speed.

Suddenly he became aware of some strange exercise on the part of the mysterious rider; and, as he swept by on the nearer side of the circle, he saw that he was throwing a lasso! A horrible thought that he was witnessing an insane rehearsal of the murder of his father flashed across his mind.

A far-off whistle from the distant woods recalled him to his calmer senses at the same moment that it seemed also to check the evolutions of the furious rider. Guest felt confident that the wretched man could not escape him now. It was the approaching train, whose appearance would undoubtedly frighten Pereo toward the entrance of the little valley guarded by him. The hill-side was already alive with the clattering echoes of the oncoming monster, when, to his horror, he saw the madman advancing rapidly towards the cutting. He put spurs to his horse, and started in pursuit; but the train was already emerging from the narrow passage, followed by the furious rider, who had wheeled abreast of the engine, and was, for a moment or two, madly keeping up with it. Guest shouted to him, but his voice was lost in the roar of the rushing caravan.

Something seemed to fly from Pereo's hand. The next moment the train had passed; rider and horse, crushed and battered out of all life, were rolling in the ditch, while the murderer's empty saddle dangled at the end of a lasso, caught on the smoke-stack of one of the murdered man's avenging improvements!

. . . .

The marriage of Maruja and the son of the late Dr.

West was received in the valley of San Antonio as one of the most admirably conceived and skillfully matured plans of that lamented genius. There were many who were ready to state that the Doctor had confided it to them years before; and it was generally accepted that the widow Saltonstall had been simply made a trustee for the benefit of the prospective young couple. Only one person perhaps, did not entirely accept these views; it was Mr. James Price—otherwise known as Aladdin. In later years, he is said to have stated authoritatively "that the only combination in business that was uncertain—was man and woman."

DRIFT FROM TWO SHORES

DRIFT FROM TWO SHORES

THE MAN ON THE BEACH

I

He lived beside a river that emptied into a great ocean. The narrow strip of land that lay between him and the estuary was covered at high tide by a shining film of water, at low tide with the cast-up offerings of sea and shore. Logs yet green, and saplings washed away from inland banks, battered fragments of wrecks and orange crates of bamboo, broken into tiny rafts yet odorous with their lost freight, lay in long successive curves,—the fringes and over-lappings of the sea. At high noon the shadow of a sea-gull's wing, or a sudden flurry and gray squall of sand-pipers, themselves but shadows, was all that broke the monotonous glare of the level sands.

He had lived there alone for a twelvemonth. Although but a few miles from a thriving settlement, during that time his retirement had never been intruded upon, his seclusion remained unbroken. In any other community he might have been the subject of rumor or criticism, but the miners at Camp Rogue and the traders at Trinidad Head, themselves individual and eccentric, were profoundly indifferent to all other forms of eccentricity or heterodoxy that did not come in contact with their own. And certainly there was no form of eccentricity less aggressive than that of a hermit, had they chosen to give him that appellation. But they did not even do that, probably from lack of interest or perception. To the various traders who supplied his small wants he was known as "Kernel," "Judge," and "Boss." To the general public "The Man on the Beach" was considered a sufficiently distinguishing title. His name, his occupation, rank, or antecedents, nobody cared to inquire. Whether this arose from a fear of reciprocal inquiry and interest, or from the profound indifference before referred to, I cannot say.

He did not look like a hermit. A man yet young, erect, well-dressed, clean-shaven, with a low voice, and a smile half melancholy, half cynical, was scarcely the conventional idea of a solitary. His dwelling, a rude improvement on a fisherman's cabin, had all the severe exterior simplicity of frontier architecture, but within it was comfortable and wholesome. Three rooms—a kitchen, a living room, and a bedroom—were all it contained.

He had lived there long enough to see the dull monotony of one season lapse into the dull monotony of the other. The bleak northwest trade-winds had brought him mornings of staring sunlight and nights of fog and silence. The warmer southwest trades had brought him clouds, rain, and the transient glories of quick grasses and odorous beach blossoms. But summer or winter, wet or dry season, on one side rose always the sharply defined hills with their changeless background of evergreens; on the other side stretched always the illimitable ocean as sharply defined against the horizon, and as unchanging in its hue. The onset of spring and autumn tides, some changes among his feathered neighbors, the footprints of certain wild animals along the river's bank, and the hanging out of party-colored signals from the wooded hillside far inland, helped him to record the slow months. On summer afternoons, when the sun sank behind a bank of fog that, moving solemnly shoreward, at last encompassed him and blotted out sea and sky, his isolation was complete. The damp gray sea that flowed above and around and about him always seemed to shut out an intangible world beyond, and to be the only real presence. The booming of breakers scarce a dozen rods from his dwelling was but a vague and unintelligible sound, or the echo of something past forever. Every morning when the sun tore away the misty curtain he awoke, dazed and bewildered, as upon a new world. The first sense of oppression over, he came to love at last this subtle spirit of oblivion; and at

night, when its cloudy wings were folded over his cabin, he
would sit alone with a sense of security he had never felt
before. On such occasions he was apt to leave his door
open, and listen as for footsteps; for what might not come
to him out of this vague, nebulous world beyond? Perhaps
even *she*,—for this strange solitary was not insane nor
visionary. He was never in spirit alone. For night and
day, sleeping or waking, pacing the beach or crouching over
his driftwood fire, a woman's face was always before him,—
the face for whose sake and for cause of whom he sat there
alone. He saw it in the morning sunlight; it was her white
hands that were lifted from the crested breakers; it
was the rustling of her skirt when the sea wind swept
through the beach grasses; it was the loving whisper of
her low voice when the long waves sank and died among
the sedge and rushes. She was as omnipresent as sea
and sky and level sand. Hence when the fog wiped them
away, she seemed to draw closer to him in the darkness.
On one or two more gracious nights in midsummer, when
the influence of the fervid noonday sun was still felt on
the heated sands, the warm breath of the fog touched his
cheek as if it had been hers, and the tears started to
his eyes.

Before the fogs came—for he arrived there in winter—he
had found surcease and rest in the steady glow of a light-
house upon the little promontory a league below his habitation. Even on the darkest nights, and in the tumults of
storm, it spoke to him of a patience that was enduring and
a steadfastness that was immutable. Later on he found a
certain dumb companionship in an uprooted tree, which,
floating down the river, had stranded hopelessly upon his
beach, but in the evening had again drifted away. Rowing
across the estuary a day or two afterward, he recognized
the tree again from a "blaze" of the settler's axe still upon
its trunk. He was not surprised a week later to find the
same tree in the sands before his dwelling, or that the next
morning it should be again launched on its purposeless wanderings. And so, impelled by wind or tide, but always
haunting his seclusion, he would meet it voyaging up the
river at the flood, or see it tossing among the breakers on

the bar, but always with the confidence of its returning sooner or later to an anchorage beside him. After the third month of his self-imposed exile, he was forced into a more human companionship, that was brief but regular. He was obliged to have menial assistance. While he might have eaten his bread "in sorrow" carelessly and mechanically, if it had been prepared for him, the occupation of cooking his own food brought the vulgarity and materialness of existence so near to his morbid sensitiveness that he could not eat the meal he had himself prepared. He did not yet wish to die, and when starvation or society seemed to be the only alternative, he chose the latter. An Indian woman, so hideous as to scarcely suggest humanity, at stated times performed for him these offices. When she did not come, which was not infrequent, he did not eat.

Such was the mental and physical condition of the Man on the Beach on the 1st of January, 1869.

It was a still, bright day, following a week of rain and wind. Low down the horizon still lingered a few white flecks—the flying squadrons of the storm—as vague as distant sails. Southward the harbor bar whitened occasionally but lazily; even the turbulent Pacific swell stretched its length wearily upon the shore. And toiling from the settlement over the low sand dunes, a carriage at last halted half a mile from the solitary's dwelling.

"I reckon ye'll hev to git out here," said the driver, pulling up to breathe his panting horses. "Ye can't git any nigher."

There was a groan of execration from the interior of the vehicle, a hysterical little shriek, and one or two shrill expressions of feminine disapprobation, but the driver moved not. At last a masculine head expostulated from the window: "Look here; you agreed to take us to the house. Why, it's a mile away at least!"

"Thar, or tharabouts, I reckon," said the driver, coolly crossing his legs on the box.

"It's no use talking; I can never walk through this sand and horrid glare," said a female voice quickly and imperatively. Then, apprehensively, "Well, of all the places!"

"Well, I never!"

"This *does* exceed everything."

"It's really *too* idiotic for anything."

It was noticeable that while the voices betrayed the difference of age and sex, they bore a singular resemblance to each other, and a certain querulousness of pitch that was dominant.

"I reckon I've gone about as fur as I allow to go with them hosses," continued the driver suggestively, "and as time's vallyble, ye'd better unload."

"The wretch does not mean to leave us here alone?" said a female voice in shrill indignation. "You'll wait for us, driver?" said a masculine voice, confidently.

"How long?" asked the driver.

There was a hurried consultation within. The words "Might send us packing!" "May take all night to get him to listen to reason," "Bother! whole thing over in ten minutes," came from the window. The driver meanwhile had settled himself back in his seat, and whistled in patient contempt of a fashionable fare that didn't know its own mind nor destination. Finally, the masculine head was thrust out, and, with a certain potential air of judicially ending a difficulty, said:—

"You're to follow us slowly, and put up your horses in the stable or barn until we want you."

An ironical laugh burst from the driver. "Oh, yes—in the stable or barn—in course. But, my eyes sorter failin' me, mebbee, now, some ev you younger folks will kindly pint out the stable or barn of the Kernel's. Woa!—will ye? —woa! Give me a chance to pick out that there barn or stable to put ye in!" This in arch confidence to the horses, who had not moved.

Here the previous speaker, rotund, dignified, and elderly, alighted indignantly, closely followed by the rest of the party, two ladies and a gentleman. One of the ladies was past the age, but not the fashion, of youth, and her Parisian dress clung over her wasted figure and well-bred bones artistically if not gracefully; the younger lady, evidently her daughter, was crisp and pretty, and carried off the aquiline nose and aristocratic emaciation of her mother with a certain piquancy and a dash that was charming. The gentleman was young, thin, with the family characteristics, but otherwise indistinctive.

With one accord they all faced directly toward the spot indicated by the driver's whip. Nothing but the bare, bleak, rectangular outlines of the cabin of the Man on the Beach met their eyes. All else was a desolate expanse, unrelieved by any structure higher than the tussocks of scant beach grass that clothed it. They were so utterly helpless that the driver's derisive laughter gave way at last to good humor and suggestion. "Look yer," he said finally, "I don't know ez it's your fault you don't know this kentry ez well ez you do Yurup; so I'll drag this yer team over to Robinson's on the river, give the horses a bite, and then meander down this yer ridge, and wait for ye. Ye'll see me from the Kernel's." And without waiting for a reply, he swung his horses' heads toward the river, and rolled away.

The same querulous protest that had come from the windows arose from the group, but vainly. Then followed accusations and recrimination. "It's *your* fault; you might have written, and had him meet us at the settlement." "You wanted to take him by surprise!" "I didn't. You know if I'd written that we were coming, he'd have taken good care to run away from us." "Yes, to some more inaccessible place." "There can be none worse than this," etc., etc. But it was so clearly evident that nothing was to be done but to go forward, that even in the midst of their wrangling they straggled on in Indian file toward the distant cabin, sinking ankle-deep in the yielding sand, punctuating their verbal altercation with sighs, and only abating it at a scream from the elder lady.

"Where's Maria?"

"Gone on ahead!" grunted the younger gentleman, in a bass voice, so incongruously large for him that it seemed to have been a ventriloquistic contribution by somebody else.

It was too true. Maria, after adding her pungency to the general conversation, had darted on ahead. But alas! that swift Camilla, after scouring the plain some two hundred feet with her demitrain, came to grief on an unbending tussock and sat down, panting but savage. As they plodded wearily toward her, she bit her red lips, smacked them on her cruel little white teeth like a festive and sprightly ghoul, and lisped:—

"You *do* look so like guys! For all the world like those English shopkeepers we met on the Righi, doing the three-guinea excursion in their Sunday clothes!"

Certainly the spectacle of these exotically plumed bipeds, whose fine feathers were already bedrabbled by sand and growing limp in the sea breeze, was somewhat dissonant with the rudeness of sea and sky and shore. A few gulls screamed at them; a loon, startled from the lagoon, arose shrieking and protesting, with painfully extended legs, in obvious burlesque of the younger gentleman. The elder lady felt the justice of her gentle daughter's criticism, and re-taliated with simple directness:—

"Your skirt is ruined, your hair is coming down, your hat is half off your head, and your shoes—in Heaven's name, Maria! what *have* you done with your shoes?"

Maria had exhibited a slim stockinged foot from under her skirt. It was scarcely three fingers broad, with an arch as patrician as her nose. "Somewhere between here and the carriage," she answered; "Dick can run back and find it, while he is looking for your brooch, mamma. Dick's so obliging."

The robust voice of Dick thundered, but the wasted figure of Dick feebly ploughed its way back, and returned with the missing buskin.

"I may as well carry them in my hand like the market girls at Saumur, for we have got to wade soon," said Miss Maria, sinking her own terrors in the delightful contempla-tion of the horror in her parent's face, as she pointed to a shining film of water slowly deepening in a narrow swale in the sands between them and the cabin.

"It's the tide," said the elder gentleman. "If we intend to go on we must hasten; permit me, my dear madam," and before she could reply he had lifted the astounded matron in his arms, and made gallantly for the ford. The gentle Maria cast an ominous eye on her brother, who, with mani-fest reluctance, performed for her the same office. But that acute young lady kept her eyes upon the preceding figure of the elder gentleman, and seeing him suddenly and mysteriously disappear to his armpits, unhesitatingly threw herself from her brother's protecting arms,—an action which instantly precipitated him into the water,—and paddled hastily to the opposite bank, where she eventually assisted in pulling the elderly gentleman out of the hollow into which he had fallen, and in rescuing her mother, who floated helplessly on the surface, upheld by her skirts, like a gigantic and variegated water-lily. Dick followed with a single gaiter. In another minute they were safe on the opposite bank.

The elder lady gave way to tears; Maria laughed hysterically; Dick mingled a bass oath with the now audible surf; the elder gentleman, whose florid face the salt water had bleached, and whose dignity seemed to have been washed away, accounted for both by saying he thought it was a quicksand.

"It might have been," said a quiet voice behind them; "you should have followed the sand dunes half a mile further to the estuary."

They turned instantly at the voice. It was that of the Man on the Beach. They all rose to their feet and uttered together, save one, the single exclamation, "James!" The elder gentleman said "Mr. North," and, with a slight resumption of his former dignity, buttoned his coat over his damp shirt front.

There was a silence, in which the Man on the Beach looked gravely down upon them. If they had intended to impress him by any suggestion of a gay, brilliant, and sensuous world beyond in their own persons, they had failed, and they knew it. Keenly alive as they had always been to external prepossession, they felt that they looked forlorn and ludicrous, and that the situation lay in his hands. The elderly lady again burst into tears of genuine distress, Maria colored over her cheek-bones, and Dick stared at the ground in sullen disquiet.

"You had better get up," said the Man on the Beach, after a moment's thought, "and come up to the cabin. I cannot offer you a change of garments, but you can dry them by the fire."

They all rose together, and again said in chorus, "James!" but this time with an evident effort to recall some speech or action previously resolved upon and committed to memory. The elder lady got so far as to clasp her hands and add, "You have not forgotten us—James, oh, James!" the younger gentleman to attempt a brusque "Why, Jim, old boy," that ended in querulous incoherence; the young lady to cast a half-searching, half-coquettish look at him; and the old gentleman to begin, "Our desire, Mr. North"—but the effort was futile. Mr. James North, standing before them with folded arms, looked from the one to the other.

"I have not thought much of you for a twelvemonth," he said, quietly, "but I have not forgotten you. Come!"

He led the way a few steps in advance, they following silently. In this brief interview they felt he had resumed the old dominance and independence, against which they had rebelled; more than that, in this half failure of their first concerted action they had changed their querulous bickerings to a sullen distrust of each other, and walked moodily apart as they followed James North into his house. A fire blazed brightly on the hearth; a few extra seats were quickly extemporized from boxes and chests, and the elder lady, with the skirt of her dress folded over her knees,—looking not unlike an exceedingly overdressed jointed doll,—dried her flounces and her tears together. Miss Maria took in the scant appointments of the house in one single glance, and then fixed her eyes upon James North, who, the least concerned of the party, stood before them, grave and patiently expectant.

"Well," began the elder lady in a high key, "after all this worry and trouble you have given us, James, haven't you anything to say? Do you know—have you the least idea what you are doing? what egregious folly you are committing? what everybody is saying? Eh? Heavens and earth!—do you know who I am?"

"You are my father's brother's widow, Aunt Mary," returned James, quietly. "If I am committing any folly it only concerns myself; if I cared for what people said I should not be here; if I loved society enough to appreciate its good report I should stay with it."

5   v. 1

"But they say you have run away from society to pine alone for a worthless creature—a woman who has used you, as she has used and thrown away others—a—"

"A woman," chimed in Dick, who had thrown himself on James's bed while his patent leathers were drying, "a woman that all the fellers know never intended"—here, however, he met James North's eye, and muttering something about "whole thing being too idiotic to talk about," relapsed into silence.

"You know," continued Mrs. North, "that while we and all our set shut our eyes to your very obvious relations with that woman, and while I myself often spoke of it to others as a simple flirtation, and averted a scandal for your sake, and when the climax was reached, and she herself gave you an opportunity to sever your relations, and nobody need have been wiser—and she'd have had all the blame—and it's only what she's accustomed to—you—you! you, James North!—you must nonsensically go, and, by this extravagant piece of idiocy and sentimental tomfoolery, let everybody see how serious the whole affair was, and how deep it hurt you! and here in this awful place, alone—where you're half drowned to get to it, and are willing to be wholly drowned to get away! Oh, don't talk to me! I won't hear it—it's just too idiotic for anything!"

The subject of this outburst neither spoke nor moved a single muscle.

"Your aunt, Mr. North, speaks excitedly," said the elder gentleman; "yet I think she does not overestimate the unfortunate position in which your odd fancy places you. I know nothing of the reasons that have impelled you to this step; I only know that the popular opinion is that the cause is utterly inadequate. You are still young, with a future before you. I need not say how your present conduct may imperil that. If you expected to achieve any good—even to your own satisfaction—but this conduct—"

"Yes—if there was anything to be gained by it!" broke in Mrs. North.

"If you ever thought she'd come back!—but that kind of woman don't. They must have change. Why"—began Dick suddenly, and as suddenly lying down again.

"Is this all you have come to say?" asked James North, after a moment's patient silence, looking from one to the other.

"All?" screamed Mrs. North; "is it not enough?"

"Not to change my mind nor my residence at present," replied North, coolly.

"Do you mean to continue this folly all your life?"

"And have a coroner's inquest, and advertisements and all the facts in the papers?"

"And have *her* read the melancholy details, and know that you were faithful and she was not?"

This last shot was from the gentle Maria, who bit her lips as it glanced from the immovable man.

"I believe there is nothing more to say," continued North, quietly. "I am willing to believe your intentions are as worthy as your zeal. Let us say no more," he added, with grave weariness; "the tide is rising, and your coachman is signaling you from the bank."

There was no mistaking the unshaken positiveness of the man, which was all the more noticeable from its gentle but utter indifference to the wishes of the party. He turned his back upon them as they gathered hurriedly around the elder gentleman, while the words, "He cannot be in his right mind," "It's your duty to do it," "It's sheer insanity," "Look at his eye!" all fell unconsciously upon his ear.

"One word more, Mr. North," said the elder gentleman, a little portentously, to conceal an evident embarrassment. "It may be that your conduct might suggest to minds more practical than your own the existence of some aberration of the intellect—some temporary mania—that might force your best friends into a quasi-legal attitude of—"

"Declaring me insane," interrupted James North, with the slight impatience of a man more anxious to end a prolix interview than to combat an argument. "I think differently. As my aunt's lawyer, you know that within the last year I have deeded most of my property to her and her family. I cannot believe that so shrewd an adviser as Mr. Edmund Carter would ever permit proceedings that would invalidate that conveyance."

Maria burst into a laugh of such wicked gratification that

James North, for the first time, raised his eyes with something of interest to her face. She colored under them, but returned his glance with another like a bayonet flash. The party slowly moved toward the door, James North following.

"Then this is your final answer?" asked Mrs. North, stopping imperiously on the threshold.

"I beg your pardon?" queried North, half abstractedly.

"Your final answer?"

"Oh, certainly."

Mrs. North flounced away a dozen rods in rage. This was unfortunate for North. It gave them the final attack in detail. Dick began: "Come along! You know you can advertise for her with a personal down there and the old woman wouldn't object as long as you were careful and put in an appearance now and then!"

As Dick limped away, Mr. Carter thought, in confidence, that the whole matter—even to suit Mr. North's sensitive nature—might be settled there. *"She* evidently expects you to return. My opinion is that she never left San Francisco. You can't tell anything about these women."

With this last sentence on his indifferent ear, James North seemed to be left free. Maria had rejoined her mother; but as they crossed the ford, and an intervening sand-hill hid the others from sight, that piquant young lady suddenly appeared on the hill and stood before him.

"And you're not coming back?" she said directly.

"No."

"Never?"

"I cannot say."

"Tell me! what is there about some women to make men love them so?"

"Love," replied North, quietly.

"No, it cannot be—it is not *that!*"

North looked over the hill and round the hill, and looked bored.

"Oh, I'm going now. But one moment, Jem! I didn't want to come. They dragged me here. Good-by."

She raised a burning face and eyes to his. He leaned forward and imprinted the perfunctory cousinly kiss of the period upon her cheek.

"Not that way," she said angrily, clutching his wrists with her long, thin fingers; "you shan't kiss me in that way, James North."

With the faintest, ghost-like passing of a twinkle in the corners of his sad eyes, he touched his lips to hers. With the contact, she caught him round the neck, pressed her burning lips and face to his forehead, his cheeks, the very curves of his chin and throat, and—with a laugh was gone.

II

HAD the kinsfolk of James North any hope that their visit might revive some lingering desire he still combated to enter once more the world they represented, that hope would have soon died. Whatever effect this episode had upon the solitary,—and he had become so self-indulgent of his sorrow, and so careless of all that came between him and it, as to meet opposition with profound indifference,—the only appreciable result was a greater attraction for the solitude that protected him, and he grew even to love the bleak shore and barren sands that had proved so inhospitable to others. There was a new meaning to the roar of the surges, an honest, loyal sturdiness in the unchanging persistency of the uncouth and blustering trade-winds, and a mute fidelity in the shining sands, treacherous to all but him. With such bandogs to lie in wait for trespassers, should he not be grateful?

If no bitterness was awakened by the repeated avowal of the unfaithfulness of the woman he loved, it was because he had always made the observation and experience of others give way to the dominance of his own insight. No array of contradictory facts ever shook his belief or unbelief; like all egotists, he accepted them as truths controlled by a larger truth of which he alone was cognizant. His simplicity, which was but another form of his egotism, was so complete as to baffle ordinary malicious cunning, and so he was spared the experience and knowledge that come to a lower nature, and help debase it.

Exercise and the stimulus of the few wants that sent him

hunting or fishing kept up his physical health. Never a
lover of rude freedom or outdoor life his sedentary pre-
dilections and nice tastes kept him from lapsing into barba-
rian excess; never a sportsman he followed the chase with
no feverish exaltation. Even dumb creatures found out his
secret, and at times, stalking moodily over the upland, the
brown deer and elk would cross his path without fear or
molestation, or, idly lounging in his canoe within the river
bar, flocks of wild fowl would settle within stroke of his
listless oar. And so the second winter of his hermitage drew
near its close, and with it came a storm that passed into
local history, and is still remembered. It uprooted giant
trees along the river, and with them the tiny rootlets of the
life he was idly fostering.

The morning had been fitfully turbulent, the wind veering
several points south and west, with suspicious lulls, unlike
the steady onset of the regular southwest trades. High overhead the long manes of racing *cirro stratus* streamed with
flying gulls and hurrying water-fowl; plover piped inces-
santly, and a flock of timorous sand-pipers sought the low
ridge of his cabin, while a wrecking crew of curlew hastily
manned the uprooted tree that tossed wearily beyond the
bar. By noon the flying clouds huddled together in masses,
and then were suddenly exploded in one vast opaque sheet
over the heavens. The sea became gray, and suddenly
wrinkled and old. There was a dumb, half-articulate cry in
the air,—rather a confusion of many sounds, as of the booming of distant guns, the clangor of a bell, the trampling of
many waves, the creaking of timbers and soughing of leaves,
that sank and fell ere you could yet distinguish them. And
then it came on to blow. For two hours it blew strongly.
At the time the sun should have set the wind had increased;
in fifteen minutes darkness shut down, even the white sands
lost their outlines, and sea and shore and sky lay in the
grip of a relentless and aggressive power.

Within his cabin, by the leaping light of his gusty fire,
North sat alone. His first curiosity passed, the turmoil
without no longer carried his thought beyond its one converging centre. *She* had come to him on the wings of the
storm, even as she had been borne to him on the summer

fog-cloud. Now and then the wind shook the cabin, but he heeded it not. He had no fears for its safety; it presented its low gable to the full fury of the wind that year by year had piled, and even now was piling, protecting buttresses of sand against it. With each succeeding gust it seemed to nestle more closely to its foundations, in the whirl of flying sand that rattled against its roof and windows. It was nearly midnight when a sudden thought brought him to his feet. What if *she* were exposed to the fury of such a night as this? What could he do to help her? Perhaps even now, as he sat there idle, she—Hark! was not that a gun—No? Yes, surely!

He hurriedly unbolted the door, but the strength of the wind and the impact of drifted sand resisted his efforts. With a new and feverish strength possessing him he forced it open wide enough to permit his egress when the wind caught him as a feather, rolled him over and over, and then, grappling him again, held him down hard and fast against the drift. Unharmed, but unable to move, he lay there, hearing the multitudinous roar of the storm, but unable to distinguish one familiar sound in the savage medley. At last he managed to crawl flat on his face to the cabin, and refastening the door, threw himself upon his bed.

He was awakened from a fitful dream of his Cousin Maria. She with a supernatural strength seemed to be holding the door against some unseen, unknown power that moaned and strove without, and threw itself in despairing force against the cabin. He could see the lithe undulations of her form as she alternately yielded to its power, and again drew the door against it, coiling herself around the log-hewn doorpost with a hideous, snake-like suggestion. And then a struggle and a heavy blow, which shook the very foundations of the structure, awoke him. He leaped to his feet, and into an inch of water! By the flickering firelight he could see it oozing and dripping from the crevices of the logs and broadening into a pool by the chimney. A scrap of paper torn from an envelope was floating idly on its current. Was it the overflow of the backed-up waters of the river? He was not left long in doubt. Another blow upon the gable of the house, and a torrent of spray leaped down the chimney, scattered the embers far and wide, and left him in utter darkness. Some of the spray clung to his lips. It was salt. The great ocean had beaten down the river bar and was upon him!

Was there aught to fly to? No! The cabin stood upon the highest point of the sand spit, and the low swale on one side crossed by his late visitors was a seething mass of breakers, while the estuary behind him was now the ocean itself. There was nothing to do but to wait.

The very helplessness of his situation was, to a man of his peculiar temperament, an element of patient strength. The instinct of self-preservation was still strong in him, but he had no fear of death, nor, indeed, any presentiment of it; yet if it came, it was an easy solution of the problem that had been troubling him, and it wiped off the slate! He thought of the sarcastic prediction of his cousin, and death in the form that threatened him was the obliteration of his home and even the ground upon which it stood. There would be nothing to record, no stain could come upon the living. The instinct that kept him true to *her* would tell her how he died; if it did not, it was equally well. And with this simple fatalism his only belief, this strange man groped his way to his bed, lay down, and in a few moments was asleep. The storm still roared without. Once again the surges leaped against the cabin, but it was evident that the wind was abating with the tide.

When he awoke it was high noon, and the sun was shining brightly. For some time he lay in a delicious languor, doubting if he was alive or dead, but feeling through every nerve and fibre an exquisite sense of peace—a rest he had not known since his boyhood—a relief he scarcely knew from what. He felt that he was smiling, and yet his pillow was wet with the tears that glittered still on his lashes. The sand blocking up his doorway, he leaped lightly from his window. A few clouds were still sailing slowly in the heavens, the trailing plumes of a great benediction that lay on sea and shore. He scarcely recognized the familiar landscape; a new bar had been formed in the river, and a narrow causeway of sand that crossed the lagoon and marshes to the river bank and the upland trail seemed to bring him nearer to humanity again. He was conscious of a fresh, childlike delight in all this, and when, a moment later, he saw the old uprooted tree, now apparently forever moored and imbedded in the sand beside his cabin, he ran to it with a sense of joy.

Its trailing roots were festooned with clinging sea-weed and the long, snaky, undulating stems of the sea-turnip; and fixed between two crossing roots was a bamboo orange crate, almost intact. As he walked toward it he heard a strange cry, unlike anything the barren sands had borne before. Thinking it might be some strange sea bird caught in the meshes of the sea-weed, he ran to the crate and looked within. It was half filled with sea-moss and feathery algæ. The cry was repeated. He brushed aside the weeds with his hands. It was not a wounded sea bird, but a living human child!

As he lifted it from its damp enwrappings he saw that it was an infant eight or nine months old. How and when it had been brought there, or what force had guided that elfish cradle to his very door, he could not determine; but it must have been left early, for it was quite warm, and its clothing almost dried by the blazing morning sun. To wrap his coat about it, to run to his cabin with it, to start out again with the appalling conviction that nothing could be done for it there, occupied some moments. His nearest neighbor was Trinidad Joe, a "logger," three miles up the river. He remembered to have heard vaguely that he was a man of family. To half strangle the child with a few drops from his whisky flask, to extricate his canoe from the marsh, and strike out into the river with his waif, was at least to do something. In half an hour he had reached the straggling cabin and sheds of Trinidad Joe, and from the few scanty flowers that mingled with the brushwood fence, and a surplus of linen fluttering on the line, he knew that his surmise as to Trinidad Joe's domestic establishment was correct.

The door at which he knocked opened upon a neat, plainly-furnished room, and the figure of a buxom woman of twenty-five. With an awkwardness new to him, North stammered out the circumstances of his finding the infant, and the object of his visit. Before he had finished, the woman, by some feminine trick, had taken the child from his hands ere he knew it; and when he paused, out of breath, burst into a fit of laughter. North tried to laugh too, but failed.

When the woman had wiped the tears from a pair of very frank blue eyes, and hidden two rows of very strong white teeth again, she said:—

"Look yar! You're that looney sort o' chap that lives alone over on the spit yonder, ain't ye?"

North hastened to admit all that the statement might imply.

"And so ye've had a baby left ye to keep you company? Lordy!" Here she looked as if dangerously near a relapse, and then added, as if in explanation of her conduct,—

"When I saw ye paddlin' down here,—you thet ez shy as elk in summer,—I sez, 'He's sick.' But a baby,—Oh, Lordy!"

For a moment North almost hated her. A woman who, in this pathetic, perhaps almost tragic, picture saw only a ludicrous image, and that image himself, was of another race than that he had ever mingled with. Profoundly indifferent as he had always been to the criticism of his equals in station, the mischievous laughter of this illiterate woman jarred upon him worse than his cousin's sarcasm. It was with a little dignity that he pointed out the fact that at present the child needed nourishment. "It's very young," he added. "I'm afraid it wants its natural nourishment."

"Whar is it to get it?" asked the woman.

James North hesitated, and looked around. There should be a baby somewhere! there *must* be a baby somewhere! "I thought that you," he stammered, conscious of an awkward coloring,—"I—that is—I—" He stopped short, for she was already cramming her apron into her mouth, too late, however, to stop the laugh that overflowed it. When she found her breath again, she said,—

"Look yar! I don't wonder they said you was looney! I'm Trinidad Joe's onmarried darter, and the only woman in this house. Any fool could have told you that. Now, ef you can rig us up a baby out o' them facts, I'd like to see it done."

Inwardly furious but outwardly polite, James North begged her pardon, deplored his ignorance, and, with a courtly bow, made a movement to take the child. But the woman as quickly drew it away.

"Not much," she said, hastily. "What! trust that poor critter to you? No, sir! Thar's more ways of feeding a baby, young man, than you knows on, with all your 'nat'ral nourishment.' But it looks kinder logy and stupid."

North freezingly admitted that he had given the infant whisky as a stimulant.

"You did? Come, now, that ain't so looney after all. Well, I'll take the baby, and when Dad comes home we'll see what can be done."

North hesitated. His dislike of the woman was intense, and yet he knew no one else and the baby needed instant care. Besides, he began to see the ludicrousness of his making a first call on his neighbors with a foundling to dispose of. She saw his hesitation, and said,—

"Ye don't know me, in course. Well, I'm Bessy Robinson, Trinidad Joe Robinson's daughter. I reckon Dad will give me a character if you want references, or any of the boys on the river."

"I'm only thinking of the trouble I'm giving you, Miss Robinson, I assure you. Any expense you may incur—"

"Young man," said Bessy Robinson, turning sharply on her heel, and facing him with her black brows a little contracted, "if it comes to expenses, I reckon I'll pay you for that baby, or not take it at all. But I don't know you well enough to quarrel with you on sight. So leave the child to me, and, if you choose, paddle down here to-morrow, after sun up—the ride will do you good—and see it, and Dad thrown in. Good by!" and with one powerful but well-shaped arm thrown around the child, and the other crooked at the dimpled elbow a little aggressively, she swept by James North and entered a bedroom, closing the door behind her.

When Mr. James North reached his cabin it was dark. As he rebuilt his fire, and tried to rearrange the scattered and disordered furniture, and remove the débris of last night's storm, he was conscious for the first time of feeling lonely. He did not miss the child. Beyond the instincts of humanity and duty he had really no interest in its welfare or future. He was rather glad to get rid of it, he would have preferred to some one else, and yet *she* looked as if she were competent. And then came the reflection that since the morning he had not once thought of the woman he loved. The like had never occurred in his twelvemonth solitude. So he set to work, thinking of her and of his sorrows, until the word "Looney," in connection with his suffering, flashed across his memory. "Looney!" It was not a nice word. It suggested something less than insanity; something that might happen to a common, unintellectual sort of person. He remembered the loon, an ungainly feathered neighbor, that was popularly supposed to have lent its name to the adjective. Could it be possible that people looked upon him as one too hopelessly and uninterestingly afflicted for sympathy or companionship, too unimportant and common for even ridicule; or was this but the coarse interpretation of that vulgar girl?

Nevertheless, the next morning "after sun up" James North was at Trinidad Joe's cabin. That worthy proprietor himself—a long, lank man, with even more than the ordinary rural Western characteristics of ill health, ill feeding, and melancholy—met him on the bank, clothed in a manner and costume that was a singular combination of the frontiersman and the sailor. When North had again related the story of his finding the child, Trinidad Joe pondered.

"It mout hev been stowed away in one of them crates for safe-keeping," he said, musingly, "and washed off the deck o' one o' them Tahiti brigs goin' down fer oranges. Leastways, it never got thar from these parts."

"But it's a miracle its life was saved at all. It must have been some hours in the water."

"Them brigs lays their course well inshore, and it was just mebbe a toss up if the vessel clawed off the reef at all! And ez to the child keepin' up, why, dog my skin! that's just the contrariness o' things," continued Joe, in sententious cynicism. "Ef an able seaman had fallen from the yard-arm that night he'd been sunk in sight o' the ship, and thet baby ez can't swim a stroke sails ashore, sound asleep, with the waves for a baby-jumper."

North, who was half relieved, yet half awkwardly disappointed at not seeing Bessy, ventured to ask how the child was doing.

"She'll do all right now," said a frank voice above, and, looking up, North discerned the round arms, blue eyes, and white teeth of the daughter at the window. "She's all hunky, and has an appetite—ef she hezn't got her 'nat'ral nourishment.' Come, Dad! heave ahead, and tell the stranger what you and me allow we'll do, and don't stand there swappin' lies with him."

"Weel," said Trinidad Joe, dejectedly, "Bess allows she can rar that baby and do justice to it. And I don't say—though I'm her father—that she can't. But when Bess wants anything she wants it all, clean down; no half-ways nor leavin's for her."

"That's me! go on, Dad—you're chippin' in the same notch every time," said Miss Robinson, with cheerful directness.

"Well, we agree to put the job up this way. We'll take the child and you'll give us a paper or writin' makin' over all your right and title. How's that?"

Without knowing exactly why he did, Mr. North objected decidedly.

"Do you think we won't take good care of it?" asked Miss Bessy, sharply.

"That is not the question," said North, a little hotly. "In the first place, the child is not mine to give. It has fallen into my hands as a trust,—the first hands that received it from its parents. I do not think it right to allow any other hands to come between theirs and mine."

Miss Bessy left the window. In another moment she appeared from the house, and, walking directly towards North, held out a somewhat substantial hand. "Good!" she said, as she gave his fingers an honest squeeze. "You ain't so looney after all. Dad, he's right! He shan't gin it up, but we'll go halves in it, he and me. He'll be father and I'll be mother 'til death do us part, or the reg'lar family turns up. Well—what do you say?"

More pleased than he dared confess to himself with the praise of this common girl, Mr. James North assented. Then would he see the baby? He would, and Trinidad Joe having already seen the baby, and talked of the baby, and felt the baby, and indeed had the baby offered to him in every way during the past night, concluded to give some of his valuable time to logging, and left them together.

Mr. North was obliged to admit that the baby was thriving. He moreover listened with polite interest to the statement that the baby's eyes were hazel, like his own; that it had five teeth; that she was, for a girl of that probable age, a robust child; and yet Mr. North lingered. Finally, with his hand on the door-lock, he turned to Bessy and said,—

"May I ask you an odd question, Miss Robinson?"

"Go on."

"Why did you think I was—'looney'?"

The frank Miss Robinson bent her head over the baby. "Why?"

"Yes, why?"

"Because you *were* looney."

"Oh!"

"But—"

"Yes—"

"You'll get over it."

And under the shallow pretext of getting the baby's food, she retired to the kitchen, where Mr. North had the supreme satisfaction of seeing her, as he passed the window, sitting on a chair with her apron over her head, shaking with l ughter.

For the next two or three days he did not visit the Robinsons, but gave himself up to past memories. On the third day he had—it must be confessed not without some effort—brought himself into that condition of patient sorrow which had been his habit. The episode of the storm and the finding of the baby began to fade, as had faded the visit of his relatives. It had been a dull, wet day and he was sitting by his fire, when there came a tap at his door. "Flora," by which juvenescent name his aged Indian handmaid was known, usually announced her presence with an imitation of a curlew's cry: it could not be her. He fancied he heard the trailing of a woman's dress against the boards, and started to his feet, deathly pale, with a name upon his lips. But the door was impatiently thrown open, and showed Bessy Robinson! And the baby!

With a feeling of relief he could not understand he offered her a seat. She turned her frank eyes on him curiously.

"You look skeert!"

"I was startled. You know I see nobody here!"

"Thet's so. But look yar, do you ever use a doctor?"

Not clearly understanding her, he in turn asked, "Why?"

"Cause you must rise up and get one now—thet's why. This yer baby of ours is sick. We don't use a doctor at our house, we don't beleeve in 'em, hain't no call for 'em—but this yer baby's parents mebbee did. So rise up out o' that cheer and get one."

James North looked at Miss Robinson and rose, albeit a little in doubt, and hesitating.

Miss Robinson saw it. "I shouldn't hev troubled ye, nor ridden three mile to do it, if ther hed been any one else to send. But Dad's over at Eureka, buying logs, and I'm alone. Hello—wher yer goin'?"

North had seized his hat and opened the door. "For a doctor," he replied amazedly.

"Did ye kalkilate to walk six miles and back?"

"Certainly—I have no horse."

"But *I* have, and you'll find her tethered outside. She ain't much to look at, but when you strike the trail she'll go."

"But *you*—how will *you* return?"

"Well," said Miss Robinson, drawing her chair to the fire, taking off her hat and shawl, and warming her knees by the blaze, "I didn't reckon to return. You'll find me here when you come back with the doctor. Go! Skedaddle quick!"

She did not have to repeat the command. In another instant James North was in Miss Bessy's seat—a man's dragoon saddle,—and pounding away through the sand. Two facts were in his mind: one was that he, the "looney," was about to open communication with the wisdom and contemporary criticism of the settlement, by going for a doctor to administer to a sick and anonymous infant in his possession; the other was that his solitary house was in the hands of a self-invited, large-limbed, illiterate, but rather comely young woman. These facts he could not gallop away from, but to his credit be it recorded that he fulfilled his mission zealously, if not coherently, to the doctor, who during the rapid ride gathered the idea that North had rescued a young married woman from drowning, who had since given birth to a child.

The few words that set the doctor right when he arrived at the cabin might in any other community have required further explanation, but Dr. Duchesne, an old army surgeon, was prepared for everything and indifferent to all. "The infant," he said, "was threatened with inflammation of the lungs; at present there was no danger, but the greatest care and caution must be exercised. Particularly exposure should be avoided." "That settles the whole matter, then," said Bessy potentially. Both gentlemen looked their surprise. "It means," she condescended to further explain, "that *you* must ride that filly home, wait for the old man to come to-morrow, and then ride back here with some of my duds, for thar's no 'day-days' nor picknicking for that baby ontil she's better. And I reckon to stay with her ontil she is."

"She certainly is unable to bear any exposure at present," said the doctor, with an amused side glance at North's perplexed face. "Miss Robinson is right. I'll ride with you over the sands as far as the trail."

"I'm afraid," said North, feeling it incumbent upon him to say something, "that you'll hardly find it as comfortable here as—"

"I reckon not," she said simply, "but I didn't expect much."

North turned a little wearily away. "Good night," she said suddenly, extending her hand, with a gentler smile of lip and eye than he had ever before noticed, "good night —take good care of Dad."

The doctor and North rode together some moments in silence. North had another fact presented to him, *i. e.* that he was going a-visiting, and that he had virtually abandoned his former life; also that it would be profanation to think of his sacred woe in the house of a stranger.

"I dare say," said the doctor, suddenly, "you are not familiar with the type of woman Miss Bessy presents so perfectly. Your life has been spent among the conventional class."

North froze instantly at what seemed to be a probing of his secret. Disregarding the last suggestion, he made answer simply and truthfully that he had never met any Western girl like Bessy.

"That's your bad luck," said the doctor. "You think her coarse and illiterate?"

Mr. North had been so much struck with her kindness that really he had not thought of it.

"That's not so," said the doctor, curtly; "although even if you told her so she would not think any the less of you—nor of herself. If she spoke rustic Greek instead of bad English, and wore a *cestus* in place of an ill-fitting corset, you'd swear she was a goddess. There's your trail. Good night."

III

JAMES NORTH did not sleep well that night. He had taken Miss Bessy's bedroom, at her suggestion, there being but two, and "Dad never using sheets and not bein' keerful in his habits." It was neat, but that was all. The scant ornamentation was atrocious; two or three highly colored prints, a shell work-box, a ghastly winter bouquet of skeleton leaves and mosses, a star-fish, and two china vases hideous enough to have been worshiped as Buddhist idols, exhibited the gentle recreation of the fair occupant, and the possible future education of the child. In the morning he was met by Joe, who received the message of his daughter with his usual dejection, and suggested that North stay with him until the child was better. That event was still remote; North found, on his return to his cabin, that the child had been worse; but he did not know, until Miss Bessy dropped a casual remark, that she had not closed her own eyes that night. It was a week before he regained his own quarters, but an active week—indeed, on the whole, a rather pleasant week. For there was a delicate flattery in being domineered by a wholesome and handsome woman, and Mr. James North had by this time made up his mind that she was both. Once or twice he found himself contemplating her splendid figure with a recollection of the doctor's compliment, and later, emulating her own frankness, told her of it.

"And what did *you* say?" she asked.

"Oh, I laughed and said—nothing."

And so did she.

A month after this interchange of frankness, she asked him if he could spend the next evening at her house. "You see," she said, "there's to be a dance down at the hall at Eureka, and I haven't kicked a fut since last spring. Hank Fisher's comin' up to take me over, and I'm goin' to let the shanty slide for the night."

"But what's to become of the baby?" asked North, a little testily.

"Well," said Miss Robinson, facing him somewhat aggressively, "I reckon it won't hurt ye to take care of it for a night. Dad can't—and if he could, he don't know how. Liked to have pizened me after mar died. No, young man, I don't propose to ask Hank Fisher to tote thet child over to Eureka and back, and spile his fun."

"Then I suppose I must make way for Mr. Hank—Hank—Fisher?" said North, with the least tinge of sarcasm in his speech.

"Of course. You've got nothing else to do, you know."

North would have given worlds to have pleaded a previous engagement on business of importance, but he knew that Bessy spoke truly. He had nothing to do. "And Fisher has, I suppose?" he asked.

"Of course—to look after *me!*"

A more unpleasant evening James North had not spent since the first day of his solitude. He almost began to hate the unconscious cause of his absurd position, as he paced up and down the floor with it. "Was there ever such egregious folly?" he began, but remembering he was quoting Maria North's favorite *résumé* of his own conduct, he

stopped. The child cried, missing, no doubt, the full
rounded curves and plump arm of its nurse. North danced
it violently, with an inward accompaniment that was not
musical, and thought of the other dancers. "Doubtless,"
he mused, "she has told this beau of hers that she has left
the baby with the 'looney' Man on the Beach. Perhaps I
may be offered a permanent engagement as a harmless sim-
pleton accustomed to the care of children. Mothers may
cry for me. The doctor is at Eureka. Of course, he will
be there to see his untranslated goddess, and condole with
her over the imbecility of the Man on the Beach." Once he
carelessly asked Joe who the company were.

"Well," said Joe, mournfully, "thar's Widder Higsby
and darter; the four Stubbs gals; in course Polly Doble
will be on hand with that feller that's clerking over at the
Head for Jones, and Jones's wife. Then thar's French
Pete, and Whisky Ben, and that chap that shot Archer,—I
disremember his name,—and the barber—what's that little
mulatto's name—that 'ar Kanaka? I swow!" continued
Joe, drearily, "I'll be forgettin' my own next—and—"

"That will do," interrupted North, only half concealing
his disgust as he rose and carried the baby to the other
room, beyond the reach of names that might shock its lady-
like ears. The next morning he met the from-dance-re-
turning Bessy abstractedly, and soon took his leave, full of
a disloyal plan, conceived in the sleeplessness of her own
bedchamber. He was satisfied that he owed a duty to its
unknown parents to remove the child from the degrading
influences of the barber Kanaka, and Hank Fisher especially, and he resolved to write to his relatives, stating
the case, asking a home for the waif and assistance to find
its parents. He addressed this letter to his cousin Maria,
partly in consideration of the dramatic farewell of that
young lady, and its possible influence in turning her sus-
ceptible heart towards his *protégé*. He then quietly settled
back to his old solitary habits, and for a week left the
Robinsons unvisited. The result was a morning call by
Trinidad Joe on the hermit. "It's a whim of my gal's,
Mr. North," he said, dejectedly, "and ez I told you before
and warned ye, when that gal hez an idee, fower yoke of

oxen and seving men can't drag it outer her. She's got a idee o' larnin'—never hevin' hed much schoolin', and we ony takin' the papers, permiskiss like—and she says *you* can teach her—not hevin' anythin' else to do. Do ye folly me?"

"Yes," said North, "certainly."

"Well, she allows ez mebbe you're proud, and didn't like her takin' care of the baby for nowt; and she reckons that ef you'll gin her some book larnin', and get her to sling some fancy talk in fash'n'ble style—why, she'll call it squar."

"You can tell her," said North, very honestly, "that I shall be only too glad to help her in any way, without ever hoping to cancel my debt of obligation to her."

"Then it's a go?" said the mystified Joe, with a desperate attempt to convey the foregoing statement to his own intellect in three Saxon words.

"It's a go," replied North, cheerfully.

And he felt relieved. For he was not quite satisfied with his own want of frankness to her. But here was a way to pay off the debt he owed her, and yet retain his own dignity. And now he could tell her what he had done, and he trusted to the ambitious instinct that prompted her to seek a better education to explain his reasons for it.

He saw her that evening and confessed all to her frankly. She kept her head averted, but when she turned her blue eyes to him they were wet with honest tears. North had a man's horror of a ready feminine lachrymal gland; but it was not like Bessy to cry, and it meant something; and then she did it in a large, goddess-like way, without sniffling, or chocking, or getting her nose red, but rather with a gentle deliquescence, a harmonious melting, so that he was fain to comfort her with nearer contact, gentleness in his own sad eyes, and a pressure of her large hand.

"It's all right, I s'pose," she said, sadly; "but I didn't reckon on yer havin' any relations, but thought you was alone, like me."

James North, thinking of Hank Fisher and the "mullater," could not help intimating that his relations were very wealthy and fashionable people, and had visited him last summer. A recollection of the manner in which they had so visited him and his own reception of them prevented his saying more. But Miss Bessy could not forego a certain feminine curiosity, and asked,—

"Did they come with Sam Baker's team?"

"Yes."

"Last July?"

"Yes."

"And Sam drove the horses here for a bite?"

"I believe so."

"And them's your relations?"

"They are."

Miss Robinson reached over the cradle and enfolded the sleeping infant in her powerful arms. Then she lifted her eyes, wrathful through her still glittering tears, and said, slowly, "They don't—have—this—child—then!"

"But why?"

"Oh, why? *I* saw them! That's why, and enough! You can't play any such gay and festive skeletons on this poor baby for flesh and blood parents. No, sir!"

"I think you judge them hastily, Miss Bessy," said North, secretly amused; "my aunt may not, at first, favorably impress strangers, yet she has many friends. But surely you do not object to my cousin Maria, the young lady?"

"What! that dried cuttle-fish, with nothing livin' about her but her eyes? James North, ye may be a fool like the old woman,—perhaps it's in the family,—but ye ain't a devil, like that gal! That ends it."

And it did. North dispatched a second letter to Maria saying that he had already made other arrangements for the baby. Pleased with her easy victory, Miss Bessy became more than usually gracious, and the next day bowed her shapely neck meekly to the yoke of her teacher, and became a docile pupil. James North could not have helped noticing her ready intelligence, even had he been less prejudiced in her favor than he was fast becoming now. If he had found it pleasant before to be admonished by her there was still more delicious flattery in her perfect trust in his omniscient skill as a pilot over this unknown sea. There was a certain enjoyment in guiding her hand over the writing-book, that I fear he could not have obtained from an intellect less graciously sustained by its physical nature. The weeks flew quickly by on gossamer wings, and when she placed a bunch of larkspurs and poppies in his hand one morning, he remembered for the first that it was spring.

I cannot say that there was more to record of Miss Bessy's education than this. Once North, half jestingly, remarked that he had never yet seen her admirer, Mr. Hank Fisher. Miss Bessy (coloring but cool)—"You never will!" North (white but hot)—"Why?" Miss Bessy (faintly)— "I'd rather not." North (resolutely)—"I insist." Bessy (yielding)—"As my teacher?" North (hesitatingly, at the limitation of the epithet)—"Y-e-e-s!" Bessy—"And you'll promise never to speak of it again?" North—"Never." Bessy (slowly—"Well, he said I did an awful thing to go over to your cabin and stay." North (in the genuine simplicity of a refined nature)—"But how?" Miss Bessy (half piqued, but absolutely admiring that nature)—"Quit! and keep your promise!"

They were so happy in these new relations that it occurred to Miss Bessy one day to take James North to task for obliging her to ask to be his pupil. "You knew how ignorant I was," she added; and Mr. North retorted by relating to her the doctor's criticism on her independence. "To tell you the truth," he added, "I was afraid you would not take it is kindly as he thought."

"That is, you thought me as vain as yourself. It seems to me you and the doctor had a great deal to say to each other."

"On the contrary," laughed North, "that was all we said."

"And you didn't make fun of me?"

Perhaps it was not necessary for North to take her hand to emphasize his denial, but he did.

Miss Bessy, being still reminiscent, perhaps, did not notice it. "It it hadn't been for that ar—I mean that thar —no, that baby—I wouldn't have known you!" she said dreamily.

"No," returned North, mischievously, "but you still would have known Hank Fisher."

No woman is perfect. Miss Bessy looked at him with a

sudden—her first and last—flash of coquetry. Then stooped and kissed—the baby.

James North was a simple gentleman, but not altogether a fool. He returned the kiss, but not vicariously.

There was a footstep on the porch. These two turned the hues of a dying dolphin, and then laughed. It was Joe. He held a newspaper in his hand. "I reckon ye woz right, Mr. North, about my takin' these yar papers reg'lar. For I allow here's suthin' that may clar up the mystery o' that baby's parents." With the hesitation of a slowly grappling intellect, Joe sat down on the table and read from the San Francisco "Herald" as follows: " 'It is now ascertained beyond doubt that the wreck reported by the Æolus was the American brig Pomare bound hence to Tahiti. The worst surmises are found correct. The body of the woman has been since identified as that of the beau-ti-ful daughter of—of—of—Terp—Terp—Terpish'—Well! I swow that name just tackles me."

"Gin it to me, Dad," said Bessy pertly. "You never had any education, any way. Hear your accomplished daughter." With a mock bow to the new schoolmaster, and a capital burlesque of a confident school girl, she strode to the middle of the room the paper held and folded book-wise in her hands. "Ahem! Where did you leave off? Oh, 'the beautiful daughter of Terpsichore—whose name was prom-i-nently connected with a mysterious social scandal of last year—the gifted but unfortunate Grace Chatterton'— No—don't stop me—there's some more! 'The body of her child, a lovely infant of six months, has not been recovered, and it is supposed was washed overboard.' There! may be that's the child, Mr. North. Why, Dad! Look, O my God! He's falling. Catch him, Dad! Quick!"

But her strong arm had anticipated her father's. She caught him, lifted him to the bed, on which he lay henceforth for many days unconscious. Then fever supervened, and delirium, and Dr. Duchesne telegraphed for his friends; but at the end of a week and the opening of a summer day the storm passed, as the other storm had passed, and he awoke, enfeebled, but at peace. Bessy was at his side—he was glad to see—alone.

"Bessy, dear," he said hesitatingly, "when I am stronger I have something to tell you."

"I know it all, Jem," she said with a trembling lip; "I heard it all—no, not from *them,* but from your own lips in your delirium. I'm glad it came from *you*—even then."

"Do you forgive me, Bessy?"

She pressed her lips to his forehead and said hastily, and then falteringly, as if afraid of her impulse:—

"Yes. Yes."

"And you will still be mother to the child?"

"*Her* child?"

"No dear, not hers, but *mine!*"

She started, cried a little, and then putting her arms around him, said: "Yes."

And as there was but one way of fulfilling that sacred promise, they were married in the autumn.

TWO SAINTS OF THE FOOT-HILLS

It never was clearly ascertained how long they had been there. The first settler of Rough-and-Ready—one Low, playfully known to his familiars as "The Poor Indian"— declared that the Saints were afore his time, and occupied a cabin in the brush when he "blazed" his way to the North Fork. It is certain that the two were present when the water was first turned on the Union Ditch and then and there received the designation of Daddy Downey and Mammy Downey, which they kept to the last. As they tottered toward the refreshment tent, they were welcomed with the greatest enthusiasm by the boys; or, to borrow the more refined language of the "Union Recorder,"—"Their gray hairs and bent figures, recalling as they did the happy paternal eastern homes of the spectators, and the blessings that fell from venerable lips when they left those homes to journey in quest of the Golden Fleece on Occidental Slopes, caused many to burst into tears." The nearer facts, that many of these spectators were orphans, that a few were unable to establish any legal parentage whatever, that others had enjoyed a State's guardianship and discipline, and that a majority had left their paternal roofs without any embarrassing preliminary formula, were mere passing clouds that did not dim the golden imagery of the writer. From that day the Saints were adopted as historical lay figures, and entered at once into possession of uninterrupted gratuities and endowment.

It was not strange that, in a country largely made up of ambitious and reckless youth, these two—types of conservative and settled forms—should be thus celebrated. Apart from any sentiment or veneration, they were admirable foils to the community's youthful progress and energy. They were put forward at every social gathering, occupied prominent seats on the platform at every public meeting, walked first in every procession, were conspicuous at the frequent funeral and rarer wedding, and were godfather and god-mother to the first baby born in Rough-and-Ready. At the first poll opened in that precinct, Daddy Downey cast the first vote, and, as was his custom on all momentous oc-casions, became volubly reminiscent. "The first vote I ever cast," said Daddy, "was for Andrew Jackson; the father o' some on your peart young chaps wasn't born then; he! he! that was 'way long in '33, wasn't it? I disremember now, but if Mammy was here, she bein' a school-gal at the time, she could say. But my memory's failin' me. I'm an old man, boys; yet I likes to see the young ones go ahead. I recklect that thar vote from a suckumstance. Squire Adams was present, and seein' it was my first vote, he put a goold piece into my hand, and, sez he, sez Squire Adams, 'Let that always be a reminder of the exercise of a glorious free-man's privilege!' He did; he! he! Lord, boys! I feel so proud of ye, that I wish I had a hundred votes to cast for ye all."

It was hardly necessary to say that the memorial tribute of Squire Adams was increased tenfold by the judges, in-spectors, and clerks, and that the old man tottered back to Mammy, considerably heavier than he came. As both of the rival candidates were equally sure of his vote, and each had called upon him and offered a conveyance, it is but fair to presume they were equally beneficent. But Daddy in-sisted upon walking to the polls,—a distance of two miles, —as a moral example, and a text for the California para-graphers, who hastened to record that such was the influence of the foot-hill climate, that "a citizen of Rough-and-Ready, aged eighty-four, rose at six o'clock, and, after milking two cows, walked a distance of twelve miles to the polls, and returned in time to chop a cord of wood before dinner."

Slightly exaggerated as this statement may have been, the fact that Daddy was always found by the visitor to be en-gaged at his wood-pile, which seemed neither to increase nor diminish under his axe, a fact, doubtless, owing to the activity of Mammy, who was always at the same time mak-ing pies, seemed to give some credence to the story. Indeed,

the wood-pile of Daddy Downey was a standing reproof to
the indolent and sluggish miner.

"Ole Daddy must use up a pow'ful sight of wood; every
time I've passed by his shanty he's been makin' the chips
fly. But what gets me is, that the pile don't seem to come
down," said Whisky Dick to his neighbor.

"Well, you derned fool!" growled his neighbor, "spose
some chap happens to pass by thar, and sees the old man
doin' a man's work at eighty, and slouches like you and me
lying round drunk, and that chap, feelin' kinder humped,
goes up some dark night and heaves a load of cut pine over
his fence, who's got anything to say about it? Say?"
Certainly not the speaker, who had done the act suggested,
nor the penitent and remorseful hearer, who repeated it
next day.

The pies and cakes made by the old woman were, I think,
remarkable rather for their inducing the same loyal and
generous spirit than for their intrinsic excellence, and it
may be said appealed more strongly to the nobler aspirations of humanity than its vulgar appetite. Howbeit, everybody ate Mammy Downey's pies, and thought of his childhood. "Take 'em, dear boys," the old lady would say; "it
does me good to see you eat 'em; reminds me kinder of my
poor Sammy, that, ef he'd lived, would hev been ez strong
and beg ez you be, but was taken down with lung fever, at
Sweetwater. I kin see him yet; that's forty year ago, dear!
comin' out o' the lot to the bake-house, and smilin' such a
beautiful smile, like yours, dear boy, as I handed him a
mince or a lemming turnover. Dear, dear, how I do run on!
and those days is past! but I seems to live in you again!"
The wife of the hotel-keeper, actuated by a low jealousy,
had suggested that she "seemed to live *off* them;" but as
that person tried to demonstrate the truth of her statement
by reference to the cost of the raw material used by the old
lady, it was considered by the camp as too practical and
economical for consideration. "Besides," added Cy Perkins,
"ef old Mammy wants to turn an honest penny in her old
age, let her do it. How would you like your old mother to
make pies on grub wages? eh?" A suggestion that so affected his hearer (who had no mother) that he bought three

on the spot. The quality of these pies had never been discussed but once. It is related that a young lawyer from San Francisco, dining at the Palmetto restaurant, pushed away one of Mammy Downey's pies with every expression of disgust and dissatisfaction. At this juncture, Whisky Dick, considerably affected by his favorite stimulant, approached the stranger's table, and, drawing up a chair, sat uninvited before him.

"Mebbee, young man," he began gravely, "ye don't like Mammy Downey's pies?"

The stranger replied curtly, and in some astonishment, that he did not, as a rule, "eat pie."

"Young man," continued Dick, with drunken gravity, "mebbee you're accustomed to Charlotte rusks and blue mange; mebbee ye can't eat unless your grub is got up by one o' them French cooks? Yet *we*—us boys yar in this camp—calls that pie—a good—a com-pe-tent pie!"

The stranger again disclaimed anything but a general dislike of that form of pastry.

"Young man," continued Dick, utterly unheeding the explanation,—"young man, mebbee you onst had an ole—a very ole mother, who, tottering down the vale o' years, made pies. Mebbee, and it's like your blank epicurean soul, ye turned up your nose on the ole woman, and went back on the pies, and on her! She that dandled ye when ye woz a baby,—a little baby! Mebbee ye went back on her, and shook her, and played off on her, and gave her away—dead away! And now, mebbee, young man—I wouldn't hurt ye for the world, but mebbee, afore ye leave this yar table, YE'LL EAT THAT PIE!"

The stranger rose to his feet, but the muzzle of a dragoon revolver in the unsteady hands of Whisky Dick, caused him to sit down again. He ate the pie, and lost his case likewise, before a Rough-and-Ready jury.

Indeed, far from exhibiting the cynical doubts and distrusts of age, Daddy Downey received always with childlike delight the progress of modern improvement and energy. "In my day, long back in the twenties, it took us nigh a week—a week, boys—to get up a barn, and all the young ones—I was one then—for miles 'round at the raisin';

and yer's you boys—rascals ye are, too—runs up this yer shanty for Mammy and me 'twixt sun-up and dark! Eh, eh, you're teachin' the old folks new tricks, are ye? Ah, get along, you!" and in playful simulation of anger he would shake his white hair and his hickory staff at the "rascals." The only indication of the conservative tendencies of age was visible in his continual protest against the extravagance of the boys. "Why," he would say, "a family, a hull family,—leavin' alone me and the old woman,—might be supported on what you young rascals throw away in a single spree. Ah, you young dogs, didn't I hear about your scattering half-dollars on the stage the other night when that Eyetalian Papist was singin'? And that money goes out of Ameriky—ivry cent!"

There was little doubt that the old couple were saving, if not avaricious. But when it was known, through the indiscreet volubility of Mammy Downey, that Daddy Downey sent the bulk of their savings, gratuities, and gifts to a dissipated and prodigal son in the East,—whose photograph the old man always carried with him,—it rather elevated him in their regard. "When ye write to that gay and festive son o' yourn, Daddy," said Joe Robinson, "send him this yer specimen. Give him my compliments, and tell him, ef he kin spend money faster than I can, I call him! Tell him, ef he wants a first-class jamboree, to kem out here, and me and the boys will show him what a square drunk is!" In vain would the old man continue to protest against the spirit of the gift; the miner generally returned with his pockets that much the lighter, and it is not improbable a little less intoxicated than he otherwise might have been. It may be premised that Daddy Downey was strictly temperate. The only way he managed to avoid hurting the feelings of the camp was by accepting the frequent donations of whisky to be used for the purposes of liniment.

"Next to snake-oil, my son," he would say, "and dilberry-juice,—and ye don't seem to pro-duce 'em hereabouts,—whisky is good for rubbin' onto old bones to make em limber. But pure cold water, 'sparklin' and bright in its liquid light,' and, so to speak, reflectin' of God's own liny-

ments on its surfiss, is the best, onless, like poor ol' Mammy
and me, ye gets the dumb-agur from over-use."

The fame of the Downey couple was not confined to the
foot-hills. The Rev. Henry Gushington, D.D., of Boston,
making a bronchial tour of California, wrote to the "Christian Pathfinder" an affecting account of his visit to them,
placed Daddy Downey's age at 102, and attributed the
recent conversions in Rough-and-Ready to their influence.
That gifted literary Hessian, Bill Smith, traveling in the
interests of various capitalists, and the trustworthy correspondent of four "only independent American journals,"
quoted him as an evidence of the longevity superinduced by
the climate, offered him as an example of the security of
helpless life and property in the mountains, used him as an
advertisement of the Union Ditch, and it is said in some
vague way cited him as proving the collateral facts of a
timber and ore-producing region existing in the foot-hills
worthy the attention of Eastern capitalists.

Praised thus by the lips of distinguished report, fostered
by the care and sustained by the pecuniary offerings of their
fellow-citizens, the Saints led for two years a peaceful life
of gentle absorption. To relieve them from the embarrassing appearance of eleemosynary receipts,—an embarrassment
felt more by the givers than the recipients,—the post-
mastership of Rough-and-Ready was procured for Daddy,
and the duty of receiving and delivering the United States
mails performed by him, with the advice and assistance of
the boys. If a few letters went astray at this time, it was
easily attributed to this undisciplined aid, and the boys
themselves were always ready to make up the value of a missing money-letter and "keep the old man's accounts square."
To these functions presently were added the treasurerships
of the Masons' and Odd Fellows' charitable funds,—the old
man being far advanced in their respective degrees,—and
even the position of almoner of their bounties was super-
added. Here, unfortunately, Daddy's habits of economy
and avaricious propensity came near making him unpopu-
lar, and very often needy brothers were forced to object to
the quantity and quality of the help extended. They always
met with more generous relief from the private hands of

the brothers themselves, and the remark, "that the ol' man was trying to set an example,—that he meant well,"—and that they would yet be thankful for his zealous care and economy. A few, I think, suffered in noble silence, rather than bring the old man's infirmity to the public notice.

And so with this honor of Daddy and Mammy, the days of the miners were long and profitable in the land of the foot-hills. The mines yielded their abundance, the winters were singularly open and yet there was no drouth nor lack of water, and peace and plenty smiled on the Sierrean foot-hills, from their highest sunny upland to the trailing *falda* of wild oats and poppies. If a certain superstition got abroad among the other camps, connecting the fortunes of Rough-and-Ready with Daddy and Mammy, it was a gentle, harmless fancy, and was not, I think, altogether rejected by the old people. A certain large, patriarchal, bountiful manner, of late visible in Daddy, and the increase of much white hair and beard, kept up the poetic illusion, while Mammy, day by day, grew more and more like somebody's fairy godmother. An attempt was made by a rival camp to emulate these paying virtues of reverence, and an aged mariner was procured from the Sailor's Snug Harbor in San Francisco, on trial. But the unfortunate seaman was more or less diseased, was not always presentable, through a weakness for ardent spirits, and finally, to use the powerful idiom of one of his disappointed foster-children, "up and died in a week, without slinging ary blessin'."

But vicissitude reaches young and old alike. Youthful Rough-and-Ready and the Saints had climbed to their meridian together, and it seemed fit that they should together decline. The first shadow fell with the immigration to Rough-and-Ready of a second aged pair. The landlady of the Independence Hotel had not abated her malevolence towards the Saints, and had imported at considerable expense her grand-aunt and grand-uncle, who had been enjoying for some years a sequestered retirement in the poorhouse at East Machias. They were indeed very old. By what miracle, even as anatomical specimens, they had been preserved during their long journey was a mystery to the camp. In some respects they had superior memories and reminiscences. The old man—Abner Trix—had shouldered a musket in the war of 1812; his wife, Abigail, had seen Lady Washington. She could sing hymns; he knew every text between "the leds" of a Bible. There is little doubt but that in many respects, to the superficial and giddy crowd of youthful spectators, they were the more interesting spectacle.

Whether it was jealousy, distrust, or timidity that overcame the Saints, was never known, but they studiously declined to meet the strangers. When directly approached upon the subject, Daddy Downey pleaded illness, kept himself in close seclusion, and the Sunday that the Trixes attended church in the school-house on the hill, the triumph of the Trix party was mitigated by the fact that the Downeys were not in their accustomed pew. "You bet that Daddy and Mammy is lying low jest to ketch them old mummies yet," explained a Downeyite. For by this time schism and division had crept into the camp; the younger and later members of the settlement adhering to the Trixes, while the older pioneers stood not only loyal to their own favorites, but even, in the true spirit of partisanship, began to seek for a principle underlying their personal feelings. "I tell ye what, boys," observed Sweetwater Joe, "if this yer camp is goin' to be run by greenhorns, and old pioneers, like Daddy and the rest of us, must take back seats, it's time we emigrated and shoved out, and tuk Daddy with us. Why, they're talkin' of rotation in offiss, and of putting that skeleton that Ma'am Decker sets up at the table, to take her boarders' appetites away, into the post-office in place o' Daddy." And, indeed, there were some fears of such a conclusion; the newer men of Rough-and-Ready were in the majority, and wielded a more than equal influence of wealth and outside enterprise. "Frisco," as a Downeyite bitterly remarked, "already owned half the town." The old friends that rallied around Daddy and Mammy were, like most loyal friends in adversity, in bad case themselves, and were beginning to look and act, it was observed, not unlike their old favorites.

At this juncture Mammy died.

The sudden blow for a few days seemed to reunite dissevered Rough-and-Ready. Both factions hastened to the bereaved Daddy with condolements, and offers of aid and assistance. But the old man received them sternly. A change had come over the weak and yielding octogenarian. Those who expected to find him maudlin, helpless, disconsolate, shrank from the cold, hard eyes and truculent voice that bade them "begone," and "leave him with his dead." Even his own friends failed to make him respond to their sympathy, and were fain to content themselves with his cold intimation that both the wishes of his dead wife and his own instincts were against any display, or the reception of any favor from the camp that might tend to keep up the divisions they had innocently created. The refusal of Daddy to accept any service offered was so unlike him as to have but one dreadful meaning! The sudden shock had turned his brain! Yet so impressed were they with his resolution that they permitted him to perform the last sad offices himself, and only a select few of his nearer neighbors assisted him in carrying the plain deal coffin from his lonely cabin in the woods to the still lonelier cemetery on the hill-top.

When the shallow grave was filled, he dismissed even these curtly, shut himself up in his cabin, and for days remained unseen. It was evident that he was no longer in his right mind.

His harmless aberration was accepted and treated with a degree of intelligent delicacy hardly to be believed of so rough a community. During his wife's sudden and severe illness, the safe containing the funds intrusted to his care by the various benevolent associations was broken into and robbed, and although the act was clearly attributable to his carelessness and preoccupation, all allusion to the fact was withheld from him in his severe affliction. When he appeared again before the camp, and the circumstances were considerately explained to him, with the remark that "the boys had made it all right," the vacant, hopeless, unintelligent eye that he turned upon the speaker showed too plainly that he had forgotten all about it. "Don't trouble the old man," said Whisky Dick, with a burst of honest poetry. "Don't ye see his memory's dead, and lying there in the

6   v. 1

coffin with Mammy?" Perhaps the speaker was nearer right than he imagined.

Failing in religious consolation, they took various means of diverting his mind with worldly amusements, and one was a visit to a traveling variety troupe, then performing in the town. The result of the visit was briefly told by Whisky Dick. "Well, sir, we went in, and I sot the old man down in a front seat, and kinder propped him up with some other of the fellers round him, and there he sot as silent and awful ez the grave. And then that fancy dancer, Miss Grace Somerset, comes in, and dern my skin, ef the old man didn't get to trembling and fidgeting all over, as she cut them pidgin wings. I tell ye what, boys, men is men, way down to their boots,—whether they're crazy or not! Well, he took on so, that I'm blamed if at last that gal *herself* didn't notice him! and she ups, suddenly, and blows him a kiss—so! with her fingers!"

Whether this narration were exaggerated or not, it is certain that the old man Downey every succeeding night of the performance was a spectator. That he may have aspired to more than that was suggested a day or two later in the following incident: A number of the boys were sitting around the stove in the Magnolia saloon, listening to the onset of a winter storm against the windows, when Whisky Dick, tremulous, excited, and bristling with rain-drops and information, broke in upon them.

"Well, boys, I've got just the biggest thing out. Ef I hadn't seed it myself, I wouldn't hev believed it!"

"It ain't thet ghost ag'in?" growled Robinson, from the depths of his arm-chair; "thet ghost's about played."

"Wot ghost?" asked a new-comer.

"Why, ole Mammy's ghost, that every feller about yer sees when he's half full and out late o' nights."

"Where?"

"Where? Why, where should a ghost be? Meanderin' round her grave on the hill, yander, in course."

"It's suthin bigger nor thet, pard," said Dick confidently; "no ghost kin rake down the pot ag'in the keerds I've got here. This ain't no bluff!"

"Well, go on!" said a dozen excited voices.

Dick paused a moment, diffidently, with the hesitation of an artistic *raconteur*.

"Well," he said, with affected deliberation, "let's see! It's nigh onto an hour ago ez I was down thar at the variety show. When the curtain was down betwixt the ax, I looks round fer Daddy. No Daddy thar! I goes out and asks some o' the boys. 'Daddy *was* there a minnit ago,' they say; 'must hev gone home.' Bein' kinder responsible for the old man, I hangs around, and goes out in the hall and sees a passage leadin' behind the scenes. Now the queer thing about this, boys, ez that suthin in my bones tells me the old man is *thar*. I pushes in, and, sure as a gun, I hears his voice. Kinder pathetic, kinder pleadin', kinder—"

"Love-makin'!" broke in the impatient Robinson.

"You've hit it, pard,—you've rung the bell every time! But she says, 'wants thet money down, or I'll—' and here I couldn't get to hear the rest. And then he kinder coaxes, and she says, sorter sassy, but listenin' all the time, —woman like, ye know, Eve and the sarpint!—and she says, 'I'll see to-morrow.' And he says, 'You won't blow on me?' and I gets excited and peeps in, and may I be teetotally durned ef I didn't see—"

"What?" yelled the crowd.

"Why, *Daddy on his knees to that there fancy dancer,* Grace Somerset! Now, if Mammy's ghost is meanderin' round, why, et's about time she left the cemetery and put in an appearance in Jackson's Hall. Thet's all!"

"Look yar, boys," said Robinson, rising, "I don't know ez it's the square thing to spile Daddy's fun. I don't object to it, provided she ain't takin' in the old man, and givin' him dead away. But ez we're his guardeens, I propose that we go down thar and see the lady, and find out ef her intentions is honorable. If she means marry, and the old man persists, why, I reckon we kin give the young couple a send-off thet won't disgrace this yer camp! Hey, boys?"

It is unnecessary to say that the proposition was received with acclamation, and that the crowd at once departed on their discreet mission. But the result was never known, for the next morning brought a shock to Rough-and-Ready before which all other interest paled to nothingness.

The grave of Mammy Downey was found violated and despoiled; the coffin opened, and half filled with the papers and accounts of the robbed benevolent associations; but the body of Mammy was gone! Nor, on examination, did it appear that the sacred and ancient form of that female had ever reposed in its recesses!

Daddy Downey was not to be found, nor is it necessary to say that the ingenuous Grace Somerset was also missing.

For three days the reason of Rough-and-Ready trembled in the balance. No work was done in the ditches, in the flume, nor in the mills. Groups of men stood by the grave of the lamented relict of Daddy Downey, as open-mouthed and vacant as that sepulchre. Never since the great earthquake of '52 had Rough-and-Ready been so stirred to its deepest foundations.

On the third day the sheriff of Calaveras—a quiet, gentle, thoughtful man—arrived in town, and passed from one to the other of excited groups, dropping here and there detached but concise and practical information.

"Yes, gentlemen, you are right, Mrs. Downey is not dead, because there wasn't any Mrs. Downey! Her part was played by George F. Fenwick, of Sydney,—a 'ticket-of-leave-man,' who was, they say, a good actor. Downey? Oh, yes! Downey was Jem Flanigan, who, in '52, used to run the variety troupe in Australia, where Miss Somerset made her *début*. Stand back a little, boys. Steady! 'The money?' Oh, yes, they've got away with that, sure! How are ye, Joe? Why, you're looking well and hearty! I rather expected ye court week. How's things your way?"

"Then they were only play-actors, Joe Hall?" broke in a dozen voices.

"I reckon!" returned the sheriff, coolly.

"And for a matter o' five blank years," said Whisky Dick, sadly, "they played this camp!"

"JINNY"

I THINK that the few who were permitted to know and love the object of this sketch spent the rest of their days not only in an attitude of apology for having at first failed to recognize her higher nature, but of remorse that they should have ever lent a credulous ear to *a priori* tradition concerning her family characteristics. She had not escaped that calumny which she shared with the rest of her sex for those youthful follies, levities, and indiscretions which belong to immaturity. It is very probable that the firmness that distinguished her maturer will in youth might have been taken for obstinacy, that her nice discrimination might at the same period have been taken for adolescent caprice, and that the positive expression of her quick intellect might have been thought youthful impertinence before her years had won respect for her judgment.

She was foaled at Indian Creek, and one month later, when she was brought over to Sawyer's Bar, was considered the smallest donkey ever seen in the foot-hills. The legend that she was brought over in one of "Dan the Quartz Crusher's" boots required corroboration from that gentleman; but his denial being evidently based upon a masculine vanity regarding the size of his foot rather than a desire to be historically accurate, it went for nothing. It is certain that for the next two months she occupied the cabin of Dan, until, perhaps incensed at this and other scandals, she one night made her way out. "I hadn't the least idee wot woz comin'," said Dan, "but about midnight I seemed to hear hail onto the roof, and a shower of rocks and stones like to a blast started in the cañon. When I got up and struck a light, thar was suthin' like onto a cord o' kindlin' wood and splinters whar she'd stood asleep, and a hole in the side o' the shanty, and—no Jinny! Lookin' at them hoofs o' hern—and mighty porty they is to look at,

165

too—you would allow she could do it!" I fear that this performance laid the foundation of her later infelicitous reputation, and perhaps awakened in her youthful breast a misplaced ambition, and an emulation which might at that time have been diverted into a nobler channel. For the fame of this juvenile performance—and its possible promise in the future—brought at once upon her the dangerous flattery and attention of the whole camp. Under intelligently directed provocation she would repeat her misguided exercise, until most of the scanty furniture of the cabin was reduced to a hopeless wreck, and sprains and callosities were developed upon the limbs of her admirers. Yet even at this early stage of her history, that penetrating intellect which was in after years her dominant quality was evident to all. She could not be made to kick at quartz tailings, at a barrel of Boston crackers, or at the head or shin of "Nigger Pete." An artistic discrimination economized her surplus energy. "Ef you'll notiss," said Dan, with a large parental softness, "she never lets herself out to onst like them mules or any jackass ez I've heerd of, but kinder holds herself in, and, so to speak, takes her bearings—sorter feels round gently with that off foot, takes her distance and her rest, and then with that ar' foot hoverin' round in the air softly, like an angel's wing, and a gentle, dreamy kind o' look in them eyes, she lites out! Don't ye, Jinny? Thar! jist ez I told ye," continued Dan, with an artist's noble forgetfulness of self, as he slowly crawled from the splintered ruin of the barrel on which he had been sitting. "Thar! did ye ever see the like! Did ye dream that all the while I was talkin' she was a meditatin' that?"

The same artistic perception and noble reticence distinguished her bray. It was one of which a less sagacious animal would have been foolishly vain or ostentatiously prodigal. It was a contralto of great compass and profundity—reaching from low G to high C—perhaps a trifle stronger in the lower register, and not altogether free from a nasal falsetto in the upper. Daring and brilliant as it was in the middle notes, it was perhaps more musically remarkable for its great sustaining power. The element of

surprise always entered into the hearer's enjoyment; long
after any ordinary strain of human origin would have
ceased, faint echoes of Jinny's last note were perpetually
recurring. But it was as an intellectual and moral expression that her bray was perfect. As far beyond her
size as were her aspirations, it was a free and running
commentary of scorn at all created things extant, with ironical and sardonic additions that were terrible. It reviled
all human endeavor, it quenched all sentiment, it suspended
frivolity, it scattered reverie, it paralyzed action. It was
omnipotent. More wonderful and characteristic than all,
the very existence of this tremendous organ was unknown
to the camp for six months after the arrival of its modest
owner, and only revealed to them under circumstances that
seemed to point more conclusively than ever to her rare
discretion.

It was the beginning of a warm night and the middle
of a heated political discussion. Sawyer's Bar had gathered in force at the Crossing, and by the light of flaring
pine torches, cheered and applauded the rival speakers who
from a rude platform addressed the excited multitude.
Partisan spirit at that time ran high in the foot-hills;
crimination and recrimination, challenge, reply, accusation,
and retort had already inflamed the meeting, and Colonel
Bungstarter, after a withering review of his opponent's
policy, culminated with a personal attack upon the career
and private character of the eloquent and chivalrous Colonel Culpepper Starbottle of Siskiyou. That eloquent and
chivalrous gentleman was known to be present; it was
rumored that the attack was expected to provoke a challenge from Colonel Starbottle which would give Bungstarter the choice of weapons, and deprive Starbottle of
his advantage as a dead shot. It was whispered also that
the sagacious Starbottle, aware of this fact, would retaliate
in kind so outrageously as to leave Bungstarter no recourse
but to demand satisfaction on the spot. As Colonel Starbottle rose, the eager crowd drew together, elbowing each
other in rapt and ecstatic expectancy. "He can't get even
on Bungstarter, onless he allows his sister ran off with a
nigger, or that he put up his grandmother at draw poker and

lost her," whispered the Quartz Crusher; "kin he?" All
ears were alert, particularly the very long and hairy ones
just rising above the railing of the speaker's platform;
for Jinny, having a feminine distrust of solitude and a
fondness for show, had followed her master to the meeting and had insinuated herself upon the platform, where
way was made for her with that frontier courtesy always
extended to her age and sex.

Colonel Starbottle, stertorous and purple, advanced to
the railing. There he unbuttoned his collar and laid his
neckcloth aside, then with his eye fixed on his antagonist
he drew off his blue frock coat, and thrusting one hand
into his ruffled shirt front, and raising the other to the dark
canopy above him, he opened his vindictive lips. The action, the attitude, were Starbottle's. But the voice was
not. For at that supreme moment, a bray—so profound,
so appalling, so utterly soul-subduing, so paralyzing that
everything else sank to mere insignificance beside it—filled
woods, and sky, and air. For a moment only the multitude
gasped in speechless astonishment—it was a moment only
—and then the welkin roared with their shouts. In vain
silence was commanded, in vain Colonel Starbottle, with a
ghastly smile, remarked that he recognized in the interruption the voice and the intellect of the opposition; the laugh
continued, the more as it was discovered that Jinny had not
yet finished, and was still recurring to her original theme.
"Gentlemen," gasped Starbottle, "any attempt by [Hee-
haw! from Jinny] brutal buffoonery to restrict the right
of free speech to all [a prolonged assent from Jinny] is
worthy only the dastardly"—but here a diminuendo so long
drawn as to appear a striking imitation of the Colonel's
own apoplectic sentences drowned his voice with shrieks of
laughter.

It must not be supposed that during this performance
a vigorous attempt was not made to oust Jinny from the
platform. But all in vain. Equally demoralizing in either
extremity, Jinny speedily cleared a circle with her flying
hoofs, smashed the speaker's table and water pitcher, sent
the railing flying in fragments over the cheering crowd,
and only succumbed to two blankets, in which, with her

head concealed, she was finally dragged, half captive, half victor, from the field. Even then a muffled and supplemental bray that came from the woods at intervals drew half the crowd away and reduced the other half to mere perfunctory hearers. The demoralized meeting was adjourned; Colonel Starbottle's withering reply remained unuttered, and the Bungstarter party were triumphant.

For the rest of the evening Jinny was the heroine of the hour, but no cajolery nor flattery could induce her to again exhibit her powers. In vain did Dean of Angel's extemporize a short harangue in the hope that Jinny would be tempted to reply; in vain was every provocation offered that might sting her sensitive nature to eloquent revolt. She replied only with her heels. Whether or not this was simple caprice, or whether she was satisfied with her maiden effort, or indignant at her subsequent treatment, she remained silent. "She made her little game," said Dan, who was a political adherent of Starbottle's, and who yet from that day enjoyed the great speaker's undying hatred, "and even if me and her don't agree on politics—*you* let her alone." Alas, it would have been well for Dan if he could have been true to his instincts, but the offer of one hundred dollars from the Bungstarter party proved too tempting. She passed irrevocably from his hands into those of the enemy. But any reader of these lines will, I trust, rejoice to hear that this attempt to restrain free political expression in the foot-hills failed signally. For, although she was again covertly introduced on the platform by the Bungstarters, and placed face to face with Colonel Starbottle at Murphy's Camp, she was dumb. Even a brass band failed to excite her emulation. Either she had become disgusted with politics or the higher prices paid by the party to other and less effective speakers aroused her jealousy and shocked her self-esteem, but she remained a passive spectator. When the Hon. Sylvester Rourback, who received, for the use of his political faculties for a single night, double the sum for which she was purchased outright, appeared on the same platform with herself, she forsook it hurriedly and took to the woods. Here she might have starved but for the intervention of one McCarty, a poor market gardener, who found

her, and gave her food and shelter under the implied contract that she should forsake politics and go to work. The
latter she for a long time resisted, but as she was considered large enough by this time to draw a cart, McCarty
broke her to single harness, with a severe fracture of his
leg and the loss of four teeth and a small spring wagon.
At length, when she could be trusted to carry his wares
to Murphy's Camp, and could be checked from entering a
shop with the cart attached to her,—a fact of which she
always affected perfect disbelief,—her education was considered as complete as that of the average California donkey. It was still unsafe to leave her alone, as she disliked
solitude, and always made it a point to join any group of
loungers with her unnecessary cart, and even to follow some
good-looking miner to his cabin. The first time this peculiarity was discovered by her owner was on his return
to the street after driving a bargain within the walls of
the Temperance Hotel. Jinny was nowhere to be seen.
Her devious course, however, was pleasingly indicated by
vegetables that strewed the road until she was at last
tracked to the veranda of the Arcade saloon, where she was
found looking through the window at a game of euchre,
and only deterred by the impeding cart from entering the
building. A visit one Sunday to the little Catholic chapel
at French Camp, where she attempted to introduce an an-
tiphonal service and the cart, brought shame and disgrace
upon her unlucky master. For the cart contained freshly-
gathered vegetables, and the fact that McCarty had been
Sabbath-breaking was painfully evident. Father Sullivan
was quick to turn an incident that provoked only the risi-
bilities of his audience into a moral lesson. "It's the poor
dumb beast that has a more Christian sowl than Michael,"
he commented; but here Jinny assented so positively that
they were fain to drag her away by main force.

To her eccentric and thoughtless youth succeeded a calm
maturity in which her conservative sagacity was steadily
developed. She now worked for her living, subject, however, to a nice discrimination by which she limited herself
to a certain amount of work, beyond which neither threats,
beatings, nor cajoleries would force her. At certain hours

she would start for the stable with or without the incumbrances of the cart or Michael, turning two long and deaf
ears on all expostulation or entreaty. "Now, God be good
to me," said Michael, one day picking himself out from a
ditch as he gazed sorrowfully after the flying heels of
Jinny, "but it's only the second load of cabbages I'm
bringin' the day, and if she's shtruck *now*, it's ruined I am
entoirely." But he was mistaken; after two hours of rumi-
nation Jinny returned of her own free will, having evidently mistaken the time, and it is said even consented to
draw an extra load to make up the deficiency. It may be
imagined from this and other circumstances that Michael
stood a little in awe of Jinny's superior intellect, and that
Jinny occasionally, with the instinct of her sex, presumed
upon it. After the Sunday episode, already referred to,
she was given her liberty on that day, a privilege she gracefully recognized by somewhat unbending her usual austerity
in the indulgence of a saturnine humor. She would visit
the mining camps, and, grazing lazily and thoughtfully before the cabins, would, by various artifices and coquet-
ries known to the female heart, induce some credulous
stranger to approach her with the intention of taking a
ride. She would submit hesitatingly to a halter, allow him
to mount her back, and, with every expression of timid
and fearful reluctance, at last permit him to guide her in a
laborious trot out of sight of human habitation. What
happened then was never clearly known. In a few moments the camp would be aroused by shouts and execrations,
and the spectacle of Jinny tearing by at a frightful pace,
with the stranger clinging with his arms around her neck,
afraid to slip off, from terror of her circumvolving heels,
and vainly imploring assistance. Again and again she
would dash by the applauding groups, adding the aggravation of her voice to the danger of her heels, until suddenly
wheeling, she would gallop to Carter's Pond, and deposit
her luckless freight in the muddy ditch. This practical joke
was repeated until one Sunday she was approached by Juan
Ramirez, a Mexican *vaquero*, booted and spurred, and carrying a *riata*. A crowd was assembled to see her discomfiture. But, to the intense disappointment of the camp,

Jinny, after quietly surveying the stranger, uttered a sardonic bray, and ambled away to the little cemetery on the hill, whose tangled chapparal effectually prevented all pursuit by her skilled antagonist. From that day she forsook the camp, and spent her Sabbaths in mortuary reflections among the pine head-boards and cold *"hic jacets"* of the dead.

Happy would it have been if this circumstance, which resulted in the one poetic episode of her life, had occurred earlier; for the cemetery was the favorite resort of Miss Jessie Lawton, a gentle invalid from San Francisco, who had sought the foot-hills for the balsam of pine and fir, and in the faint hope that the freshness of the wild roses might call back her own. The extended views from the cemetery satisfied Miss Lawton's artistic taste, and here frequently, with her sketch-book in hand, she indulged that taste and a certain shy reserve which kept her from contact with strangers. On one of the leaves of that sketch-book appears a study of a donkey's head, being none other than the grave features of Jinny, as once projected timidly over the artist's shoulder. The preliminaries of this intimacy have never transpired, nor is it a settled fact if Jinny made the first advances. The result was only known to the men of Sawyer's Bar by a vision which remained fresh in their memories long after the gentle lady and her four-footed friend had passed beyond their voices. As two of the tunnel-men were returning from work one evening, they chanced to look up the little trail, kept sacred from secular intrusion, that led from the cemetery to the settlement. In the dim twilight, against a sunset sky, they beheld a pale-faced girl riding slowly toward them. With a delicate instinct, new to those rough men, they drew closer in the shadow of the bushes until she passed. There was no mistaking the familiar grotesqueness of Jinny; there was no mistaking the languid grace of Miss Lawton. But a wreath of wild roses was around Jinny's neck, from her long ears floated Miss Jessie's hat ribbons, and a mischievous, girlish smile was upon Miss Jessie's face, as fresh as the azaleas in her hair. By the next day the story of this gentle apparition was known to a dozen miners in camp, and all were sworn to secrecy. But the next evening, and the next, from the safe shadows of the woods they watched and drank in the beauty of that fanciful and all unconscious procession. They kept their secret, and never a whisper or footfall from these rough men broke its charm or betrayed their presence. The man who could have shocked the sensitive reserve of the young girl would have paid for it with his life.

And then one day the character of the procession changed, and this little incident having been told, it was permitted that Jinny should follow her friend, caparisoned even as before, but this time by the rougher but no less loving hands of men. When the cortège reached the ferry where the gentle girl was to begin her silent journey to the sea, Jinny broke from those who held her, and after a frantic effort to mount the barge fell into the swiftly rushing Stanislaus. A dozen stout arms were stretched to save her, and a rope skilfully thrown was caught around her feet. For an instant she was passive, and, as it seemed, saved. But the next moment her dominant instinct returned, and with one stroke of her powerful heel she snapped the rope in twain and so drifted with her mistress to the sea.

ROGER CATRON'S FRIEND

I THINK that, from the beginning, we all knew how it would end. He had always been so quiet and conventional, although by nature an impulsive man; always so temperate and abstemious, although a man with a quick appreciation of pleasure; always so cautious and practical, although an imaginative man, that when, at last, one by one he loosed these bands, and gave himself up to a life, perhaps not worse than other lives which the world has accepted as the natural expression of their various owners, we at once decided that the case was a hopeless one. And when one night we picked him up out of the Union Ditch, a begrimed and weather-worn drunkard, a hopeless debtor, a self-confessed spendthrift, and a half-conscious, maudlin imbecile, we knew that the end had come. The wife he had abandoned had in turn deserted him; the woman he had misled had already realized her folly, and left him with her reproaches; the associates of his reckless life, who had used and abused him, had found him no longer of service, or even amusement, and clearly there was nothing left to do but to hand him over to the state, and we took him to the nearest penitential asylum. Conscious of the Samaritan deed, we went back to our respective wives, and told his story. It is only just to say that these sympathetic creatures were more interested in the philanthropy of their respective husbands than in its miserable object. "It was good and kind in you, dear," said loving Mrs. Maston to her spouse, as returning home that night he flung his coat on a chair with an air of fatigued righteousness; "it was like your kind heart to care for that beast; but after he left that good wife of his—that perfect saint—to take up with that awful woman, I think I'd have left him to die in the ditch. Only to think of it, dear, a woman that you wouldn't speak to!" Here Mr. Maston coughed slightly, colored a little, mumbled

174

something about "women not understanding some things,"
"that men were men," etc., and then went comfortably to
sleep, leaving the outcast, happily oblivious of all things,
and especially this criticism, locked up in Hangtown Jail.

For the next twelve hours he lay there, apathetic and
half-conscious. Recovering from this after a while, he became furious, vengeful, and unmanageable, filling the cell
and corridor with maledictions of friend and enemy; and
again sullen, morose, and watchful. Then he refused food,
and did not sleep, pacing his limits with the incessant, feverish tread of a caged tiger. Two physicians, diagnosing his
case from the scant facts, pronounced him insane, and he
was accordingly transported to Sacramento. But on the
way thither he managed to elude the vigilance of his guards,
and escaped. The alarm was given, a hue and cry followed
him, the best detectives of San Francisco were on his track,
and finally recovered his dead body—emaciated and wasted
by exhaustion and fever—in the Stanislaus Marshes, identified it, and, receiving the reward of $1,000 offered by his
surviving relatives and family, assisted in legally estab-
lishing the end we had predicted.

Unfortunately for the moral, the facts were somewhat inconsistent with the theory. A day or two after the remains
were discovered and identified, the real body of "Roger
Catron, aged 52 years, slight, iron-gray hair, and shabby in
apparel," as the advertisement read, dragged itself, travel-
worn, trembling, and disheveled, up the steep slope of Deadwood Hill. How he should do it, he had long since
determined,—ever since he had hidden his Derringer, a mere
baby pistol, from the vigilance of his keepers. Where he
should do it, he had settled within his mind only within
the last few moments. Deadwood Hill was seldom fre-
quented; his body might lie there for months before it was
discovered. He had once thought of the river, but he remembered it had an ugly way of exposing its secrets on
sandbar and shallow, and that the body of Whisky Jim,
bloated and disfigured almost beyond recognition, had been
once delivered to the eyes of Sandy Bar, before breakfast,
on the left bank of the Stanislaus. He toiled up through
the chimisal that clothed the southern slope of the hill until

he reached the bald, storm-scarred cap of the mountain, ironically decked with the picked, featherless plumes of a few dying pines. One, stripped of all but two lateral branches, brought a boyish recollection to his fevered brain. Against a background of dull sunset fire, it extended two gaunt arms—black, rigid, and pathetic. Calvary!

With the very word upon his lips, he threw himself, face downwards, on the ground beneath it, and, with his fingers clutched in the soil, lay there for some moments, silent and still. In this attitude, albeit a skeptic and unorthodox man, he prayed. I cannot say—indeed I *dare* not say—that his prayer was heard, or that God visited him thus. Let us rather hope that all there was of God in him, in this crucial moment of agony and shame, strove outward and upward. Howbeit, when the moon rose he rose too, perhaps a trifle less steady than the planet, and began to descend the hill with feverish haste, yet with this marked difference between his present haste and his former recklessness, that it seemed to have a well-defined purpose. When he reached the road again, he struck into a well-worn trail, where, in the distance, a light faintly twinkled. Following this beacon, he kept on, and at last flung himself heavily against the door of the little cabin from whose window the light had shone. As he did so, it opened upon the figure of a square, thickset man, who, in the impetuosity of Catron's onset, received him, literally, in his arms.

"Captain Dick," said Roger Catron, hoarsely, "Captain Dick, save me! For God's sake, save me!"

Captain Dick, without a word, placed a large, protecting hand upon Catron's shoulder, allowed it to slip to his waist, and then drew his visitor quietly, but firmly, within the cabin. Yet, in the very movement, he had managed to gently and unobtrusively possess himself of Catron's pistol.

"Save ye! From which?" asked Captain Dick, as quietly and unobtrusively dropping the Derringer in a flour sack.

"From everything," gasped Catron, "from the men that are hounding me, from my family, from my friends, but most of all—from, from—myself!"

He had, in turn, grasped Captain Dick, and forced him

frenziedly against the wall. The captain released himself, and, taking the hands of his excited visitor, said slowly,—

"Ye want some blue mass—suthin' to unload your liver. I'll get it up for ye."

"But, Captain Dick, I'm an outcast, shamed, disgraced—"

"Two on them pills taken now, and two in the morning," continued the captain, gravely, rolling a bolus in his fingers, "will bring yer head to the wind again. Yer fallin' to leeward all the time, and ye want to brace up."

"But, Captain," continued the agonized man, again clutching the sinewy arms of his host, and forcing his livid face and fixed eyes within a few inches of Captain Dick's, "hear me! You must and shall hear me. I've been in jail—do you hear?—in jail, like a common felon. I've been sent to the asylum, like a demented pauper. I've—"

"Two now, and two in the morning," continued the captain, quietly releasing one hand only to place two enormous pills in the mouth of the excited Catron, "thar now—a drink o' whisky—thar, that'll do—just enough to take the taste out of yer mouth, wash it down, and belay it, so to speak. And how are the mills running, gin'rally, over at the Bar?"

"Captain Dick, hear me—if you *are* my friend, for God's sake hear me! An hour ago I should have been a dead man—"

"They say that Sam Bolin hez sold out of the Excelsior—"

"Captain Dick! Listen, for God's sake; I have suffered—"

But Captain Dick was engaged in critically examining his man. "I guess I'll ladle ye out some o' that soothin' mixture I bought down at Simpson's t' other day," he said, reflectively. "And I onderstand the boys up on the Bar think the rains will set in airly."

But here Nature was omnipotent. Worn by exhaustion, excitement, and fever, and possibly a little affected by Captain Dick's later potion, Roger Catron turned white, and lapsed against the wall. In an instant Captain Dick had caught him, as a child, lifted him in his stalwart arms, wrapped a blanket around him, and deposited him in his bunk. Yet, even in his prostration, Catron made one more despairing appeal for mental sympathy from his host.

"I know I'm sick—dying, perhaps," he gasped, from under the blankets; "but promise me, whatever comes, tell my wife—say to—"

"It has been lookin' consid'ble like rain, lately, here-abouts," continued the captain, coolly, in a kind of am-phibious slang, characteristic of the man, "but in these yer latitudes no man kin set up to be a weather sharp."

"Captain! will you hear me?"

"Yer goin' to sleep, now," said the captain, potentially.

"But, Captain, they are pursuing me! If they should track me here?"

"Thar is a rifle over thar, and yer's my navy revolver. When I've emptied them, and want you to bear a hand, I'll call ye. Just now your lay is to turn in. It's my watch."

There was something so positive, strong, assuring, and a little awesome in the captain's manner, that the trembling, nervously-prostrated man beneath the blankets forbore to question further. In a few moments his breathing, albeit hurried and irregular, announced that he slept. The cap-tain then arose, for a moment critically examined the sleep-ing man, holding his head a little on one side, whistling softly, and stepping backwards to get a good perspective, but always with contemplative good humor, as if Catron were a work of art, which he (the captain) had created, yet one that he was not yet entirely satisfied with. Then he put a large pea-jacket over his flannel blouse, dragged a Mexican *serapé* from the corner, and putting it over his shoulders, opened the cabin door, sat down on the door-step, and leaning back against the door-post, composed himself to meditation. The moon lifted herself slowly over the crest of Deadwood Hill, and looked down, not unkindly, on his broad, white, shaven face, round and smooth as her own disc, encircled with a thin fringe of white hair and whiskers. Indeed, he looked so like the prevailing carica-tures in a comic almanac of planets, with dimly outlined features, that the moon would have been quite justified in flirting with him, as she clearly did, insinuating a twinkle into his keen, gray eyes, making the shadow of a dimple on his broad, fat chin, and otherwise idealizing him after the fashion of her hero-worshiping sex. Touched by these benign influences, Captain Dick presently broke forth in melody. His song was various, but chiefly, I think, confined to the recital of the exploits of one "Lorenzo," who, as related by himself,—

> "Shipped on board of a Liner,
> 'Renzo, boys, Renzo,"—

a fact that seemed to have deprived him at once of all metre, grammar, or even the power of coherent narration. At times a groan or a half-articulate cry would come from the "bunk" whereon Roger Catron lay, a circumstance that always seemed to excite Captain Dick to greater effort and more rapid vocalization. Toward morning, in the midst of a prolonged howl from the captain, who was finishing the "Starboard Watch, ahoy!" in three different keys, Roger Catron's voice broke suddenly and sharply from his enwrappings:—

"Dry up, you d—d old fool, will you?"

Captain Dick stopped instantly. Rising to his feet, and looking over the landscape, he took all nature into his confidence in one inconceivably arch and crafty wink. "He's coming up to the wind," he said softly, rubbing his hands. "The pills is fetchin' him. Steady now, boys, steady. Steady as she goes on her course," and with another wink of ineffable wisdom, he entered the cabin and locked the door.

Meanwhile, the best society of Sandy Bar was kind to the newly-made widow. Without being definitely expressed, it was generally felt that sympathy with her was now safe, and carried no moral responsibility with it. Even practical and pecuniary aid, which before had been withheld, lest it should be diverted from its proper intent, and, perhaps through the weakness of the wife, made to minister to the wickedness of the husband,—even that was now openly suggested. Everybody felt that somebody should do something for the widow. A few did it. Her own sex rallied to her side, generally with large sympathy, but, unfortunately, small pecuniary or practical result. At last, when the feasibility of her taking a boarding-house in San Francisco, and identifying herself with that large class of American gentlewomen who have seen better days, but clearly are on the road never to see them again, was suggested, a few of her own and her husband's rich relatives came to the front to rehabilitate her. It was easier to take her into their homes as an equal than to refuse to call upon her as the mistress of a lodging-house in the adjoining street. And upon inspection it was found that she was still quite an eligible *partie,* prepossessing, and withal, in her widow's weeds, a kind of poetical and sentimental presence, as necessary in a wealthy and fashionable American family as a work of art. "Yes, poor Caroline has had a sad, sad history," the languid Mrs. Walker Catron would say, "and we all sympathize with her deeply; Walker always regards her as a sister." What was this dark history never came out, but its very mystery always thrilled the visitor, and seemed to indicate plainly the respectability of the hostess. An American family without a genteel skeleton in its closet could scarcely add to that gossip which keeps society from forgetting its members. Nor was it altogether unnatural that presently Mrs. Roger Catron lent herself to this sentimental deception, and began to think that she really was a more exquisitely aggrieved woman than she had imagined. At times, when this vague load of iniquity put upon her dead husband assumed, through the mystery of her friends, the rumor of murder and highway robbery, and even an attempt upon her own life, she went to her room, a little frightened, and had "a good cry," reappearing more mournful and pathetic than ever, and corroborating the suspicions of her friends. Indeed, one or two impulsive gentlemen, fired by her pathetic eyelids, openly regretted that the deceased had not been hanged, to which Mrs. Walker Catron responded that, "Thank Heaven, they were spared at least that disgrace!" and so sent conviction into the minds of her hearers.

It was scarcely two months after this painful close of her matrimonial life that one rainy February morning the servant brought a card to Mrs. Roger Catron, bearing the following inscription:—

" Richard Graeme Macleod."

Women are more readily affected by names than we are, and there was a certain Highland respectability about this that, albeit, not knowing its possessor, impelled Mrs. Catron to send word that she "would be down in a few moments." At the end of this femininely indefinite period,—a quarter of an hour by the French clock on the mantel-piece,—Mrs. Roger Catron made her appearance in the reception-room. It was a dull, wet day, as I have said before, but on the Contra Costa hills the greens and a few flowers were already showing a promise of rejuvenescence and an early spring. There was something of this, I think, in Mrs. Catron's presence, shown perhaps in the coquettish bow of a ribbon, in a larger and more delicate ruche, in a tighter belting of her black cashmere gown; but still there was a suggestion of recent rain in the eyes, and threatening weather. As she entered the room, the sun came out, too, and revealed the prettiness and delicacy of her figure, and I regret to state, also, the somewhat obtrusive plainness of her visitor.

"I knew ye'd be sorter disapp'inted at first, not gettin' the regular bearings o' my name, but I'm 'Captain Dick.' Mebbe ye've heard your husband—that is, your husband ez waz, Roger Catron—speak o' me?"

Mrs. Catron, feeling herself outraged and deceived in belt, ruche, and ribbon, freezingly admitted that she had heard of him before.

"In course," said the captain; "why, Lord love ye, Mrs. Catron,—ez waz,—he used to be all the time talkin' of ye. And allers in a free, easy, confidential way. Why, one night—don't ye remember?—when he came home, carryin', mebbee, more canvas than was seamanlike, and you shet him out the house, and laid for him with a broomstick, or one o' them crokay mallets, I disremember which, and he kem over to me, ole Captain Dick, and I sez to him, sez I, 'Why, Roger, them's only love pats, and yer condishun is such ez to make any woman mad-like.' Why, Lord bless ye! there ain't enny of them mootool differences you and him hed ez I doesn't knows on, and didn't always stand by, and lend ye a hand, and heave in a word or two of advice when called on."

Mrs. Catron, ice everywhere but in her pink cheeks, was glad that Mr. Catron seemed to have always a friend to whom he confided *everything*, even the base falsehoods he had invented.

"Mebbe now they *waz* falsehoods," said the captain, thoughtfully. "But don't ye go to think," he added conscientiously, "that he kept on that tack all the time. Why, that day he made a raise, gambling, I think, over at Dutch Flat, and give ye them bracelets,—regular solid gold,—why, it would have done your heart good to have heard him talk about you—said you had the prettiest arm in Californy. Well," said the captain, looking around for a suitable climax, "well, you'd have thought that he was sorter proud of ye! Why, I woz with him in 'Frisco when he bought that A 1 prize bonnet for ye for $75, and not hevin' over $50 in his pocket, borryed the other $25 outer me. Mebbe it was a little fancy for a bonnet; but I allers thought he took it a little too much to heart when you swopped it off for that Dollar Varden dress, just because that Lawyer Maxwell said the Dollar Vardens was becomin' to ye. Ye know, I reckon, he was always sorter jealous of that thar shark—"

"May I venture to ask what your business is with me?" interrupted Mrs. Catron, sharply.

"In course," said the captain, rising. "Ye see," he said, apologetically, "we got to talking o' Roger and ole times, and I got a little out o' my course. It's a matter of—" he began to fumble in his pockets, and finally produced a small memorandum-book, which he glanced over—"it's a matter of $250."

"I don't understand you," said Mrs. Catron, in indignant astonishment.

"On the 15th of July," said the captain, consulting his memorandum-book, "Roger sold his claim at Nye's Ford for $1,500. Now, le's see. Thar was nigh on $350 ez he admitted to me he lost at poker, and we'll add $50 to that for treating, suppers, and drinks gin'rally—put Roger down for $400. Then there was *you*. Now you spent $250 on your trip to 'Frisco thet summer; then $200 went for them presents you sent your Aunt Jane, and thar was $400 for house expenses. Well, thet foots up $1,250. Now, what's become of thet other $250?"

Mrs. Catron's woman's impulse to retaliate sharply overcame her first natural indignation at her visitor's impudence.

Therein she lost, woman-like, her ground of vantage.

"Perhaps the woman he fled with can tell you," she said savagely.

"Thet," said the captain, slowly, "is a good, a reasonable idee. But it ain't true; from all I can gather *she* lent *him* money. It didn't go *thar*."

"Roger Catron left me penniless," said Mrs. Catron, hotly.

"Thet's jist what gets me. You oughter have $250 somewhar lying round."

Mrs. Catron saw her error. "May I ask what right you have to question me? If you have any, I must refer you to my lawyer or my brother-in-law; if you have none, I hope you will not oblige me to call the servants to put you from the house."

"Thet sounds reasonable and square, too," said the captain, thoughtfully; "I've a power of attorney from Roger Catron to settle up his affairs and pay his debts, given a week afore them detectives handed ye over his dead body. But I thought that you and me might save lawyer's fees and all fuss and feathers, ef, in a sociable, sad-like way,— lookin' back sorter on Roger ez you and me once knew him, —we had a quiet talk together."

"Good morning, sir," said Mrs. Catron, rising stiffly. The captain hesitated a moment, a slight flush of color came in his face as he at last rose as the lady backed out of the room. "Good morning, ma'am," said the captain, and departed.

Very little was known of this interview except the general impression in the family that Mrs. Catron had successfully resisted a vague attempt at blackmail from one of her husband's former dissolute companions. Yet it is only fair to say that Mrs. Catron snapped up, quite savagely, two male sympathizers on this subject, and cried a good deal for two days afterward, and once, in the hearing of her sister-in-law, to that lady's great horror, "wished she was dead."

A week after this interview, as Lawyer Phillips sat in his office, he was visited by Macleod. Recognizing, possibly, some practical difference between the widow and the lawyer, Captain Dick this time first produced his credentials, —a "power of attorney." "I need not tell you," said Phillips, "that the death of your principal renders this instrument invalid, and I suppose you know that, leaving no will, and no property, his estate has not been administered upon."

"Mebbe it is, and mebbe it isn't. But I hain't askin' for anythin' but information. There was a bit o' prop'ty and a mill onto it, over at Heavytree, ez sold for $10,000. I don't see," said the captain, consulting his memorandum-book, "ez *he* got anything out of it."

"It was mortgaged for $7,000," said the lawyer, quickly, and the interest and fees amount to about $3,000 more."

"The mortgage was given as security for a note?"

"Yes, a gambling debt," said the lawyer, sharply.

"Thet's so, and my belief ez that it wasn't a square game. He shouldn't hev given no note. Why, don't ye mind, 'way back in '60, when you and me waz in Marysville, that night that you bucked agin faro, and lost seving hundred dollars, and then refoosed to take up your checks, saying it was fraud and a gambling debt? And don't ye mind when that chap kicked ye, and I helped to drag him off ye—and—"

"I'm busy now, Mr. Macleod," said Phillips, hastily; "my clerk will give you all the information you require. Good morning."

"It's mighty queer," said the captain, thoughtfully, as he descended the stairs, "but the moment the conversation gets limber and sociable-like, and I gets to runnin' free under easy sail, it's always 'Good morning, Captain,' and we're becalmed."

By some occult influence, all the foregoing conversation, slightly exaggerated, and the whole interview of the captain with the widow with sundry additions, became the common property of Sandy Bar, to the great delight of the boys. There was scarcely a person who had ever had business or social relations with Roger Catron, whom "The Frozen Truth," as Sandy Bar delighted to designate the captain, had not "interviewed," as simply and directly. It is said that he closed a conversation with one of the San Francisco detectives, who had found Roger Catron's body, in these words: "And now hevin' got throo' bizness, I was goin' to ask ye what's gone of Matt. Jones, who was with ye in the bush in Austraily. Lord, how he got me quite interested in ye, telling me how you and him got out on a ticket-of-leave, and was chased by them milishy guards, and at last swam out to a San Francisco bark and escaped;" but here the inevitable pressure of previous business always stopped the captain's conversational flow. The natural result of this was a singular reaction in favor of the late Roger Catron in the public sentiment of Sandy Bar, so strong, indeed, as to induce the Rev. Mr. Joshua McSnagly, the next Sunday, to combat it with the moral of Catron's life. After the service, he was approached in the vestibule, and in the hearing of some of his audience, by Captain Dick, with the following compliment: "In many pints ye hed jess got Roger Catron down to a hair. I knew ye'd do it: why, Lord love ye, you and him had pints in common; and when he giv' ye that hundred dollars arter the fire in Sacramento, to help ye rebuild the parsonage, he said to me,—me not likin' ye on account o' my being on the committee that invited ye to resign from Marysville all along o' that affair with Deacon Pursell's darter; and a piece she was, parson! eh?—well, Roger, he ups and sez to me, 'Every man hez his faults,' sez he; and sez he, 'there's no reason why a parson ain't a human being like us, and that gal o' Pursell's is pizen, ez I know.' So ye see, I seed that ye was hittin' yourself over Catron's shoulder, like them early martyrs." But here, as Captain Dick was clearly blocking up all egress from the church, the sexton obliged him to move on, and again he was stopped in his conversational career.

But only for a time. Before long, it was whispered that Captain Dick had ordered a meeting of the creditors, debtors, and friends of Roger Catron at Robinson's Hall. It was suggested, with some show of reason, that this had

been done at the instigation of various practical jokers of
Sandy Bar, who had imposed on the simple directness of
the captain, and the attendance that night certainly indicated something more than a mere business meeting. All
of Sandy Bar crowded into Robinson's Hall, and long before Captain Dick made his appearance on the platform,
with his inevitable memorandum-book, every inch of floor
was crowded.

The captain began to read the expenditures of Roger
Catron with relentless fidelity of detail. The several losses
by poker, the whisky bills, and the record of a "jamboree"
at Tooley's, the vague expenses whereof footed up $275,
were received with enthusiastic cheers by the audience. A
single milliner's bill for $125 was hailed with delight; $100
expended in treating the Vestal Virgin Combination Troupe
almost canonized his memory; $50 for a simple buggy ride
with Deacon Fisk brought down the house; $500 advanced,
without security, and unpaid, for the electioneering expenses of Assemblyman Jones, who had recently introduced
a bill to prevent gambling and the sale of lager beer on
Sundays, was received with an ominous groan. One or
two other items of money loaned occasioned the withdrawal
of several gentlemen from the audience amidst the hisses
or ironical cheers of the others.

At last Captain Dick stopped and advanced to the foot-
lights.

"Gentlemen and friends," he said, slowly. "I foots up
$25,000 as Roger Catron hez *made,* fair and square, in this
yer county. I foots up $27,000 ez he has *spent* in this yer
county. I puts it to you ez men,—far-minded men,—ef this
man was a pauper and debtor? I put it to you ez far-
minded men,—ez free and easy men,—ez political economists,—ez this the kind of men to impoverish a county?"

An overwhelming and instantaneous "No!" almost
drowned the last utterance of the speaker.

"Thar is only one item," said Captain Dick, slowly,
"only one item, that ez men,—ez far-minded men,—ez
political economists,—it seems to me we hez the right to
question. It's this: Thar is an item, read to you by me,
of $2,000 paid to certing San Francisco detectives, paid

out o' the assets o' Roger Catron, for the finding of Roger Catron's body. Gentlemen of Sandy Bar and friends, *I* found that body, and yer it is!"

And Roger Catron, a little pale and nervous, but palpably in the flesh, stepped upon the platform.

Of course the newspapers were full of it the next day. Of course, in due time, it appeared as a garbled and romantic item in the San Francisco press. Of course Mrs. Catron, on reading it, fainted, and for two days said that this last cruel blow ended all relations between her husband and herself. On the third day she expressed her belief that, if he had had the slightest feeling for her, he would, long since, for the sake of mere decency, have communicated with her. On the fourth day she thought she had been, perhaps, badly advised, had an open quarrel with her relatives, and intimated that a wife had certain obligations, etc. On the sixth day, still not hearing from him, she quoted Scripture, spoke of a seventy-times-seven forgiveness, and went generally into mild hysterics. On the seventh, she left in the morning train for Sandy Bar.

And really I don't know as I have anything more to tell. I dined with them recently, and, upon my word, a more decorous, correct, conventional, and dull dinner I never ate in my life.

"WHO WAS MY QUIET FRIEND?"

"STRANGER!"

The voice was not loud, but clear and penetrating. I looked vainly up and down the narrow, darkening trail. No one in the fringe of alder ahead; no one on the gullied slope behind.

"O! stranger!"

This time a little impatiently. The California classical vocative, "O," always meant business.

I looked up, and perceived for the first time on the ledge, thirty feet above me, another trail parallel with my own, and looking down upon me through the buckeye bushes a small man on a black horse.

Five things to be here noted by the circumspect mountaineer. *First,* the locality,—lonely and inaccessible, and away from the regular faring of teamsters and miners. *Secondly,* the stranger's superior knowledge of the road, from the fact that the other trail was unknown to the ordinary traveler. *Thirdly,* that he was well armed and equipped. *Fourthly,* that he was better mounted. *Fifthly,* that any distrust or timidity arising from the contemplation of these facts had better be kept to one's self.

All this passed rapidly through my mind as I returned his salutation.

"Got any tobacco?" he asked.

I had, and signified the fact, holding up the pouch inquiringly.

"All right, I'll come down. Ride on, and I'll jine ye on the slide."

"The slide!" Here was a new geographical discovery as odd as the second trail. I had ridden over the trail a dozen times, and seen no communication between the ledge and trail. Nevertheless, I went on a hundred yards or so, when there was a sharp crackling in the underbrush, a shower of stones on the trail, and my friend plunged through the bushes to my side, down a grade that I should scarcely have dared to lead my horse. There was no doubt he was an accomplished rider,—another fact to be noted.

As he ranged beside me, I found I was not mistaken as to his size; he was quite under the medium height, and but for a pair of cold, gray eyes, was rather commonplace in feature.

"You've got a good horse there," I suggested.

He was filling his pipe from my pouch, but looked up a little surprised, and said, "Of course." He then puffed away with the nervous eagerness of a man long deprived of that sedative. Finally, between the puffs, he asked me whence I came.

I replied, "From Lagrange."

He looked at me a few moments curiously, but on my adding that I had only halted there for a few hours, he said: "I thought I knew every man between Lagrange and Indian Spring, but somehow I sorter disremember your face and your name."

Not particularly caring that he should remember either, I replied half laughingly, that, as I lived the other side of Indian Spring, it was quite natural. He took the rebuff, if such it was, so quietly that as an act of mere perfunctory politeness I asked him where he came from.

"Lagrange."

"And you are going to—"

"Well! that depends pretty much on how things pan out, and whether I can make the riffle." He let his hand rest quite unconsciously on the leathern holster of his dragoon revolver, yet with a strong suggestion to me of his ability "to make the riffle" if he wanted to, and added: "But just now I was reck'nin' on taking a little *pasear* with you."

There was nothing offensive in his speech save its familiarity, and the reflection, perhaps, that whether I objected or not, he was quite able to do as he said. I only replied that if our *pasear* was prolonged beyond Heavytree Hill, I should have to borrow his beast. To my surprise he replied quietly, "That's so," adding that the horse was at my disposal when he wasn't using it, and *half* of it when he was. "Dick has carried double many a time before this," he continued, "and kin do it again; when your mustang gives out I'll give you a lift and room to spare."

I could not help smiling at the idea of appearing before the boys at Red Gulch *en croupe* with the stranger; but neither could I help being oddly affected by the suggestion that his horse had done double duty before. "On what occasion, and why?" was a question I kept to myself. We were ascending the long, rocky flank of the divide; the narrowness of the trail obliged us to proceed slowly, and in file, so that there was little chance for conversation, had he been disposed to satisfy my curiosity.

We toiled on in silence, the buckeye giving way to chimisal, the westering sun, reflected again from the blank walls beside us, blinding our eyes with its glare. The pines in the cañon below were olive gulfs of heat, over which a hawk here and there drifted lazily, or, rising to our level, cast a weird and gigantic shadow of slowly moving wings on the mountain side. The superiority of the stranger's horse led him often far in advance, and made me hope that he might forget me entirely, or push on, growing weary of waiting. But regularly he would halt by a bowlder, or reappear from some chimisal, where he had patiently halted. I was beginning to hate him mildly, when at one of those reappearances he drew up to my side, and asked me how I liked Dickens!

Had he asked my opinion of Huxley or Darwin, I could not have been more astonished. Thinking it were possible that he referred to some local celebrity of Lagrange, I said, hesitatingly:—

"You mean—"

"Charles Dickens. Of course you've read him? Which of his books do you like best?"

I replied with considerable embarrassment that I liked them all,—as I certainly did.

He grasped my hand for a moment with a fervor quite unlike his usual phlegm, and said, "That's me, old man. Dickens ain't no slouch. You can count on him pretty much all the time."

With this rough preface, he launched into a criticism of the novelist, which for intelligent sympathy and hearty appreciation I had rarely heard equaled. Not only did he dwell upon the exuberance of his humor, but upon the power of his pathos and the all-pervading element of his poetry. I looked at the man in astonishment. I had considered myself a rather diligent student of the great master of fiction, but the stranger's felicity of quotation and illustration staggered me. It is true, that his thought was not always clothed in the best language, and often appeared in the slouching, slangy undress of the place and period, yet it never was rustic nor homespun, and sometimes struck me with its precision and fitness. Considerably softened toward him, I tried him with other literature. But vainly. Beyond a few of the lyrical and emotional poets, he knew nothing. Under the influence and enthusiasm of his own speech, he himself had softened considerably; offered to change horses with me, readjusted my saddle with professional skill, transferred my pack to his own horse, insisted upon my sharing the contents of his whisky flask, and, noticing that I was unarmed, pressed upon me a silver-mounted Derringer, which he assured me he could "warrant." These various offices of good will and the diversion of his talk beguiled me from noticing the fact that the trail was beginning to become obscure and unrecognizable. We were evidently pursuing a route unknown before to me. I pointed out the fact to my companion, a little impatiently. He instantly resumed his old manner and dialect.

"Well, I reckon one trail's as good as another, and what hev ye got to say about it?"

I pointed out, with some dignity, that I preferred the old trail.

"Mebbe you did. But you're jiss now takin' a *pasear* with *me*. This yer trail will bring you right into Indian Spring, and *onnoticed,* and no questions asked. Don't you mind now, I'll see you through."

It was necessary here to make some stand against my strange companion. I said firmly, yet as politely as I could, that I had proposed stopping over night with a friend.

"Whar?"

I hesitated. The friend was an eccentric Eastern man, well known in the locality for his fastidiousness and his habits as a recluse. A misanthrope, of ample family and ample means, he had chosen a secluded but picturesque valley in the Sierras where he could rail against the world without opposition. "Lone Valley," or "Boston Ranch," as it was familiarly called, was the one spot that the average miner both respected and feared. Mr. Sylvester, its proprietor, had never affiliated with "the boys," nor had he ever lost their respect by any active opposition to their ideas. If seclusion had been his object, he certainly was gratified. Nevertheless, in the darkening shadows of the night, and on a lonely and unknown trail, I hesitated a little at repeating his name to a stranger of whom I knew so little. But my mysterious companion took the matter out of my hands.

"Look yar," he said, suddenly, "thar ain't but one place twixt yer and Indian Spring whar ye can stop, and that is Sylvester's."

I assented, a little sullenly.

"Well," said the stranger, quietly, and with a slight suggestion of conferring a favor on me, "ef yer pointed for Sylvester's—why—*I don't mind stopping thar with ye.* It's a little off the road—I'll lose some time—but taking it by and large, I don't much mind."

I stated, as rapidly and as strongly as I could, that my acquaintance with Mr. Sylvester did not justify the introduction of a stranger to his hospitality; that he was unlike most of the people here,—in short, that he was a queer man, etc., etc.

To my surprise my companion answered quietly: "Oh, that's all right. I've heerd of him. Ef you don't feel like checking me through, or if you'd rather put 'C. O. D.' on my back, why it's all the same to me. I'll play it alone. Only you just count me in. Say 'Sylvester' all the time. That's me!"

What could I oppose to this man's quiet assurance? I felt myself growing red with anger and nervous with embarrassment. What would the correct Sylvester say to me?

What would the girls,—I was a young man then, and had won an *entrée* to their domestic circle by my reserve,—known by a less complimentary adjective among "the boys," —what would they say to my new acquaintance? Yet I certainly could not object to his assuming all risks on his own personal recognizances, nor could I resist a certain feeling of shame at my embarrassment.

We were beginning to descend. In the distance below us already twinkled the lights in the solitary rancho of Lone Valley. I turned to my companion. "But you have forgotten that I don't even know your name. What am I to call you?"

"That's so," he said, musingly. "Now, let's see. 'Kearney' would be a good name. It's short and easy like. Thar's a street in 'Frisco the same title; Kearney it is."

"But—" I began impatiently.

"Now you leave all that to me," he interrupted, with a superb self-confidence that I could not but admire. "The name ain't no account. It's the man that's responsible. Ef I was to lay for a man that I reckoned was named Jones, and after I fetched him I found out on the inquest that his real name was Smith, that wouldn't make no matter, as long as I got the man."

The illustration, forcible as it was, did not strike me as offering a prepossessing introduction, but we were already at the rancho. The barking of dogs brought Sylvester to the door of the pretty little cottage which his taste had adorned.

I briefly introduced Mr. Kearney. "Kearney will do—Kearney's good enough for me," commented the *soi-disant* Kearney half-aloud, to my own horror and Sylvester's evident mystification, and then he blandly excused himself for a moment that he might personally supervise the care of his own beast. When he was out of ear-shot I drew the puzzled Sylvester aside.

"I have picked up—I mean I have been picked up on the road by a gentle maniac, whose name is not Kearney. He is well armed and quotes Dickens. With care, acquiescence in his views on all subjects, and general submission to his commands, he may be placated. Doubtless the spectacle

7   v. 1

of your helpless family, the contemplation of your daughter's beauty and innocence, may touch his fine sense of humor and pathos. Meanwhile, Heaven help you, and forgive me."

I ran upstairs to the little den that my hospitable host had kept always reserved for me in my wanderings. I lingered some time over my ablutions, hearing the languid, gentlemanly drawl of Sylvester below, mingled with the equally cool, easy slang of my mysterious acquaintance. When I came down to the sitting-room I was surprised, however, to find the self-styled Kearney quietly seated on the sofa, the gentle May Sylvester, the "Lily of Lone Valley," sitting with maidenly awe and unaffected interest on one side of him, while on the other that arrant flirt, her cousin Kate, was practicing the pitiless archery of her eyes, with an excitement that seemed almost real.

"Who is your deliciously cool friend?" she managed to whisper to me at supper, as I sat utterly dazed and bewildered between the enrapt May Sylvester, who seemed to hang upon his words, and this giddy girl of the period, who was emptying the battery of her charms in active rivalry upon him. "Of course we know his name isn't Kearney. But how romantic! And isn't he perfectly lovely? And who is he?"

I replied with severe irony that I was not aware what foreign potentate was then traveling *incognito* in the Sierras of California, but that when his royal highness was pleased to inform me, I should be glad to introduce him properly. "Until then," I added, "I fear the acquaintance must be Morganatic."

"You're only jealous of him," she said pertly. "Look at May—she is completely fascinated. And her father, too." And actually, the languid, world-sick, cynical Sylvester was regarding him with a boyish interest and enthusiasm almost incompatible with his nature. Yet I submit honestly to the clear-headed reason of my own sex, that I could see nothing more in the man than I have already delivered to the reader.

In the middle of an exciting story of adventure, of which he, to the already prejudiced mind of his fair auditors, was evidently the hero, he stopped suddenly.

"It's only some pack train passing the bridge on the lower trail," explained Sylvester; "go on."

"It may be my horse is a trifle oneasy in the stable," said the alleged Kearney; "he ain't used to boards and covering." Heaven only knows what wild and delicious revelation lay in the statement of this fact, but the girls looked at each other with cheeks pink with excitement as Kearney arose, and, with quiet absence of ceremony, quitted the table.

"Ain't he just lovely?" said Kate, gasping for breath, "and so witty."

"Witty!" said the gentle May, with just the slightest trace of defiance in her sweet voice; "witty, my dear? why, don't you see that his heart is just breaking with pathos? Witty, indeed; why, when he was speaking of that poor Mexican woman that was hung, I saw the tears gather in his eyes. Witty, indeed!"

"Tears," laughed the cynical Sylvester, "tears, idle tears. Why, you silly children, the man is a man of the world, a philosopher, quiet, observant, unassuming."

"Unassuming!" Was Sylvester intoxicated, or had the mysterious stranger mixed the "insane verb" with the family pottage? He returned before I could answer this self-asked inquiry, and resumed coolly his broken narrative. Finding myself forgotten in the man I had so long hesitated to introduce to my friends, I retired to rest early, only to hear, through the thin partitions, two hours later, enthusiastic praises of the new guest from the voluble lips of the girls, as they chatted in the next room before retiring.

At midnight I was startled by the sound of horses' hoofs and the jingling of spurs below. A conversation between my host and some mysterious personage in the darkness was carried on in such a low tone that I could not learn its import. As the cavalcade rode away I raised the window.

"What's the matter?"

"Nothing," said Sylvester, coolly, "only another one of those playful homicidal freaks peculiar to the country. A man was shot by Cherokee Jack over at Lagrange this morning, and that was the sheriff of Calaveras and his posse hunting him. I told him I'd seen nobody but you and your friend. By the way, I hope the cursed noise hasn't disturbed him. The poor fellow looked as if he wanted rest."

I thought so, too. Nevertheless, I went softly to his room. It was empty. My impression was that he had distanced the sheriff of Calaveras about two hours.

A GHOST OF THE SIERRAS

It was a vast silence of pines, redolent with balsamic breath, and muffled with the dry dust of dead bark and matted mosses. Lying on our backs, we looked upward through a hundred feet of clear, unbroken interval to the first lateral branches that formed the flat canopy above us. Here and there the fierce sun, from whose active persecution we had just escaped, searched for us through the woods, but its keen blade was dulled and turned aside by intercostal boughs, and its brightness dissipated in nebulous mists throughout the roofing of the dim, brown aisles around us. We were in another atmosphere, under another sky; indeed, in another world than the dazzling one we had just quitted. The grave silence seemed so much a part of the grateful coolness, that we hesitated to speak, and for some moments lay quietly outstretched on the pine tassels where we had first thrown ourselves. Finally, a voice broke the silence:—

"Ask the old Major; he knows all about it!"

The person here alluded to under that military title was myself. I hardly need explain to any Californian that it by no means followed that I was a "Major," or that I was "old," or that I knew anything about "it," or indeed what "it" referred to. The whole remark was merely one of the usual conventional feelers to conversation,—a kind of social preamble, quite common to our slangy camp intercourse. Nevertheless, as I was always known as the Major, perhaps for no better reason than that the speaker, an old journalist, was always called Doctor, I recognized the fact so far as to kick aside an intervening saddle, so that I could see the speaker's face on a level with my own, and said nothing

"About ghosts!" said the Doctor, after a pause, which nobody broke or was expected to break. "Ghosts, sir! That's what we want to know. What are we doing here

197

in this blanked old mausoleum of Calaveras County, if it isn't to find out something about 'em, eh?"

Nobody replied.

"Thar's that haunted house at Cave City. Can't be more than a mile or two away, anyhow. Used to be just off the trail."

A dead silence.

The Doctor (addressing space generally): "Yes, sir; it *was* a mighty queer story."

Still the same reposeful indifference. We all knew the Doctor's skill as a *raconteur;* we all knew that a story was coming, and we all knew that any interruption would be fatal. Time and time again, in our prospecting experience, had a word of polite encouragement, a rash expression of interest, even a too eager attitude of silent expectancy, brought the Doctor to a sudden change of subject. Time and time again have we seen the unwary stranger stand amazed and bewildered between our own indifference and the sudden termination of a promising anecdote, through his own unlucky interference. So we said nothing. "The Judge"—another instance of arbitrary nomenclature—pretended to sleep. Jack began to twist a *cigarrito.* Thornton bit off the ends of pine needles reflectively.

"Yes, sir," continued the Doctor, coolly resting the back of his head on the palms of his hands, "it *was* rather curious. All except the murder. *That's* what gets me, for the murder had no new points, no fancy touches, no sentiment, no mystery. Was just one of the old style, 'sub-head' paragraphs. Old-fashioned miner scrubs along on hardtack and beans, and saves up a little money to go home and see relations. Old-fashioned assassin sharpens up knife, old style; loads old flint-lock, brass-mounted pistol; walks in on old-fashioned miner one dark night, sends him home to his relations away back to several generations, and walks off with the swag. No mystery *there;* nothing to clear up; subsequent revelations only impertinence. Nothing for any ghost to do—who meant business. More than that, over forty murders, same old kind, committed every year in Calaveras, and no spiritual post obits coming due every anniversary; no assessments made on the peace and quiet of the surviving community. I tell you what, boys, I've always been inclined to throw off on the Cave City ghost for that alone. It's a bad precedent, sir. If that kind o' thing is going to obtain in the foot-hills, we'll have the trails full of chaps formerly knocked over by Mexicans and road agents; every little camp and grocery will have stock enough on hand to go into business, and where's there any security for surviving life and property, eh? What's your opinion, Judge, as a fair-minded legislator?"

Of course there was no response. Yet it was part of the Doctor's system of aggravation to become discursive at these moments, in the hope of interruption, and he continued for some moments to dwell on the terrible possibility of a state of affairs in which a gentleman could no longer settle a dispute with an enemy without being subjected to succeeding spiritual embarrassment. But all this digression fell upon apparently inattentive ears.

"Well, sir, after the murder, the cabin stood for a long time deserted and tenantless. Popular opinion was against it. One day a ragged prospector, savage with hard labor and harder luck, came to the camp, looking for a place to live and a chance to prospect. After the boys had taken his measure, they concluded that he'd already tackled so much in the way of difficulties that a ghost more or less wouldn't be of much account. So they sent him to the haunted cabin. He had a big yellow dog with him, about as ugly and as savage as himself; and the boys sort o' congratulated themselves, from a practical view-point, that while they were giving the old ruffian a shelter, they were helping in the cause of Christianity against ghosts and goblins. They had little faith in the old man, but went their whole pile on that dog. That's where they were mistaken.

"The house stood almost three hundred feet from the nearest cave, and on dark nights, being in a hollow, was as lonely as if it had been on the top of Shasta. If you ever saw the spot when there was just moon enough to bring out the little surrounding clumps of chapparal until they looked like crouching figures, and make the bits of broken quartz glisten like skulls, you'd begin to understand how big a contract that man and that yellow dog undertook.

"They went into possession that afternoon, and old Hard Times set out to cook his supper. When it was over he sat down by the embers and lit his pipe, the yellow dog lying at his feet. Suddenly 'Rap! rap!' comes from the door. 'Come in,' says the man, gruffly. 'Rap!' again. 'Come in and be d—d to you,' says the man, who has no idea of getting up to open the door. But no one responded, and the next moment smash goes the only sound pane in the only window. Seeing this, old Hard Times gets up, with the devil in his eye, and a revolver in his hand, followed by the yellow dog, with every tooth showing, and swings open the door. No one there! But as the man opened the door, that yellow dog, that had been so chipper before, suddenly begins to crouch and step backward, step by step, trembling and shivering, and at last crouches down in the chimney, without even so much as looking at his master. The man slams the door shut again, but there comes another smash.

This time it seems to come from inside the cabin, and it isn't until the man looks around and sees everything quiet that he gets up, without speaking, and makes a dash for the door, and tears round outside the cabin like mad, but finds nothing but silence and darkness. Then he comes back swearing and calls the dog. But that great yellow dog that the boys would have staked all their money on is crouching under the bunk, and has to be dragged out like a coon from a hollow tree, and lies there, his eyes starting from their sockets; every limb and muscle quivering with fear, and his very hair drawn up in bristling ridges. The man calls him to the door. He drags himself a few steps, stops, sniffs, and refuses to go further. The man calls him again, with an oath and a threat. Then, what does that yellow dog do? He crawls edgewise towards the door, crouching himself against the bunk till he's flatter than a knife blade; then, half way, he stops. Then that d—d yellow dog begins to walk gingerly—lifting each foot up in the air, one after the other, still trembling in every limb. Then he stops again. Then he crouches. Then he gives one little shuddering leap—not straight forward, but up,—clearing the floor about six inches, as if—"

"Over something," interrupted the Judge, hastily, lifting himself on his elbow.

The Doctor stopped instantly. "Juan," he said coolly, to one of the Mexican packers, "quit foolin' with that *riata*. You'll have that stake out and that mule loose in another minute. Come over this way!"

The Mexican turned a scared, white face to the Doctor, muttering something, and let go the deer-skin hide. We all up-raised our voices with one accord, the Judge most penitently and apologetically, and implored the Doctor to go on. "I'll shoot the first man who interrupts you again," added Thornton, persuasively.

But the Doctor, with his hands languidly under his head, had lost his interest. "Well, the dog ran off to the hills, and neither the threats nor cajoleries of his master could ever make him enter the cabin again. The next day the man left the camp. What time is it? Getting on to sundown, ain't it? Keep off my leg, will you, you d—d Greaser, and stop stumbling round there! Lie down."

But we knew that the Doctor had not completely finished his story, and we waited patiently for the conclusion. Meanwhile the old, gray silence of the woods again asserted itself, but shadows were now beginning to gather in the heavy beams of the roof above, and the dim aisles seemed to be narrowing and closing in around us. Presently the Doctor recommenced lazily, as if no interruption had occurred.

"As I said before, I never put much faith in that story, and shouldn't have told it, but for a rather curious experience of my own. It was in the spring of '62, and I was one of a party of four, coming up from O'Neill's, when we had been snowed up. It was awful weather; the snow had changed to sleet and rain after we crossed the divide, and the water was out everywhere; every ditch was a creek, every creek a river. We had lost two horses on the North Fork, we were dead beat, off the trail, and sloshing round, with night coming on, and the level hail like shot in our faces. Things were looking bleak and scary when, riding a little ahead of the party, I saw a light twinkling in a hollow beyond. My horse was still fresh, and calling out to the boys to follow me and bear for the light, I struck out for it. In another moment I was before a little cabin that half burrowed in the black chapparal; I dismounted and rapped at the door. There was no response. I then tried to force the door, but it was fastened securely from within. I was all the more surprised when one of the boys, who had overtaken me, told me that he had just seen through a window a man reading by the fire. Indignant at this inhospitality, we both made a resolute onset against the door, at the same time raising our angry voices to a yell. Suddenly there was a quick response, the hurried withdrawing of a bolt, and the door opened.

"The occupant was a short, thick-set man, with a pale, careworn face, whose prevailing expression was one of gentle good humor and patient suffering. When we entered, he asked us hastily why we had not 'sung out' before.

" 'But we *knocked!*' I said, impatiently, 'and almost drove your door in.'

" 'That's nothing,' he said, patiently. 'I'm used to *that.*'

"I looked again at the man's patient, fateful face, and then around the cabin. In an instant the whole situation flashed before me. 'Are we not near Cave City?' I asked.

" 'Yes,' he replied, 'it's just below. You must have passed it in the storm.'

" 'I see.' I again looked around the cabin. 'Isn't this what they call the haunted house?'

"He looked at me curiously. 'It is,' he said, simply.

"You can imagine my delight! Here was an opportunity to test the whole story, to work down to the bed rock, and see how it would pan out! We were too many and too well armed to fear tricks or dangers from outsiders. If —as one theory had been held—the disturbance was kept up by a band of concealed marauders or road agents, whose purpose was to preserve their haunts from intrusion, we were quite able to pay them back in kind for any assault. I need not say that the boys were delighted with this prospect when the fact was revealed to them. The only one doubtful or apathetic spirit there was our host, who quietly resumed his seat and his book, with his old expression of patient martyrdom. It would haev been easy for me to have drawn him out, but I felt that I did not want to corroborate anybody else's experience; only to record my own. And I thought it better to keep the boys from any predisposing terrors.

"We ate our supper, and then sat, patiently and expectant, around the fire. An hour slipped away, but no disturbance; another hour passed as monotonously. Our host read his book; only the dash of hail against the roof broke the silence. But—"

The Doctor stopped. Since the last interruption, I noticed he had changed the easy slangy style of his story to a more perfect, artistic, and even studied manner. He dropped now suddenly into his old colloquial speech, and quietly said: "If you don't quit stumbling over those *riatas*, Juan, I'll hobble *you*. Come here, there; lie down, will you?"

We all turned fiercely on the cause of this second dangerous interruption, but a sight of the poor fellow's pale and frightened face withheld our vindictive tongues. And the Doctor, happily, of his own accord, went on:—

"But I had forgotten that it was no easy matter to keep these high-spirited boys, bent on a row, in decent subjection; and after the third hour passed without a supernatural exhibition, I observed, from certain winks and whispers, that they were determined to get up indications of their own. In a few moments violent rappings were heard from all parts of the cabin; large stones (adroitly thrown up the chimney) fell with a heavy thud on the roof. Strange groans and ominous yells seemed to come from the outside (where the interstices between the logs were wide enough). Yet, through all this uproar, our host sat still and patient, with no sign of indignation or reproach upon his good-humored but haggard features. Before long it became evident that this exhibition was exclusively for *his* benefit. Under the thin disguise of asking him to assist them in discovering the disturbers *outside* the cabin, those inside took advantage of his absence to turn the cabin topsy-turvy.

" 'You see what the spirits have done, old man,' said the arch leader of this mischief. 'They've upset that there flour barrel while we wasn't looking, and then kicked over the water jug and spilled all the water!'

"The patient man lifted his head and looked at the flour-strewn walls. Then he glanced down at the floor, but drew back with a slight tremor.

" 'It ain't water!' he said, quietly.

" 'What is it, then?'

" 'It's BLOOD! Look!'

"The nearest man gave a sudden start and sank back white as a sheet.

"For there, gentlemen, on the floor, just before the door, where the old man had seen the dog hesitate and lift his feet, there! there!—gentlemen—upon my honor, slowly widened and broadened a dark red pool of human blood! Stop him! Quick! Stop him, I say!"

There was a blinding flash that lit up the dark woods, and a sharp report! When we reached the Doctor's side he was holding the smoking pistol, just discharged, in one hand, while with the other he was pointing to the rapidly disappearing figure of Juan, our Mexican vaquero!

"Missed him! by G—d!" said the Doctor. "But did you hear him? Did you see his livid face as he rose up at the name of blood? Did you see his guilty conscience in his face. Eh? Why don't you speak? What are you staring at?"

"Was it the murdered man's ghost, Doctor?" we all panted in one quick breath.

"Ghost be d—d! No! But in that Mexican vaquero—that cursed Juan Ramirez!—I saw and shot at his murderer!"

THE HOODLUM BAND

OR

THE BOY CHIEF, THE INFANT POLITICIAN, AND THE PIRATE PRODIGY

BY JACK WHACKAWAY

Author of "The Boy Slaver," "The Immature Incendiary," "The Precocious Pugilist," etc., etc.

CHAPTER I

IT was a quiet New England village. Nowhere in the valley of the Connecticut the autumn sun shone upon a more peaceful, pastoral, manufacturing community. The wooden nutmegs were slowly ripening on the trees, and the white pine hams for Western consumption were gradually rounding into form under the deft manipulation of the hardy American artisan. The honest Connecticut farmer was quietly gathering from his threshing floor the shoe-pegs, which, when intermixed with a fair proportion of oats, offered a pleasing substitute for fodder to the effete civilizations of Europe. An almost Sabbath-like stillness prevailed. Doemville was only seven miles from Hartford, and the surrounding landscape smiled with the conviction of being fully insured.

Few would have thought that this peaceful village was the home of the three young heroes whose exploits would hereafter—but we anticipate.

Doemville Academy was the principal seat of learning in the county. Under the grave and gentle administration of the venerable Doctor Context, it had attained just popularity. Yet the increasing infirmities of age obliged the doctor to relinquish much of his trust to his assistants, who, it is needless to say, abused his confidence. Before long their brutal tyranny and deep-laid malevolence became apparent. Boys were absolutely forced to study their lessons. The sickening fact will hardly be believed, but during school hours they were obliged to remain in their seats with the appearance at least of discipline. It is stated by good authority that the rolling of croquet balls across the floor during recitation was objected to, under the fiendish excuse of its interfering with their studies. The breaking of windows by base balls, and the beating of small scholars with bats, were declared against. At last, bloated and arrogant with success, the under-teachers threw aside all disguise and revealed themselves in their true colors. A cigar was actually taken out of a day scholar's mouth during prayers! A flask of whisky was dragged from another's desk, and then thrown out of the window. And finally, Profanity, Hazing, Theft, and Lying were almost discouraged!

Could the youth of America, conscious of their power and a literature of their own, tamely submit to this tyranny? Never! We repeat it firmly. Never! We repeat it to parents and guardians. Never! But the fiendish tutors, chuckling in their glee, little knew what was passing through the cold, haughty intellect of Charles Fanuel Hall Golightly, aged ten; what curled the lip of Benjamin Franklin Jenkins, aged seven; or what shone in the bold blue eyes of Bromley Chitterlings, aged six and a half, as they sat in the corner of the playground at recess. Their only other companion and confidant was the negro porter and janitor of the school, known as "Pirate Jim."

Fitly, indeed, was he named, as the secrets of his early wild career—confessed freely to his noble young friends—plainly showed. A slaver at the age of seventeen, the ringleader of a mutiny on the African Coast at the age of twenty, a privateersman during the last war with England, the commander of a fire-ship and its sole survivor at twenty-five, with a wild intermediate career of unmixed piracy, until the Rebellion called him to civil service again as a blockade-runner, and peace and a desire for rural repose led him to seek the janitorship of the Doemville Academy, where no questions were asked and references not exchanged: he was, indeed, a fit mentor for our daring youth.

Although a man whose days had exceeded the usual space allotted to humanity, the various episodes of his career footing his age up to nearly one hundred and fifty-nine years, he scarcely looked it, and was still hale and vigorous.

"Yes," continued Pirate Jim, critically, "I don't think he was any bigger nor you, Master Chitterlings, if as big, when he stood on the fork'stle of my ship, and shot the captain o' that East Injymen dead. We used to call him little Weevils, he was so young-like. But, bless your hearts, boys! he wa'n't anything to little Sammy Barlow, ez once crep' up inter the captain's stateroom on a Rooshin frigate, stabbed him to the heart with a jack-knife, then put on the captain's uniform and his cocked hat, took command of the ship and fout her hisself."

"Wasn't the captain's clothes big for him?" asked B. Franklin Jenkins, anxiously.

The janitor eyed young Jenkins with pained dignity.

"Didn't I say the Rooshin captain was a small, a very small man? Rooshins is small, likewise Greeks."

A noble enthusiasm beamed in the faces of the youthful heroes.

"Was Barlow as large as me?" asked C. F. Hall Golightly, lifting his curls from his Jove-like brow.

"Yes; but then he hed hed, so to speak, experiences. It was allowed that he had pizened his schoolmaster afore he went to sea. But it's dry talking, boys."

Golightly drew a flask from his jacket and handed it to the janitor. It was his father's best brandy. The heart of the honest old seaman was touched.

"Bless ye, my own pirate boy!" he said, in a voice suffocating with emotion.

"I've got some tobacco," said the youthful Jenkins, "but it's fine-cut; I use only that now."

"I kin buy some plug at the corner grocery," said Pirate Jim, "only I left my port-money at home."

"Take this watch," said young Golightly; "it is my father's. Since he became a tyrant and usurper, and forced me to join a corsair's band, I've began by dividing the property."

"This is idle trifling," said young Chitterlings, mildly.

"Every moment is precious. Is this an hour to give to wine and wassail? Ha, we want action—action! We must strike the blow for freedom to-night—aye, this very night. The scow is already anchored in the mill-dam, freighted with provisions for a three months' voyage. I have a black flag in my pocket. Why, then, this cowardly delay?"

The two elder youths turned with a slight feeling of awe and shame to gaze on the glowing cheeks, and high, haughty crest of their youngest comrade—the bright, the beautiful Bromley Chitterlings. Alas! that very moment of forgetfulness and mutual admiration was fraught with danger. A thin, dyspeptic, half-starved tutor approached.

"It is time to resume your studies, young gentlemen," he said, with fiendish politeness.

They were his last words on earth.

"Down, tyrant!" screamed Chitterlings.

"Sic him—I mean, *Sic semper tyrannis!*" said the classical Golightly.

A heavy blow on the head from a base-ball bat, and the rapid projection of a base ball against his empty stomach, brought the tutor a limp and lifeless mass to the ground. Golightly shuddered. Let not my young readers blame him too rashly. It was his first homicide.

"Search his pockets," said the practical Jenkins.

They did so, and found nothing but a Harvard Triennial Catalogue.

"Let us fly," said Jenkins.

"Forward to the boats!" cried the enthusiastic Chitterlings.

But C. F. Hall Golightly stood gazing thoughtfully at the prostrate tutor.

"This," he said calmly, "is the result of a too free government and the common school system. What the country needs is reform. I cannot go with you, boys."

"Traitor!" screamed the others.

C. F. H. Golightly smiled sadly.

"You know me not. I shall not become a pirate—but a Congressman!"

Jenkins and Chitterlings turned pale.

"I have already organized two caucuses in a base ball

club, and bribed the delegates of another. Nay, turn not away. Let us be friends, pursuing through various ways one common end. Farewell!" They shook hands.

"But where is Pirate Jim?" asked Jenkins.

"He left us but for a moment to raise money on the watch to purchase armament for the scow. Farewell!"

And so the gallant, youthful spirits parted, bright with the sunrise of hope.

That night a conflagration raged in Doemville. The Doemville Academy, mysteriously fired, first fell a victim to the devouring element. The candy shop and cigar store, both holding heavy liabilities against the academy, quickly followed. By the lurid gleams of the flames, a long, low, sloop-rigged scow, with every mast gone except one, slowly worked her way out of the mill-dam towards the Sound. The next day three boys were missing—C. F. Hall Golightly, B. F. Jenkins, and Bromley Chitterlings. Had they perished in the flames Who shall say? Enough that never more under these names did they again appear in the homes of their ancestors.

Happy, indeed, would it have been for Doemville had the mystery ended here. But a darker interest and scandal rested upon the peaceful village. During that awful night the boarding-school of Madam Brimborion was visited stealthily, and two of the fairest heiresses of Connecticut— daughters of the president of a savings bank, and insurance director—were the next morning found to have eloped. With them also disappeared the entire contents of the Savings Bank, and on the following day the Flamingo Fire Insurance Company failed.

CHAPTER II

LET my young readers now sail with me to warmer and more hospitable climes. Off the coast of Patagonia a long, low, black schooner proudly rides the seas, that breaks softly upon the vine-clad shores of that luxuriant land. Who is this that, wrapped in Persian rugs, and dressed in the most expensive manner, calmly reclines on the quarter-deck of the schooner, toying lightly ever and anon with the luscious fruits of the vicinity, held in baskets of solid gold by Nubian slaves? or at intervals, with daring grace, guides an ebony velocipede over the polished black walnut decks, and in and out the intricacies of the rigging. Who is it? well may be asked. What name is it that blanches with terror the cheeks of the Patagonian navy? Who but the Pirate Prodigy—the relentless Boy Scourer of Patagonian seas? Voyagers slowly drifting by the Silurian beach, coasters along the Devonian shore, still shudder at the name of Bromley Chitterlings—the Boy Avenger, late of Hartford, Connecticut.

It has been often asked by the idly curious, Why Avenger, and of what? Let us not seek to disclose the awful secret hidden under that youthful jacket. Enough that there may have been that of bitterness in his past life that he

" Whose soul would sicken o'er the heaving wave,"

or "whose soul would heave above the sickening wave," did not understand. Only one knew him, perhaps too well —a queen of the Amazons, taken prisoner off Terra del Fuego a week previous. She loved the Boy Avenger. But in vain; his youthful heart seemed obdurate.

"Hear me," at last he said, when she had for the seventh time wildly proffered her hand and her kingdom in marriage, "and know once and forever why I must decline your flattering proposal: I love another."

With a wild, despairing cry, she leaped into the sea, but was instantly rescued by the Pirate Prodigy. Yet, even in that supreme moment, such was his coolness that on his way to the surface he captured a mermaid, and, placing her in charge of his steward, with directions to give her a stateroom, with hot and cold water, calmly resumed his place by the Amazon's side. When the cabin door closed on his faithful servant, bringing champagne and ices to the interesting stranger, Chitterlings resumed his narrative with a choking voice:—

"When I first fled from the roof of a tyrannical parent, I loved the beautiful and accomplished Eliza J. Sniffen. Her father was president of the Workingmen's Savings

Bank, and it was perfectly understood that in the course of time the entire deposits would be his. But, like a vain fool, I wished to anticipate the future, and in a wild moment persuaded Miss Sniffen to elope with me; and, with the entire cash assets of the bank, we fled together." He paused, overcome with emotion. "But fate decreed it otherwise. In my feverish haste, I had forgotten to place among the stores of my pirate craft that peculiar kind of chocolate caramel to which Eliza Jane was most partial. We were obliged to put into New Rochelle on the second day out, to enable Miss Sniffen to procure that delicacy at the nearest confectioner's, and match some zephyr worsteds at the first fancy shop. Fatal mistake. She went—she never returned!" In a moment he resumed in a choking voice, "After a week's weary waiting, I was obliged to put to sea again, bearing a broken heart and the broken bank of her father. I have never seen her since."

"And you still love her?" asked the Amazon queen, excitedly.

"Aye, forever!"

"Noble youth. Here take the reward of thy fidelity, for know, Bromley Chitterlings, that I am Eliza Jane. Wearied with waiting, I embarked on a Peruvian guano ship—but it's a long story, dear."

"And altogether too thin," said the Boy Avenger, fiercely, releasing himself from her encircling arms. "Eliza Jane's age, a year ago, was only thirteen, and you are forty, if a day."

"True," she returned, sadly, "but I have suffered much, and time passes rapidly, and I've grown. You would scarcely believe that this is my own hair."

"I know not," he replied, in gloomy abstraction.

"Forgive my deceit," she returned. "If you are affianced to another, let me at least be—a mother to you."

The Pirate Prodigy started, and tears came to his eyes. The scene was affecting in the extreme. Several of the oldest seamen—men who had gone through scenes of suffering with tearless eyes and unblanched cheeks—now retired to the spirit-room to conceal their emotion. A few went into caucus in the forecastle, and returned with the request that the Amazonian queen should hereafter be known as the "Queen of the Pirates' Isle."

"Mother!" gasped the Pirate Prodigy.

"My son!" screamed the Amazonian queen.

They embraced. At the same moment a loud flop was heard on the quarter-deck. It was the forgotten mermaid, who, emerging from her state-room and ascending the companion-way at that moment, had fainted at the spectacle. The Pirate Prodigy rushed to her side with a bottle of smelling-salts.

She recovered slowly. "Permit me," she said, rising with dignity, "to leave the ship. I am unaccustomed to such conduct."

"Hear me—she is my mother!"

"She certainly is old enough to be," replied the mermaid; "and to speak of that being her own hair!" she added with a scornful laugh, as she rearranged her own luxuriant tresses with characteristic grace, a comb, and a small hand-mirror.

"If I couldn't afford any other clothes, I might wear a switch, too!" hissed the Amazonian queen. "I suppose you don't dye it on account of the salt water. But perhaps you prefer green, dear?"

"A little salt water might improve your own complexion, love."

"Fishwoman!" screamed the Amazonian queen.

"Bloomerite!" shrieked the mermaid.

In another instant they had seized each other.

"Mutiny! Overboard with them!" cried the Pirate Prodigy, rising to the occasion, and casting aside all human affection in the peril of the moment.

A plank was brought and two women placed upon it.

"After you, dear," said the mermaid, significantly, to the Amazonian queen; "you're the oldest."

"Thank you!" said the Amazonian queen, stepping back. "Fish is always served first."

Stung by the insult, with a wild scream of rage, the mermaid grappled her in her arms and leaped into the sea.

As the waters closed over them forever, the Pirate Prodigy sprang to his feet. "Up with the black flag, and bear away for New London," he shouted in trumpet-like tones. "Ha, ha! Once more the Rover is free!"

Indeed it was too true. In that fatal moment he had again loosed himself from the trammels of human feeling, and was once more the Boy Avenger.

CHAPTER III

AGAIN I must ask my young friends to mount my hippogriff and hie with me to the almost inaccessible heights of the Rocky Mountains. There, for years, a band of wild and untamable savages, known as the "Pigeon Feet," had resisted the blankets and Bibles of civilization. For years the trails leading to their camp were marked by the bones of teamsters and broken wagons, and the trees were decked with the drying scalp locks of women and children. The boldest of military leaders hesitated to attack them in their fortresses, and prudently left the scalping knives, rifles, powder, and shot, provided by a paternal government for their welfare, lying on the ground a few miles from their encampment, with the request that they were not to be used until the military had safely retired. Hitherto, save an occasional incursion into the territory of the "Knock-knees," a rival tribe, they had limited their depredations to the vicinity.

But lately a baleful change had come over them. Acting under some evil influence, they now pushed their warfare into the white settlements, carrying fire and destruction with them. Again and again had the government offered them a free pass to Washington and the privilege of being photographed, but under the same evil guidance they refused. There was a singular mystery in their mode of aggression. School-houses were always burned, the school-masters taken into captivity, and never again heard from. A palace car on the Union Pacific Railway, containing an excursion party of teachers *en route* to San Francisco, was surrounded, its inmates captured, and—their vacancies in the school catalogue never again filled. Even a Board of Educational Examiners, proceeding to Cheyenne, were taken prisoners, and obliged to answer questions they themselves had proposed, amidst horrible tortures. By degrees these atrocities were traced to the malign influence of a new chief of the tribe. As yet little was known of him but through his baleful appellations, "Young Man who Goes for his Teacher," and "He Lifts the Hair of the School Marm." He was said to be small and exceedingly youthful in appearance. Indeed, his earlier appellative, "He Wipes his Nose on his Sleeve," was said to have been given to him to indicate his still boy-like habits.

It was night in the encampment and among the lodges of the "Pigeon Toes." Dusky maidens flitted in and out among the camp-fires like brown moths, cooking the toothsome buffalo hump, frying the fragrant bear's meat, and stewing the esculent bean for the braves. For a few favored ones spitted grasshoppers were reserved as a rare delicacy, although the proud Spartan soul of their chief scorned all such luxuries.

He was seated alone in his wigwam, attended only by the gentle Mushymush, fairest of the "Pigeon Feet" maidens. Nowhere were the characteristics of her great tribe more plainly shown than in the little feet that lapped over each other in walking. A single glance at the chief was sufficient to show the truth of the wild rumors respecting his youth. He was scarcely twelve, of proud and lofty bearing, and clad completely in wrappings of various-colored scalloped cloths, which gave him the appearance of a somewhat extra-sized pen-wiper. An enormous eagle's feather, torn from the wing of a bald eagle who once attempted to carry him away, completed his attire. It was also the memento of one of his most superhuman feats of courage. He would undoubtedly have scalped the eagle but that nature had anticipated him.

"Why is the Great Chief sad?" asked Mushymush, softly. "Does his soul still yearn for the blood of the pale-faced teachers? Did not the scalping of two professors of geology in the Yale exploring party satisfy his warrior's heart yesterday? Has he forgotten that Hayden and Clarence King are still to follow? Shall his own Mushymush bring him a botanist to-morrow? Speak, for the silence of my brother lies on my heart like the snow on the mountain, and checks the flow of my speech."

Still the proud Boy Chief sat silent. Suddenly he said: "Hist!" and rose to his feet. Taking a long rifle from the ground he adjusted its sight. Exactly seven miles away on the slope of the mountain the figure of a man was seen walking. The Boy Chief raised the rifle to his unerring eye and fired. The man fell.

A scout was dispatched to scalp and search the body. He presently returned.

"Who was the pale face?" eagerly asked the chief.

"A life insurance agent."

A dark scowl settled on the face of the chief.

"I thought it was a book-peddler."

"Why is my brother's heart sore against the book-peddler?" asked Mushymush.

"Because," said the Boy Chief, fiercely, "I am again without my regular dime novel, and I thought he might have one in his pack. Hear me, Mushymush; the United States mails no longer bring me my 'Young America,' or my 'Boys' and Girls' Weekly.' I find it impossible, even with my fastest scouts, to keep up with the rear of General Howard, and replenish my literature from the sutler's wagon. Without a dime novel or a 'Young America,' how am I to keep up this Injin business?"

Mushymush remained in meditation a single moment. Then she looked up proudly.

"My brother has spoken. It is well. He shall have his dime novel. He shall know what kind of a hair-pin his sister Mushymush is."

And she arose and gamboled lightly as the fawn out of his presence.

In two hours she returned. In one hand she held three small flaxen scalps, in the other "The Boy Marauder," complete in one volume, price ten cents.

"Three pale-faced children," she gasped, "were reading it in the tail end of an emigrant wagon. I crept up to them softly. Their parents are still unaware of the accident," and she sank helpless at his feet.

"Noble girl!" said the Boy Chief, gazing proudly on her

prostrate form; "and these are the people that a military despotism expects to subdue!"

CHAPTER IV

BUT the capture of several wagon-loads of commissary whisky, and the destruction of two tons of stationery intended for the general commanding, which interfered with his regular correspondence with the War Department, at last awakened the United States military authorities to active exertion. A quantity of troops were massed before the "Pigeon Feet" encampment, and an attack was hourly imminent.

"Shine your boots, sir?"

It was the voice of a youth in humble attire, standing before the flap of the commanding general's tent.

The General raised his head from his correspondence.

"Ah," he said, looking down on the humble boy, "I see; I shall write that the appliances of civilization move steadily forward with the army. Yes," he added, "you may shine my military boots. You understand, however, that to get your pay you must first—"

"Make a requisition on the commissary-general, have it certified to by the quartermaster, countersigned by the post-adjutant, and submitted by you to the War Department—"

"And charged as stationery," added the General, gently. "You are, I see, an intelligent and thoughtful boy. I trust you neither use whisky, tobacco, nor are ever profane?"

"I promised my sainted mother—"

"Enough! Go on with your blacking; I have to lead the attack on the 'Pigeon Feet' at eight precisely. It is now half-past seven," said the General, consulting a large kitchen clock that stood in the corner of his tent.

The little boot-black looked up; the General was absorbed in his correspondence. The boot-black drew a tin putty blower from his pocket, took unerring aim, and nailed in a single shot the minute hand to the dial. Going on with his blacking, yet stopping ever and anon to glance over the General's plan of campaign, spread on the table before him, he was at last interrupted by the entrance of an officer.

"Everything is ready for the attack, General. It is now eight o'clock."

"Impossible! It is only half-past seven."

"But my watch and the watches of your staff—"

"Are regulated by my kitchen clock, that has been in my family for years. Enough! It is only half-past seven."

The officer retired; the boot-black had finished one boot. Another officer appeared.

"Instead of attacking the enemy, General, we are attacked ourselves. Our pickets are already driven in."

"Military pickets should not differ from other pickets," interrupted the boot-black, modestly. "To stand firmly they should be well driven in."

"Ha! there is something in that," said the General, thoughtfully. "But who are you, who speak thus?"

Rising to his full height, the boot-black threw off his outer rags, and revealed the figure of the Boy Chief of the "Pigeon Feet."

"Treason!" shrieked the General; "order an advance along the whole line."

But in vain. The next moment he fell beneath the tomahawk of the Boy Chief, and within the next quarter of an hour the United States Army was dispersed. Thus ended the battle of Boot-black Creek.

CHAPTER V

AND yet the Boy Chief was not entirely happy. Indeed, at times he seriously thought of accepting the invitation extended by the Great Chief at Washington, immediately after the massacre of the soldiers, and once more revisiting the haunts of civilization. His soul sickened in feverish inactivity; schoolmasters palled on his taste; he had introduced base ball, blind hooky, marbles, and peg-top among his Indian subjects, but only with indifferent suc-

cess. The squaws insisted in boring holes through the
china alleys and wearing them as necklaces; his warriors
stuck spikes in their base ball bats and made war clubs of
them. He could not but feel, too, that the gentle Mushymush, although devoted to her pale-faced brother, was
deficient in culinary education. Her mince pies were
abominable; her jam far inferior to that made by his Aunt
Sally of Doemville. Only an unexpected incident kept
him equally from the extreme of listless Sybaritic indulgence, or of morbid cynicism. Indeed, at the age of
twelve, he already had become disgusted with existence.

He had returned to his wigwam after an exhausting
buffalo hunt in which he had slain two hundred and seventy-
five buffalos with his own hand, not counting the individual
buffalo on which he had leaped so as to join the herd, and
which he afterward led into the camp a captive and a
present to the lovely Mushymush. He had scalped two express riders and a correspondent of the "New York Herald";
had despoiled the Overland Mail Stage of a quantity of
vouchers which enabled him to draw double rations from
the government, and was reclining on a bear skin, smoking
and thinking of the vanity of human endeavor, when a
scout entered, saying that a pale-face youth had demanded
access to his person.

"Is he a commissioner? If so, say that the red man is
rapidly passing to the happy hunting-grounds of his fathers, and now desires only peace, blankets, and ammunition;
obtain the latter and then scalp the commissioner."

"But it is only a youth who asks an interview."

"Does he look like an insurance agent? If so, say that
I have already policies in three Hartford companies.
Meanwhile prepare the stake, and see that the squaws are
ready with their implements of torture."

The youth was admitted; he was evidently only half the
age of the Boy Chief. As he entered the wigwam and
stood revealed to his host they both started. In another
moment they were locked in each other's arms.

"Jenky, old boy!"

"Bromley, old fel!"

B. F. Jenkins, for such was the name of the Boy Chief,

was the first to recover his calmness. Turning to his warriors he said, proudly—

"Let my children retire while I speak to the agent of our Great Father in Washington. Hereafter no latch keys will be provided for the wigwams of the warriors. The practice of late hours must be discouraged."

"How!" said the warriors, and instantly retired.

"Whisper," said Jenkins, drawing his friend aside; "I am known here only as the Boy Chief of the 'Pigeon Toes.'"

"And I," said Bromley Chitterlings, proudly, "am known everywhere as the Pirate Prodigy—the Boy Avenger of the Patagonian Coast."

"But how came you here?"

"Listen! My pirate brig, the 'Lively Mermaid,' now lies at Meiggs's Wharf in San Francisco, disguised as a Mendocino lumber vessel. My pirate crew accompanied me here in a palace car from San Francisco."

"It must have been expensive," said the prudent Jenkins.

"It was, but they defrayed it by a collection from the other passengers—you understand, an enforced collection. The papers will be full of it to-morrow. Do you take the 'New York Sun'?"

"No; I dislike their Indian policy. But why are you here?"

"Hear me, Jenk! 'Tis a long and a sad story. The lovely Eliza J. Sniffen, who fled with me from Doemville, was seized by her parents and torn from my arms at New Rochelle. Reduced to poverty by the breaking of the savings bank of which he was president,—a failure to which I largely contributed, and the profits of which I enjoyed, —I have since ascertained that Eliza Jane Sniffen was forced to become a schoolmistress, departed to take charge of a seminary in Colorado, and since then has never been heard from."

Why did the Boy Chief turn pale, and clutch at the tent-pole for support? Why, indeed!

"Eliza J. Sniffen," gasped Jenkins, "aged fourteen, red-haired, with a slight tendency to strabismus?"

"The same."

"Heaven help me! She died by my mandate!"

"Traitor!" shrieked Chitterlings, rushing at Jenkins with a drawn poniard.

But a figure interposed. The slight girlish form of Mushymush with outstretched hands stood between the exasperated Pirate Prodigy and the Boy Chief.

"Forbear," she said sternly to Chitterlings; "you know not what you do."

The two youths paused.

"Hear me," she said rapidly. "When captured in a confectioner's shop at New Rochelle, E. J. Sniffen was taken back to poverty. She resolved to become a schoolmistress. Hearing of an opening in the West, she proceeded to Colorado to take exclusive charge of the *pensionnat* of Mad. Choflie, late of Paris. On the way thither she was captured by the emissaries of the Boy Chief—"

"In consummation of a fatal vow I made never to spare educational instructors," interrupted Jenkins.

"But in her captivity," continued Mushymush, "she managed to stain her face with poke-berry juice, and mingling with the Indian maidens was enabled to pass for one of the tribe. Once undetected, she boldly ingratiated herself with the Boy Chief,—how honestly and devotedly he best can tell,—for I, Mushymush, the little sister of the Boy Chief, am Eliza Jane Sniffen."

The Pirate Prodigy clasped her in his arms. The Boy Chief, raising his hand, ejaculated:—

"Bless you, my children!"

"There is but one thing wanting to complete this reunion," said Chitterlings, after a pause, but the hurried entrance of a scout stopped his utterance.

"A commissioner from the Great Father in Washington."

"Scalp him!" shrieked the Boy Chief; "this is no time for diplomatic trifling."

"We have, but he still insists upon seeing you, and has sent in his card."

The Boy Chief took it, and read aloud, in agonized accents:—

"Charles F. Hall Golightly, late Page in United States Senate, and Acting Commissioner of United States."

In another moment, Golightly, pale, bleeding, and, as it were, prematurely bald, but still cold and intellectual, entered the wigwam. They fell upon his neck and begged his forgiveness.

"Don't mention it," he said, quietly; "these things must and will happen under our present system of government. My story is brief. Obtaining political influence through caucuses, I became at last Page in the Senate. Through the exertions of political friends I was appointed clerk to the commissioner whose functions I now represent. Knowing through political spies in your own camp who you were, I acted upon the physical fears of the commissioner, who was an ex-clergyman, and easily induced him to deputize me to consult with you. In doing so, I have lost my scalp, but as the hirsute signs of juvenility have worked against my political progress I do not regret it. As a partially bald young man I shall have more power. The terms that I have to offer are simply this: you can do everything you want, go anywhere you choose, if you will only leave this place. I have a hundred thousand-dollar draft on the United States Treasury in my pocket at your immediate disposal."

"But what's to become of me?" asked Chitterlings.

"Your case has already been under advisement. The Secretary of State, who is an intelligent man, is determined to recognize you as *de jure* and *de facto* the only loyal representative of the Patagonian government. You may safely proceed to Washington as its envoy extraordinary. I dine with the secretary next week."

"And yourself, old fellow?"

"I only wish that twenty years from now you will recognize by your influence and votes the rights of C. F. H. Golightly to the presidency."

And here ends our story. Trusting that my dear young friends may take whatever example or moral their respective parents and guardians may deem fittest from these pages, I hope in future years to protray further the career of those three young heroes I have already introduced in the spring-time of life to their charitable consideration.

THE MAN WHOSE YOKE WAS
NOT EASY

HE was a spare man, and, physically, an ill-conditioned man, but at first glance scarcely a seedy man. The indications of reduced circumstances in the male of the better class are, I fancy, first visible in the boots and shirt; the boots offensively exhibiting a degree of polish inconsistent with their dilapidated condition, and the shirt showing an extent of ostentatious surface that is invariably fatal to the threadbare waist-coat that it partially covers. He was a pale man, and, I fancied, still paler from his black clothes.

He handed me a note.

It was from a certain physician; a man of broad culture and broader experience; a man who had devoted the greater part of his active life to the alleviation of sorrow and suffering; a man who had lived up to the noble vows of a noble profession; a man who locked in his honorable breast the secrets of a hundred families, whose face was as kindly, whose touch was as gentle, in the wards of the great public hospitals as it was beside the laced curtains of the dying Narcissa; a man who, through long contact with suffering, had acquired a universal tenderness and breadth of kindly philosophy; a man who, day and night, was at the beck and call of anguish; a man who never asked the creed, belief, moral or worldly standing of the sufferer, or even his ability to pay the few coins that enabled him (the physician) to exist and practice his calling; in brief, a man who so nearly lived up to the example of the Great Master that it seems strange I am writing of him as a doctor of medicine and not of divinity.

The note was in pencil, characteristically brief, and ran thus:—

"Here is the man I spoke of. He ought to be good material for you."

For a moment I sat looking from the note to the man, and sounding the "dim perilous depths" of my memory for the meaning of this mysterious communication. The good "material," however, soon relieved my embarrassment by putting his hand on his waistcoat, coming toward me, and saying, "It is just here, you can feel it."

It was not necessary for me to do so. In a flash I remembered that my medical friend had told me of a certain poor patient, once a soldier, who, among his other trials and uncertainties, was afflicted with an aneurism caused by the buckle of his knapsack pressing upon the arch of the aorta. It was liable to burst at any shock or any moment. The poor fellow's yoke had indeed been too heavy.

In the presence of such a tremendous possibility I think for an instant I felt anxious only about myself. What *I* should do; how dispose of the body; how explain the circumstance of his taking off; how evade the ubiquitous reporter and the coroner's inquest; how a suspicion might arise that I had in some way, through negligence or for some dark purpose, unknown to the jury, precipitated the catastrophe, all flashed before me. Even the note, with its darkly suggestive offer of "good material" for me, looked diabolically significant. What might not an intelligent lawyer make of it?

I tore it up instantly, and with feverish courtesy begged him to be seated.

"You don't care to feel it?" he asked, a little anxiously.

"No."

"Nor see it?"

"No."

He sighed, a trifle sadly, as if I had rejected the only favor he could bestow. I saw at once that he had been under frequent exhibition to the doctors, and that he was, perhaps, a trifle vain of this attention. This perception was corroborated a moment later by his producing a copy of a medical magazine, with a remark that on the sixth page I would find a full statement of his case.

"Could I serve him in any way?" I asked.

It appeared that I could. If I could help him to any light employment, something that did not require any great physical exertion or mental excitement, he would be thankful. But he wanted me to understand that he was not, strictly speaking, a poor man; that some years before the discovery of his fatal complaint he had taken out a life insurance policy for five thousand dollars, and that he had raked and scraped enough together to pay it up, and that he would not leave his wife and four children destitute. "You see," he added, "if I could find some sort of light work to do, and kinder sled along, you know—until—"

He stopped, awkwardly.

I have heard several noted actors thrill their audiences with a single phrase. I think I never was as honestly moved by any spoken word as that "until," or the pause that followed it. He was evidently quite unconscious of its effect, for as I took a seat beside him on the sofa, and looked more closely in his waxen face, I could see that he was evidently embarrassed, and would have explained himself further, if I had not stopped him.

Possibly it was the dramatic idea, or possibly chance, but a few days afterward, meeting a certain kind-hearted theatrical manager, I asked him if he had any light employment for a man who was an invalid? "Can he walk?" "Yes." "Stand up for fifteen minutes?" "Yes." "Then I'll take him. He'll do for the last scene in the 'Destruction of Sennacherib'—it's a tremendous thing, you know. We'll have two thousand people on the stage." I was a trifle alarmed at the title, and ventured to suggest (without betraying my poor friend's secret that he could not actively engage in the "Destruction of Sennacherib," and that even the spectacle of it might be too much for him. "Needn't see it at all," said my managerial friend; "put him in front, nothing to do but march in and march out, and dodge curtain."

He was engaged. I admit I was at times haunted by grave doubts as to whether I should not have informed the manager of his physical condition, and the possibility that he might some evening perpetrate a real tragedy on the mimic stage, but on the first performance of "The Destruction of Sennacherib," which I conscientiously attended, I was somewhat relieved. I had often been amused with the placid way in which the chorus in the opera invariably received the most astounding information, and witnessed the most appalling tragedies by poison or the block, without anything more than a vocal protest or command, always delivered to the audience and never to the actors, but I think my poor friend's utter impassiveness to the wild carnage and the terrible exhibitions of incendiarism that were going on around him transcended even that. Dressed in a costume that seemed to be the very soul of anachronism, he stood a little outside the proscenium, holding a spear, the other hand pressed apparently upon the secret within his breast, calmly surveying, with his waxen face, the gay auditorium. I could not help thinking that there was a certain pride visible even in his placid features, as of one who was conscious that at any moment he might change this simulated catastrophe into real terror. I could not help saying this to the Doctor, who was with me. "Yes," he said with professional exactitude; "when it happens he'll throw his arms up above his head, utter an ejaculation, and fall forward on his face,—it's a singular thing, they always fall forward on their face,—and they'll pick up the man as dead as Julius Cæsar."

After that, I used to go night after night, with a certain hideous fascination; but, while it will be remembered the "Destruction of Sennacherib" had a tremendous run, it will also be remembered that not a single life was really lost during its representation.

It was only a few weeks after this modest first appearance on the boards of "The Man with an Aneurism," that, happening to be at dinner party of practical business men, I sought to interest them with the details of the above story, delivered with such skill and pathos as I could command. I regret to say that, as a pathetic story, it for a moment seemed to be a dead failure. At last a prominent banker sitting next to me turned to me with the awful question: "Why don't your friend try to realize on his life insurance?" I begged his pardon, I didn't quite understand. "Oh, discount, sell out. Look here—(after a pause). Let

8   v. 1

him assign his policy to me, it's not much of a risk, on
your statement. Well—I'll give him his five thousand
dollars, clear."

And he did. Under the advice of this cool-headed—I
think I may add warm-hearted—banker, "The Man with
an Aneurism" invested his money in the name of and for
the benefit of his wife in certain securities that paid him
a small but regular stipend. But he still continued upon
the boards of the theatre.

By reason of some business engagements that called me
away from the city, I did not see my friend the physician
for three months afterward. When I did I asked tidings
of The Man with the Aneurism. The Doctor's kind face
grew sad. "I'm afraid—that is, I don't exactly know
whether I've good news or bad. Did you ever see his wife?"

I never had.

"Well, she was younger than he, and rather attractive.
One of those doll-faced women. You remember, he settled
that life insurance policy on her and the children: she
might have waited; she didn't. The other day she eloped
with some fellow, I don't remember his name, with the children and the five thousand dollars."

"And the shock killed him," I said with poetic prompti-
tude.

"No—that is—not yet; I saw him yesterday," said the
Doctor, with conscientious professional precision, looking
over his list of calls.

"Well, where is the poor fellow now?"

"He's still at the theatre. James, if these powders are
called for, you'll find them here in this envelope. Tell
Mrs. Blank I'll be there at seven—and she can give the baby
this until I come. Say there's no danger. These women
are an awful bother! Yes, he's at the theatre yet. Which
way are you going? Down town? Why can't you step
into my carriage, and I'll give you a lift, and we'll talk on
the way down? Well—he's at the theatre yet. And—and
—do you remember the 'Destruction of Sennacherib?' No?
Yes you do. You remember that woman in pink, who
pirouetted in the famous ballet scene! You don't? Why,
yes you do! Well, I imagine, of course I don't know, it's

only a summary diagnosis, but I imagine that our friend with the aneurism has attached himself to her."

"Doctor, you horrify me."

"There are more things, Mr. Poet, in heaven and earth than are yet dreamt of in your philosophy. Listen. My diagnosis may be wrong, but that woman called the other day at my office to ask about him, his health, and general condition. I told her the truth—and she *fainted*. It was about as dead a faint as I ever saw; I was nearly an hour in bringing her out of it. Of course it was the heat of the room, her exertions the preceding week, and I prescribed for her. Queer, wasn't it? Now, if I were a writer, and had your faculty, I'd make something out of that."

"But how is his general health?"

"Oh, about the same. He can't evade what will come, you know, at any moment. He was up here the other day. Why, the pulsation was as plain—why, the entire arch of the aorta— What! you get out here? Good-by."

Of course no moralist, no man writing for a sensitive and strictly virtuous public, could further interest himself in this man. So I dismissed him at once from my mind, and returned to the literary contemplation of virtue that was clearly and positively defined, and of Sin, that invariably commenced with a capital letter. That this man, in his awful condition, hovering on the verge of eternity, should allow himself to be attracted by—but it was horrible to contemplate.

Nevertheless, a month afterwards, I was returning from a festivity with my intimate friend Smith, my distinguished friend Jobling, my most respectable friend Robinson, and my wittiest friend Jones. It was a clear, star-lit morning, and we seemed to hold the broad, beautiful avenue to ourselves; and I fear we acted as if it were so. As we hilariously passed the corner of Eighteenth Street, a coupé rolled by, and I suddenly heard my name called from its gloomy depths.

"I beg your pardon," said the Doctor, as his driver drew up by the sidewalk, "but I've some news for you. I've just been to see our poor friend ——. Of course I was too late. He was gone in a flash."

"What! dead?"

"As Pharaoh! In an instant, just as I said. You see, the rupture took place in the descending arch of—"

"But, Doctor!"

"It's a queer story. Am I keeping you from your friends? No? Well, you see she—that woman I spoke of —had written a note to him based on what I had told her. He got it, and dropped in his dressing-room, dead as a herring."

"How could she have been so cruel, knowing his condition? She might, with woman's tact, have rejected him less abruptly."

"Yes; but you're all wrong. By Jove! she *accepted* him! was willing to marry him!"

"What?"

"Yes. Don't you see? It was joy that killed him. Gad, we never thought of *that!* Queer, ain't it? See here, don't you think you might make a story out of it?"

"But, Doctor, it hasn't got any moral."

"Humph! That's so. Good morning. Drive on, John."

MY FRIEND, THE TRAMP

I HAD been sauntering over the clover downs of a certain noted New England seaport. It was a Sabbath morning, so singularly reposeful and gracious, so replete with the significance of the seventh day of rest, that even the Sabbath bells ringing a mile away over the salt marshes had little that was monitory, mandatory, or even supplicatory in their drowsy voices. Rather they seemed to call from their cloudy towers, like some renegade muezzin: "Sleep is better than prayer; sleep on, O sons of the Puritans! Slumber still, O deacons and vestrymen! Let, oh let those feet that are swift to wickedness curl up beneath thee! those palms that are itching for the shekels of the ungodly lie clasped beneath thy pillow! Sleep is better than prayer."

And, indeed, though it was high morning, sleep was still in the air. Wrought upon at last by the combined influences of sea and sky and atmosphere, I succumbed, and lay down on one of the boulders of a little stony slope that gave upon the sea. The great Atlantic lay before me, not yet quite awake, but slowly heaving the rhythmical expiration of slumber. There was no sail visible in the misty horizon. There was nothing to do but to lie and stare at the unwinking ether.

Suddenly I became aware of the strong fumes of tobacco. Turning my head, I saw a pale blue smoke curling up from behind an adjacent boulder. Rising, and climbing over the intermediate granite, I came upon a little hollow, in which, comfortably extended on the mosses and lichens, lay a powerfully-built man. He was very ragged; he was very dirty; there was a strong suggestion about him of his having too much hair, too much nail, too much perspiration; too much of those superfluous excrescences and exudations that society and civilization strive to keep under. But it was noticeable that he had not much of anything else. It was The Tramp.

With that swift severity with which we always visit rebuke upon the person who happens to present any one of our vices offensively before us, in his own person, I was deeply indignant at his laziness. Perhaps I showed it in my manner, for he rose to a half-sitting attitude, returned my stare apologetically, and made a movement toward knocking the fire from his pipe against the granite.

"Shure, sur, and if I'd belaved that I was trispassin on yer honor's grounds, it's meself that would hev laid down on the say shore and takin' the salt waves for me blankits. But it's sivinteen miles I've walked this blessed noight, with nothin' to sustain me, and hevin' a mortal wakeness to fight wid in me bowels, by reason of starvation, and only a bit o' baccy that the Widdy Maloney gi' me at the cross roads, to kape me up entoirley. But it was the dark day I left me home in Milwaukee to walk to Boston; and if ye'll oblige a lone man who has left a wife and six children in Milwaukee, wid the loan of twenty-five cints, furninst the time he gits worruk, God'll be good to ye."

It instantly flashed through my mind that the man before me had the previous night partaken of the kitchen hospitality of my little cottage, two miles away. That he presented himself in the guise of a distressed fisherman, mulcted of his wages by an inhuman captain; that he had a wife lying sick of consumption in the next village, and two children, one of whom was a cripple, wandering in the streets of Boston. I remembered that this tremendous indictment against Fortune touched the family, and that the distressed fisherman was provided with clothes, food, and some small change. The food and small change had disappeared, but the garments for the consumptive wife, where were they? He had been using them for a pillow.

I instantly pointed out this fact, and charged him with the deception. To my surprise, he took it quietly, and even a little complacently.

"Bedad, yer roight; ye see, sur" (confidentially), "ye see, sur, until I get worruk—and it's worruk I'm lukin' for—I have to desave now and thin to shute the locality. Ah, God save us! but on the say-coast thay'r that har-rud upon thim that don't belong to the say."

I ventured to suggest that a strong, healthy man like him might have found work somewhere between Milwaukee and Boston.

"Ah, but ye see I got free passage on a freight train, and didn't sthop. It was in the Aist that I expected to find worruk."

"Have you any trade?"

"Trade, is it? I'm a brickmaker, God knows, and many's the lift I've had at makin' bricks in Milwaukee. Shure, I've as aisy a hand at it as any man. Maybe yer honor might know of a kill hereabout?"

Now to my certain knowledge, there was not a brick kiln within fifty miles of that spot, and of all unlikely places to find one would have been this sandy peninsula, given up to the summer residences of a few wealthy people. Yet I could not help admiring the assumption of the scamp, who knew this fact as well as myself. But I said, "I can give you work for a day or two;" and, bidding him gather up his sick wife's apparel, led the way across the downs to my cottage. At first I think the offer took him by surprise, and gave him some consternation, but he presently recovered his spirits, and almost instantly his speech. "Ah, worruk, is it? God be praised! it's meself that's ready and willin'. 'Though maybe me hand is spoilt wid brick-makin'."

I assured him that the work I would give him would require no delicate manipulation, and so we fared on over the sleepy downs. But I could not help noticing that, although an invalid, I was a much better pedestrian than my companion, frequently leaving him behind, and that even as a "tramp," he was etymologically an impostor. He had a way of lingering beside the fences we had to climb over, as if to continue more confidentially the history of his misfortunes and troubles, which he was delivering to me during our homeward walk, and I noticed that he could seldom resist the invitation of a mossy boulder or a tussock of salt grass. "Ye see, sur," he would say, suddenly sitting down, "it's along uv me misfortunes beginnin' in Milwaukee that—" and it was not until I was out of hearing that he would languidly gather his traps again and saunter after me. When I reached my own garden gate he leaned for a moment over it, with both of his powerful arms extended downward, and said, "Ah, but it's a blessin' that Sunday comes to give rest fur the wake and the weary, and them as walks sivinteen miles to get it." Of course I took the hint. There was evidently no work to be had from my friend, the Tramp, that day. Yet his countenance brightened as he saw the limited extent of my domain, and observed that the garden, so called, was only a flower-bed about twenty-five by ten. As he had doubtless before this been utilized, to the extent of his capacity, in digging, he had probably expected that kind of work; and I daresay I discomfitted him by pointing him to an almost leveled stone wall, about twenty feet long, with the remark that his work would be the rebuilding of that stone wall, with stone brought from the neighboring slopes. In a few moments he was comfortably provided for in the kitchen, where the cook, a woman of his own nativity, apparently, "chaffed" him with a raillery that was to me quite unintelligible. Yet I noticed that when, at sunset, he accompanied Bridget to the spring for water, ostentatiously flourishing the empty bucket in his hand, when they returned in the gloaming Bridget was carrying the water, and my friend, the Tramp, was some paces behind her, cheerfully "colloguing," and picking blackberries.

At seven the next morning he started in cheerfully to work. At nine, A. M., he had placed three large stones on the first course in position, an hour having been spent in looking for a pick and hammer, and in the incidental "chaffing" with Bridget. At ten o'clock I went to overlook his work; it was a rash action, as it caused him to respectfully doff his hat, discontinue his labors, and lean back against the fence in cheerful and easy conservation. "Are you fond uv blackberries, Captain?" I told him that the children were in the habit of getting them from the meadow beyond, hoping to estop the suggestion I knew was coming. "Ah, but, Captain, it's meself that with wanderin' and havin' nothin' to pass me lips but the berries I'd pick from the hedges,—it's meself knows where to find thim. Sure, it's yer childer, and foine boys they are, Captain, that's besaching me to go wid 'em to the place, known'st only to meself." It is unnecessary to say that he triumphed. After the manner of vagabonds of all degrees, he had enlisted the women and children on his side—and my friend, the Tramp, had his own way. He departed at eleven and returned at four, P. M., with a tin dinner-pail half filled. On interrogating the boys it appeared that they had had a "bully time," but on cross-examination it came out that *they* had picked the berries. From four to six, three more stones were laid, and the arduous labors of the day were over. As I stood looking at the first course of six stones, my friend, the Tramp, stretched his strong arms out to their fullest extent and said: "Ay, but it's worruk that's good for me; give me worruk, and it's all I'll be askin' fur."

I ventured to suggest that he had not yet accomplished much.

"Wait till to-morror. Ah, but ye'll see thin. It's me hand that's yet onaisy wid brick-makin' and sthrange to the shtones. An ye'll wait till to-morror?"

Unfortunately I did not wait. An engagement took me away at an early hour, and when I rode up to my cottage at noon my eyes were greeted with the astonishing spectacle of my two boys hard at work laying the courses of the stone wall, assisted by Bridget and Norah, who were dragging stones from the hillsides, while comfortably stretched on the top of the wall lay my friend, the Tramp, quietly overseeing the operation with lazy and humorous comment. For an instant I was foolishly indignant, but he soon brought me to my senses. "Shure, sur, it's only larnin' the boys the habits uv industhry I was—and may they niver know, be the same token, what it is to worruk fur the bread betune their lips. Shure it's but makin' 'em think it play I was. As fur the colleens beyint in the kitchen, sure isn't it betther they was helping your honor here than colloguing with themselves inside?"

Nevertheless, I thought it expedient to forbid henceforth any interruption of servants or children with my

friend's "worruk." Perhaps it was the result of this em-
bargo that the next morning early the Tramp wanted to
see me.

"And it's sorry I am to say it to ye, sur," he began,
"but it's the handlin' of this stun that's desthroyin' me
touch at the brick-makin', and it's better I should lave ye
and find worruk at me own thrade. For it's worruk I am
nadin'. It isn't meself, Captain, to ate the bread of oidle-
ness here. And so good-by to ye, and if it's fifty cints ye
can be givin' me ontil I'll find a kill—it's God that'll
repay ye."

He got the money. But he got also conditionally a note
from me to my next neighbor, a wealthy retired physician,
possessed of a large domain, a man eminently practical
and businesslike in his management of it. He employed
many laborers on the sterile waste he called his "farm,"
and it occurred to me that if there really was any work in
my friend, the Tramp, which my own indolence and preoccupation had failed to bring out, he was the man to do it.

I met him a week after. It was with some embarrassment that I inquired after my friend, the Tramp. "Oh,
yes," he said, reflectively, "let's see: he came Monday and
left me Thursday. He was, I think, a stout, strong man,
a well-meaning, good-humored fellow, but afflicted with a
most singular variety of diseases. The first day I put
him at work in the stables he developed chills and fever
caught in the swamps of Louisiana—"

"Excuse me," I said hurriedly, "you mean in Milwaukee!"

"I know what I'm talking about," returned the Doctor,
testily; "he told me his whole wretched story—his escape
from the Confederate service, the attack upon him by armed
negroes, his concealment in the bayous and swamps—"

"Go on, Doctor," I said, feebly; "you were speaking of
his work."

"Yes. Well, his system was full of malaria; the first day
I had him wrapped up in blankets, and dosed with quinine.
The next day he was taken with all the symptoms of
cholera morbus, and I had to keep him up on brandy and
capsicum. Rheumatism set in on the following day, and
incapacitated him for work, and I concluded I had better

give him a note to the director of the City Hospital than keep him here. As a pathological study he was good; but as I was looking for a man to help about the stable, I couldn't afford to keep him in both capacities."

As I never could really tell when the Doctor was in joke or in earnest, I dropped the subject. And so my friend, the Tramp, gradually faded from my memory, not however without leaving behind him in the barn where he had slept a lingering flavor of whisky, onions, and fluffiness. But in two weeks this had gone, and the "Shebang" (as my friends irreverently termed my habitation) knew him no more. Yet it was pleasant to think of him as having at last found a job at brick-making, or having returned to his family at Milwaukee, or making his Louisiana home once more happy with his presence, or again tempting the fish-producing main—this time with a noble and equitable captain.

It was a lovely August morning when I rode across the sandy peninsula to visit a certain noted family, whereof all the sons were valiant and the daughters beautiful. The front of the house was deserted, but on the rear veranda I heard the rustle of gowns, and above it arose what seemed to be the voice of Ulysses, reciting his wanderings. There was no mistaking that voice, it was my friend, the Tramp!

From what I could hastily gather from his speech, he had walked from St. John, N. B., to rejoin a distressed wife in New York, who was, however, living with opulent but objectionable relatives. "An' shure, miss, I wouldn't be askin' ye the loan of a cint if I could get worruk at me trade of carpet-wavin'—and maybe ye know of some manufacthory where they wave carpets beyant here. Ah, miss, and if ye don't give me a cint, it's enough for the loikes of me to know that me troubles has brought the tears in the most beautiful oiyes in the wurruld, and God bless ye for it, miss!"

Now I knew that the Most Beautiful Eyes in the World belonged to one of the most sympathetic and tenderest hearts in the world, and I felt that common justice demanded my interference between it and one of the biggest scamps in the world. So, without waiting to be announced by the servant, I opened the door, and joined the group on the veranda.

If I expected to touch the conscience of my friend, the Tramp, by a dramatic entrance, I failed utterly; for no sooner did he see me, than he instantly gave vent to a howl of delight, and, falling on his knees before me, grasped my hand, and turned oratorically to the ladies.

"Oh, but it's himself—himself that has come as a witness to me carrakther! Oh, but it's himself that lifted me four wakes ago, when I was lyin' with a mortal wakeness on the say-coast, and tuk me to his house. Oh, but it's himself that shupported me over the faldes, and whin the chills and faver came on me and I shivered wid the cold, it was himself, God bless him, as sthripped the coat off his back, and giv it me, sayin', 'Take it, Dinnis, it's shtarved with the cowld say air ye'll be entoirely.' Ah, but look at him —will ye, miss! Look at his swate, modist face—a blushin' like your own, miss. Ah! look at him, will ye? He'll be denyin' of it in a minit—may the blessin' uv God folly him. Look at him, miss! Ah, but it's a swate pair ye'd make! (the rascal knew I was a married man). Ah, miss, if you could see him wroightin' day and night with such an illigant hand of his own—(he had evidently believed from the gossip of my servants that I was a professor of chirography)—if ye could see him, miss, as I have, ye'd be proud of him."

He stopped out of breath. I was so completely astounded I could say nothing: the tremendous indictment I had framed to utter as I opened the door vanished completely. And as the Most Beautiful Eyes in the Wurruld turned gratefully to mine—well—

I still retained enough principle to ask the ladies to withdraw, while I would take upon myself the duty of examining into the case of my friend, the Tramp, and giving him such relief as was required. (I did not know until afterward, however, that the rascal had already despoiled their scant purses of three dollars and fifty cents.) When the door was closed upon them I turned upon him.

"You infernal rascal!"

"Ah, Captain, and would ye be refusin' *me* a carrakther

and me givin' *ye* such a one as Oi did! God save us! but if ye'd hav' seen the luk that the purty one give ye. Well, before the chills and faver bruk me spirits entirely, when I was a young man, and makin' me tin dollars a week brick-makin', it's meself that wud hav' given—"

"I consider," I broke in, "that a dollar is a fair price for your story, and as I shall have to take it all back and expose you before the next twenty-four hours pass, I think you had better hasten to Milwaukee, New York, or Louisiana."

I handed him the dollar. "Mind, I don't want to see your face again."

"Ye wun't, Captain."

And I did not.

But it so chanced that later in the season, when the migratory inhabitants had flown to their hot-air registers in Boston and Providence, I breakfasted with one who had lingered. It was a certain Boston lawyer,—replete with principle, honesty, self-discipline, statistics, æsthetics, and a perfect consciousness of possessing all these virtues, and a full recognition of their market values. I think he tolerated me as a kind of foreigner, gently but firmly waiving all argument on any topic, frequently distrusting my facts, generally my deductions, and always my ideas. In conversation he always appeared to descend only half way down a long moral and intellectual staircase, and always delivered his conclusions over the balusters.

I had been speaking of my friend, the Tramp. "There is but one way of treating that class of impostors; it is simply to recognize the fact that the law calls him a 'vagrant,' and makes his trade a misdemeanor. Any sentiment on the other side renders you *particeps criminis*. I don't know but an action would lie against you for encouraging tramps. Now, I have an efficacious way of dealing with these gentry." He rose and took a double-barreled fowling-piece from the chimney. "When a tramp appears on my property, I warn him off. If he persists, I fire on him—as I would on any criminal trespasser."

"Fire on him?" I echoed in alarm.

"Yes—*but with powder only!* Of course *he* doesn't know that. But he doesn't come back."

It struck me for the first time that possibly many other of my friend's arguments might be only blank cartridges, and used to frighten off other trespassing intellects.

"Of course, if the tramp still persisted, I would be justified in using shot. Last evening I had a visit from one. He was coming over the wall. My shot gun was efficacious; you should have seen him run!"

It was useless to argue with so positive a mind, and I dropped the subject. After breakfast I strolled over the downs, my friend promising to join me as soon as he arranged some household business.

It was a lovely, peaceful morning, not unlike the day when I first met my friend, the Tramp. The hush of a great benediction lay on land and sea. A few white sails twinkled afar, but sleepily; one or two large ships were creeping in lazily, like my friend, the Tramp. A voice behind me startled me.

My host had rejoined me. His face, however, looked a little troubled.

"I just now learned something of importance," he began. "It appears that with all my precautions that Tramp has visited my kitchen, and the servants have entertained him. Yesterday morning, it appears, while I was absent, he had the audacity to borrow my gun to go duck-shooting. At the end of two or three hours he returned with two ducks and—the gun."

"That was, at least, honest."

"Yes—but! That fool of a girl says that, as he handed back the gun, he told her it was all right, and that he had loaded it up again to save the master trouble."

I think I showed my concern in my face, for he added, hastily: "It was only duck-shot; a few wouldn't hurt him!"

Nevertheless, we both walked on in silence for a moment.

"I thought the gun kicked a little," he said at last, musingly; "but the idea of— Hallo! what's this?"

He stopped before the hollow where I had first seen my Tramp. It was deserted, but on the mosses there were spots of blood and fragments of an old gown, blood-stained, as if used for bandages. I looked at it closely: it was the gown intended for the consumptive wife of my friend, the Tramp.

But my host was already nervously tracking the blood-stains that on rock, moss, and boulder were steadily leading toward the sea. When I overtook him at last on the shore, he was standing before a flat rock, on which lay a bundle I recognized, tied up in a handkerchief, and a crooked grape-vine stick.

"He may have come here to wash his wounds—salt is a styptic," said my host, who had recovered his correct precision of statement.

I said nothing, but looked toward the sea. Whatever secret lay hid in its breast, it kept it fast. Whatever its calm eyes had seen that summer night, it gave no reflection now. It lay there passive, imperturbable, and reticent. But my friend, the Tramp, was gone!

THE MAN FROM SOLANO

HE came toward me out of an opera lobby, between the acts,—a figure as remarkable as anything in the performance. His clothes, no two articles of which were of the same color, had the appearance of having been purchased and put on only an hour or two before,—a fact more directly established by the clothes-dealer's ticket which still adhered to his coat-collar, giving the number, size, and general dimensions of that garment somewhat obtrusively to an uninterested public. His trousers had a straight line down each leg, as if he had been born flat but had since developed; and there was another crease down his back, like those figures children cut out of folded paper. I may add that there was no consciousness of this in his face, which was good-natured, and, but for a certain squareness in the angle of his lower jaw, utterly uninteresting and commonplace.

"You disremember me," he said, briefly, as he extended his hand, "but I'm from Solano, in Californy. I met you there in the spring of '57. I was tendin' sheep, and you was burnin' charcoal."

There was not the slightest trace of any intentional rudeness in the reminder. It was simply a statement of fact, and as such to be accepted.

"What I hailed ye for was only this," he said, after I had shaken hands with him. "I saw you a minnit ago standin' over in yon box—chirpin' with a lady—a young lady, peart and pretty. Might you be telling me her name?"

I gave him the name of a certain noted belle of a neighboring city, who had lately stirred the hearts of the metropolis, and who was especially admired by the brilliant and fascinating young Dashboard, who stood beside me.

The Man from Solano mused for a moment, and then said, "Thet's so! thet's the name! It's the same gal!"

"You have met her, then?" I asked, in surprise.

"Ye-es," he responded, slowly: "I met her about fower months ago. She'd bin makin' a tour of Californy with some friends, and I first saw her aboard the cars this side of Reno. She lost her baggage-checks, and I found them on the floor and gave 'em back to her, and she thanked me. I reckon now it would be about the square thing to go over thar and sorter recognize her." He stopped a moment, and looked at us inquiringly.

"My dear sir," struck in the brilliant and fascinating Dashboard, "if your hesitation proceeds from any doubt as to the propriety of your attire, I beg you to dismiss it from your mind at once. The tyranny of custom, it is true, compels your friend and myself to dress peculiarly, but I assure you nothing could be finer than the way that the olive green of your coat melts in the delicate yellow of your cravat, or the pearl gray of your trousers blends with the bright blue of your waistcoat, and lends additional brilliancy to that massive oroide watch-chain which you wear."

To my surprise, the Man from Solano did not strike him. He looked at the ironical Dashboard with grave earnestness, and then said quietly:—

"Then I reckon you wouldn't mind showin' me in thar?"

Dashboard was, I admit, a little staggered at this. But he recovered himself, and, bowing ironically, led the way to the box. I followed him and the Man from Solano.

Now, the belle in question happened to be a gentle-woman—descended from gentlewomen—and after Dashboard's ironical introduction, in which the Man from Solano was not spared, she comprehended the situation instantly. To Dashboard's surprise she drew a chair to her side, made the Man from Solano sit down, quietly turned her back on Dashboard, and in full view of the brilliant audience and the focus of a hundred lorgnettes, entered into conversation with him.

Here, for the sake of romance, I should like to say he became animated, and exhibited some trait of excellence, —some rare wit or solid sense. But the fact is he was dull and stupid to the last degree. He persisted in keeping the conversation upon the subject of the lost baggage-checks,

and every bright attempt of the lady to divert him failed
signally. At last, to everybody's relief, he rose, and leaning over her chair, said:—

"I calklate to stop over here some time, miss, and you
and me bein' sorter strangers here, maybe when there's
any show like this goin' on you'll let me—"

Miss X. said somewhat hastily that the multiplicity of
her engagements and the brief limit of her stay in New
York she feared would, etc., etc. The two other ladies had
their handkerchiefs over their mouths, and were staring intently on the stage, when the Man from Solano continued:—

"Then, maybe, miss, whenever there is a show goin' on
that you'll attend, you'll just drop me word to Earle's
Hotel, to this yer address," and he pulled from his pocket
a dozen well-worn letters, and taking the buff envelope
from one, handed it to her with something like a bow.

"Certainly," broke in the facetious Dashboard, "Miss X.
goes to the Charity Ball to-morrow night. The tickets are
but a trifle to an opulent Californian, and a man of your
evident means, and the object a worthy one. You will, no
doubt, easily secure an invitation."

Miss X. raised her handsome eyes for a moment to Dashboard. "By all means," she said, turning to the Man from
Solano; "and as Mr. Dashboard is one of the managers and
you are a stranger, he will, of course, send you a complimentary ticket. I have known Mr. Dashboard long enough
to know that he is invariably courteous to strangers and a
gentleman." She settled herself in her chair again and
fixed her eyes upon the stage.

The Man from Solano thanked the Man of New York,
and then, after shaking hands with everybody in the box,
turned to go. When he had reached the door he looked
back to Miss X., and said,—

"It *was* one of the queerest things in the world, miss,
that my findin' them checks—"

But the curtain had just then risen on the garden scene
in "Faust," and Miss X. was absorbed. The Man from
Solano carefully shut the box door and retired. I followed him.

He was silent until he reached the lobby, and then he

said, as if renewing a previous conversation, "She *is* a mighty peart gal—that's so. She's just my kind, and will make a stavin' good wife."

I thought I saw danger ahead for the Man from Solano, so I hastened to tell him that she was beset by attentions, that she could have her pick and choice of the best of society, and finally, that she was, most probably, engaged to Dashboard.

"That's so," he said quietly, without the slightest trace of feeling. "It would be mighty queer if she wasn't. But I reckon I'll steer down to the ho-tel. I don't care much for this yellin'." (He was alluding to a cadenza of that famous cantatrice, Signora Batti Batti.) "What's the time?"

He pulled out his watch. It was such a glaring chain, so obviously bogus, that my eyes were fascinated by it. "You're looking at that watch," he said; "it's purty to look at, but she don't go worth a cent. And yet her price was $125, gold. I gobbled her up in Chatham Street day before yesterday, where they were selling 'em very cheap at auction."

"You have been outrageously swindled," I said, indignantly. "Watch and chain are not worth twenty dollars."

"Are they worth fifteen?" he asked, gravely.

"Possibly."

"Then I reckon it's a fair trade. Ye see, I told 'em I was a Californian from Solano, and hadn't anything about me of greenbacks. I had three slugs with me. Ye remember them slugs?" (I did; the "slug" was a "token" issued in the early days—a hexagonal piece of gold a little over twice the size of a twenty-dollar gold piece—worth and accepted for fifty dollars.)

"Well, I handed them that, and they handed me the watch. You see them slugs I had made myself outer brass filings and iron pyrites, and used to slap 'em down on the boys for a bluff in a game of draw poker. You see, not being reg'lar gov-ment money, it wasn't counterfeiting. I reckon they cost me, counting time and anxiety, about fifteen dollars. So, if this yer watch is worth that, it's about a square game, ain't it?"

I began to understand the Man from Solano, and said it

was. He returned his watch to his pocket, toyed playfully with the chain, and remarked, "Kinder makes a man look fash'nable and wealthy, don't it?"

I agreed with him. "But what do you intend to do here?" I asked.

"Well, I've got a cash capital of nigh on seven hundred dollars. I guess until I get into reg'lar business I'll skirmish round Wall Street, and sorter lay low." I was about to give him a few words of warning, but I remembered his watch, and desisted. We shook hands and parted.

A few days after I met him on Broadway. He was attired in another new suit, but I think I saw a slight improvement in his general appearance. Only five distinct colors were visible in his attire. But this, I had reason to believe afterwards, was accidental.

I asked him if he had been to the ball. He said he had. "That gal, and a mighty peart gal she was too, was there, but she sorter fought shy of me. I got this new suit to go in, but those waiters sorter run me into a private box, and I didn't get much chance to continner our talk about them checks. But that young feller, Dashboard, was mighty perlite. He brought lots of fellers and young women round to the box to see me, and he made up a party that night to take me round Wall Street and in them Stock Boards. And the next day he called for me and took me, and I invested about five hundred dollars in them stocks— may be more. You see, we sorter swopped stocks. You know I had ten shares in the Peacock Copper Mine, that you was once secretary of."

"But those shares are not worth a cent. The whole thing exploded ten years ago."

"That's so, may be; *you* say so. But then I didn't know anything more about Communipaw Central, or the Naphtha Gaslight Company, and so I thought it was a square game. Only I realized on the stocks I bought, and I kem up outer Wall Street about four hundred dollars better. You see it was a sorter risk, after all, for them Peacock stocks *might* come up!"

I looked into his face: it was immeasurably serene and commonplace. I began to be a little afraid of the man, or, rather, of my want of judgment of the man; and after a few words we shook hands and parted.

It was some months before I again saw the Man from Solano. When I did, I found that he had actually become a member of the Stock Board, and had a little office on Broad Street, where he transacted a fair business. My remembrance going back to the first night I met him, I inquired if he had renewed his acquaintance with Miss X. "I heerd that she was in Newport this summer, and I ran down there fur a week."

"And you talked with her about the baggage-checks?"

"No," he said, seriously; "she gave me a commission to buy some stocks for her. You see, I guess them fash'nable fellers sorter got to runnin' her about me, and so she put our acquaintance on a square business footing. I tell you, she's a right peart gal. Did ye hear of the accident that happened to her?"

I had not.

"Well, you see, she was out yachting, and I managed through one of those fellers to get an invite, too. The whole thing was got up by a man that they say is going to marry her. Well, one afternoon the boom swings round in a little squall and knocks her overboard. There was an awful excitement,—you've heard about it, may be?"

"No!" But I saw it all with a romancer's instinct in a flash of poetry! This poor fellow, debarred through uncouthness from expressing his affection for her, had at last found his fitting opportunity. He had—

"Thar was an awful row," he went on. "I ran out on the taffrail, and there a dozen yards away was that purty creature, that peart gal, and—I—"

"You jumped for her," I said, hastily.

"No!" he said gravely. "I let the other man do the jumping. I sorter looked on."

I stared at him in astonishment.

"No," he went on, seriously. "He was the man who jumped—that was just then his 'put'—his line of business. You see, if I had waltzed over the side of that ship, and cavoorted in, and flummuxed round and finally flopped to the bottom, that other man would have jumped nateral-like and saved her; and ez he was going to marry her anyway, I don't exactly see where *I'd* hev been represented in the transaction. But don't you see, ef, after he'd jumped and hadn't got her, he'd gone down himself, I'd hev had the next best chance, and the advantage of heving him outer the way. You see, you don't understand me—I don't think you did in Californy."

"Then he did save her?"

"Of course. Don't you see she was all right. If he'd missed her, I'd have chipped in. Thar warn't no sense in my doing his duty onless he failed."

Somehow the story got out. The Man from Solano as a butt became more popular than ever, and of course received invitations to burlesque receptions, and naturally met a great many people whom otherwise he would not have seen. It was observed also that his seven hundred dollars were steadily growing, and that he seemed to be getting on in his business. Certain California stocks which I had seen quietly interred in the old days in the tombs of their fathers were magically revived; and I remember, as one who has seen a ghost, to have been shocked as I looked over the quotations one morning to have seen the ghostly face of the "Dead Beat Beach Mining Co.," rouged and plastered, looking out from the columns of the morning paper. At last a few people began to respect, or suspect, the Man from Solano. At last, suspicion culminated with this incident:—

He had long expressed a wish to belong to a certain "fash'n'ble" club, and with a view of burlesque he was invited to visit the club, where a series of ridiculous entertainments were given him, winding up with a card party. As I passed the steps of the club-house early next morning, I overheard two or three members talking excitedly,—

"He cleaned everybody out." "Why, he must have raked in nigh on $40,000."

"Who?" I asked.

"The Man from Solano."

As I turned away, one of the gentlemen, a victim, noted for his sporting propensities, followed me, and laying his hand on my shoulders, asked:—

"Tell me fairly now. What business did your friend follow in California?"

"He was a shepherd."

"A what?"

"A shepherd. Tended his flocks on the honey-scented hills of Solano."

"Well, all I can say is, d—n your California pastorals!"

THE OFFICE SEEKER

HE asked me if I had ever seen the "Remus Sentinel."

I replied that I had not, and would have added that I did not even know where Remus was, when he continued by saying it was strange the hotel proprietor did not keep the "Sentinel" on his files, and that he, himself, should write to the editor about it. He would not have spoken about it, but he, himself, had been an humble member of the profession to which I belonged, and had often written for its columns. Some friends of his—partial, no doubt—had said that his style somewhat resembled Junius's; but of course, you know—well, what he could say was that in the last campaign his articles were widely sought for. He did not know but he had a copy of one. Here his hand dived into the breast-pocket of his coat, with a certain deftness that indicated long habit, and, after depositing on his lap a bundle of well-worn documents, every one of which was glaringly suggestive of certificates and signatures, he concluded he had left it in his trunk.

I breathed more freely. We were sitting in the rotunda of a famous Washington hotel, and only a few moments before had the speaker, an utter stranger to me, moved his chair beside mine and opened a conversation. I noticed that he had that timid, lonely, helpless air which invests the bucolic traveler who, for the first time, finds himself among strangers, and his identity lost, in a world so much larger, so much colder, so much more indifferent to him than he ever imagined. Indeed, I think that what we often attribute to the impertinent familiarity of countrymen and rustic travelers on railways or in cities is largely due to their awful loneliness and nostalgia. I remember to have once met in a smoking-car on a Kansas railway one of these lonely ones, who, after plying me with a thousand useless questions, finally elicited the fact that I knew slightly a man who had once dwelt in his native town in Illinois. During the rest of our journey the conversation turned chiefly upon his fellow-townsman, whom it afterwards appeared that my Illinois friend knew no better than I did. But he had established a link between himself and his far-off home through me, and was happy.

While this was passing through my mind I took a fair look at him. He was a spare young fellow, not more than thirty, with sandy hair and eyebrows, and eyelashes so white as to be almost imperceptible. He was dressed in black, somewhat to the "rearward o' the fashion," and I had an odd idea that it had been his wedding suit, and it afterwards appeared I was right. His manner had the precision and much of the dogmatism of the country school-master, accustomed to wrestle with the feeblest intellects. From his history, which he presently gave me, it appeared I was right here also.

He was born and bred in a Western State, and, as school-master of Remus and Clerk of Supervisors, had married one of his scholars, the daughter of a clergyman, and a man of some little property. He had attracted some attention by his powers of declamation, and was one of the principal members of the Remus Debating Society. The various questions then agitating Remus,—"Is the doctrine of immortality consistent with an agricultural life?" and, "Are round dances morally wrong?"—afforded him an opportunity of bringing himself prominently before the country people. Perhaps I might have seen an extract copied from the "Remus Sentinel" in the "Christian Recorder" of May 7, 1875? No? He would get it for me. He had taken an active part in the last campaign. He did not like to say it, but it had been universally acknowledged that he had elected Gashwiler.

Who?

Gen. Pratt C. Gashwiler, member of Congress from our deestrict.

Oh!

A powerful man, sir—a very powerful man; a man whose influence will presently be felt here, sir—*here!* Well, he had come on with Gashwiler, and—well, he did not know why—Gashwiler did not know why he should not, you know (a feeble, half-apologetic laugh here), receive that reward, you know, for these services which, etc., etc.

I asked him if he had any particular or definite office in view.

Well, no. He had left that to Gashwiler. Gashwiler had said—he remembered his very words: "Leave it all to me; I'll look through the different departments, and see what can be done for a man of your talents."

And—

He's looking. I'm expecting him back here every minute. He's gone over to the Department of Tape, to see what can be done there. Ah! here he comes.

A large man approached us. He was very heavy, very unwieldy, very unctuous and oppressive. He affected the "honest farmer," but so badly that the poorest husbandman would have resented it. There was a suggestion of a cheap lawyer about him that would have justified any self-respecting judge in throwing him over the bar at once. There was a military suspicion about him that would have entitled him to a court-martial on the spot. There was an introduction, from which I learned that my office-seeking friend's name was Expectant Dobbs. And then Gashwiler addressed me:—

"Our young friend here is waiting, waiting. Waiting, I may say, on the affairs of State. Youth," continued the Hon. Mr. Gashwiler, addressing an imaginary constituency, "is nothing but a season of waiting—of preparation—ha, ha!"

As he laid his hand in a fatherly manner—a fatherly manner that was as much of a sham as anything else about him—I don't know whether I was more incensed at him or his victim, who received it with evident pride and satisfaction. Nevertheless he ventured to falter out:—

"Has anything been done yet?"

"Well, no; I can't say that anything—that is, that anything has been *completed;* but I may say we are in excellent position for an advance—ha, ha! But we must wait, my young friend, wait. What is it the Latin philosopher says? 'Let us by all means hasten slowly'—ha, ha!"

and he turned to me as if saying confidentially, "Observe the impatience of these boys!" "I met, a moment ago, my old friend and boyhood's companion, Jim McGlasher, chief of the Bureau for the Dissemination of Useless Information, and," lowering his voice to a mysterious but audible whisper, "I shall see him again to-morrow."

The "All aboard!" of the railway omnibus at this moment tore me from the presence of this gifted legislator and his *protégé;* but as we drove away I saw through the open window the powerful mind of Gashwiler operating, so to speak, upon the susceptibilities of Mr. Dobbs.

I did not meet him again for a week. The morning of my return I saw the two conversing together in the hall, but with the palpable distinction between this and their former interviews, that the gifted Gashwiler seemed to be anxious to get away from his friend. I heard him say something about "committees" and "to-morrow," and when Dobbs turned his freckled face toward me I saw that he had got at last some expression into it—disappointment.

I asked him pleasantly how he was getting on.

He had not lost his pride yet. He was doing well, although such was the value set upon his friend Gashwiler's abilities by his brother members that he was almost always occupied with committee business. I noticed that his clothes were not in as good case as before, and he told me that he had left the hotel, and taken lodgings in a by-street, where it was less expensive. Temporarily of course.

A few days after this I had business in one of the great departments. From the various signs over the doors of its various offices and bureaus it always oddly reminded me of Stewart's or Arnold and Constable's. You could get pensions, patents, and plants. You could get land and the seeds to put in it, and the Indians to prowl round it, and what not. There was a perpetual clanging of office desk bells, and a running hither and thither of messengers strongly suggestive of "Cash 47."

As my business was with the manager of this Great National Fancy Shop, I managed to push by the sad-eyed, eager-faced crowd of men and women in the anteroom, and entered the secretary's room, conscious of having left behind me a great deal of envy and uncharitableness of spirit. As I opened the door I heard a monotonous flow of Western speech which I thought I recognized. There was no mistaking it. It was the voice of the Gashwiler.

"The appointment of this man, Mr. Secretary, would be most acceptable to the people in my deestrict. His family are wealthy and influential, and it's just as well in the fall elections to have the supervisors and county judge pledged to support the administration. Our delegates to the State Central Committee are to a man"—but here, perceiving from the wandering eye of Mr. Secretary that there was another man in the room, he whispered the rest with a familiarity that must have required all the politician in the official's breast to keep from resenting.

"You have some papers, I suppose?" asked the secretary, wearily.

Gashwiler was provided with a pocketful, and produced them. The secretary threw them on the table among the other papers, where they seemed instantly to lose their identity, and looked as if they were ready to recommend anybody but the person they belonged to. Indeed, in one corner the entire Massachusetts delegation, with the Supreme Bench at their head, appeared to be earnestly advocating the manuring of Iowa waste lands; and to the inexperienced eye, a noted female reformer had apparently appended her signature to a request for a pension for wounds received in battle.

"By the way," said the secretary, "I think I have a letter here from somebody in your district asking an appointment, and referring to you? Do you withdraw it?"

"If anybody has been presuming to speculate upon my patronage," said the Hon. Mr. Gashwiler, with rising rage.

"I've got the letter somewhere here," said the secretary, looking dazedly at his table. He made a feeble movement among the papers, and then sank back hopelessly in his chair, and gazed out of the window as if he thought and rather hoped it might have flown away. "It was from a Mr. Globbs, or Gobbs, or Dobbs, of Remus," he said finally, after a superhuman effort of memory.

"Oh, that's nothing—a foolish fellow who has been boring me for the last month."

"Then I am to understand that this application is withdrawn?"

"As far as my patronage is concerned, certainly. In fact, such an appointment would not express the sentiments—indeed, I may say, would be calculated to raise active opposition in the deestrict."

The secretary uttered a sigh of relief, and the gifted Gashwiler passed out. I tried to get a good look at the honorable scamp's eye, but he evidently did not recognize me.

It was a question in my mind whether I ought not to expose the treachery of Dobbs's friend, but the next time I met Dobbs he was in such good spirits that I forebore. It appeared that his wife had written to him that she had discovered a second cousin in the person of the Assistant Superintendent of the Envelope Flap Moistening Bureau of the Department of Tape, and had asked his assistance; and Dobbs had seen him, and he had promised it. "You see," said Dobbs, "in the performance of his duties he is often very near the person of the secretary, frequently in the next room, and he is a powerful man, sir—a powerful man to know, sir—a *very* powerful man."

How long this continued I do not remember. Long enough, however, for Dobbs to become quite seedy, for the giving up of wrist cuffs, for the neglect of shoes and beard, and for great hollows to form round his eyes, and a slight flush on his cheek-bones. I remember meeting him in all the departments, writing letters or waiting patiently in anterooms from morning till night. He had lost all his old dogmatism, but not his pride. "I might as well be here as anywhere, while I'm waiting," he said, "and then I'm getting some knowledge of the details of official life."

In the face of this mystery I was surprised at finding a note from him one day, inviting me to dine with him at a certain famous restaurant. I had scarce got over my amazement, when the writer himself overtook me at my hotel. For a moment I scarcely recognized him. A new suit of fashionably-cut clothes had changed him, without, however,

entirely concealing his rustic angularity of figure and outline. He even affected a fashionable dilettante air, but so
mildly and so innocently that it was not offensive.

"You see," he began, explanatory-wise, "I've just found
out the way to do it. None of these big fellows, these cabinet officers, know me except as an applicant. Now, the way
to do this thing is to meet 'em fust sociably; wine 'em and
dine 'em. Why, sir,"—he dropped into the schoolmaster
again here,—"I had two cabinet ministers, two judges, and
a general at my table last night."

"On *your* invitation?"

"Dear, no! all I did was to pay for it. Tom Soufflet gave
the dinner and invited the people. Everybody knows Tom.
You see, a friend of mine put me up to it, and said that
Soufflet had fixed up no end of appointments and jobs in
that way. You see, when these gentlemen get sociable over
their wine, he says carelessly, 'By the way, there's So-and-so
—a good fellow—wants something; give it to him.' And
the first thing you know, or they know, he gets a promise
from them. They get a dinner—and a good one—and he
gets an appointment."

"But where did you get the money?"

"Oh,"—he hesitated,—"I wrote home, and Fanny's father
raised fifteen hundred dollars some way, and sent it to me.
I put it down to political expenses." He laughed a weak,
foolish laugh here, and added, "As the old man don't drink
nor smoke, he'd lift his eyebrows to know how the money
goes. But I'll make it all right when the office comes—and
she's coming, sure pop."

His slang fitted as poorly on him as his clothes, and his
familiarity was worse than his former awkward shyness.
But I could not help asking him what had been the result
of this expenditure.

"Nothing just yet. But the Secretary of Tape and the
man at the head of the Inferior Department, both spoke to
me, and one of them said he thought he'd heard my name
before. He might," he added, with a forced laugh, "for
I've written him fifteen letters."

Three months passed. A heavy snow-storm stayed my
chariot wheels on a Western railroad, ten miles from a

nervous lecture committee and a waiting audience; there was nothing to do but to make the attempt to reach them in a sleigh. But the way was long and the drifts deep, and when at last four miles out we reached a little village, the driver declared his cattle could hold out no longer, and we must stop there. Bribes and threats were equally of no avail. I had to accept the fact.

"What place is this?"

"Remus."

"Remus, Remus," where had I heard that name before? But while I was reflecting he drove up before the door of the tavern. It was a dismal, sleep-forbidding place, and only nine o'clock, and here was the long winter's night before me. Failing to get the landlord to give me a team to go further, I resigned myself to my fate and a cigar, behind the red-hot stove. In a few moments one of the loungers approached me, calling me by name, and in a rough but hearty fashion condoled with me for my mishap, advised me to stay at Remus all night, and added: "The quarters ain't the best in the world yer at this hotel. But thar's an old man yer—the preacher that was—that for twenty years hez taken in such fellers as you and lodged 'em free gratis for nothing, and hez been proud to do it. The old man used to be rich; he ain't so now; sol his big house on the cross roads, and lives in a little cottage with his darter right over yan. But ye couldn't do him a better turn than to go over thar and stay, and if he thought I'd let ye go out o' Remus without axing ye, he'd give me h—ll. Stop, I'll go with ye."

I might at least call on the old man, and I accompanied my guide through the still falling snow until we reached a little cottage. The door opened to my guide's knock, and with the brief and discomposing introduction, "Yer, ole man, I've brought you one o' them snow-bound lecturers," he left me on the threshold, as my host, a kindly-faced, white-haired man of seventy, came forward to greet me.

His frankness and simple courtesy overcame the embarrassment left by my guide's introduction, and I followed him passively as he entered the neat, but plainly-furnished sitting-room. At the same moment a pretty, but faded young woman arose from the sofa and was introduced to me as his daughter. "Fanny and I live here quite alone, and if you knew how good it was to see somebody from the great outside world now and then, you would not apologize for what you call your intrusion."

During this speech I was vaguely trying to recall where and when and under what circumstances I had ever before seen the village, the house, the old man or his daughter. Was it in a dream, or in one of those dim reveries of some previous existence to which the spirit of mankind is subject? I looked at them again. In the careworn lines around the once pretty girlish mouth of the young woman, in the furrowed seams over the forehead of the old man, in the ticking of the old-fashioned clock on the shelf, in the faint whisper of the falling snow outside, I read the legend, "Patience, patience; Wait and Hope."

The old man filled a pipe, and offering me one, continued, "Although I seldom drink myself, it was my custom to always keep some nourishing liquor in my house for passing guests, but to-night I find myself without any." I hastened to offer him my flask, which, after a moment's coyness, he accepted, and presently under its benign influence at least ten years dropped from his shoulders, and he sat up in his chair erect and loquacious.

"And how are affairs at the National Capital, sir?" he began.

Now, if there was any subject of which I was profoundly ignorant, it was this. But the old man was evidently bent on having a good political talk. So I said vaguely, yet with a certain sense of security, that I guessed there wasn't much being done.

"I see," said the old man, "in the matters of resumption; of the sovereign rights of States and federal interference, you would imply that a certain conservative tentative policy is to be promulgated until after the electoral committee have given their verdict." I looked for help towards the lady, and observed feebly that he had very clearly expressed my views.

The old man, observing my look, said: "Although my daughter's husband holds a federal position in Washington, the pressure of his business is so great that he has little time to give us mere gossip—I beg your pardon, did you speak?"

I had unconsciously uttered an exclamation. This, then, was Remus—the home of Expectant Dobbs—and these his wife and father; and the Washington banquet-table, ah me! had sparkled with the yearning heart's blood of this poor wife, and had been upheld by this tottering Caryatid of a father.

"Do you know what position he has?"

The old man did not know positively, but thought it was some general supervising position. He had been assured by Mr. Gashwiler that it was a first-class clerkship; yes, a *first* class.

I did not tell him that in this, as in many other official regulations in Washington, they reckoned backward, but said:—

"I suppose that your M. C., Mr.—Mr. Gashwiler—"

"Don't mention his name," said the little woman, rising to her feet hastily; "he never brought Expectant anything but disappointment and sorrow. I hate, I despise the man."

"Dear Fanny," expostulated the old man, gently, "this is unchristian and unjust. Mr. Gashwiler is a powerful, a very powerful man! His work is a great one; his time is preoccupied with weightier matters.

"His time was not so preoccupied but he could make use of poor Expectant," said this wounded dove, a little spitefully.

Nevertheless it was some satisfaction to know that Dobbs had at last got a place, no matter how unimportant, or who had given it to him; and when I went to bed that night in the room that had been evidently prepared for their conjugal chamber, I felt that Dobbs's worst trials were over. The walls were hung with souvenirs of their ante-nuptial days. There was a portrait of Dobbs, *aetat.* 25; there was a faded bouquet in a glass case, presented by Dobbs to Fanny on examination-day; there was a framed resolution of thanks to Dobbs from the Remus Debating Society; there was a certificate of Dobbs's election as President of the Remus Philomathean Society; there was his commission as

Captain in the Remus Independent Contingent of Home
Guards; there was a Freemason's chart, in which Dobbs
was addressed in epithets more fulsome and extravagant
than any living monarch. And yet all these cheap glories
of a narrow life and narrower brain were upheld and made
sacred by the love of the devoted priestess who worshiped
at this lonely shrine, and kept the light burning through
gloom and doubt and despair. The storm tore round the
house, and shook its white fists in the windows. A dried
wreath of laurel that Fanny had placed on Dobbs's head
after his celebrated centennial address at the school-house,
July 4, 1876, swayed in the gusts, and sent a few of its
dead leaves down on the floor, and I lay in Dobbs's bed
and wondered what a first-class clerkship was.

I found out early the next summer. I was strolling
through the long corridors of a certain great department,
when I came upon a man accurately yoked across the shoulders, and supporting two huge pails of ice on either side,
from which he was replenishing the pitchers in the various
offices. As I passed I turned to look at him again. It was
Dobbs!

He did not set down his burden; it was against the rules,
he said. But he gossiped cheerily, said he was beginning
at the foot of the ladder, but expected soon to climb up.
That it was Civil Service Reform, and of course he would
be promoted soon.

"Had Gashwiler procured the appointment?"

No. He believed it was *me*. *I* had told his story to
Assistant-secretary Blank, who had, in turn related it to
Bureau-director Dash—both good fellows—but this was all
they could do. Yes, it was a foothold. But he must go now.

Nevertheless, I followed him up and down, and, cheered
up with a rose-colored picture of his wife and family, and
my visit there, and promising to come and see him the next
time I came to Washington, I left him with his self-imposed
yoke.

With a new administration, Civil Service Reform came
in, crude and ill-digested, as all sudden and sweeping reforms must be; cruel to the individual, as all crude reforms
will ever be; and among the list of helpless men and women,

incapacitated for other work by long service in the dull routine of federal office, who were decapitated, the weak, foolish, emaciated head of Expectant Dobbs went to the block. It afterward appeared that the gifted Gashwiler was responsible for the appointment of twenty clerks, and that the letter of poor Dobbs, in which he dared to refer to the now powerless Gashwiler, had sealed his fate. The country made an example of Gashwiler and—Dobbs.

From that moment he disappeared. I looked for him in vain in anterooms, lobbies, and hotel corridors, and finally came to the conclusion that he had gone home.

How beautiful was that July Sabbath, when the morning train from Baltimore rolled into the Washington depot. How tenderly and chastely the morning sunlight lay on the east front of the Capitol until the whole building was hushed in a grand and awful repose. How difficult it was to think of a Gashwiler creeping in and out of those enfiling columns, or crawling beneath that portico, without wondering that yon majestic figure came not down with flat of sword to smite the fat rotundity of the intruder. How difficult to think that parricidal hands have ever been lifted against the Great Mother, typified here in the graceful white chastity of her garments, in the noble tranquillity of her face, in the gathering up her white-robed children within her shadow.

This led me to think of Dobbs, when, suddenly a face flashed by my carriage window. I called to the driver to stop, and, looking again, saw that it was a woman standing bewildered and irresolute on the street corner. As she turned her anxious face toward me I saw that it was Mrs. Dobbs.

What was she doing here, and where was Expectant?

She began an incoherent apology, and then burst into explanatory tears. When I had got her in the carriage she said, between her sobs, that Expectant had not returned; that she had received a letter from a friend here saying he was sick,—oh very, very sick,—and father could not come with her, so she came alone. She was so frightened, so lonely, so miserable.

Had she his address?

Yes, just here! It was on the outskirts of Washington, near Georgetown. Then I would take her there, if I could, for she knew nobody.

On our way I tried to cheer her up by pointing out some of the children of the Great Mother before alluded to, but she only shut her eyes as we rolled down the long avenues, and murmured, "Oh, these cruel, cruel distances!"

At last we reached the locality, a negro quarter, yet clean and neat in appearance. I saw the poor girl shudder slightly as we stopped at the door of a low, two-story frame house, from which the unwonted spectacle of a carriage brought a crowd of half-naked children and a comely, cleanly, kind-faced mulatto woman.

Yes, this was the house. He was upstairs, rather poorly, but asleep, she thought.

We went upstairs. In the first chamber, clean, though poorly furnished, lay Dobbs. On a pine table near his bed were letters and memorials to the various departments, and on the bed-quilt, unfinished, but just as the weary fingers had relaxed their grasp upon it, lay a letter to the Tape Department.

As we entered the room he lifted himself on his elbow. "Fanny!" he said, quickly, and a shade of disappointment crossed his face. "I thought it was a message from the secretary," he added, apologetically.

The poor woman had suffered too much already to shrink from this last crushing blow. But she walked quietly to his side without a word or cry, knelt, placed her loving arms around him, and I left them so together.

When I called again in the evening he was better; so much better that, against the doctor's orders, he had talked to her quite cheerfully and hopefully for an hour, until suddenly raising her bowed head in his two hands, he said, "Do you know, dear, that in looking for help and influence there was one, dear, I had forgotten; one who is very potent with kings and councilors, and I think, love, I shall ask Him to interest Himself in my behalf. It is not too late yet, darling, and I shall seek Him to-morrow."

And before the morrow came he had sought and found Him, and I doubt not got a good place.

A SLEEPING-CAR EXPERIENCE

It was in a Pullman sleeping-car on a Western road. After that first plunge into unconsciousness which the weary traveler takes on getting into his berth, I awakened to the dreadful revelation that I had been asleep only two hours. The greater part of a long winter night was before me to face with staring eyes.

Finding it impossible to sleep, I lay there wondering a number of things: why, for instance, the Pullman sleeping-car blankets were unlike other blankets; why they were like squares cut out of cold buckwheat cakes, and why they clung to you when you turned over, and lay heavy on you without warmth; why the curtains before you could not have been made opaque, without being so thick and suffocating; why it would not be as well to sit up all night half asleep in an ordinary passenger-car as to lie awake all night in a Pullman. But the snoring of my fellow-passengers answered this question in the negative.

With the recollection of last night's dinner weighing on me as heavily and coldly as the blankets, I began wondering why, over the whole extent of the continent, there was no local dish; why the bill of fare at restaurant and hotel was invariably only a weak reflex of the metropolitan hostelries; why the *entrées* were always the same, only more or less badly cooked; why the traveling American always was supposed to demand turkey and cold cranberry sauce; why the pretty waiter-girl apparently shuffled your plates behind your back, and then dealt them over your shoulder in a semi-circle, as if they were a hand at cards, and not always a good one? Why, having done this, she instantly retired to the nearest wall, and gazed at you scornfully, as one who would say, "Fair sir, though lowly, I am proud; if thou dost imagine that I would permit undue familiarity of speech, beware!" And then I began to think of and dread the coming breakfast; to wonder why the ham was always cut half an inch thick, and why the fried egg always resembled a glass eye that visibly winked at you with diabolical dyspeptic suggestions; to wonder if the buckwheat cakes, the eating of which requires a certain degree of artistic preparation and deliberation, would be brought in as usual one minute before the train started. And then I had a vivid recollection of a fellow-passenger who, at a certain breakfast station in Illinois, frantically enwrapped his portion of this national pastry in his red bandana handkerchief, took it into the smoking-car, and quietly devoured it *en route*.

Lying broad awake, I could not help making some observations which I think are not noticed by the day traveler. First, that the speed of a train is not equal or continuous. That at certain times the engine apparently starts up, and says to the baggage train behind it, "Come, come, this won't do! Why, it's nearly half-past two; how in h—ll shall we get through? Don't you talk to *me*. Pooh, pooh!" delivered in that rhythmical fashion which all meditation assumes on a railway train. *Exempli gratia:* One night, having raised my window-curtain to look over a moonlit snowy landscape, as I pulled it down the lines of a popular comic song flashed across me. Fatal error! The train instantly took it up, and during the rest of the night I was haunted by this awful refrain: "Pull down the bel-lind, pull down the bellind; simebody's klink klink, O don't be shoo-shoo!" Naturally this differs on the different railways. On the New York Central, where the road-bed is quite perfect and the steel rails continuous, I have heard this irreverent train give the words of a certain popular revival hymn after this fashion: "Hold the fort, for I am Sankey; Moody slingers still. Wave the swish swash back from klinky, klinky klanky kill." On the New York and New Haven, where there are many switches, and the engine whistles at every cross road, I have often heard, "Tommy make room for your whooopy! that's a little clang; bumpity, bumpity, boopy, clikitty, clikitty, clang." Poetry, I fear, fared little better. One starlit night, coming from Quebec, as we slipped by a virgin forest, the opening lines of Evangeline flashed upon me. But all I could make of them was this: "This is the forest primeval-eval; the groves of the pines and the hemlocks-locks-locks-locks-loooock!" The train was only "slowing" or "braking" up at a station. Hence the jar in the metre.

I had noticed a peculiar Æolian harp-like cry that ran through the whole train as we settled to rest at last after a long run—an almost sigh of infinite relief, a musical sigh that began in C and ran gradually up to F natural, which I think most observant travelers have noticed day and night. No railway official has ever given me a satisfactory explanation of it. As the car, in a rapid run, is always slightly projected forward of its trucks, a practical friend once suggested to me that it was the gradual settling back of the car body to a state of inertia, which, of course, every poetical traveler would reject. Four o'clock the sound of boot-blacking by the porter faintly apparent from the toilet-room. Why not talk to him? But, fortunately, I remembered that any attempt at extended conversation with conductor or porter was always resented by them as implied disloyalty to the company they represented. I recalled that once I had endeavored to impress upon a conductor the absolute folly of a midnight inspection of tickets, and had been treated by him as an escaped lunatic. No, there was no relief from this suffocating and insupportable loneliness to be gained then. I raised the window-blind and looked out. We were passing a farm-house. A light, evidently the lantern of a farm-hand, was swung beside a barn. Yes, the faintest tinge of rose in the far horizon. Morning, surely, at last.

We had stopped at a station. Two men had got into the car, and had taken seats in the one vacant section, yawning occasionally and conversing in a languid, perfunctory sort of way. They sat opposite each other, occasionally looking out of the window, but always giving the strong impression that they were tired of each other's company. As I looked out of my curtains at them, the One Man said, with a feebly concealed yawn:—

"Yes, well, I reckon he was at one time as poplar an ondertaker ez I knew."

The Other Man (inventing a question rather than giving an answer, out of some languid, social impulse): "But was he—this yer ondertaker—a Christian—hed he jined the church?"

The One Man (reflectively): "Well, I don't know ez you might call him a purfessin' Christian; but he hed—yes, he hed conviction. I think Dr. Wylie hed him under conviction. Et least that was the way I got it from *him.*"

A long, dreary pause. The Other Man (feeling it was incumbent upon him to say something): "But why was he poplar ez an ondertaker?"

The One Man (lazily): "Well, he was kinder poplar with widders and widderers—sorter soothen 'em a kinder, keerless way; slung 'em suthin' here and there, sometimes outer the Book, sometimes outer hisself, ez a man of experience as hed hed sorror. Hed, they say (*very cautiously*), lost three wives hisself, and five children by this yer new disease—dipthery—out in Wisconsin. I don't know the facts, but that's what's got round."

The Other Man: "But how did he lose his poplarity?"

The One Man: "Well, that's the question. You see he interduced some things into ondertaking that waz new. He hed, for instance, a way, as he called it, of manniperlating the features of the deceased."

The Other Man (quietly): "How manniperlating?"

The One Man (struck with a bright and aggressive thought): "Look yer, did ye ever notiss how, generally speakin', onhandsome a corpse is?"

The Other Man had noticed this fact.

The One Man (returning to his fact): "Why there was Mary Peebles, ez was daughter of my wife's bosom friend —a mighty pooty girl and a professing Christian—died of scarlet fever. Well, that gal—I was one of the mourners, being my wife's friend—well, that gal, though I hedn't, perhaps, oughter say—lying in that casket, fetched all the way from some A1 establishment in Chicago, filled with flowers and furbelows—didn't really seem to be of much account. Well, although my wife's friend, and me a mourner—well, now, I was—disappointed and discouraged."

The Other Man (in palpably affected sympathy): "Sho! now!"

"Yes, *sir!* Well, you see, this yer ondertaker, this Wilkins, hed a way of correctin' all thet. And just by manniperlation. He worked over the face of the deceased ontil he perduced what the survivin' relatives called a look of resignation,—you know, a sort of smile, like. When he wanted to put in any extrys, he perduced what he called— hevin' reglar charges for this kind of work—a Christian's hope."

The Other Man: "I want to know."

"Yes. Well, I admit, at times it was a little startlin'. And I've allers said (a little confidentially) that I had my doubts of its being Scriptoorl, or sacred, we being, ez you know, worms of the yearth; and I relieved my mind to our pastor, but he didn't feel like interferin', ez long ez it was confined to church membership. But the other day, when Cy Dunham died—you disremember Cy Dunham?"

A long interval of silence. The Other Man was looking out of the window, and had apparently forgotten his companion completely. But as I stretched my head out of the curtain I saw four other heads as eagerly reached out from other berths to hear the conclusion of the story. One head, a female one, instantly disappeared on my looking around, but a certain tremulousness of her window-curtain showed an unabated interest. The only two utterly disinterested men were the One Man and the Other Man.

The Other Man (detaching himself languidly from the window): "Cy Dunham?"

"Yes; Cy never hed hed either convictions or purfessions. Uster get drunk and go round with permiscous women. Sorter like the prodigal son, only a little more so, ez fur ez I kin judge from the facks ez stated to me. Well, Cy one day petered out down at Little Rock, and was sent up yer for interment. The fammerly, being proud-like, of course didn't spare no money on that funeral, and it waz—now between you and me—about ez shapely and first-class and prime-mess affair ez I ever saw. Wilkins hed put in his extrys. He hed put onto that prodigal's face the A1 touch,—hed him fixed up with a 'Christian's hope.' Well, it waz about the turning-point, for thar waz some of the members and the pastor hisself thought that the line oughter to be drawn somewhere, and thar waz some talk at Deacon Tibbet's about a reg'lar conference meetin' regardin' it. But it wasn't thet which made him onpoplar."

Another silence; no expression nor reflection from the face of the Other Man of the least desire to know what ultimately settled the unpopularity of the undertaker. But from the curtains of the various berths several eager and one or two even wrathful faces, anxious for the result.

The Other Man (lazily recurring to the fading topic): "Well, what made him onpoplar?"

The One Man (quietly): "Extrys, I think—that is, I suppose, not knowin'" (cautiously) "all the facts. When Mrs. Widdecombe lost her husband, 'bout two months ago, though she'd been through the valley of the shadder of death twice—this bein' her third marriage, hevin' been John Barker's widder—"

The Other Man (with an intense expression of interest): "No, you're foolin' me!"

The One Man (solemnly): "Ef I was to appear before my Maker to-morrow, yes! she was the widder of Barker."

The Other Man: "Well, I swow."

The One Man: "Well, this Widder Widdecombe, she put up a big funeral for the deceased. She hed Wilkins, and thet ondertaker just laid hisself out. Just spread hisself. Onfort'natly,—perhaps fort'natly in the ways of Providence,—one of Widdecombe's old friends, a doctor up thar in Chicago, comes down to the funeral. He goes up with the friends to look at the deceased, smilin' a peaceful sort o' heavinly smile, and everybody sayin' he's gone to meet his reward, and this yer friend turns round, short and sudden on the widder settin' in her pew, and kinder enjoyin', as wimen will, all the compliments paid the corpse, and he says, says he:—

"'What did you say your husband died of, marm?'

"'Consumption,' she says, wiping her eyes, poor critter. 'Consumption—gallopin' consumption.'

"'Consumption be d—d,' sez he, bein' a profane kind of Chicago doctor, and not bein' ever under conviction. 'Thet man died of strychnine. Look at thet face. Look at thet contortion of them fashal muscles. Thet's strychnine. Thet's *risers Sardonikus'* (thet's what he said; he was always sorter profane).

" 'Why, doctor,' says the widder, 'thet—thet is his last smile. It's a Christian's resignation.'

" 'Thet be blowed; don't tell me,' sez he. 'Hell is full of thet kind of resignation. It's pizon. And I'll—' Why, dern my skin, yes we are; yes, it's Joliet. Wall, now, who'd hev thought we'd been nigh onto an hour."

Two or three anxious passengers from their berths: "Say; look yer, stranger! Old man! What became of—"

But the One Man and the Other Man had vanished.

MORNING ON THE AVENUE

NOTES BY AN EARLY RISER.

I HAVE always been an early riser. The popular legend that "Early to bed and early to rise," invariably and rhythmically resulted in healthfulness, opulence, and wisdom, I beg here to solemnly protest against. As an "unhealthy" man, as an "unwealthy" man, and doubtless by virtue of this protest an "unwise" man, I am, I think, a glaring example of the untruth of the proposition.

For instance, it is my misfortune, as an early riser, to live upon a certain fashionable avenue, where the practice of early rising is confined exclusively to domestics. Consequently, when I issue forth on this broad, beautiful thoroughfare at six A. M., I cannot help thinking that I am, to a certain extent, desecrating its traditional customs.

I have more than once detected the milkman winking at the maid with a diabolical suggestion that I was returning from a carouse, and Roundsman 9999 has once or twice followed me a block or two with the evident impression that I was a burglar returning from a successful evening out. Nevertheless, these various indiscretions have brought me into contact with a kind of character and phenomena whose existence I might otherwise have doubted.

First, let me speak of a large class of working-people whose presence is, I think, unknown to many of those gentlemen who are in the habit of legislating or writing about them. A majority of these early risers in the neighborhood of which I may call my "beat" carry with them unmistakable evidences of the American type. I have seen so little of that foreign element that is popularly supposed to be the real working class of the great metropolis, that I have often been inclined to doubt statistics. The ground that my morning rambles cover extends from Twenty-third

Street to Washington Park, and laterally from Sixth Avenue to Broadway. The early rising artisans that I meet
here, crossing three avenues,—the milkmen, the truck-driv-
ers, the workman, even the occasional tramp,—wherever they
may come from or go to, or what their real *habitat* may be,
—are invariably Americans. I give it as an honest record,
whatever its significance or insignificance may be, that during the last year, between the hours of six and eight A. M.,
in and about the locality I have mentioned, I have met with
but two unmistakable foreigners, an Irishman and a Ger-
man. Perhaps it may be necessary to add to this statement that the people I have met at those early hours I have
never seen at any other time in the same locality.

As to their quality, the artisans were always cleanly
dressed, intelligent, and respectful. I remember, however,
one morning, when the ice storm of the preceding night
had made the sidewalks glistening, smiling and impassable,
to have journeyed down the middle of Twelfth Street with
a mechanic so sooty as to absolutely leave a legible track in
the snowy pathway. He was the fireman attending the engine in a noted manufactory, and in our brief conversation
he told me many facts regarding his profession which I fear
interested me more than the after-dinner speeches of some
distinguished gentlemen I had heard the preceding night.
I remember that he spoke of his engine as "she," and related certain circumstances regarding her inconsistency, her
aberrations, her pettishnesses, that seemed to justify the
feminine gender. I have a grateful recollection of him as
being one who introduced me to a restaurant where chicory,
thinly disguised as coffee, was served with bread at five
cents a cup, and that he honorably insisted on being the
host, and paid his ten cents for our mutual entertainment
with the grace of a Barmecide. I remember, in a more
genial season,—I think early summer,—to have found upon
the benches of Washington Park a gentleman who informed
me that his profession was that of a "pigeon catcher";
that he contracted with certain parties in this city to fur-
nish these birds for what he called their "pigeon-shoots";
and that in fulfilling this contract he often was obliged to
go as far west as Minnesota. The details he gave—his

methods of entrapping the birds, his study of their habits, his evident belief that the city pigeon, however well provided for by parties who fondly believed the bird to be their own, was really *ferae naturae,* and consequently "game" for the pigeon-catcher—were all so interesting that I listened to him with undisguised delight. When he had finished, however, he said, "And now, sir, being a poor man, with a large family, and work bein' rather slack this year, if ye could oblige me with the loan of a dollar and your address, until remittances what I'm expecting come in from Chicago, you'll be doin' me a great service," etc., etc. He got the dollar, of course (his information was worth twice the money), but I imagine he lost my address. Yet it is only fair to say that some days after, relating his experience to a prominent sporting man, he corroborated all its details, and satisfied me that my pigeon-catching friend, although unfortunate, was not an impostor.

And this leads me to speak of the birds. Of all early risers, my most importunate, aggressive, and obtrusive companions are the English sparrows. Between six and seven A. M. they seem to possess the avenue, and resent my intrusion. I remember, one chilly morning, when I came upon a flurry of them, chattering, quarreling, skimming, and alighting just before me. I stopped at last, fearful of stepping on the nearest. To my great surprise, instead of flying away, he contested the ground inch by inch before my advancing foot, with his wings outspread and open bill outstretched, very much like that ridiculous burlesque of the American eagle which the common canary-bird assumes when teased. "Did you ever see 'em wash in the fountain in the square?" said Roundsman 9999, early one summer morning. I had not. "I guess they're there yet. Come and see 'em," he said, and complacently accompanied me two blocks. I don't know which was the finer sight,—the thirty or forty winged sprites, dashing in and out of the basin, each the very impersonation of a light-hearted, mischievous Puck, or this grave policeman, with badge and club and shield, looking on with delight. Perhaps my visible amusement, or the spectacle of a brother policeman just then going past with a couple of "drunk and disorderlies," recalled his official responsibilities and duties. "They say them foreign sparrows drive all the other birds away," he added, severely; and then walked off with a certain reserved manner, as if it were not impossible for him to be called upon some morning to take the entire feathered assembly into custody, and if so called upon he should do it.

Next, I think, in procession among the early risers, and surely next in fresh and innocent exterior, were the workwomen or shop-girls. I have seen this fine avenue on gala afternoons bright with the beauty and elegance of an opulent city, but I have see no more beautiful faces than I have seen among these humbler sisters. As the mere habits of dress in America, except to a very acute critic, give no suggestion of the rank of the wearer, I can imagine an inexperienced foreigner utterly mystified and confounded by these girls, who perhaps work a sewing-machine or walk the long floors of a fashionable dry-goods shop. I remember one face and figure, faultless and complete,—modestly yet most becomingly dressed,—indeed, a figure that Compte-Calix might have taken for one of his exquisite studies, which, between seven and eight A. M. passed through Eleventh Street, between Sixth Avenue and Broadway. So exceptionally fine was her carriage, so chaste and virginal her presence, and so refined and even spiritual her features, that, as a literary man, I would have been justified in taking her for the heroine of a society novel. Indeed, I had already woven a little romance about her, when one morning she overtook me, accompanied by another girl—pretty, but of a different type—with whom she was earnestly conversing. As the two passed me, there fell from her faultless lips the following astounding sentence: "And I told him, if he didn't like it he might lump it, and he traveled off on his left ear, you bet!" Heaven knows what indiscretion this speech saved me from; but the reader will understand what a sting the pain of rejection might have added to it by the above formula.

The "morning-cocktail" men come next in my experience of early rising. I used to take my early cup of coffee in the café of a certain fashionable restaurant that had a bar attached. I could not help noticing that, unlike the usual social libations of my countrymen, the act of taking a morning cocktail was a solitary one. In the course of my experience I cannot recall the fact of two men taking an ante-breakfast cocktail together. On the contrary, I have observed the male animal rush savagely at the bar, demand his drink of the bar-keeper, swallow it, and hasten from the scene of his early debauchery, or else take it in a languid, perfunctory manner, which, I think, must have been insulting to the bar-keeper. I have observed two men, whom I had seen drinking amicably together the preceding night, standing gloomily at the opposite corners of the bar, evidently trying not to see each other and making the matter a confidential one with the bar-keeper. I have seen even a thin disguise of simplicity assumed. I remember an elderly gentleman, of most respectable exterior, who used to enter the café as if he had strayed there accidentally. After looking around carefully, and yet unostentatiously, he would walk to the bar, and, with an air of affected carelessness, state that "not feeling well this morning, he guessed he would take—well, he would leave it to the bar-keeper." The bar-keeper invariably gave him a stiff brandy cocktail. When the old gentleman had done this half a dozen times, I think I lost faith in him. I tried afterwards to glean from the bar-keeper some facts regarding those experiences, but I am proud to say that he was honorably reticent. Indeed, I think it may be said truthfully that there is no record of a bar-keeper who has been "interviewed." Clergymen and doctors have, but it is well for the weakness of humanity that the line should be drawn somewhere.

And this reminds me that one distressing phase of early rising is the incongruous and unpleasant contact of the preceding night. The social yesterday is not fairly over before nine A. M. to-day, and there is always a humorous, sometimes a pathetic, lapping over the edges. I remember one morning at six o'clock to have been overtaken by a carriage that drew up beside me. I recognized the coachman, who touched his hat apologetically, as if he wished me to understand that he was not at all responsible for the condition of his master, and I went to the door of the carriage. I was astonished to find two young friends of mine, in correct evening dress, reclining on each other's shoulders and sleeping the sleep of the justly inebriated. I stated this fact to the coachman. Not a muscle of his well-trained face answered to my smile. But he said: "You see, sir, we've been out all night, and more than four blocks below they saw you, and wanted me to hail you, but you know you stopped to speak to a gentleman, and so I sorter lingered, and I drove round the block once or twice, and I guess I've got 'em quiet again." I looked in the carriage door once more on these sons of Belial. They were sleeping quite unconsciously. A *bouttonnière* in the lappel of the younger one's coat had shed its leaves, which were scattered over him with a ridiculous suggestion of the "Babes in the Wood," and I closed the carriage door softly. "I suppose I'd better take 'em home, sir?" queried the coachman, gravely. "Well, yes, John, perhaps you had."

There is another picture in my early rising experience that I wish was as simply and honestly ludicrous. It was at a time when the moral sentiment of the metropolis, expressed through ordinance and special legislation, had declared itself against a certain form of "variety" entertainment, and had, as usual, proceeded against the performers, and not the people who encouraged them. I remember, one frosty morning, to have encountered in Washington Park my honest friend Sergeant X. and Roundsman 9999 conveying a party of these derelicts to the station. One of the women, evidently, had not had time to change her apparel, and had thinly disguised the flowing robe and loose *cestus* of Venus under a ragged "waterproof"; while the other, who had doubtless posed for Mercury, hid her shapely tights in a plaid shawl, and changed her winged sandals for a pair of "arctics." Their rouged faces were streaked and stained with tears. The man who was with them, the male of their species, had but hastily washed himself of his Ethiopian presentment, and was still black behind the ears; while an exaggerated shirt collar and frilled shirt made his occasional indignant profanity irresistibly ludicrous. So they fared on over the glittering snow, against the rosy sunlight of the square, the gray front of the University building, with a few twittering sparrows in the foreground, beside the two policemen, quiet and impassive as fate. I could not help thinking of the distinguished A., the most fashionable B., the wealthy and respectable C., the sentimental D., and the man of the world E., who were present at the performance, whose distinguished patronage had called it into life, and who were then resting quietly in their beds, while these haggard servants of their pleasaunce were haled over the snow to punishment and ignominy.

Let me finish by recalling one brighter picture of that same season. It was early; so early that the cross of Grace Church had, when I looked up, just caught the morning sun, and for a moment flamed like a crusader's symbol. And then the grace and glory of that exquisite spire became slowly visible. Fret by fret the sunlight stole slowly down, quivering and dropping from each, until at last the whole church beamed in rosy radiance. Up and down the long avenue the street lay in shadow; by some strange trick of the atmosphere the sun seemed to have sought out only that graceful structure for its blessing. And then there was a dull rumble. It was the first omnibus,—the first throb in the great artery of the reviving city. I looked up. The church was again in shadow.

WITH THE ENTRÉES

"ONCE, when I was a pirate—!"

The speaker was an elderly gentleman in correct evening dress, the room a tasteful one, the company of infinite respectability, the locality at once fashionable and exclusive, the occasion an unexceptionable dinner. To this should be added that the speaker was also the host.

With these conditions self-evident, all that good breeding could do was to receive the statement with a vague smile that might pass for good-humored incredulity or courteous acceptation of a simple fact. Indeed, I think we all rather tried to convey the impression that our host, when he *was* a pirate,—if he ever really was one,—was all that a self-respecting pirate should be, and never violated the canons of good society. This idea was, to some extent, crystallized by the youngest Miss Jones in the exclamation, "Oh, how nice!"

"It was, of course, many years ago, when I was quite a lad."

We all murmured "Certainly," as if piracy were a natural expression of the exuberance of youth.

"I ought, perhaps, explain the circumstances that led me into this way of life."

Here Legrande, a courteous attaché of the Patagonian legation, interposed in French and an excess of politeness, "that it was not of a necessity," a statement to which his English neighbor hurriedly responded, *"Oui, oui."*

"There ess a boke," he continued, in a well-bred, rapid whisper, "from Captain Canot,—a Frenchman,—most eenteresting—he was—oh, a fine man of education—and what you call a 'slavair,'" but here he was quietly nudged into respectful silence.

"I ran away from home," continued our host. He paused, and then added, appealingly, to the two distinguished foreigners present: "I do not know if I can make you understand that this is a peculiarly American predilection. The exodus of the younger males of an American family against the parents' wishes does not, with us, necessarily carry any obloquy with it. To the average American the prospect of fortune and a better condition lies *outside* of his home; with you the home means the estate, the succession of honors or titles, the surety that the conditions of life shall all be kept intact. With us the children who do not expect, and generally succeed in improving the fortunes of the house, are marked exceptions. Do I make myself clear?"

The French-Patagonian attaché thought it was "charming and progressif." The Baron Von Pretzel thought he had noticed a movement of that kind in Germany, which was expressed in a single word of seventeen syllables. Viscount Piccadilly said to his neighbor: "That, you know now, the younger sons, don't you see, go to Australia, you know in some beastly trade—stock-raising or sheep—you know; but, by Jove! them fellahs—"

"My father always treated me well," continued our host. "I shared equally with my brothers the privileges and limitations of our New England home. Nevertheless, I ran away and went to sea—"

"To see—what?" asked Legrande.

"*Aller sur mer,*" said his neighbor, hastily.

"Go on with your piracy!" said Miss Jones.

The distinguished foreigners looked at each other and then at Miss Jones. Each made a mental note of the average cold-blooded ferocity of the young American female.

"I shipped on board of a Liverpool 'liner,'" continued our host.

"What ess a 'liner'?" interrupted Legrande, *sotto voce*, to his next neighbor, who pretended not to hear him.

"I need not say that these were the days when we had not lost our carrying trade, when American bottoms—"

"*Que est cé,* 'bot toom'?" said Legrande, imploringly, to his other friend.

"When American bottoms still carried the bulk of freight, and the supremacy of our flag—"

Here Legrande recognized a patriotic sentiment and responded to it with wild republican enthusiasm, nodding his head violently. Piccadilly noticed it, too, and, seeing an opening for some general discussion on free trade, began half audibly to *his* neighbor: "Most extraordinary thing, you know, your American statesmen—"

"I deserted the ship at Liverpool—"

But here two perfunctory listeners suddenly turned toward the other end of the table, where another guest, our Nevada Bonanza lion, was evidently in the full flood of pioneer anecdote and narration. Calmly disregarding the defection, he went on:—

"I deserted the ship at Liverpool in consequence of my ill-treatment by the second mate,—a man selected for his position by reason of his superior physical strength and recognized brutality. I have been since told that he graduated from the state prison. On the second day out I saw him strike a man senseless with a belaying pin for some trifling breach of discipline. I saw him repeatedly beat and kick sick men—"

"Did you ever read Dana's 'Two Years before the Mast'?" asked Lightbody, our heavy literary man, turning to *his* neighbor, in a distinctly audible whisper. "Ah! there's a book! Got all this sort of thing in it. Dev'lishly well written, too."

The Patagonian (alive for information): "What ess this Dana, eh?"

His left hand neighbor (shortly): "Oh, that man!"

His right hand neighbor (curtly): "The fellah who wrote the Encyclopædia and edits 'The Sun'? that was put up in Boston for the English mission and didn't get it."

The Patagonian (making a mental diplomatic note of the fact that the severe discipline of the editor of "The Sun," one of America's profoundest scholars, while acting from patriotic motives, as the second mate of an American "bottom," had unfitted him for diplomatic service abroad): *"Ah, ciel!"*

"I wandered on the quays for a day or two, until I was picked up by a Portuguese sailor, who, interesting himself in my story, offered to procure me a passage to Fayal and Lisbon, where, he assured me, I could find more comfortable and profitable means of returning to my own land. Let me say here that this man, although I knew him afterward as one of the most unscrupulous and heartless of pirates,—in fact the typical buccaneer of the books,—was to me always kind, considerate, and, at times, even tender. He was a capital seaman. I give this evidence in favor of a much ridiculed race, who have been able seamen for centuries."

"Did you ever read that Portuguese Guide-book?" asked Lightbody of his neighbor; "it's the most exquisitely ridiculous thing—"

"Will the great American pirate kindly go on, or resume his original functions," said Miss Jones, over the table, with a significant look in the direction of Lightbody. But her anxiety was instantly misinterpreted by the polite and fair-play loving Englishman: "I say, now, don't you know that the fact is these Portuguese fellahs are always ahead of us in the discovery business? Why, you know—"

"I shipped with him on a brig, ostensibly bound to St. Kitts and a market. We had scarcely left port before I discovered the true character of the vessel. I will not terrify you with useless details. Enough that all that tradition and romance has given you of the pirate's life was ours. Happily, through the kindness of my Portuguese friend, I was kept from being an active participant in scenes of which I was an unwilling witness. But I must always bear my testimony to one fact. Our discipline, our *esprit de corps,* if I may so term it, was perfect. No benevolent society, no moral organization, was ever so personally self-sacrificing, so honestly loyal to one virtuous purpose, as we were to our one vice. The individual was always merged in the purpose. When our captain blew out the brains of our quartermaster, one day—"

"That reminds me—*did* you read of that Georgia murder?" began Lightbody; "it was in all the papers I think. Oh, I beg pardon—"

"For simply interrupting him in a conversation with our second officer," continued our host, quietly. "The act, although harsh and perhaps unnecessarily final, was, I think, indorsed by the crew. James, pass the champagne to Mr. Lightbody."

He paused a moment for the usual casual interruption, but even the active Legrande was silent.

Alas! from the other end of the table came the voice of the Bonanza man:—

"The rope was around her neck. Well, gentlemen, that Mexican woman standing there, with that crowd around her, eager for her blood, dern my skin! if she didn't call out to the sheriff to hold on a minit. And what fer? Ye can't guess! Why, one of them long braids she wore was under the noose, and kinder in the way. I remember her raising her hand to her neck and givin' a spiteful sort of jerk to the braid that fetched it outside the slip-knot, and then saying to the sheriff: 'There, d—n ye, go on.' There was a sort o' thoughtfulness in the act, a kind o' keerless, easy way, that jist fetched the boys—even them thet hed the rope in their hands, and they—" (suddenly recognizing the silence): "Oh, beg pardon, old man; didn't know I'd chipped into your yarn—heave ahead; don't mind me."

"What I am trying to tell you is this: One night, in the Caribbean Sea, we ran into one of the Leeward Islands, that had been in olden time a rendezvous for our ship. We were piloted to our anchorage outside by my Portuguese friend, who knew the locality thoroughly, and on whose dexterity and skill we placed the greatest reliance. If anything more had been necessary to fix this circumstance in my mind, it would have been the fact that two or three days before he had assured me that I should presently have the means of honorable discharge from the pirate's crew, and a return to my native land. A launch was sent from the ship to communicate with our friends on the island, who supplied us with stores, provisions, and general information. The launch was manned by eight men, and officered by the first mate,—a grim, Puritanical, practical New Englander, if I may use such a term to describe a pirate, of great courage, experience, and physical strength. My Portuguese friend, acting as pilot, prevailed upon them to allow me to accompany the party as coxswain. I was naturally anxious, you can readily comprehend, to see—"

"Certainly," "Of course," "Why shouldn't you?" went round the table.

"Two trustworthy men were sent ashore with instructions. We, meanwhile, lay off the low, palm-fringed beach, our crew lying on their oars, or giving way just enough to keep the boat's head to the breakers. The mate and myself sat in the stern sheets, looking shoreward for the signal. The night was intensely black. Perhaps for this reason never before had I seen the phosphorescence of a tropical sea so strongly marked. From the great open beyond, luminous crests and plumes of pale fire lifted themselves, ghost-like, at our bows, sank, swept by us with long, shimmering, undulating trails, broke on the beach in silvery crescents, or shattered their brightness on the black rocks of the promontory. The whole vast sea shone and twinkled like another firmament, against which the figures of our men, sitting with their faces toward us, were outlined darkly. The grim, set features of our first mate, sitting beside me, were faintly illuminated. There was no sound but the whisper of passing waves against our lap-streak, and the low, murmuring conversation of the men. I had my face toward the shore. As I looked over the glimmering expanse, I suddenly heard the whispered name of our first mate. As suddenly, by the phosphorescent light that surrounded it, I saw the long trailing hair and gleaming shoulders of a woman floating beside us. Legrande, you are positively drinking nothing. Lightbody, you are shirking the Burgundy—you used to like it!"

He paused, but no one spoke.

"I—let me see! where was I? Oh, yes! Well, I saw the woman, and when I turned to call the attention of the first mate to this fact, I knew instantly, by some strange instinct, that he had seen and heard her, too. So, from that moment to the conclusion of our little drama, we were silent, but enforced spectators.

"She swam gracefully—silently! I remember noticing through that odd, half-weird, phosphorescent light which broke over her shoulders as she rose and fell with each quiet stroke of her splendidly rounded arms, that she was a mature, perfectly-formed woman. I remember, also, that when she reached the boat, and, supporting herself with one small hand on the gunwale, she softly called the mate in a whisper by his Christian name, I had a boyish idea that she was—the—er—er—female of his species—his—er —natural wife! I'm boring you—am I not?"

Two or three heads shook violently and negatively. The youngest, and, I regret to say, the *oldest*, Miss Jones uttered together sympathetically, "Go on—please; do!"

"The—woman told him in a few rapid words that he had been betrayed; that the two men sent ashore were now in the hands of the authorities; that a force was being organized to capture the vessel; that instant flight was necessary, and that the betrayer and traitor was—my friend, the Portuguese, Fernandez!

"The mate raised the dripping, little brown hand to his lips, and whispered some undistinguishable words in her ear. I remember seeing her turn a look of ineffable love and happiness upon his grim, set face, and then she was gone. She dove as a duck dives, and I saw her shapely head, after a moment's suspense, reappear a cable's length away toward the shore.

"I ventured to raise my eyes to the mate's face; it was cold and impassive. I turned my face toward the crew; they were conversing in whispers with each other, with their faces toward us, yet apparently utterly oblivious of the scene that had just taken place in the stern. There was a moment of silence, and then the mate's voice came out quite impassively, but distinctly:—

" 'Fernandez!'

" 'Aye, aye, sir!'

" 'Come aft and—bring your oar with you.'

"He did so, stumbling over the men, who, engaged in their whispered yarns, didn't seem to notice him.

" 'See if you can find soundings here.'

"Fernandez leaned over the stern and dropped his oar to its shaft in the phosphorescent water. But he touched no bottom; the current brought the oar at right angles presently to the surface.

" 'Send it down, man,' said the mate, imperatively; 'down, down. Reach over there. What are you afraid of? So; steady there; I'll hold you.'

"Frenandez leaned over the stern and sent the oar and

half of his bared brown arm into the water. In an instant the mate caught him with one tremendous potential grip at his elbows, and forced him and his oar head downward in the waters. The act was so sudden, yet so carefully premeditated, that no outcry escaped the doomed man. Even the launch scarcely dipped her stern to the act. In that awful moment I heard a light laugh from one of the men in response to a wanton yarn from his comrade,— James, bring the vichy to Mr. Lightbody! You'll find that a dash of cognac will improve it wonderfully.

"Well—to go on—a few bubbles arose to the surface. Fernandez seemed unreasonably passive, until I saw that when the mate had gripped his elbows with his hands he had also firmly locked the traitor's knees within his own. In a few moments—it seemed to me, then, a century—the mate's grasp relaxed; the body of Fernandez, a mere limp, leaden mass, slipped noiselessly and heavily into the sea. There was no splash. The ocean took it calmly and quietly to its depths. The mate turned to the men, without deigning to cast a glance on me.

" 'Oars!' The men raised their oars apeak.

" 'Let fall!' There was a splash in the water, encircling the boat in concentric lines of molten silver.

" 'Give way!'

"Well, of course, that's all. *We* got away in time. I knew I bored you awfully! Eh? Oh, you want to know what became of the woman—really, I don't know! And myself—oh, I got away at Havana! Eh? Certainly; James, you'll find some smelling salts in my bureau. Gentlemen, I fear we have kept the ladies too long."

But they had already risen, and were slowly filing out of the room. Only one lingered—the youngest Miss Jones.

"That was a capital story," she said, pausing beside our host, with a special significance in her usual audacity. "Do you know you absolutely sent cold chills down my spine a moment ago. Really, now, you ought to write for the magazines!"

Our host looked up at the pretty, audacious face. Then he said, *sotto voce,*—

"I do!"

BY SHORE AND SEDGE

AN APOSTLE OF THE TULES

I

ON October 10, 1856, about four hundred people were camped in Tasajara Valley, California. It could not have been for the prospect, since a more barren, dreary, monotonous, and uninviting landscape never stretched before human eye; it could not have been for convenience or contiguity, as the nearest settlement was thirty miles away; it could not have been for health or salubrity, as the breath of the ague-haunted *tules* in the outlying Stockton marshes swept through the valley; it could not have been for space or comfort, for, encamped on an unlimited plain, men and women were huddled together as closely as in an urban tenement-house, without the freedom or decency of rural isolation; it could not have been for pleasant companionship, as dejection, mental anxiety, tears, and lamentation were the dominant expression; it was not a hurried flight from present or impending calamity, for the camp had been deliberately planned, and for a week pioneer wagons had been slowly arriving; it was not an irrevocable exodus, for some had already returned to their homes that others might take their places. It was simply a religious revival of one or two denominational sects, known as a "camp-meeting."

A large central tent served for the assembling of the principal congregation; smaller tents served for prayer-meetings and class-rooms, known to the few unbelievers as "side-shows"; while the actual dwellings of the worshipers were rudely extemporized shanties of boards and canvas, sometimes mere *corrals* or inclosures open to the cloudless sky, or more often the unhitched covered wagon which had brought them there. The singular resemblance to a circus, already profanely suggested, was carried out by a straggling fringe of boys and half-grown men on the outskirts of the encampment, acrimonious with disappointed curiosity, lazy without the careless ease of vagrancy, and vicious without the excitement of dissipation. For the coarse poverty and brutal economy of the larger arrangements, the dreary panorama of unlovely and unwholesome domestic details always before the eyes, were hardly exciting to the senses. The circus might have been more dangerous, but scarcely more brutalizing. The actors themselves, hard and aggressive through practical struggles, often warped and twisted with chronic forms of smaller diseases, or malformed and crippled through carelessness and neglect, and restless and uneasy through some vague mental distress and inquietude that they had added to their burdens, were scarcely amusing performers. The rheumatic Parkinsons, from Green Springs; the ophthalmic Filgees, from Alder Creek; the ague-stricken Harneys, from Martinez Bend; and the feeble-limbed Steptons, from Sugar Mill, might, in their combined families, have suggested a hospital, rather than any other social assemblage. Even their companionship, which had little of cheerful fellowship in it, would have been grotesque but for the pathetic instinct of some mutual vague appeal from the hardness of their lives and the helplessness of their conditions that had brought them together. Nor was this appeal to a Higher Power any the less pathetic that it bore no reference whatever to their respective needs or deficiencies, but was always an invocation for a light which, when they believed they had found it, to unregenerate eyes scarcely seemed to illumine the rugged path in which their feet were continually stumbling. One might have smiled at the idea of the vendetta-following Ferguses praying for "justification by Faith," but the actual spectacle of old Simon Fergus, whose shot-gun was still in his wagon, offering up that appeal with streaming eyes and agonized features was painful beyond a doubt. To seek and obtain an exaltation of feeling vaguely known as "It," or less vaguely veiling a sacred name, was the burden of the general appeal.

The large tent had been filled, and between the exhortations a certain gloomy enthusiasm had been kept up by singing, which had the effect of continuing in an easy, rhythmical, impersonal, and irresponsible way the sympathies of the meeting. This was interrupted by a young man who rose suddenly, with that spontaneity of impulse which characterized the speakers, but unlike his predecessors, he remained for a moment mute, trembling and irresolute. The fatal hesitation seemed to check the unreasoning, monotonous flow of emotion, and to recall to some extent the reason and even the criticism of the worshipers. He stammered a prayer whose earnestness was undoubted, whose humility was but too apparent, but his words fell on faculties already benumbed by repetition and rhythm. A slight movement of curiosity in the rear benches, and a whisper that it was the maiden effort of a new preacher, helped to prolong the interruption. A heavy man of strong physical expression sprang to the rescue with a hysterical cry of "Glory!" and a tumultuous fluency of epithet and sacred adjuration. Still the meeting wavered. With one final paroxysmal cry, the powerful man threw his arms around his nearest neighbor and burst into silent tears. An anxious hush followed; the speaker still continued to sob on his neighbor's shoulder. Almost before the fact could be commented upon, it was noticed that the entire rank of worshipers on the bench beside him were crying also; the second and third rows were speedily dissolved in tears, until even the very youthful scoffers in the last benches suddenly found their half-hysterical laughter turned to sobs. The danger was averted, the reaction was complete; the singing commenced, and in a few moments the hapless cause of the interruption and the man who had retrieved the disaster stood together outside the tent. A horse was picketed near them.

The victor was still panting from his late exertions, and was more or less diluvial in eye and nostril, but neither eye nor nostril bore the slightest tremor of other expression. His face was stolid and perfectly in keeping with his physique,—heavy, animal, and unintelligent.

"Ye oughter trusted in the Lord," he said to the young preacher.

"But I did," responded the young man, earnestly.

"That's it. Justifyin' yourself by works instead o' leanin' onto Him! Find Him, sez you! Git Him, sez you! Works is vain. Glory! glory!" he continued, with fluent vacuity and wandering, dull, observant eyes.

"But if I had a little more practice in class, Brother Silas, more education?"

"The letter killeth," interrupted Brother Silas. Here his wandering eyes took dull cognizance of two female faces peering through the opening of the tent. "No, yer mishun, Brother Gideon, is to seek Him in the by-ways, in the wilderness,—where the foxes hev holes and the ravens hev their young,—but not in the Temples of the people. Wot sez Sister Parsons?"

One of the female faces detached itself from the tent flaps, which it nearly resembled in color, and brought forward an angular figure clothed in faded fustian that had taken the various shades and odors of household service.

"Brother Silas speaks well," said Sister Parsons, with stridulous fluency. "It's fore-ordained. Fore-ordinashun is better nor ordinashun, saith the Lord. He shall go forth, turnin' neither to the right hand nor the left hand, and seek Him among the lost tribes and the ungodly. He shall put aside the temptashun of Mammon and the flesh." Her eyes and those of Brother Silas here both sought the other female face, which was that of a young girl of seventeen.

"Wot sez little Sister Meely,—wot sez Meely Parsons?" continued Brother Silas, as if repeating an unctuous formula.

The young girl came hesitatingly forward, and with a nervous cry of "Oh, Gideon!" threw herself on the breast of the young man.

For a moment they remained locked in each other's arms. In the promiscuous and fraternal embracings which were a part of the devotional exercises of the hour, the act passed without significance. The young man gently raised her face. She was young and comely, albeit marked with a half-frightened, half-vacant sorrow. "Amen," said Brother Gideon, gravely.

He mounted his horse and turned to go. Brother Silas had clasped his powerful arms around both women and was holding them in a ponderous embrace.

"Go forth, young man, into the wilderness."

The young man bowed his head, and urged his horse forward in the bleak and barren plain. In half an hour every vestige of the camp and its unwholesome surroundings was lost in the distance. It was as if the strong desiccating wind, which seemed to spring up at his horse's feet, had cleanly erased the flimsy structures from the face of the plain, swept away the lighter breath of praise and plaint, and dried up the easy-flowing tears. The air was harsh but pure; the grim economy of form and shade and color in the level plain was coarse but not vulgar; the sky above him was cold and distant but not repellent; the moisture that had been denied his eyes at the prayer-meeting here; the words that had choked his utterance an hour ago now rose to his lips. He threw himself from his horse, and kneeling in the withered grass— a mere atom in the boundless plain—lifted his pale face against the irresponsive blue and prayed.

He prayed that the unselfish dream of his bitter boyhood, his disappointed youth, might come to pass. He prayed that he might in higher hands become the humble instrument of good to his fellow-man. He prayed that the deficiencies of his scant education, his self-taught learning, his helpless isolation, and his inexperience might be overlooked or reinforced by grace. He prayed that the Infinite Compassion might enlighten his ignorance and solitude with a manifestation of the Spirit; in his very weakness he prayed for some special revelation, some sign or token, some visitation or gracious unbending from that coldly lifting sky. The low sun burned the black edge of the distant *tules* with dull eating fires as he prayed, lit the dwarfed hills with a brief but ineffectual radiance, and then died out. The lingering trade winds fired a few volleys over its grave and then lapsed into a chilly silence. The young man staggered to his feet; it was quite dark now, but the coming night had advanced a few starry vedettes so near the plain they looked like human watch-fires. For an instant he could not remember where he was. Then a light trembled far down at the entrance of the valley. Brother Gideon recognized it. It was in the lonely farmhouse of the widow of the last Circuit preacher.

II

The abode of the late Reverend Marvin Hiler remained in the disorganized condition he had left it when removed from his sphere of earthly uselessness and continuous accident. The straggling fence that only half inclosed the house and barn had stopped at that point where the two deacons who had each volunteered to do a day's work on it had completed their allotted time. The building of the barn had been arrested when the half load of timber contributed by Sugar Mill brethren was exhausted, and three windows given by "Christian Seekers" at Martinez painfully accented the boarded spaces for the other three that "Unknown Friends" in Tasajara had promised but not yet supplied. In the clearing some trees that had been felled but not taken away added to the general incompleteness.

Something of this unfinished character clung to the Widow Hiler and asserted itself in her three children, one of whom was consistently posthumous. Prematurely old and prematurely disappointed, she had all the inexperience of girlhood with the cares of maternity, and kept in her family circle the freshness of an old maid's misogynistic antipathies with a certain guilty and remorseful consciousness of widowhood. She supported the meagre household to which her husband had contributed only the extra mouths to feed with reproachful astonishment and weary incapacity. She had long since grown tired of trying to make both ends meet, of which she declared "the Lord had taken one." During her two years' widowhood she had waited on Providence, who by a pleasing local fiction had been made responsible for the disused and cast-off furniture and clothing which, accompanied with scriptural texts, found their way mysteriously into her few habitable rooms. The providential manna was not always fresh; the ravens who fed her and her little ones with flour from the Sugar Mills did not always select the best quality. Small wonder that, sitting by her lonely hearthstone,—a borrowed stove that supplemented the unfinished fireplace,—surrounded by her mismatched furniture and clad in misfitting garments, she had contracted a habit of sniffling during her dreary watches. In her weaker moments she attributed it to grief; in her stronger intervals she knew that it sprang from damp and draught.

In her apathy the sound of horses' hoofs at her unprotected door even at that hour neither surprised nor alarmed her. She lifted her head as the door opened and the pale face of Gideon Deane looked into the room. She moved aside the cradle she was rocking, and, taking a saucepan and tea-cup from a chair beside her, absently dusted it with her apron, and pointing to the vacant seat said, "Take a chair," as quietly as if he had stepped from the next room instead of the outer darkness.

"I'll put up my horse first," said Gideon gently.

"So do," responded the widow briefly.

Gideon led his horse across the inclosure, stumbling over the heaps of rubbish, dried chips, and weather-beaten shavings with which it was strewn, until he reached the unfinished barn, where he temporarily bestowed his beast. Then taking a rusty axe, by the faint light of the stars, he attacked one of the fallen trees with such energy that at the end of ten minutes he reappeared at the door with an armful of cut boughs and chips, which he quietly deposited behind the stove. Observing that he was still standing as if looking for something, the widow lifted her eyes and said, "Ef it's the bucket, I reckon ye'll find it at the spring, where one of them foolish Filgee boys left it. I've been that tuckered out sens sundown, I ain't had the ambition to go and tote it back." Without a word Gideon repaired to the spring, filled the missing bucket, replaced the hoop on the loosened staves of another he found lying useless beside it, and again returned to the house. The widow once more pointed to the chair, and Gideon sat down. "It's quite a spell sens you wos here," said the Widow Hiler, returning her foot to the cradle-rocker; "not sens yer was ordained. Be'n practicin', I reckon, at the meetin'."

A slight color came into his cheek. "My place is not there, Sister Hiler," he said gently; "it's for those with the gift o' tongues. I go forth only a common laborer in the vineyard." He stopped and hesitated; he might have said more, but the widow, who was familiar with that kind of humility as the ordinary perfunctory expression of her class, suggested no sympathetic interest in his mission.

"Thar's a deal o' talk over there," she said dryly, "and thar's folks ez thinks thar's a deal o' money spent in picnicking the Gospel that might be given to them ez wish to spread it, or to their widows and children. But that don't consarn you, Brother Gideon. Sister Parsons hez money enough to settle her darter Meely comfortably on her own land; and I've heard tell that you and Meely was only waitin' till you was ordained to be jined together. You'll hev an easier time of it, Brother Gideon, than poor Marvin Hiler had," she continued, suppressing her tears with a certain astringency that took the place of her lost pride; "but the Lord wills that some should be tried and some not."

"But I am not going to marry Meely Parsons," said Gideon quietly.

The widow took her foot from the rocker. "Not marry Meely!" she repeated vaguely. But relapsing into her despondent mood she continued: "Then I reckon it's true what other folks sez of Brother Silas Braggley makin' up to her and his powerful exhortin' influence over her ma. Folks sez ez Sister Parsons hez just resigned her soul inter his keepin'."

"Brother Silas hez a heavenly gift," said the young man, with gentle enthusiasm; "and perhaps it may be so. If it is, it is the Lord's will. But I do not marry Meely because my life and my ways henceforth must lie far beyond her sphere of strength. I oughtn't to drag a young inexperienced soul with me to battle and struggle in the thorny paths that I must tread."

"I reckon you know your own mind," said Sister Hiler grimly. "But thar's folks ez might allow that Meely Parsons ain't any better than others, that she shouldn't have her share o' trials and keers and crosses. Riches and bringin' up don't exempt folks from the shadder. I married Marvin Hiler outer a house ez good ez Sister Parsons', and at a time when old Cyrus Parsons hadn't a roof to his head but the cover of the emigrant wagon he kem across the plains in. I might say ez Marvin knowed pretty well wot it was to have a helpmeet in his ministration, if it wasn't vanity of sperit to say it now. But the flesh is weak, Brother Gideon." Her influenza here resolved itself into unmistakable tears, which she wiped away with the first article that was accessible in the work-bag before her. As it chanced to be a black silk neckerchief of the deceased Hiler, the result was funereal, suggestive, but practically ineffective.

"You were a good wife to Brother Hiler," said the young man gently. "Everybody knows that."

"It's suthin' to think of since he's gone," continued the widow, bringing her work nearer to her eyes to adjust it to their tear-dimmed focus. "It's suthin' to lay to heart in the lonely days and nights when thar's no man round to fetch water and wood and lend a hand to doin' chores; it's suthin' to remember, with his three children to feed, and little Selby, the eldest, that vain and useless that he can't even tote the baby round while I do the work of a hired man."

"It's a hard trial, Sister Hiler," said Gideon, "but the Lord has His appointed time."

Familiar as consolation by vague quotation was to Sister Hiler, there was an occult sympathy in the tone in which this was offered that lifted her for an instant out of her narrower self. She raised her eyes to his. The personal abstraction of the devotee had no place in the deep dark eyes that were lifted from the cradle to hers with a sad, discriminating, and almost womanly sympathy. Surprised out of her selfish preoccupation, she was reminded of her apparent callousness to what might be his present disappointment. Perhaps it seemed strange to her, too, that those tender eyes should go a-begging.

"Yer takin' a Christian view of yer own disappointment, Brother Gideon," she said, with less astringency of manner; "but every heart knoweth its own sorrer. I'll be gettin' supper now that the baby's sleepin' sound, and ye'll sit by and eat."

"If you let me help you, Sister Hiler," said the young man with a cheerfulness that belied any overwhelming

heart affection, and awakened in the widow a feminine
curiosity as to his real feelings to Meely. But her further
questioning was met with a frank, amiable, and simple
brevity that was as puzzling as the most artful periphrase
of tact. Accustomed as she was to the loquacity of grief
and the confiding prolixity of disappointed lovers, she could
not understand her guest's quiescent attitude. Her curiosity, however, soon gave way to the habitual contemplation
of her own sorrows, and she could not forego the op-
portune presence of a sympathizing auditor to whom she
could relieve her feelings. The preparations for the evening meal were therefore accompanied by a dreary monotone
of lamentation. She bewailed her lost youth, her brief
courtship, the struggles of her early married life, her premature widowhood, her penurious and helpless existence,
the disruption of all her present ties, the hopelessness of
the future. She rehearsed the unending plaint of those
long evenings, set to the music of the restless wind around
her bleak dwelling, with something of its stridulous re-
iteration. The young man listened, and replied with softly
assenting eyes, but without pausing in the material aid that
he was quietly giving her. He had removed the cradle of
the sleeping child to the bedroom, quieted the sudden wakefulness of "Pinkey," rearranged the straggling furniture
of the sitting-room with much order and tidiness, repaired
the hinges of a rebellious shutter and the lock of an un-
yielding door, and yet had apparently retained an unabated
interest in her spoken woes. Surprised once more into
recognizing this devotion, Sister Hiler abruptly arrested
her monologue.

"Well, if you ain't the handiest man I ever seed about
a house!"

"Am I?" said Gideon, with suddenly sparkling eyes.
"Do you really think so?"

"I do."

"Then you don't know how glad I am." His frank face
so unmistakably showed his simple gratification that the
widow, after gazing at him for a moment, was suddenly
seized with a bewildering fancy. The first effect of it was
the abrupt withdrawal of her eyes, then a sudden effusion of

blood to her forehead that finally extended to her cheek-bones, and then an interval of forgetfulness where she remained with a plate held vaguely in her hand. When she succeeded at last in putting it on the table instead of the young man's lap, she said in a voice quite unlike her own,—

"Sho!"

"I mean it," said Gideon, cheerfully. After a pause, in which he unostentatiously rearranged the table which the widow was abstractedly disorganizing, he said gently, "After tea, when you're not so much flustered with work and worry, and more composed in spirit, we'll have a little talk, Sister Hiler. I'm in no hurry to-night, and if you don't mind I'll make myself comfortable in the barn with my blanket until sun-up to-morrow. I can get up early enough to do some odd chores round the lot before I go."

"You know best, Brother Gideon," said the widow, faintly, "and if you think it's the Lord's will, and no speshal trouble to you, so do. But sakes alive! it's time I tidied myself a little," she continued, lifting one hand to her hair, while with the other she endeavored to fasten a buttonless collar; "leavin' alone the vanities o' dress, it's ez much as one can do to keep a clean rag on with the children climbin' over ye. Sit by, and I'll be back in a minit." She retired to the back room, and in a few moments returned with smoothed hair and a palm-leaf broché shawl thrown over her shoulders, which not only concealed the ravages made by time and maternity on the gown beneath, but to some extent gave her the suggestion of being a casual visitor in her own household. It must be confessed that for the rest of the evening Sister Hiler rather lent herself to this idea, possibly from the fact that it temporarily obliterated the children, and quite removed her from any responsibility in the unpicturesque household. This effect was only marred by the absence of any impression upon Gideon, who scarcely appeared to notice the change, and whose soft eyes seemed rather to identify the miserable woman under her forced disguise. He prefaced the meal with a fervent grace, to which the widow listened with something of the conscious attitude she had adopted at church during her late husband's ministration, and during the meal she ate with a like consciousness of "company manners."

Later that evening Selby Hiler woke up in his little truckle bed, listening to the rising midnight wind, which in his childish fancy he confounded with the sound of voices that came through the open door of the living-room. He recognized the deep voice of the young minister, Gideon, and the occasional tearful responses of his mother, and he was fancying himself again at church when he heard a step, and the young preacher seemed to enter the room, and going to the bed leaned over it and kissed him on the forehead, and then bent over his little brother and sister and kissed them too. Then he slowly reëntered the living-room. Lifting himself softly on his elbow, Selby saw him go up towards his mother, who was crying, with her head on the table, and kiss her also on the forehead. Then he said "Good-night," and the front door closed, and Selby heard his footsteps crossing the lot towards the barn. His mother was still sitting with her face buried in her hands when he fell asleep.

She sat by the dying embers of the fire until the house was still again; then she rose and wiped her eyes. "Et's a good thing," she said, going to the bedroom door, and looking in upon her sleeping children; "et's a mercy and a blessing for them and—for—me. But—but—he might—hev—said—he——loved me!"

III

Although Gideon Deane contrived to find a nest for his blanket in the mouldy straw of the unfinished barn loft, he could not sleep. He restlessly watched the stars through the cracks of the boarded roof, and listened to the wind that made the half-open structure as vocal as a sea-shell, until past midnight. Once or twice he had fancied he heard the tramp of horse-hoofs on the far-off trail, and now it seemed to approach nearer, mingled with the sound of voices. Gideon raised his head and looked through the doorway of the loft. He was not mistaken: two men had

halted in the road before the house, and were examining
it as if uncertain if it were the dwelling they were seeking, and were hesitating if they should rouse the inmates.
Thinking he might spare the widow this disturbance to
her slumbers, and possibly some alarm, he rose quickly,
and descending to the inclosure walked towards the house.
As he approached the men advanced to meet him, and
by accident or design ranged themselves on either
side. A glance showed him they were strangers to the
locality.

"We're lookin' fer the preacher that lives here," said
one, who seemed to be the elder. "A man by the name o'
Hiler, I reckon!"

"Brother Hiler has been dead two years," responded Gideon. "His widow and children live here."

The two men looked at each other. The younger one
laughed; the elder mumbled something about its being
"three years ago," and then turning suddenly on Gideon,
said:

"P'r'aps *you're* a preacher?"

"I am."

"Can you come to a dying man?"

"I will."

The two men again looked at each other. "But," continued Gideon, softly, "you'll please keep quiet so as not
to disturb the widow and her children, while I get my
horse." He turned away; the younger man made a movement as if to stop him, but the elder quickly restrained his
hand. "He isn't goin' to run away," he whispered. "Look,"
he added, as Gideon a moment later reappeared mounted
and equipped.

"Do you think we'll be in time?" asked the young
preacher as they rode quickly away in the direction of the
tules.

The younger repressed a laugh; the other answered
grimly, "I reckon."

"And is he conscious of his danger?"

"I reckon."

Gideon did not speak again. But as the onus of that
silence seemed to rest upon the other two, the last speaker,

after a few moments' silent and rapid riding, continued abruptly, "You don't seem curious?"

"Of what?" said Gideon, lifting his soft eyes to the speaker. "You tell me of a brother at the point of death, who seeks the Lord through an humble vessel like myself. *He* will tell me the rest."

A silence still more constrained on the part of the two strangers followed, which they endeavored to escape from by furious riding; so that in half an hour the party had reached a point where the tules began to sap the arid plain, while beyond them broadened the lagoons of the distant river. In the foreground, near a clump of dwarfed willows, a camp-fire was burning, around which fifteen or twenty armed men were collected, their horses picketed in an outer circle guarded by two mounted sentries. A blasted cotton-wood with a single black arm extended over the tules stood ominously against the dark sky.

The circle opened to receive them and closed again. The elder man dismounted and leading Gideon to the blasted cotton-wood, pointed to a pinioned man seated at its foot with an armed guard over him. He looked up at Gideon with an amused smile.

"You said it was a dying man," said Gideon, recoiling.

"He will be a dead man in half an hour," returned the stranger.

"And you?"

"We are the Vigilantes from Alamo. This man," pointing to the prisoner, "is a gambler who killed a man yesterday. We hunted him here, tried him an hour ago, and found him guilty. The last man we hung here, three years ago, asked for a parson. We brought him the man who used to live where we found you. So we thought we'd give this man the same show, and brought you."

"And if I refuse?" said Gideon.

The leader shrugged his shoulders.

"That's *his* lookout, not ours. We've given him the chance. Drive ahead, boys," he added, turning to the others; "the parson allows he won't take a hand."

"One moment," said Gideon, in desperation, "one moment, for the sake of that God you have brought me here to invoke in behalf of this wretched man. One moment, for the sake of Him in whose presence you must stand one day as he does now." With passionate earnestness he pointed out the vindictive impulse they were mistaking for Divine justice; with pathetic fervency he fell upon his knees and implored their mercy for the culprit. But in vain. As at the camp-meeting of the day before, he was chilled to find his words seemed to fall on unheeding and unsympathetic ears. He looked around on their abstracted faces; in their gloomy savage enthusiasm for expiatory sacrifice, he was horrified to find the same unreasoning exaltation that had checked his exhortations then. Only one face looked upon his, half mischievously, half compassionately. It was the prisoner's.

"Yer wastin' time on us," said the leader, dryly; "wastin' *his* time. Hadn't you better talk to him?"

Gideon rose to his feet, pale and cold. "He may have something to confess. May I speak with him alone?" he said gently.

The leader motioned to the sentry to fall back. Gideon placed himself before the prisoner so that in the faint light of the camp-fire the man's figure was partly hidden by his own. "You meant well with your little bluff, pardner," said the prisoner, not unkindly, "but they've got the cards to win."

"Kneel down with your back to me," said Gideon, in a low voice. The prisoner fell on his knees. At the same time he felt Gideon's hand and the gliding of steel behind his back, and the severed cords hung loosely on his arms and legs.

"When I lift my voice to God, brother," said Gideon, softly, "drop on your face and crawl as far as you can in a straight line in my shadow, then break for the tules. I will stand between you and their first fire."

"Are you mad?" said the prisoner. "Do you think they won't fire lest they should hurt you? Man! they'll kill *you*, the first thing."

"So be it—if your chance is better."

Still on his knees, the man grasped Gideon's two hands in his own and devoured him with his eyes.

"You mean it?"

"I do."

"Then," said the prisoner, quietly, "I reckon I'll stop and hear what you've got to say about God until they're ready."

"You refuse to fly?"

"I reckon I was never better fitted to die than now," said the prisoner, still grasping his hand. After a pause he added in a lower tone, "I can't pray—but—I think," he hesitated, "I think I could manage to ring in a hymn."

"Will you try, brother?"

"Yes."

With their hands tightly clasped together, Gideon lifted his gentle voice. The air was a common one, familiar in the local religious gatherings, and after the first verse one or two of the sullen lookers-on joined unkindly in the refrain. But, as he went on, the air and words seemed to offer a vague expression to the dull lowering animal emotion of the savage concourse, and at the end of the second verse the refrain, augmented in volume and swelled by every voice in the camp, swept out over the hollow plain.

It was met in the distance by a far-off cry. With an oath taking the place of his supplication, the leader sprang to his feet. But too late! The cry was repeated as a nearer slogan of defiance—the plain shook—there was the tempestuous onset of furious hoofs—a dozen shots—the scattering of the embers of the camp-fire into a thousand vanishing sparks even as the lurid gathering of savage humanity was dispersed and dissipated over the plain, and Gideon and the prisoner stood alone. But as the sheriff of Contra Costa with his rescuing *posse* swept by, the man they had come to save fell forward in Gideon's arms with a bullet in his breast—the Parthian shot of the flying Vigilante leader.

The eager crowd that surged around him with outstretched helping hands would have hustled Gideon aside. But the wounded man roused himself, and throwing an arm around the young preacher's neck, warned them back with the other. "Stand back!" he gasped. "He risked his life for mine! Look at him, boys! Wanted ter stand up 'twixt them hounds and me and draw their fire on himself! Ain't he just hell?" he stopped; an apologetic smile crossed his lips. "I clean forgot, pardner; but it's all right. I said I was ready to go; and I am." His arm slipped from Gideon's neck; he slid to the ground; he had fainted.

A dark, military-looking man pushed his way through the crowd—the surgeon, one of the *posse*, accompanied by a younger man fastidiously dressed. The former bent over the unconscious prisoner, and tore open his shirt; the latter followed his movements with a flush of anxious inquiry in his handsome, careless face. After a moment's pause the surgeon, without looking up, answered the young man's mute questioning. "Better send the sheriff here at once, Jack."

"He is here," responded the official, joining the group.

The surgeon looked up at him. "I am afraid they've put the case out of your jurisdiction, Sheriff," he said grimly. "It's only a matter of a day or two at best— perhaps only a few hours. But he won't live to be taken back to jail."

"Will he live to go as far as Martinez?" asked the young man addressed as Jack.

"With care, perhaps."

"Will you be responsible for him, Jack Hamlin?" said the sheriff, suddenly.

"I will."

"Then take him. Stay, he's coming to."

The wounded man slowly opened his eyes. They fell upon Jack Hamlin with a pleased look of recognition, but almost instantly and anxiously glanced around as if seeking another. Leaning over him, Jack said gayly, "They've passed you over to me, old man; are you willing?"

The wounded man's eyes assented, but still moved restlessly from side to side.

"Is there any one you want to go with you?"

"Yes," said the eyes.

"The doctor, of course?"

The eyes did not answer. Gideon dropped on his knees beside him. A ray of light flashed in the helpless man's eyes and transfigured his whole face.

"You want *him?*" said Jack incredulously.

"Yes," said the eyes.

"What—the preacher?"

The lips struggled to speak. Everybody bent down to hear his reply.

"You bet," he said faintly.

IV

It was early morning when the wagon containing the wounded man, Gideon, Jack Hamlin, and the surgeon crept slowly through the streets of Martinez and stopped before the door of the "Palmetto Shades." The upper floor of this saloon and hostelry was occupied by Mr. Hamlin as his private lodgings, and was fitted up with the usual luxury and more than the usual fastidiousness of his extravagant class. As the dusty and travel-worn party trod the soft carpets and brushed aside their silken hangings in their slow progress with their helpless burden to the lace-canopied and snowy couch of the young gambler, it seemed almost a profanation of some feminine seclusion. Gideon, to whom such luxury was unknown, was profoundly troubled. The voluptuous ease and sensuousness, the refinements of a life of irresponsible indulgence, affected him with a physical terror to which in his late moment of real peril he had been a stranger; the gilding and mirrors blinded his eyes; even the faint perfume seemed to him an unhallowed incense, and turned him sick and giddy. Accustomed as he had been to disease and misery in its humblest places and meanest surroundings, the wounded desperado lying in laces and fine linen seemed to him monstrous and unnatural. It required all his self-abnegation, all his sense of duty, all his deep pity, and all the instinctive tact which was born of his gentle thoughtfulness for others, to repress a shrinking. But when the miserable cause of all again opened his eyes and sought Gideon's hand, he forgot it all. Happily, Hamlin, who had been watching him with wondering but critical eyes, mistook his concern. "Don't you worry about that gin-mill and hash-gymnasium downstairs," he said. "I've given the proprietor a thousand dollars to shut up shop as long as this thing lasts." That this was done from some delicate sense of respect to the preacher's domiciliary presence, and not entirely to secure complete quiet and seclusion for the invalid, was evident from the fact that Mr. Hamlin's drawing and dining rooms, and even the hall, were filled with eager friends and inquirers. It was discomposing to Gideon to find himself almost an equal subject of interest and curiosity to the visitors. The story of his simple devotion had lost nothing by report; hats were doffed in his presence that might have grown to their wearers' heads; the boldest eyes dropped as he passed by; he had only to put his pale face out of the bedroom door and the loudest discussion, heated by drink or affection, fell to a whisper. The surgeon, who had recognized the one dominant wish of the hopelessly sinking man, gravely retired, leaving Gideon a few simple instructions and directions for their use. "He'll last as long as he has need of you," he said respectfully. "My art is only second here. God help you both! When he wakes, make the most of your time."

In a few moments he did waken, and as before turned his fading look almost instinctively on the faithful, gentle eyes that were watching him. How Gideon made the most of his time did not transpire, but at the end of an hour, when the dying man had again lapsed into unconsciousness, he softly opened the door of the sitting-room.

Hamlin started hastily to his feet. He had cleared the room of his visitors, and was alone. He turned a moment towards the window before he faced Gideon with inquiring but curiously-shining eyes.

"Well?" he said, hesitatingly.

"Do you know Kate Somers?" asked Gideon.

Hamlin opened his brown eyes. "Yes."

"Can you send for her?"

"What, *here?*"

"Yes, here."

"What for?"

"To marry him," said Gideon, gently. "There's no time to lose."

"To *marry* him?"

"He wishes it."

"But say—oh, come, now," said Hamlin confidentially, leaning back with his hands on the top of a chair. "Ain't this playing it a little—just a *little*—too low down? Of course you mean well, and all that; but come, now, say— couldn't you just let up on him there? Why, she"—Hamlin softly closed the door—"she's got no character."

"The more reason he should give her one."

A cynical knowledge of matrimony imparted to him by the wives of others evidently colored Mr. Hamlin's views. "Well, perhaps it's all the same if he's going to die. But isn't it rather rough on *her*? I don't know," he added, reflectively; "she was sniveling round here a little while ago, until I sent her away."

"You sent her away!" echoed Gideon.

"I did."

"Why?"

"Because *you* were here."

Nevertheless Mr. Hamlin departed, and in half an hour reappeared with two brilliantly dressed women. One, hysterical, tearful, frightened, and pallid, was the destined bride; the other, highly colored, excited, and pleasedly observant, was her friend. Two men hastily summoned from the anteroom as witnesses completed the group that moved into the bedroom and gathered round the bed.

The ceremony was simple and brief. It was well, for of all who took part in it none was more shaken by emotion than the officiating priest. The brilliant dresses of the women, the contrast of their painted faces with the waxen pallor of the dying man; the terrible incongruity of their voices, inflections, expressions, and familiarity; the mingled perfume of cosmetics and the faint odor of wine; the eyes of the younger woman following his movements with strange absorption, so affected him that he was glad when he could fall on his knees at last and bury his face in the pillow of the sufferer. The hand that had been placed in the bride's cold fingers slipped from them and mechanically sought Gideon's again. The significance of the unconscious act brought the first spontaneous tears into the woman's eyes.

It was his last act, for when Gideon's voice was again lifted in prayer, the spirit for whom it was offered had risen with it, as it were, still lovingly hand in hand, from the earth forever.

The funeral was arranged for two days later, and Gideon found that his services had been so seriously yet so humbly counted upon by the friends of the dead man that he could scarce find it in his heart to tell them that it was the function of the local preacher—an older and more experienced man than himself. "If it is," said Jack Hamlin, coolly, "I'm afraid he won't get a yaller dog to come to his church; but if you say you'll preach at the grave, there ain't a man, woman, or child that will be kept away. Don't you go back on your luck, now; it's something awful and nigger-like. You've got this crowd where the hair is short; excuse me, but it's so. Talk of revivals! You could give that one-horse show in Tasajara a hundred points, and skunk them easily." Indeed, had Gideon been accessible to vanity, the spontaneous homage he met with everywhere would have touched him more sympathetically and kindly than it did; but in the utter unconsciousness of his own power and the quality they worshiped in him, he felt alarmed and impatient of what he believed to be their weak sympathy with his own human weakness. In the depth of his unselfish heart, lit, it must be confessed, only by the scant, inefficient lamp of his youthful experience, he really believed he had failed in his apostolic mission because he had been unable to touch the hearts of the Vigilantes by oral appeal and argument. Feeling thus the reverence of these irreligious people that surrounded him, the facile yielding of their habits and prejudices to his half-uttered wish, appeared to him only a temptation of the flesh. No one had sought him after the manner of the camp-meeting; he had converted the wounded man through a common weakness of their humanity. More than that, he was conscious of a growing fascination for the truthfulness and sincerity of that class; particularly of Mr. Jack Hamlin, whose conversion he felt he could never attempt, yet whose strange friendship alternately thrilled and frightened him.

It was the evening before the funeral. The coffin, half

smothered in wreaths and flowers, stood upon trestles in the anteroom; a large silver plate bearing an inscription on which for the second time Gideon read the name of the man he had converted. It was a name associated on the frontier so often with reckless hardihood, dissipation, and blood, that even now Gideon trembled at his presumption, and was chilled by a momentary doubt of the efficiency of his labor. Drawing unconsciously nearer to the mute subject of his thoughts, he threw his arms across the coffin and buried his face between them.

A stream of soft music, the echo of some forgotten song, seemed to Gideon to suddenly fill and possess the darkened room, and then to slowly die away, like the opening and shutting of a door upon a flood of golden radiance. He listened with hushed breath and a beating heart. He had never heard anything like it before. Again the strain arose, the chords swelled round him, until from their midst a tenor voice broke high and steadfast, like a star in troubled skies. Gideon scarcely breathed. It was a hymn—but such a hymn. He had never conceived there could be such beautiful words, joined to such exquisite melody, and sung with a grace so tender and true. What were all other hymns to this ineffable yearning for light, for love, and for infinite rest? Thrilled and exalted, Gideon felt his doubts pierced and scattered by that illuminating cry. Suddenly he rose, and with a troubled thought pushed open the door to the sitting-room. It was Mr. Jack Hamlin sitting before a parlor organ. The music ceased.

"It was *you*," stammered Gideon.

Jack nodded, struck a few chords by way of finish, and then wheeled round on the music-stool towards Gideon. His face was slightly flushed. "Yes. I used to be the organist and tenor in our church in the States. I used to snatch the sinners bald-headed with that. Do you know I reckon I'll sing that to-morrow, if you like, and maybe afterwards we'll—but"—he stopped—"we'll talk of that after the funeral. It's business." Seeing Gideon still glancing with a troubled air from the organ to himself, he said: "Would you like to try that hymn with me? Come on!"

He again struck the chords. As the whole room seemed

to throb with the music, Gideon felt himself again carried away. Glancing over Jack's shoulders, he could read the words but not the notes; yet, having a quick ear for rhythm, he presently joined in with a deep but uncultivated baritone. Together they forgot everything else, and at the end of an hour were only recalled by the presence of a silently admiring concourse of votive-offering friends who had gathered round them.

The funeral took place the next day at the grave dug in the public cemetery—a green area fenced in by the palisading tules. The words of Gideon were brief but humble; the strongest partisan of the dead man could find no fault in a confession of human frailty in which the speaker humbly confessed his share; and when the hymn was started by Hamlin and taken up by Gideon, the vast multitude, drawn by interest and curiosity, joined as in a solemn Amen.

Later, when those two strangely-assorted friends had returned to Mr. Hamlin's rooms previous to Gideon's departure, the former, in a manner more serious than his habitual cynical good-humor, began: "I said I had to talk business with you. The boys about here want to build a church for you, and are ready to plank the money down if you'll say it's a go. You understand they aren't asking you to run in opposition to that Gospel sharp—excuse me—that's here now, nor do they want you to run a side show in connection with it. They want you to be independent. They don't pin you down to any kind of religion, you know; whatever you care to give them—Methodist, Roman Catholic, Presbyterian—is mighty good enough for them, if you'll expound it. You might give a little of each, or one on one day and one another—they'll never know the difference if you only mix the drinks yourself. They'll give you a house and guarantee you fifteen hundred dollars the first year."

He stopped and walked towards the window. The sunlight that fell upon his handsome face seemed to call back the careless smile to his lips and the reckless fire to his brown eyes. "I don't suppose there's a man among them that wouldn't tell you all this in a great deal better way than I do. But the darned fools—excuse me—would have *me* break it to you. Why, I don't know. I needn't tell you I like you—not only for what you did for George—but I like you for your style—for yourself. And I want you to accept. You could keep these rooms till they got a house ready for you. Together—you and me—we'd make that organ howl. But because I like it—because it's everything to us—and nothing to you, it don't seem square for me to ask it. Does it?"

Gideon replied by taking Hamlin's hand. His face was perfectly pale, but his look collected. He had not expected this offer, and yet when it was made he felt as if he had known it before—as if he had been warned of it—as if it was the great temptation of his life. Watching him with an earnestness only slightly overlaid by his usual manner, Hamlin went on.

"I know it would be lonely here, and a man like you ought to have a wife for—" he slightly lifted his eyebrows —"for example's sake. I heard there was a young lady in the case over there in Tasajara—but the old people didn't see it on account of your position. They'd jump at it now. Eh? No? Well," continued Jack, with a decent attempt to conceal his cynical relief, "perhaps those boys have been so eager to find out all they could do for you that they've been sold. Perhaps we're making equal fools of ourselves now in asking you to stay. But don't say no just yet—take a day or a week to think of it."

Gideon still pale but calm, cast his eyes around the elegant room, at the magic organ, then upon the slight handsome figure before him. "I *will* think of it," he said, in a low voice, as he pressed Jack's hand. "And if I accept you will find me here to-morrow afternoon at this time; if I do not you will know that I keep with me wherever I go the kindness, the brotherly love, and the grace of God that prompts your offer, even though He withholds from me His blessed light, which alone can make me know His wish." He stopped and hesitated. "If you love me, Jack, don't ask me to stay, but pray for that light which alone can guide my feet back to you, or take me hence for ever."

He once more tightly pressed the hand of the embarrassed man before him and was gone.

Passers-by on the Martinez road that night remembered a mute and ghostly rider who, heedless of hail or greeting, moved by them as in a trance or vision. But the Widow Hiler the next morning, coming from the spring, found no abstraction or preoccupation in the soft eyes of Gideon Deane as he suddenly appeared before her, and gently relieved her of the bucket she was carrying. A quick flash of color over her brow and cheek-bone, as if a hot iron had passed there, and a certain astringent coyness, would have embarrassed any other man than him.

"Sho, it's *you*. I reck'ned I'd seen the last of you."

"You don't mean that, Sister Hiler?" said Gideon, with a gentle smile.

"Well, what with the report of your goin's on at Martinez and improvin' the occasion of that sinner's death, and leadin' a revival, I reckoned you'ld hev forgotten low folks at Tasajara. And if your goin' to be settled there in a new church, with new hearers, I reckon you'll want new surroundings too. Things change and young folks change with 'em."

They had reached the house. Her breath was quick and short as if she and not Gideon had borne the burden. He placed the bucket in its accustomed place, and then gently took her hand in his. The act precipitated the last drop of feeble coquetry she had retained, and the old tears took its place. Let us hope for the last time. For as Gideon stooped and lifted her ailing babe in his strong arms, he said softly, "Whatever God has wrought for me since we parted, I know now He has called me to but one work."

"And that work?" she asked, tremulously.

"To watch over the widow and fatherless. And with God's blessing, sister, and His holy ordinance, I am here to stay."

SARAH WALKER

It was very hot. Not a breath of air was stirring throughout the western wing of the Greyport Hotel, and the usual feverish life of its four hundred inmates had succumbed to the weather. The great veranda was deserted; the corridors were desolated; no footfall echoed in the passages; the lazy rustle of a wandering skirt, or a passing sigh that was half a pant, seemed to intensify the heated silence. An intoxicated bee, disgracefully unsteady in wing and leg, who had been holding an inebriated conversation with himself in the corner of my window pane, had gone to sleep at last and was snoring. The errant prince might have entered the slumberous halls unchallenged, and walked into any of the darkened rooms whose open doors gaped for more air, without awakening the veriest Greyport flirt with his salutation. At times a drowsy voice, a lazily interjected sentence, an incoherent protest, a long-drawn phrase of saccharine tenuity suddenly broke off with a gasp, came vaguely to the ear, as if indicating a half-suspended, half-articulated existence somewhere, but not definite enough to indicate conversation. In the midst of this, there was the sudden crying of a child.

I looked up from my work. Through the camera of my jealously guarded window I could catch a glimpse of the vivid, quivering blue of the sky, the glittering intensity of the ocean, the long motionless leaves of the horse-chestnut in the road,—all utterly inconsistent with anything as active as this lamentation. I stepped to the open door and into the silent hall.

Apparently the noise had attracted the equal attention of my neighbors. A vague chorus of "Sarah Walker," in querulous recognition, of "O Lord! that child again!" in hopeless protest, rose faintly from the different rooms. As the lamentations seemed to approach nearer, the visitors' doors were successively shut, swift footsteps hurried along the hall; past my open door came a momentary vision of a heated nursemaid carrying a tumultuous chaos of frilled skirts, flying sash, rebellious slippers, and tossing curls; there was a moment's rallying struggle before the room nearly opposite mine, and then a door opened and shut upon the vision. It was Sarah Walker!

Everybody knew her; few had ever seen more of her than this passing vision. In the great hall, in the dining-room, in the vast parlors, in the garden, in the avenue, on the beach, a sound of lamentation had always been followed by this same brief apparition. Was there a sudden pause among the dancers and a subjugation of the loudest bassoons in the early evening "hop," the explanation was given in the words "Sarah Walker." Was there a wild confusion among the morning bathers on the sands, people whispered "Sarah Walker." A panic among the waiters at dinner, an interruption in the Sunday sacred concert, a disorganization of the after-dinner promenade on the veranda, was instantly referred to Sarah Walker. Nor were her efforts confined entirely to public life. In cozy corners and darkened recesses, bearded lips withheld the amorous declaration to mutter "Sarah Walker" between their clenched teeth; coy and bashful tongues found speech at last in the rapid formulation of "Sarah Walker." Nobody ever thought of abbreviating her full name. The two people in the hotel, otherwise individualized, but known only as "Sarah Walker's father" and "Sarah Walker's mother," and never as Mr. and Mrs. Walker, addressed her only as "Sarah Walker"; two animals that were occasionally a part of this passing pageant were known as "Sarah Walker's dog" and "Sarah Walker's cat," and later it was my proud privilege to sink my own individuality under the title of "that friend of Sarah Walker's."

It must not be supposed that she had attained this baleful eminence without some active criticism. Every parent in the Greyport Hotel had held his or her theory of the particular defects of Sarah Walker's education; every virgin and bachelor had openly expressed views of the peculiar discipline that was necessary to her subjugation. It may be roughly estimated that she would have spent the entire nine years of her active life in a dark cupboard on an exclusive diet of bread and water, had this discipline obtained; while, on the other hand, had the educational theories of the parental assembly prevailed, she would have ere this shone an etherealized essence in the angelic host. In either event she would have "ceased from troubling," which was the general Greyport idea of higher education. A paper read before our Literary Society on "Sarah Walker and other infantile diseases," was referred to in the catalogue as "Walker, Sarah, Prevention and Cure," while the usual burlesque legislation of our summer season culminated in the Act entitled "An Act to amend an Act entitled an Act for the abatement of Sarah Walker." As she was hereafter exclusively to be fed "on the *provisions* of this Act," some idea of its general tone may be gathered. It was a singular fact in this point of her history that her natural progenitors not only offered no resistance to the doubtful celebrity of their offspring, but, by hopelessly accepting the situation, to some extent *posed* as Sarah Walker's victims. Mr. and Mrs. Walker were known to be rich, respectable, and indulgent to their only child. They themselves had been evolved from a previous generation of promiscuously acquired wealth into the repose of inherited property, but it was currently accepted that Sarah had "cast back" and reincarnated some waif on the deck of an emigrant ship at the beginning of the century.

Such was the child separated from me by this portentous history, a narrow passage, and a closed nursery door. Presently, however, the door was partly opened again as if to admit the air. The crying had ceased, but in its place the monotonous Voice of Conscience, for the moment personated by Sarah Walker's nursemaid, kept alive a drowsy recollection of Sarah Walker's transgressions.

"You see," said the Voice, "what a dreadful thing it is for a little girl to go on as you do. I am astonished at you, Sarah Walker. So is everybody; so is the good ladies next door; so is the kind gentleman opposite; so is all! Where you expect to go to, 'Evin only knows! How you expect to be forgiven, saints alone can tell! But so it is always, and yet you keep it up. And wouldn't you like it different, Sarah Walker? Wouldn't you like to have everybody love you? Wouldn't you like them good ladies next door, and that nice gentleman opposite, all to kinder rise up and say, 'Oh, what a dear good little girl Sarah Walker is?'" The interpolation of a smacking sound of lips, as if in unctuous anticipation of Sarah Walker's virtue, here ensued—"Oh, what a dear, good, sw-e-et, lovely little girl Sarah Walker is!"

There was a dead silence. It may have been fancy, but I thought that some of the doors in the passage creaked softly as if in listening expectation. Then the silence was broken by a sigh. Had Sarah Walker ingloriously succumbed? Rash and impotent conclusion!

"I don't," said Sarah Walker's voice, slowly rising until it broke on the crest of a mountainous sob, "I—don't—want—'em—to—love me. I—don't want—'em—to say—what a—dear—good—little girl—Sarah Walker is!" She caught her breath. "I—want—'em—to say—what a naughty — bad — dirty — horrid — filthy — little girl Sarah Walker is—so I do. There!"

The doors slammed all along the passages. The dreadful issue was joined. I softly crossed the hall and looked into Sarah Walker's room.

The light from a half-opened shutter fell full upon her rebellious little figure. She had stiffened herself in a large easy-chair into the attitude in which she had been evidently deposited there by the nurse whose torn-off apron she still held rigidly in one hand. Her shapely legs stood out before her, jointless and inflexible to the point of her tiny shoes—a *pose* copied with pathetic fidelity by the French doll at her feet. The attitude must have been dreadfully uncomfortable, and maintained only as being replete with some vague insults to the person who had put her down, as exhibiting a wild indecorum of silken stocking. A mystified kitten—Sarah Walker's inseparable—was held as rigidly under one arm with equal dumb aggressiveness. Following the stiff line of her half-recumbent figure, her head suddenly appeared perpendicularly erect—yet the only mobile part of her body. A dazzling sunburst of silky hair, the color of burnished copper, partly hid her neck and shoulders and the back of the chair. Her eyes were a darker shade of the same color—the orbits appearing deeper and larger from the rubbing in of habitual tears from long wet lashes. Nothing so far seemed inconsistent with her infelix reputation, but, strange to say, her other features were marked by delicacy and refinement, and her mouth—that sorely exercised and justly dreaded member—was small and pretty, albeit slightly dropped at the corners.

The immediate effect of my intrusion was limited solely to the nursemaid. Swooping suddenly upon Sarah Walker's too evident *déshabillé,* she made two or three attempts to pluck her into propriety; but the child, recognizing the cause as well as the effect, looked askance at me and only stiffened herself the more. "Sarah Walker, I'm shocked."

"It ain't *his* room anyway," said Sarah, eying me malevolently. "What's he doing here?"

There was so much truth in this that I involuntarily drew back abashed. The nurse-maid ejaculated "Sarah!" and lifted her eyes in hopeless protest.

"And he needn't come seeing *you,*" continued Sarah, lazily rubbing the back of her head against the chair; "my papa don't allow it. He warned you 'bout the other gentleman, you know."

"Sarah Walker!"

I felt it was necessary to say something. "Don't you want to come with me and look at the sea?" I said with utter feebleness of invention. To my surprise, instead of actively assaulting me Sarah Walker got up, shook her hair over her shoulders, and took my hand.

"With your hair in that state?" almost screamed the domestic. But Sarah Walker had already pulled me into the hall. What particularly offensive form of opposition to authority was implied in this prompt assent to my proposal I could only darkly guess. For myself I knew I must appear to her a weak impostor. What would there possibly be in the sea to interest Sarah Walker? For the moment I prayed for a water-spout, a shipwreck, a whale, or any marine miracle to astound her and redeem my

character. I walked guiltily down the hall, holding her hand
bashfully in mine. I noticed that her breast began to
heave convulsively; if she cried I knew I should mingle
my tears with hers. We reached the veranda in gloomy
silence. As I expected, the sea lay before us glittering in
the sun—vacant, staring, flat, and hopelessly and unques-
tionably uninteresting.

"I knew it all along," said Sarah Walker, turning down
the corners of her mouth; "there never was anything to
see. I know why you got me to come here. You want to
tell me if I'm a good girl you'll take me to sail some day.
You want to say if I'm bad the sea will swallow me up.
That's all you want, you horrid thing, you!"

"Hush!" I said, pointing to the corner of the veranda.

A desperate idea of escape had just seized me. Bolt
upright in the recess of a window sat a nursemaid who had
succumbed to sleep equally with her helpless charge in the
perambulator beside her. I instantly recognized the infant
—a popular organism known as "Baby Buckly"—the prodigy of the Greyport Hotel, the pet of its enthusiastic wo-
manhood. Fat and featureless, pink and pincushiony, it
was borrowed by gushing maidenhood, exchanged by idiotic
maternity, and had grown unctuous and tumefacient under
the kisses and embraces of half the hotel. Even in its
present repose it looked moist and shiny from indiscrim-
inate and promiscuous osculation.

"Let's borrow Baby Buckly," I said recklessly.

Sarah Walker at once stopped crying. I don't know
how she did it, but the cessation was instantaneous, as if
she had turned off a tap somewhere.

"And put it in Mr. Peters' bed!" I continued.

Peters being notoriously a grim bachelor, the bare sug-
geston bristled with outrage. Sarah Walker's eyes sparkled.

"You don't mean it!—go 'way!"—she said with affected
coyness.

"But I do! Come."

We extracted it noiselessly together—that is, Sarah
Walker did, with deft womanliness—carried it darkly along
the hall to No. 27, and deposited it in Peters' bed, where
it lay like a freshly opened oyster. We then returned

hand in hand to my room, where we looked out of the window on the sea. It was observable that there was no lack of interest in Sarah Walker now.

Before five minutes had elapsed some one breathlessly passed the open door while we were still engaged in marine observation. This was followed by return footsteps and a succession of swiftly rustling garments, until the majority of the women in our wing had apparently passed our room, and we saw an irregular stream of nursemaids and mothers converging towards the hotel out of the grateful shadow of arbors, trees, and marquees. In fact we were still engaged in observation when Sarah Walker's nurse came to fetch her away, and to inform her that "by rights" Baby Buckly's nurse and Mr. Peters should both be made to leave the hotel that very night. Sarah Walker permitted herself to be led off with dry but expressive eyes. That evening she did not cry, but, on being taken into the usual custody for disturbance, was found to be purple with suppressed laughter.

This was the beginning of my intimacy with Sarah Walker. But while it was evident that whatever influence I obtained over her was due to my being *particeps criminis*, I think it was accepted that a regular abduction of infants might become in time monotonous if not dangerous. So she was satisfied with the knowledge that I could not now, without the most glaring hypocrisy, obtrude a moral superiority upon her. I do not think she would have turned state evidence and accused me, but I was by no means assured of her disinterested regard. She contented herself, for a few days afterwards, with meeting me privately and mysteriously communicating unctuous reminiscences of our joint crime, without suggesting a repetition. Her intimacy with me did not seem to interfere with her general relations to her own species in the other children in the hotel. Perhaps I should have said before that her popularity with them was by no means prejudiced by her infelix reputation. But while she was secretly admired by all, she had few professed followers and no regular associates. Whether the few whom she selected for that baleful preëminence were either torn from her by horrified guardians, or came to grief through her dangerous counsels, or whether she really did not care for them, I could not say. Their elevation was brief, their retirement unregretted. It was however permitted me, through felicitous circumstances, to become acquainted with the probable explanation of her unsociability.

The very hot weather culminated one afternoon in a dead faint of earth and sea and sky. An Alpine cloudland of snow that had mocked the upturned eyes of Greyport for hours, began to darken under the folding shadow of a black and velvety wing. The atmosphere seemed to thicken as the gloom increased; the lazy dust, thrown up by hurrying feet that sought a refuge, hung almost motionless in the air. Suddenly it was blown to the four quarters in one fierce gust that as quickly dispersed the loungers drooping in shade and cover. For a few seconds the long avenue was lost in flying clouds of dust, and then was left bare of life or motion. Raindrops in huge stars and rosettes appeared noiselessly and magically upon the sidewalks— gouts of moisture apparently dropped from mid-air. And then the ominous hush returned.

A mile away along the rocks, I turned for shelter into a cavernous passage of the overhanging cliff, where I could still watch the coming storm upon the sea. A murmur of voices presently attracted my attention. I then observed that the passage ended in a kind of open grotto, where I could dimly discern the little figures of several children, who, separated from their nurses in the sudden onset of the storm, had taken refuge there. As the gloom deepened they became silent again, until the stillness was broken by a familiar voice. There was no mistaking it.—It was Sarah Walker's. But it was not lifted in lamentation, it was raised only as if resuming a suspended narrative.

"Her name," said Sarah Walker gloomily, "was Kribbles. She was the only child—of—of orphaned parentage, and fair to see, but she was bad, and God did not love her. And one day she was separated from her nurse on a desert island like to this. And then came a hidgeous thunderstorm. And a great big thunderbolt came galumping after her. And it ketched her and rolled all over her—so! and then it came back and ketched her and rolled her over—so! And when they came to pick her up there was not so much as *that* left of her. All burnt up!"

"Wasn't there just a little bit of her shoe?" suggested a cautious auditor.

"Not a bit," said Sarah Walker firmly. All the other children echoed "Not a bit," indignantly, in evident gratification at the completeness of Kribbles' catastrophe. At this moment the surrounding darkness was suddenly filled with a burst of blue celestial fire; the heavy inky sea beyond, the black-edged mourning horizon, the gleaming sands, each nook and corner of the dripping cave, with the frightened faces of the huddled group of children, started into vivid life for an instant, and then fell back with a deafening crash into the darkness.

There was a slight sound of whimpering. Sarah Walker apparently pounced upon the culprit, for it ceased.

"Sniffling 'tracts 'lectricity," she said sententiously.

"But you thaid it wath Dod!" lisped a casuist of seven.

"It's all the same," said Sarah sharply, "and so's asking questions."

This obscure statement was however apparently understood, for the casuist lapsed into silent security. "Lots of things 'tracts it," continued Sarah Walker. "Gold and silver, and metals and knives and rings."

"And pennies?"

"And pennies most of all! Kribbles was that vain, she used to wear jewelry and fly in the face of Providence."

"But you thaid—"

"Will you?—There! you hear that?" There was another blinding flash and bounding roll of thunder along the shore. "I wonder you didn't ketch it. You would—only I'm here."

All was quiet again, but from certain indications it was evident that a collection of those dangerous articles that had proved fatal to the unhappy Kribbles was being taken up. I could hear the clink of coins and jingle of ornaments. That Sarah herself was the custodian was presently shown. "But won't the lightning come to you now?" asked a timid voice.

"No," said Sarah, promptly, " 'cause I ain't afraid!
Look!"

A frightened protest from the children here ensued, but
the next instant she appeared at the entrance of the grotto
and ran down the rocks towards the sea. Skipping from
bowlder to bowlder she reached the furthest projection of
the ledge, now partly submerged by the rising surf, and
then turned half triumphantly, half defiantly, towards the
grotto. The weird phosphorescence of the storm lit up
the resolute little figure standing there, gorgeously bedecked
with the chains, rings, and shiny trinkets of her companions.
With a tiny hand raised in mock defiance of the elements,
she seemed to lean confidingly against the panting breast
of the gale, with fluttering skirt and flying tresses. Then
the vault behind her cracked with three jagged burning
fissures, a weird flame leaped upon the sand, there was a
cry of terror from the grotto, echoed by a scream of
nurses on the cliff, a deluge of rain, a terrific onset from
the gale—and—Sarah Walker was gone? Nothing of the
kind! When I reached the ledge, after a severe struggle
with the storm, I found Sarah on the leeward side, drenched
but delighted. I held her tightly, while we waited for a
lull to regain the cliff, and took advantage of the sympathetic situation.

"But you know you *were* frightened, Sarah," I whispered; "you thought of what happened to poor Kribbles."

"Do you know who Kribbles was?" she asked confidentially.

"No."

"Well," she whispered, "I made Kribbles up. And the
hidgeous storm and thunderbolt—and the burning! All out
of my own head."

The only immediate effect of this escapade was apparently
to precipitate and bring into notoriety the growing affection of an obscure lover of Sarah Walker's, hitherto un-
suspected. He was a mild inoffensive boy of twelve, known
as "Warts," solely from an inordinate exhibition of these
youthful excrescences. On the day of Sarah Walker's adventure his passion culminated in a sudden and illogical
attack upon Sarah's nurse and parents while they were

bewailing her conduct, and in assaulting them with his feet
and hands. Whether he associated them in some vague
way with the cause of her momentary peril, or whether he
only wished to impress her with the touching flattery of a
general imitation of her style, I cannot say. For his love-
making was peculiar. A day or two afterwards he came
to my open door and remained for some moments bashfully looking at me. The next day I found him standing
by my chair in the piazza with an embarrassed air and in
utter inability to explain his conduct. At the end of a
rapid walk on the sand one morning, I was startled by the
sound of hurried breath, and looking around, discovered
the staggering Warts quite exhausted by endeavoring to
keep up with me on his short legs. At last the daily recurrence of his haunting presence forced a dreadful suspicion upon me. Warts was courting *me* for Sarah Walker!
Yet it was impossible to actually connect her with these
mute attentions. "You want me to give them to Sarah
Walker," I said cheerfully one afternoon, as he laid upon
my desk some peculiarly uninviting crustacea which looked
not unlike a few detached excrescences from his own hands.
He shook his head decidedly. "I understand," I continued,
confidently; "you want me to keep them for her." "No,"
said Warts, doggedly. "Then you only want me to tell
her how nice they are?" The idea was apparently so
shamelessly true that he blushed himself hastily into the
passage, and ceased any future contribution. Naturally
still more ineffective was the slightest attempt to bring his
devotion into the physical presence of Sarah Walker. The
most ingenious schemes to lure him into my room while she
was there failed utterly. Yet he must have at one time
basked in her baleful presence. "Do you like Warts?"
I asked her one day bluntly. "Yes," said Sarah Walker
with cheerful directness; "ain't *he* got a lot of 'em?—
though he used to have more. But," she added reflectively,
"do you know the little Ilsey boy?" I was compelled to
admit my ignorance. "Well!" she said with a reminiscent sigh of satisfaction, *"he's* got only two toes on his left
foot—showed 'em to me. And he was born so." Need it
be said that in these few words I read the dismal sequel

of Warts' unfortunate attachment? His accidental eccentricity was no longer attractive. What were his evanes-
cent accretions, subject to improvement or removal, beside
the hereditary and settled malformations of his rival?

Once only, in this brief summer episode, did Sarah
Walker attract the impulsive and general sympathy of
Greyport. It is only just to her consistency to say it was
through no fault of hers, unless a characteristic exposure
which brought on a chill and diphtheria could be called
her own act. Howbeit, towards the close of the season,
when a sudden suggestion of the coming autumn had crept,
one knew not how, into the heart of a perfect day; when
even a return of the summer warmth had a suspicion of
hectic,—on one of these days Sarah Walker was missed
with the bees and the butterflies. For two days her voice
had not been heard in hall or corridor, nor had the sunshine of her French marigold head lit up her familiar
places. The two days were days of relief, yet mitigated
with a certain uneasy apprehension of the return of Sarah
Walker, or—more alarming thought!—the Sarah Walker
element in a more appalling form. So strong was this impression that an unhappy infant who unwittingly broke this
interval with his maiden outcry was nearly lynched. "We're
not going to stand that from *you,* you know," was the crystallized sentiment of a brutal bachelor. In fact, it began
to be admitted that Greyport had been accustomed to Sarah
Walker's ways. In the midst of this, it was suddenly whispered that Sarah Walker was lying dangerously ill, and
was not expected to live.

Then occurred one of those strange revulsions of human
sentiment which at first seem to point the dawning of a
millennium of poetic justice, but which, in this case, ended
in merely stirring the languid pulses of society into a hectic
fever, and in making sympathy for Sarah Walker an in-
sincere and exaggerated fashion. Morning and afternoon
visits to her apartment, with extravagant offerings, were
de rigueur; bulletins were issued three times a day; an allusion to her condition was the recognized preliminary to
all conversation; advice, suggestions, and petitions to re-
store the baleful existence, flowed readily from the same

facile invention that had once proposed its banishment;
until one afternoon the shadow had drawn so close that
even Folly withheld its careless feet before it, and laid down
its feeble tinkling bells and gaudy cap tremblingly on the
threshold. But the sequel must be told in more vivid words
than mine.

"Whin I saw that angel lyin' there," said Sarah Walker's
nurse, "as white, if ye plaze, as if the whole blessed blood
of her body had gone to make up the beautiful glory of
her hair; speechless as she was, I thought I saw a sort of
longin' in her eyes.

"'Is it anythin' you'll be wantin', Sarah darlint', sez her
mother with a tremblin' voice, 'afore it's lavin' us ye are?
Is it the ministher yer askin' for, love?' sez she.

"And Sarah looked at me, and if it was the last words
I spake, her lips moved and she whispered 'Scotty.'

"'Wirra! wirra!' sez the mother, 'it's wanderin' she is,
the darlin';' for Scotty, don't ye see, was the grand bar-
keeper of the hotel.

"'Savin' yer presence, ma'am,' sez I, 'and the child's here,
ez is half a saint already, it's thruth she's spakin'—it's
Scotty she wants.' And with that my angel blinks wid
her black eyes 'yes.'

"'Bring him,' says the docthor, 'at once.'

"And they bring him in wid all the mustachios and
moighty fine curls of him, and his diamonds, rings, and
pins all a-glistening just like his eyes when he set 'em on
that suffering saint.

"'Is it anythin' you're wantin,' Sarah dear?' sez he,
thryin' to spake firm. And Sarah looks at him, and then
looks at a tumbler on the table.

"'Is it a bit of a cocktail, the likes of the one I made
for ye last Sunday unbeknownst?' sez he, looking round
mortal afraid of the parents. And Sarah Walker's eyes
said, 'It is.' Then the ministher groaned, but the docthor
jumps to his feet.

"'Bring it,' sez he, 'and howld your jaw, an ye's a Christian sowl.' And he brought it. An' afther the first sip,
the child lifts herself up on one arm, and sez, with a swate
smile and a toss of the glass:

" 'I looks towards you, Scotty,' sez she.

" 'I observes you and bows, miss,' sez he, makin' as if he was dhrinkin' wid her.

" 'Here's another nail in yer coffin, old man,' sez she winkin'.

" 'And here's the hair all off your head, miss,' sez he quite aisily, tossin' back the joke betwixt 'em.

"And with that she dhrinks it off, and lies down and goes to sleep like a lamb, and wakes up wid de rosy dawn in her cheeks, and the morthal seekness gone forever."

.   .   .   .

Thus Sarah Walker recovered. Whether the fact were essential to the moral conveyed in these pages, I leave the reader to judge.

I was leaning on the terrace of the Kronprinzen-Hof at Rolandseck one hot summer afternoon, lazily watching the groups of tourists strolling along the road that ran between the Hof and the Rhine. There was certainly little in the place or its atmosphere to recall the Greyport episode of twenty years before, when I was suddenly startled by hearing the name of "Sarah Walker."

In the road below me were three figures,—a lady, a gentleman, and a little girl. As the latter turned towards the lady who addressed her, I recognized the unmistakable copper-colored tresses, trim figure, delicate complexion, and refined features of the friend of my youth! I seized my hat, but by the time I had reached the road, they had disappeared.

The utter impossibility of its being Sarah Walker herself, and the glaring fact that the very coincidence of name would be inconsistent with any conventional descent from the original Sarah, I admit confused me. But I examined the book of the Kronprinzen-Hof and the other hotels, and questioned my *portier*. There was no "Mees" nor "Madame Walkiere" extant in Rolandseck. Yet might not Monsieur have heard incorrectly? The Czara Walka was evidently Russian, and Rolandseck was a resort for Russian princes. But pardon! Did Monsieur really mean the young demoiselle now approaching? Ah! that was a different affair. She was the daughter of the Italian Prince and Princess

Monte Castello staying here. The lady with her was not the Princess, but a foreign friend. The gentleman was the Prince. Would he present Monsieur's card?

They were entering the hotel. The Prince was a little, inoffensive-looking man, the lady an evident countrywoman of my own, and the child—was, yet was *not,* Sarah! There was the face, the outline, the figure—but the life, the verve, the audacity, was wanting! I could contain myself no longer.

"Pardon an inquisitive compatriot, madam," I said; "but I heard you a few moments ago address this young lady by the name of a very dear young friend, whom I knew twenty years ago—Sarah Walker. Am I right?"

The Prince stopped and gazed at us both with evident affright; then suddenly recognizing in my freedom some wild American indecorum, doubtless provoked by the presence of another of my species, which he really was not expected to countenance, retreated behind the *portier*. The circumstance by no means increased the good-will of the lady, as she replied somewhat haughtily:—

"The Principessina is named Sarah Walker, after her mother's maiden name."

"Then this *is* Sarah Walker's daughter!" I said joyfully.

"She is the daughter of the Prince and Princess of Monte Castello," corrected the lady frigidly.

"I had the pleasure of knowing her mother very well." I stopped and blushed. Did I really know Sarah Walker very well? And would Sarah Walker know me now? Or would it not be very like her to go back on me? There was certainly anything but promise in the feeble-minded, vacuous copy of Sarah before me. I was yet hesitating, when the Prince, who had possibly received some quieting assurance from the *portier,* himself stepped forward, stammered that the Princess would, without doubt, be charmed to receive me later, and skipped upstairs, leaving the impression on my mind that he contemplated ordering his bill at once. There was no excuse for further prolonging the interview. "Say good-by to the strange gentleman, Sarah," suggested Sarah's companion stiffly. I looked at the child in the wild hope of recognizing some prompt resistance to the suggestion that would have identified her with the lost Sarah of my youth—but in vain. "Good-by, sir," said the affected little creature, dropping a mechanical curtsey. "Thank you very much for remembering my mother." "Good-by, Sarah!" It was indeed good-by forever.

For on my way to my room I came suddenly upon the Prince, in a recess of the upper hall, addressing somebody through an open door with a querulous protest, whose wild extravagance of statement was grotesquely balanced by its utter feeble timidity of manner. "It is," said the Prince, "indeed a grave affair. We have here hundreds of socialists, emissaries from lawless countries and impossible places, who travel thousands of miles to fall upon our hearts and embrace us. They establish an espionage over us; they haunt our walks in incredible numbers; they hang in droves upon our footsteps; Heaven alone saves us from a public osculation at any moment! They openly allege that they have dandled us on their knees at recent periods; washed and dressed us, and would do so still. Our happiness, our security—"

"Don't be a fool, Prince. Do shut up!"

The Prince collapsed and shrank away, and I hurried past the open door. A tall, magnificent-looking woman was standing before a glass, arranging her heavy red hair. The face, which had been impatiently turned towards the door, had changed again to profile, with a frown still visible on the bent brow. Our eyes met as I passed. The next moment the door slammed, and I had seen the last of Sarah Walker.

A SHIP OF '49

IT had rained so persistently in San Francisco during the first week of January, 1854, that a certain quagmire in the roadway of Long Wharf had become impassable, and a plank was thrown over its dangerous depth. Indeed, so treacherous was the spot that it was alleged, on good authority, that a hastily embarking traveler had once hopelessly lost his portmanteau, and was fain to dispose of his entire interest in it for the sum of two dollars and fifty cents to a speculative stranger on the wharf. As the stranger's search was rewarded afterwards only by the discovery of the body of a casual Chinaman, who had evidently endeavored wickedly to anticipate him, a feeling of commercial insecurity was added to the other eccentricities of the locality.

The plank led to the door of a building that was a marvel even in the chaotic frontier architecture of the street. The houses on either side—irregular frames of wood or corrugated iron—bore evidence of having been quickly thrown together, to meet the requirements of the goods and passengers who were once disembarked on what was the muddy beach of the infant city. But the building in question exhibited a certain elaboration of form and design utterly inconsistent with this idea. The structure obtruded a bowed front to the street, with a curving line of small windows, surmounted by elaborate carvings and scroll work of vines and leaves, while below, in faded gilt letters, appeared the legend "Pontiac—Marseilles." The effect of this incongruity was startling. It is related that an inebriated miner, impeded by mud and drink before its door, was found gazing at its remarkable façade with an expression of the deepest despondency. "I hev lived a free life, pardner," he explained thickly to the Samaritan who succored him, "and every time since I've been on this six weeks' jamboree might have kalkilated it would come to this. Snakes I've seen afore now, and rats I'm not unfamiliar with, but when it comes to the starn of a ship risin' up out of the street, I reckon it's time to pass in my checks." "It *is* a ship, you blasted old soaker," said the Samaritan curtly.

It was indeed a ship. A ship run ashore and abandoned on the beach years before by her gold-seeking crew, with the *débris* of her scattered stores and cargo, overtaken by the wild growth of the strange city and the reclamation of the muddy flat, wherein she lay hopelessly imbedded; her retreat cut off by wharves and quays and breakwater, jostled at first by sheds, and then impacted in a block of solid warehouses and dwellings, her rudder, port, and counter boarded in, and now gazing hopelessly through her cabin windows upon the busy street before her. But still a ship despite her transformation. The faintest line of contour yet left visible spoke of the buoyancy of another element; the balustrade of her roof was unmistakably a taffrail. The rain slipped from her swelling sides with a certain lingering touch of the sea; the soil around her was still treacherous with its suggestions, and even the wind whistled nautically over her chimney. If, in the fury of some southwesterly gale, she had one night slipped her strange moorings and left a shining track through the lower town to the distant sea, no one would have been surprised.

Least of all, perhaps, her present owner and possessor, Mr. Abner Nott. For by the irony of circumstances, Mr. Nott was a Far Western farmer who had never seen a ship before, nor a larger stream of water than a tributary of the Missouri River. In a spirit, half of fascination, half of speculation, he had bought her at the time of her abandonment, and had since mortgaged his ranch at Petaluma with his live stock, to defray the expenses of filling in the land where she stood, and the improvements of the vicinity. He had transferred his household goods and his only daughter to her cabin, and had divided the space "between decks" and her hold into lodging-rooms, and lofts for the storage of goods. It could hardly be said that the investment had been profitable. His tenants vaguely recognized that his occupancy was a sentimental rather than a

commercial speculation, and often generously lent themselves to the illusion by not paying their rent. Others
treated their own tenancy as a joke,—a quaint recreation
born of the childlike familiarity of frontier intercourse.
A few had left; carelessly abandoning their unsalable goods
to their landlord, with great cheerfulness and a sense of
favor. Occasionally Mr. Abner Nott, in a practical relapse,
raged against the derelicts, and talked of dispossessing
them, or even dismantling his tenement, but he was easily
placated by a compliment to the "dear old ship," or an
effort made by some tenant to idealize his apartment. A
photographer who had ingeniously utilized the forecastle
for a gallery (accessible from the bows in the next street),
paid no further tribute than a portrait of the pretty face
of Rosey Nott. The superstitious reverence in which Abner
Nott held his monstrous fancy was naturally enhanced by
his purely bucolic exaggeration of its real functions and
its native element. "This yer keel has sailed, and sailed,
and sailed," he would explain with some incongruity of
illustration, "in a bee line, makin' tracks for days runnin'.
I reckon more storms and blizzards hez tackled her then
you ken shake a stick at. She's stampeded whales afore
now, and sloshed round with pirates and freebooters in and
outer the Spanish Main, and across lots from Marcelleys
where she was rared. And yer she sits peaceful-like just
ez if she'd never been outer a pertater patch, and hadn't
ploughed the sea with fo'sails and studdin' sails and them
things cavortin' round her masts."

Abner Nott's enthusiasm was shared by his daughter,
but with more imagination, and an intelligence stimulated
by the scant literature of her father's emigrant wagon and
the few books found on the cabin shelves. But to her
the strange shell she inhabited suggested more of the great
world than the rude, chaotic civilization she saw from the
cabin windows or met in the persons of her father's lodgers.
Shut up for days in this quaint tenement, she had seen it
change from the enchanted playground of her childish
fancy to the theatre of her active maidenhood, but without
losing her ideal romance in it. She had translated its
history in her own way, read its quaint nautical hieroglyphics

after her own fashion, and possessed herself of its secrets. She had in fancy made voyages in it to foreign lands, had heard the accents of a softer tongue on its decks, and on summer nights, from the roof of the quarter-deck, had seen mellower constellations take the place of the hard metallic glitter of the Californian skies. Sometimes, in her isolation, the long, cylindrical vault she inhabited seemed, like some vast sea-shell, to become musical with the murmurings of the distant sea. So completely had it taken the place of the usual instincts of feminine youth that she had forgotten she was pretty, or that her dresses were old in fashion and scant in quantity. After the first surprise of admiration her father's lodgers ceased to follow the abstracted nymph except with their eyes,—partly respecting her spiritual shyness, partly respecting the jealous supervision of the paternal Nott. She seldom penetrated the crowded centre of the growing city; her rare excursions were confined to the old ranch at Petaluma, whence she brought flowers and plants, and even extemporized a hanging-garden on the quarter-deck.

It was still raining, and the wind, which had increased to a gale, was dashing the drops against the slanting cabin windows with a sound like spray when Mr. Abner Nott sat before a table seriously engaged with his accounts. For it was "steamer night,"—as that momentous day of reckoning before the sailing of the regular mail steamer was briefly known to commercial San Francisco,—and Mr. Nott was subject at such times to severely practical relapses. A swinging light seemed to bring into greater relief that peculiar encased casket-like security of the low-timbered, tightly-fitting apartment, with its toy-like utilities of space, and made the pretty oval face of Rosey Nott appear a characteristic ornament. The sliding door of the cabin communicated with the main deck, now roofed in and partitioned off so as to form a small passage that led to the open starboard gangway, where a narrow, inclosed staircase built on the ship's side took the place of the ship's ladder under her counter, and opened in the street.

A dash of rain against the window caused Rosey to lift her eyes from her book.

"It's much nicer here than at the ranch, father," she said coaxingly, "even leaving alone its being a beautiful ship instead of a shanty; the wind don't whistle through the cracks and blow out the candle when you're reading, nor the rain spoil your things hung up against the wall. And you look more like a gentleman sitting in his own— ship—you know, looking over his bills and getting ready to give his orders."

Vague and general as Miss Rosey's compliment was, it had its full effect upon her father, who was at times dimly conscious of his hopeless rusticity and its incongruity with his surroundings. "Yes," he said awkwardly, with a slight relaxation of his aggressive attitude; "yes, in course it's more bang-up style, but it don't pay—Rosey—it don't pay. Yer's the Pontiac that oughter be bringin' in, ez rents go, at least three hundred a month, don't make her taxes. I bin thinkin' seriously of sellin' her."

As Rosey knew her father had experienced this serious contemplation on the first of every month for the last two years, and cheerfully ignored it the next day, she only said, "I'm sure the vacant rooms and lofts are all rented, father."

"That's it," returned Mr. Nott thoughtfully, plucking at his bushy whiskers with his fingers and thumb as if he were removing dead and sapless incumbrances in their growth, "that's just what it is—them's ez in it themselves don't pay, and them ez haz left their goods—the goods don't pay. The feller ez stored them iron sugar kettles in the forehold, after trying to get me to make another advance on 'em, sez he believes he'll have to sacrifice 'em to me after all, and only begs I'd give him a chance of buying back the half of 'em ten years from now, at double what I advanced him. The chap that left them five hundred cases of hair dye 'tween decks and then skipped out to Sacramento, met me the other day in the street and advised me to use a bottle ez an advertisement, or try it on the starn of the Pontiac for fire-proof paint. That foolishness ez all he's good for. And yet thar might be suthin' in the paint, if a feller had nigger luck. Ther's that New York chap ez bought up them damaged boxes of plug terbaker for fifty dollars a thousand, and sold 'em for foundations for that

new building in Sansome Street at a thousand clear profit.
It's all luck, Rosey."

The girl's eyes had wandered again to the pages of her
book. Perhaps she was already familiar with the text of
her father's monologue. But recognizing an additional
querulousness in his voice, she laid the book aside and
patiently folded her hands in her lap.

"That's right—for I've suthin' to tell ye. The fact is
Sleight wants to buy the Pontiac out and out just ez she
stands with the two fifty vara lots she stands on."

"Sleight wants to buy her? Sleight?" echoed Rosey
incredulously.

"You bet! Sleight—the big financier, the smartest man
in 'Frisco."

"What does he want to buy her for?" asked Rosey,
knitting her pretty brows.

The apparently simple question suddenly puzzled Mr.
Nott. He glanced feebly at his daughter's face, and
frowned in vacant irritation. "That's so," he said, drawing a long breath; "there's suthin' in that."

"What did he *say?*" continued the young girl, impatiently.

"Not much. 'You've got the Pontiac, Nott,' sez he.
'You bet!' sez I. 'What'll you take for her and the lot
she stands on?' sez he, short and sharp. Some fellers,
Rosey," said Nott, with a cunning smile, "would hev blurted
out a big figger and been cotched. That ain't my style.
I just looked at him. 'I'll wait fur your figgers until next
steamer day,' sez he, and off he goes like a shot. He's
awfully sharp, Rosey."

"But if he is sharp, father, and he really wants to buy
the ship," returned Rosey, thoughtfully, "it's only because
he knows it's valuable property, and not because he likes
it as we do. He can't take that value away even if we
don't sell it to him, and all the while we have the comfort
of the dear old Pontiac, don't you see?"

This exhaustive commercial reasoning was so sympathetic
to Mr. Nott's instincts that he accepted it as conclusive.
He, however, deemed it wise to still preserve his practical
attitude. "But that don't make it pay by the month, Rosey.

Suthin' must be done. I'm thinking I'll clean out that photographer."

"Not just after he's taken such a pretty view of the cabin front of the Pontiac from the street, father! No! He's going to give us a copy, and put the other in a shop window in Montgomery Street."

"That's so," said Mr. Nott, musingly; "it's no slouch of an advertisement. 'The Pontiac,' the property of A. Nott, Esq., of St. Jo, Missouri. Send it on to your Aunt Phœbe; sorter make the old folks open their eyes—oh? Well, seein' he's been to some expense fittin' up an entrance from the other street, we'll let him slide. But as to that d——d old Frenchman Ferrers, in the next loft, with his stuck-up airs and high-falutin style, we must get quit of him; he's regularly gouged me in that ere horsehair spekilation."

"How can you say that, father!" said Rosey, with a slight increase of color. "It was your own offer. You know those bales of curled horsehair were left behind by the late tenant to pay his rent. When Mr. de Ferrières rented the room afterwards, you told him you'd throw them in in the place of repairs and furniture. It was your own offer."

"Yes, but I didn't reckon ther'd ever be a big price per pound paid for the darned stuff for sofys and cushions and sich."

"How do you know *he* knew it, father?" responded Rosey.

"Then why did he look so silly at first, and then put on airs when I joked him about it, eh?"

"Perhaps he didn't understand your joking, father. He's a foreigner, and shy and proud, and—not like the others. I don't think he knew what you meant then, any more than he believed he was making a bargain before. He may be poor, but I think he's been—a—a—gentleman."

The young girl's animation penetrated even Mr. Nott's slow comprehension. Her novel opposition, and even the prettiness it enhanced, gave him a dull premonition of pain. His small round eyes became abstracted, his mouth remained partly open, even his fresh color slightly paled.

"You seem to have been takin' stock of this yer man,

Rosey," he said, with a faint attempt at archness; "if he warn't ez old ez a crow, for all his young feathers, I'd think he was makin' up to you."

But the passing glow had faded from her young cheeks, and her eyes wandered again to her book. "He pays his rent regularly every steamer night," she said, quietly, as if dismissing an exhausted subject, "and he'll be here in a moment, I dare say." She took up her book, and leaning her head on her hand, once more became absorbed in its pages.

An uneasy silence followed. The rain beat against the windows, the ticking of a clock became audible, but still Mr. Nott sat with vacant eyes fixed on his daughter's face, and the constrained smile on his lips. He was conscious that he had never seen her look so pretty before, yet he could not tell why this was no longer an unalloyed satisfaction. Not but that he had always accepted the admiration of others for her as a matter of course, but for the first time he became conscious that she not only had an interest in others, but apparently a superior knowledge of them. How did she know these things about this man, and why had she only now accidentally spoken of them? *He* would have done so. All this passed so vaguely through his unreflective mind, that he was unable to retain any decided impression, but the far-reaching one that his lodger had obtained some occult influence over her through the exhibition of his baleful skill in the horsehair speculation. "Them tricks is likely to take a young girl's fancy. I must look arter her," he said to himself softly.

A slow regular step in the gangway interrupted his paternal reflections. Hastily buttoning across his chest the pea-jacket which he usually wore at home as a single concession to his nautical surroundings, he drew himself up with something of the assumption of a ship-master, despite certain bucolic suggestions of his boots and legs. The footsteps approached nearer, and a tall figure suddenly stood in the doorway.

It was a figure so extraordinary that even in the strange masquerade of that early civilization it was remarkable; a figure with whom father and daughter were already fa-

miliar without abatement of wonder—the figure of a re-
juvenated old man, padded, powdered, dyed, and painted to
the verge of caricature, but without a single suggestion of
ludicrousness or humor. A face so artificial that it seemed
almost a mask, but, like a mask, more pathetic than amusing. He was dressed in the extreme of fashion of a dozen
years before; his pearl gray trousers strapped tightly over
his varnished boots, his voluminous satin cravat and high
collar embraced his rouged cheeks and dyed whiskers, his
closely-buttoned frock coat clinging to a waist that seemed
accented by stays.

He advanced two steps into the cabin with an upright
precision of motion that might have hid the infirmities of
age, and said deliberately with a foreign accent:—

"You-r-r ac-coumpt?"

In the actual presence of the apparition Mr. Nott's
dignified resistance wavered. But glancing uneasily at his
daughter and seeing her calm eyes fixed on the speaker
without embarrassment, he folded his arms stiffly, and with
a lofty simulation of examining the ceiling, said,—

"Ahem! Rosa! The gentleman's account."

It was an infelicitous action. For the stranger, who
evidently had not noticed the presence of the young girl
before, started, took a step quickly forward, bent stiffly
but profoundly over the little hand that held the account,
raised it to his lips, and with "a thousand pardons,
mademoiselle," laid a small canvas bag containing the rent
before the disorganized Mr. Nott and stiffly vanished.

That night was a troubled one to the simple-minded
proprietor of the good ship Pontiac. Unable to voice his
uneasiness by further discussion, but feeling that his late
discomposing interview with his lodger demanded some
marked protest, he absented himself on the plea of business during the rest of the evening, happily to his daughter's utter obliviousness of the reason. Lights were burning
brilliantly in counting-rooms and offices, the feverish life
of the mercantile city was at its height. With a vague idea
of entering into immediate negotiations with Mr. Sleight
for the sale of the ship—as a direct way out of his present
perplexity, he bent his steps towards the financier's office,

but paused and turned back before reaching the door. He made his way to the wharf and gazed abstractedly at the lights reflected in the dark, tremulous, jelly-like water. But wherever he went he was accompanied by the absurd figure of his lodger—a figure he had hitherto laughed at or half pitied, but which now, to his bewildered comprehension, seemed to have a fateful significance. Here a new idea seized him, and he hurried back to the ship, slackening his pace only when he arrived at his own doorway. Here he paused a moment and slowly ascended the staircase. When he reached the passage he coughed slightly and paused again. Then he pushed open the door of the darkened cabin and called softly :—

"Rosey!"

"What is it, father?" said Rosey's voice from the little state-room on the right—Rosey's own bower.

"Nothing!" said Mr. Nott, with an affectation of languid calmness; "I only wanted to know if you was comfortable. It's an awful busy night in town."

"Yes, father."

"I reckon thar's tons o' gold goin' to the States to-morrow."

"Yes, father."

"Pretty comfortable, eh?"

"Yes, father."

"Well, I'll browse round a spell, and turn in myself, soon."

"Yes father."

Mr. Nott took down a hanging lantern, lit it, and passed out into the gangway. Another lamp hung from the companion hatch to light the tenants to the lower deck, whence he descended. This deck was divided fore and aft by a partitioned passage,—the lofts or apartments being lighted from the ports, and one or two by a door cut through the ship's side communicating with an alley on either side. This was the case with the loft occupied by Mr. Nott's strange lodger, which, besides a door in the passage, had this independent communication with the alley. Nott had never known him to make use of the latter door; on the contrary, it was his regular habit to issue from his apartment at three o'clock every afternoon, dressed as he has been described, stride deliberately through the passage to the upper deck and thence into the street, where his strange figure was a feature of the principal promenade for two or three hours, returning as regularly at eight o'clock to the ship and the seclusion of his loft. Mr. Nott paused before the door, under the pretence of throwing the light before him into the shadows of the forecastle; all was silent within. He was turning back when he was impressed by the regular recurrence of a peculiar rustling sound which he had at first referred to the rubbing of the wires of the swinging lantern against his clothing. He set down the light and listened; the sound was evidently on the other side of the partition; the sound of some prolonged, rustling, scraping movement, with regular intervals. Was it due to another of Mr. Nott's unprofitable tenants—the rats? No. A bright idea flashed upon Mr. Nott's troubled mind. It was de Ferrières snoring! He smiled grimly. "Wonder if Rosey'd call him a gentleman if she heard that," he chuckled to himself as he slowly made his way back to the cabin and the small state-room opposite to his daughter's. During the rest of the night he dreamed of being compelled to give Rosey in marriage to his strange lodger, who added insult to the outrage by snoring audibly through the marriage service.

Meantime, in her cradle-like nest in her nautical bower, Miss Rosey slumbered as lightly. Waking from a vivid dream of Venice—a child's Venice—seen from the swelling deck of the proudly-riding Pontiac, she was so impressed as to rise and cross on tiptoe to the little slanting port-hole. Morning was already dawning over the flat, straggling city, but from every counting-house and magazine the votive tapers of the feverish worshipers of trade and mammon were still flaring fiercely.

II

The day following "steamer night" was usually stale and flat at San Francisco. The reaction from the feverish exaltation of the previous twenty-four hours was seen in the listless faces and lounging feet of promenaders, and was notable in the deserted offices and warehouses still redolent of last night's gas, and strewn with the dead ashes of last night's fires.

There was a brief pause before the busy life which ran its course from "steamer day" to steamer day was once more taken up. In that interval a few anxious speculators and investors breathed freely, some critical situation was relieved, or some impending catastrophe momentarily averted. In particular, a singular stroke of good fortune that morning befell Mr. Nott. He not only secured a new tenant, but, as he sagaciously believed, introduced into the Pontiac a counteracting influence to the subtle fascinations of de Ferrières.

The new tenant apparently possessed a combination of business shrewdness and brusque frankness that strongly impressed his landlord. "You see, Rosey," said Nott, complacently describing the interview to his daughter, "when I sorter intimated in a keerless kind o' way that sugar kettles and hair dye was about played out ez securities, he just planked down the money for two months in advance. 'There,' sez he, 'that's *your* security—now where's *mine?*' 'I reckon I don't hitch on, pardner,' sez I; 'security what for?' ''Spose you sell the ship?' sez he, 'afore the two months is up. I've heard that old Sleight wants to buy her.' 'Then you gets back your money,' sez I. 'And lose my room,' sez he; 'not much, old man. You sign a paper that whoever buys the ship inside o' two months hez to buy *me* ez a tenant with it; that's on the square.' So I sign the paper. It was mighty cute in the young feller, wasn't it?" he said, scanning his daughter's pretty puzzled face a little anxiously; "and don't you see ez I ain't goin' to sell the Pontiac, it's just about ez cute in me, eh? He's a contractor somewhere around yer, and wants to be near his work. So he takes the room next to the Frenchman, that that ship captain quit for the mines, and succeeds naterally to his chest and things. He's might peartlookin, that young feller, Rosey—long black moustaches, all his own color, Rosey—and he's a regular high-stepper, you bet. I reckon he's not only been a gentleman, but ez *now*. Some o' them contractors are very high-toned!"

"I don't think we have any right to give him the captain's chest, father," said Rosey; "there may be some private things in it. There were some letters and photographs in the hair-dye man's trunk that you gave the photographer."

"That's just it, Rosey," returned Abner Nott with sublime unconsciousness, "photographs and love letters you can't sell for cash, and I don't mind givin' 'em away, if they kin make a feller creature happy."

"But, father, have we the *right* to give 'em away?"

"They're collateral security, Rosey," said her father grimly. "Co-la-te-ral," he continued, emphasizing each syllable by tapping the fist of one hand in the open palm of the other. "Co-la-te-ral is the word the big business sharps yer about call 'em. You can't get round that." He paused a moment, and then, as a new idea seemed to be painfully borne in his round eyes, continued cautiously: "Was that the reason why you woudn't touch any of them dresses from the trunks of that opery gal ez skedaddled for Sacramento? And yet them trunks I regularly bought at auction—Rosey—at auction, on spec—and they didn't realize the cost of drayage."

A slight color mounted to Rosey's face. "No," she said, hastily, "not that." Hesitating a moment she then drew softly to his side, and, placing her arms around his neck, turned his broad, foolish face towards her own. "Father," she began, "when mother died, would *you* have liked anybody to take her trunks and paw around her things and wear them?"

"When your mother died, just this side o' Sweetwater, Rosey," said Mr. Nott, with beaming unconsciousness, "she hadn't any trunks. I reckon she hadn't even an extra gown hanging up in the wagin, 'cept the petticoat ez she had wrapped around yer. It was about ez much ez we could do to skirmish round with Injins, alkali, and cold, and we sorter forgot to dress for dinner. She never thought, Rosey, that you and me would live to be inhabitin' a paliss of a real ship. Ef she had she would have died a proud woman."

He turned his small, loving, boar-like eyes upon her as a preternaturally innocent and trusting companion of Ulysses might have regarded the transforming Circe. Rosey turned away with the faintest sigh. The habitual look of abstraction returned to her eyes as if she had once more taken refuge in her own ideal world. Unfortunately the change did not escape either the sensitive observation or the fatuous misconception of the sagacious parent. "Ye'll be mountin' a few furbelows and fixins, Rosey, I reckon, ez only natural. Mabbee ye'll have to prink up a little now that we've got a gentleman contractor in the ship. I'll see what I kin pick up in Montgomery Street." And indeed he succeeded a few hours later in accomplishing with equal infelicity his generous design. When she returned from her household tasks she found on her berth a purple velvet bonnet of extraordinary make, and a pair of white satin slippers. "They'll do for a start off, Rosey," he explained, "and I got 'em at my figgers."

"But I go out so seldom, father, and a bonnet—"

"That's so," interrupted Mr. Nott, complacently, "it might be jest ez well for a young gal like yer to appear ez if she *did* go out, or would go out if she wanted to. So you kin be wearin' that ar headstall kinder like this evening when the contractor's here, ez if you'd jest come in from a *pasear*."

Miss Rosey did not however immediately avail herself of her father's purchase, but contented herself with the usual scarlet ribbon that like a snood confined her brown hair, when she returned to her tasks. The space between the galley and the bulwarks had been her favorite resort in summer when not actually engaged in household work. It was now lightly roofed over with boards and tarpaulin against the winter rain, but still afforded her a veranda-like space before the gallery door, where she could read or sew, looking over the bow of the Pontiac to the tossing bay or the further range of the Contra Costa hills.

Hither Miss Rosey brought the purple prodigy, partly to please her father, partly with a view of subjecting it to violent radical changes. But after trying it on before the tiny mirror in the galley once or twice, her thoughts wandered away, and she fell into one of her habitual reveries seated on a little stool before the galley door.

She was roused from it by the slight shaking and rattling of the doors of a small hatch on the deck, not a dozen yards from where she sat. It had been evidently fastened from below during the wet weather, but as she gazed, the fastenings were removed, the doors were suddenly lifted, and the head and shoulders of a young man emerged from the deck. Partly from her father's description, and partly from the impossibility of its being anybody else, she at once conceived it to be the new lodger. She had time to note that he was young and good-looking, graver perhaps than became his sudden pantomimic appearance, but before she could observe him closely, he had turned, closed the hatch with a certain familiar dexterity, and walked slowly towards the bows. Even in her slight bewilderment, she observed that his step upon the deck seemed different to her father's or the photographer's, and that he laid his hand on various objects with a half-caressing ease and habit. Presently he paused and turned back, and glancing at the galley door for the first time encountered her wondering eyes.

It seemed so evident that she had been a curious spectator of his abrupt entrance on deck that he was at first disconcerted and confused. But after a second glance at her he appeared to resume his composure, and advanced a little defiantly towards the galley.

"I suppose I frightened you, popping up the fore hatch just now?"

"The what?" asked Rosey.

"The fore hatch," he repeated impatiently, indicating it with a gesture.

"And that's the fore hatch?" she said abstractedly. "You seem to know ships."

"Yes—a little," he said quietly. "I was below, and unfastened the hatch to come up the quickest way and take a look round. I've just hired a room here," he added explanatorily.

"I thought so," said Rosey simply; "you're the contractor?"

" The contractor !—oh, yes ! You seem to know it all."

" Father's told me."

"Oh, he's your father—Nott? Certainly. I see now," he continued, looking at her with a half repressed smile. "Certainly, Miss Nott, good morning," he half added and walked towards the companion way. Something in the direction of his eyes as he turned away made Rosey lift her hands to her head. She had forgotten to remove her father's baleful gift.

She snatched it off and ran quickly to the companion way. "Sir !" she called.

The young man turned half way down the steps and looked up. There was a faint color in her cheeks, and her pretty brown hair was slightly disheveled from the hasty removal of the bonnet.

" Father's very particular about strangers being on this deck," she said a little sharply.

" Oh—ah—I'm sorry I intruded."

" I—I—thought I'd tell you," said Rosey, frightened by her boldness into a feeble anti-climax.

" Thank you."

She came back slowly to the galley and picked up the unfortunate bonnet with a slight sense of remorse. Why should she feel angry with her poor father's unhappy offering? And what business had this strange young man to use the ship so familiarly? Yet she was vaguely conscious that she and her father, with all their love and their domestic experience of it, lacked a certain instinctive ease in its possession that the half indifferent stranger had shown on first treading its deck, She walked to the hatchway and examined it with a new interest. Succeeding in lifting the hatch, she gazed at the lower deck. As she already knew the ladder had long since been removed to make room for one of the partitions, the only way the stranger could have reached it was by leaping to one of the rings. To make sure of this she let herself down holding on to the rings, and dropped a couple of feet to the deck below. She was in the narrow passage her father had penetrated the previous night. Before her was the door leading to de Ferrieres's loft, always locked. It was silent within; it was the hour when the old Frenchman made his habitual promenade in the city. But the light from the newly-opened hatch allowed her to see more of the mysterious recesses of the forward bulkhead than she had known before, and she was startled by observing another yawning hatch-way at her feet from which the closely-fitting door had been lifted, and which the new lodger had evidently forgotten to close again. The young girl stooped 'down and peered cautiously into the black abyss. Nothing was to be seen, nothing heard but the distant gurgle and click of water in some remoter depth. She replaced the hatch and returned by way of the passage to the cabin.

When her father came home that night she briefly recounted the interview with the new lodger, and her discovery of his curiosity. She did this with a possible increase of her usual shyness and abstraction, and apparently more as a duty than a colloquial recreation. But it pleased Mr. Nott also to give it more than his usual misconception. "Looking round the ship, was he—eh, Rosey?" he said with infinite archness. "In course, kinder sweepin' round the galley, and offerin' to fetch you wood and water, eh?" Even when the young girl had picked up her book with the usual faint smile of affectionate tolerance, and then drifted away in its pages, Mr. Nott chuckled audibly. "I reckon old Frenchy didn't come by when the young one was bedevlin' you there."

"What, father?" said Rosey, lifting her abstracted eyes to his face.

At the moment it seemed impossible that any human intelligence could have suspected deceit or duplicity in Rosey's clear gaze. But Mr. Nott's intelligence was superhuman. "I was sayin' that Mr. Ferrières didn't happen in while the young feller was there—eh?"

"No, father," answered Rosey, with an effort to follow him out of the pages of her book. "Why?"

But Mr. Nott did not reply. Later in the evening he awkwardly waylaid the new lodger before the cabin door as that gentleman would have passed on to his room.

"I'm afraid," said the young man, glancing at Rosey, "that I intruded upon your daughter to-day. I was a little curious to see the old ship, and I didn't know what part of it was private."

"There ain't no private part to this yer ship—that ez, 'cepting the rooms and lofts," said Mr. Nott, authoritatively. Then, subjecting the anxious look of his daughter to his usual faculty for misconception, he added, "Thar ain't no place whar you haven't as much right to go ez any other man; thar ain't any man, furriner or Amerykan, young or old, dyed or undyed, ez hev got any better rights. You hear me, young fellow. Mr. Renshaw—my darter. My darter—Mr. Renshaw. Rosey, give the gentleman a chair. She's only jest come in from a promeynade, and hez jest taken off her bonnet," he added, with an arch look at Rosey, and a hurried look around the cabin, as if he hoped to see the missing gift visible to the general eye. "So take a seat a minit, won't ye?"

But Mr. Renshaw, after an observant glance at the young girl's abstracted face, brusquely excused himself. "I've got a letter to write," he said, with a half bow to Rosey. "Good night."

He crossed the passage to the room that had been assigned to him, and closing the door gave way to some irritability of temper in his efforts to light the lamp and adjust his writing materials. For his excuse to Mr. Nott was more truthful than most polite pretexts. He had, indeed, a letter to write, and one that, being yet young in duplicity, the near presence of his host rendered difficult. For it ran as follows:—

"DEAR SLEIGHT,

"As I found I couldn't get a chance to make any examination of the ship except as occasion offered, I just went in to rent lodgings in her from the God-forsaken old ass who owns her, and here I am a tenant for two months. I contracted for that time in case the old fool should sell out to some one else before. Except that she's cut up a little between decks by the partitions for lofts that that Pike County idiot has put into her, she looks but little changed, and her *fore-hold,* as far as I can judge, is intact. It seems that Nott bought her just as she stands, with her cargo half out, but he wasn't here when she broke cargo. If anybody else had bought her but this cursed Missourian, who hasn't got the hayseed out of his hair, I might have found out something from him, and saved myself this kind of fooling, which isn't in my line. If I could get possession of a loft on the main deck, well forward, just over the fore-hold, I could satisfy myself in a few hours, but the loft is rented by that crazy Frenchman who parades Montgomery Street every afternoon, and though old Pike County wants to turn him out, I'm afraid I can't get it for a week to come.

"If anything should happen to me, just you waltz down here and corral my things at once, for this old frontier pirate has a way of confiscating his lodgers' trunks.

"Yours, DICK."

III

If Mr. Renshaw indulged in any further curiosity regarding the interior of the Pontiac, he did not make his active researches manifest to Rosey. Nor, in spite of her father's invitation, did he again approach the galley—a fact which gave her her first vague impression in his favor. He seemed also to avoid the various advances which Mr. Nott appeared impelled to make, whenever they met in the passage, but did so without seemingly avoiding *her*, and marked his half contemptuous indifference to the elder Nott by an increase of respect to the young girl. She would have liked to ask him something about ships, and was sure his conversation would have been more interesting than that of old Captain Bower, to whose cabin he had succeeded, who had once told her a ship was the "devil's hen-coop." She would have liked also to explain to him that she was not in the habit of wearing a purple bonnet. But her thoughts were presently engrossed by an experience which interrupted the even tenor of her young life.

She had been, as she afterwards remembered, impressed with a nervous restlessness one afternoon, which made it impossible for her to perform her ordinary household duties, or even to indulge her favorite recreation of reading or castle building. She wandered over the ship, and, impelled by the same vague feeling of unrest, descended to the lower deck and the forward bulkhead where she had discovered the open hatch. It had not been again disturbed, nor was there any trace of further exploration. A little ashamed, she knew not why, of revisiting the scene of Mr. Renshaw's researches, she was turning back when she noticed that the door which communicated with de Ferrières's loft was partly open. The circumstance was so unusual that she stopped before it in surprise. There was no sound from within; it was the hour when its queer occupant was always absent; he must have forgotten to lock the door or it had been unfastened by other hands. After a moment of hesitation she pushed it further open and stepped into the room.

By the dim light of two port-holes she could see that the floor was strewn and piled with the contents of a broken bale of curled horse hair, of which a few untouched bales still remained against the wall. A heap of morocco skins, some already cut in the form of chair cushion covers, and a few cushions unfinished and unstuffed lay in the light of the ports, and gave the apartment the appearance of a cheap workshop. A rude instrument for combing the horse hair, awls, buttons, and thread heaped on a small bench showed that active work had been but recently interrupted. A cheap earthenware ewer and basin on the floor, and a pallet made of an open bale of horse hair, on which a ragged quilt and blanket were flung, indicated that the solitary worker dwelt and slept beside his work.

The truth flashed upon the young girl's active brain, quickened by seclusion and fed by solitary books. She read with keen eyes the miserable secret of her father's strange guest in the poverty-stricken walls, in the mute evidences of menial handicraft performed in loneliness and privation, in this piteous adaptation of an accident to save the conscious shame of premeditated toil. She knew now why he had stammeringly refused to receive her father's offer to buy back the goods he had given him; she knew now how hardly gained was the pittance that paid his rent and supported his childish vanity and grotesque pride. From a peg in the corner hung the familiar masquerade that hid his poverty—the pearl-gray trousers, the black frock coat, the tall shining hat—in hideous contrast to the penury of his surroundings. But if *they* were here, where was *he,* and in what new disguise had he escaped from his poverty? A vague uneasiness caused her to hesitate and return to the open door. She had nearly reached it when her eye fell on the pallet which it partly illuminated. A singular resemblance in the ragged heap made her draw closer. The faded quilt was a dressing-gown, and clutching its folds lay a white, wasted hand.

The emigrant childhood of Rose Nott had been more than once shadowed by scalping knives, and she was acquainted with Death. She went fearlessly to the couch, and found that the dressing-gown was only an enwrapping of the emaciated and lifeless body of de Ferrières. She did not retreat or call for help, but examined him closely. He was unconscious, but not pulseless; he had evidently been strong enough to open the door for air or succor, but had afterward fallen in a fit on the couch. She flew to her father's locker and the galley fire, returned, and shut the door behind her, and by the skillful use of hot water and whisky soon had the satisfaction of seeing a faint color take the place of the faded rouge in the ghastly cheeks. She was still chafing his hands when he slowly opened his eyes. With a start, he made a quick attempt to push aside her hands and rise. But she gently restrained him.

"Eh—what!" he stammered, throwing his face back from hers with an effort and trying to turn it to the wall.

"You have been ill," she said quietly. "Drink this."

With his face still turned away he lifted the cup to his chattering teeth. When he had drained it he threw a trembling glance around the room and at the door.

"There's no one been here but myself," she said quickly. "I happened to see the door open as I passed. I didn't think it worth while to call any one."

The searching look he gave her turned into an expression of relief, which, to her infinite uneasiness, again feebly lightened into one of antiquated gallantry. He drew the dressing-gown around him with an air.

"Ah! it is a goddess, Mademoiselle, that has deigned to enter the cell where—where—I—amuse myself. It is droll —is it not? I came here to make—what you call—the experiment of your father's fabric. I make myself—ha! ha! —like a workman. Ah, bah! the heat, the darkness, the plebeian motion make my head to go round. I stagger, I faint, I cry out, I fall. But what of that? The great God hears my cry and sends me an angel. *Voilà!*"

He attempted an easy gesture of gallantry, but overbalanced himself and fell sideways on the pallet with a gasp. Yet there was so much genuine feeling mixed with his grotesque affectation, so much piteous consciousness of the ineffectiveness of his falsehood, that the young girl, who had turned away, came back and laid her hand upon his arm.

"You must lie still and try to sleep," she said gently. "I will return again. Perhaps," she added, "there is some one I can send for?"

He shook his head violently. Then in his old manner added, "After Mademoiselle—no one."

"I mean—" she hesitated—"have you no friends?"

"Friends,—ah! without doubt." He shrugged his shoulders. "But Mademoiselle will comprehend—"

"You are better now," said Rosey quickly, "and no one need know anything if you don't wish it. Try to sleep. You need not lock the door when I go; I will see that no one comes in."

He flushed faintly and averted his eyes. "It is too droll, Mademoiselle, is it not?"

"Of course it is," said Rosey, glancing round the miserable room.

"And Mademoiselle is an angel."

He carried her hand to his lips humbly—his first purely unaffected action. She slipped through the door, and softly closed it behind her.

Reaching the upper deck she was relieved to find her father had not returned, and her absence had been unnoticed. For she had resolved to keep de Ferrières's secret to herself from the moment that she had unwittingly discovered it, and to do this and still be able to watch over him without her father's knowledge required some caution. She was conscious of his strange aversion to the unfortunate man without understanding the reason, but as she was in the habit of entertaining his caprices more from affectionate tolerance of his weakness than reverence of his judgment, she saw no disloyalty to him in withholding a confidence that might be disloyal to another. "It won't do father any good to know it," she said to herself, "and if it *did* it oughtn't to," she added with triumphant feminine logic. But the impression made upon her by the spectacle she had just witnessed was stronger than any other consideration. The revelation of de Ferrières's secret poverty seemed a chapter from a romance of her own weaving; for a moment it lifted the miserable hero out of the depths of his folly and selfishness. She forgot the weakness of the man in the strength of his dramatic surroundings. It partly satisfied a craving she had felt; it was not exactly the story of the ship, as she had dreamed it, but it was an episode in her experience of it that broke its monotony. That she should soon learn, perhaps from de Ferrières's own lips, the true reason of his strange seclusion, and that it involved more than appeared to her now, she never for a moment doubted.

At the end of an hour she again knocked softly at the door, carrying some light nourishment she had prepared for him. He was asleep, but she was astounded to find that in the interval he had managed to dress himself completely in his antiquated finery. It was a momentary shock to the illusion she had been fostering, but she forgot it in the pitiable contrast between his haggard face and his pomatumed hair and beard, the jauntiness of his attire, and the collapse of his invalid figure. When she had satisfied herself that his sleep was natural, she busied herself softly in arranging the miserable apartment. With a few feminine touches she removed the slovenliness of misery, and placed the loose material and ostentatious evidences of his work on one side. Finding that he still slept, and knowing the importance of this natural medication, she placed the refreshment she had brought by his side and noiselessly quitted the apartment. Hurrying through the gathering darkness between decks, she once or twice thought she had heard footsteps, and paused, but encountering no one, attributed the impression to her over-consciousness. Yet she thought it prudent to go to the galley first, where she lingered a few moments before returning to the cabin. On entering she was a little startled at observing a figure seated at her father's desk, but was relieved at finding it was Mr. Renshaw.

He rose and put aside the book he had idly picked up. "I am afraid I am an intentional intruder this time, Miss Nott. But I found no one here, and I was tempted to look into this ship-shape little snuggery. You see the temptation got the better of me."

His voice and smile were so frank and pleasant, so free from his previous restraint, yet still respectful, so youthful yet manly, that Rosey was affected by them even in her preoccupation. Her eyes brightened and then dropped before his admiring glance. Had she known that the excitement of the last few hours had brought a wonderful charm into her pretty face, had aroused the slumbering life of her half-awakened beauty, she would have been more confused. As it was, she was only glad that the young man should turn out to be "nice." Perhaps he might tell her something about ships; perhaps if she had only known him longer she might, with de Ferrières's permission, have shared her confidence with him, and enlisted his sympathy and assistance. She contented herself with showing this anticipatory gratitude in her face as she begged him, with the timidity of a maiden hostess, to resume his seat.

But Mr. Renshaw seemed to talk only to make her talk, and I am forced to admit that Rosey found this almost as pleasant. It was not long before he was in possession of her simple history from the day of her baby emigration to California to the transfer of her childish life to the old ship, and even of much of the romantic fancies she had woven into her existence there. Whatever ulterior purpose he had in view, he listened as attentively as if her artless chronicle was filled with practical information. Once, when she had paused for breath, he said gravely, "I must ask you to show me over this wonderful ship some day that I may see it with your eyes."

"But I think you know it already better than I do," said Rosey with a smile.

Mr. Renshaw's brow clouded slightly. "Ah," he said, with a touch of his former restraint; "and why?"

"Well," said Rosey timidly, "I thought you went round and touched things in a familiar way as if you had handled them before."

The young man raised his eyes to Rosey's and kept them there long enough to bring back his gentler expression. "Then, because I found you trying on a very queer bonnet the first day I saw you," he said, mischievously, "I ought to believe you were in the habit of wearing one."

In the first flush of mutual admiration young people are apt to find a laugh quite as significant as a sigh for an expression of sympathetic communion, and this master-stroke of wit convulsed them both. In the midst of it Mr. Nott entered the cabin. But the complacency with which he viewed the evident perfect understanding of the pair was destined to suffer some abatement. Rosey, suddenly conscious that she was in some way participating in ridicule of her father through his unhappy gift, became embarrassed. Mr. Renshaw's restraint returned with the presence of the old man. In vain, at first, Abner Nott strove with profound levity to indicate his arch comprehension of the situation, and in vain, later, becoming alarmed, he endeavored, with cheerful gravity, to indicate his utter obliviousness of any but a business significance in their *tête-à-tête*.

"I oughtn't to hev intruded, Rosey," he said, "when you and the gentleman were talkin' of contracts, mebbee; but don't mind me. I'm on the fly, anyhow, Rosey dear, hevin' to see a man round the corner."

But even the attitude of withdrawing did not prevent the exit of Renshaw to his apartment and of Rosey to the galley. Left alone in the cabin, Abner Nott felt in the knots and tangles of his beard for a reason. Glancing down at his prodigious boots which, covered with mud and gravel, strongly emphasized his agricultural origin, and gave him a general appearance of standing on his own broad acres, he was struck with an idea. "It's them boots," he whispered to himself, softly; "they somehow don't seem 'xactly to trump or follow suit in this yer cabin; they don't hitch into anythin', but jist slosh round loose, and, so to speak, play it alone. And them young critters nat'rally feels it and gets out o' the way." Acting upon this instinct with his usual precipitate caution, he at once proceeded to the nearest second-hand shop, and, purchasing a pair of enormous carpet slippers, originally the property of a gouty sea-captain, reappeared with a strong suggestion of newly upholstering the cabin. The improvement, however, was fraught with a portentous circumstance. Mr. Nott's footsteps, which usually announced his approach all over the ship, became stealthy and inaudible.

Meantime Miss Rosey had taken advantage of the absence of her father to visit her patient. To avoid attracting attention she did not take a light, but groped her way to the lower deck and rapped softly at the door. It was instantly opened by de Ferrières. He had apparently appreciated the few changes she had already made in the room, and had himself cleared away the pallet from which he had risen to make two low seats against the wall. Two bits of candle placed on the floor illuminated the beams above, the dressing-gown was artistically draped over the solitary chair, and a pile of cushions formed another seat. With elaborate courtesy he handed Miss Rosey to the chair. He looked pale and weak, though the gravity of the attack had evidently passed. Yet he persisted in remaining standing. "If I sit," he explained with a gesture, "I shall again disgrace myself by sleeping in Mademoiselle's presence. Yes! I shall sleep—I shall dream—and wake to find her gone?"

More embarrassed by his recovery than when he was lying helplessly before her, she said hesitatingly that she was glad he was better, and that she hoped he liked the broth.

"It was manna from heaven, Mademoiselle. See, I have taken it all—every precious drop. What else could I have done for Mademoiselle's kindness?"

He showed her the empty bowl. A swift conviction came upon her that the man had been suffering from want of food. The thought restored her self-possession even while it brought the tears to her eyes. "I wish you would let me speak to father—or some one," she said impulsively, and stopped.

A quick and half insane gleam of terror and suspicion lit up his deep eyes. "For what, Mademoiselle! For an accident—that is nothing—absolutely nothing, for I am strong and well now—see!" he said tremblingly. "Or for a whim—for a folly you may say, that they will misunderstand. No, Mademoiselle is good, is wise. She will say to herself, 'I understand, my friend Monsieur de Ferrières for the moment has a secret. He would seem poor, he would take the *rôle* of artisan, he would shut himself up in these walls—perhaps I may guess why, but it is his secret. I think of it no more.'" He caught her hand in his with a gesture that he would have made one of gallantry, but that in its tremulous intensity became a piteous supplication.

"I have said nothing, and will say nothing, if you wish it," said Rosey hastily; "but others may find out how you live here. This is not fit work for you. You seem to be a—a gentleman. You ought to be a lawyer, or a doctor, or in a bank," she continued timidly, with a vague enumeration of the prevailing degrees of local gentility.

He dropped her hand. "Ah! does not Mademoiselle comprehend that it is *because* I am a gentleman that there is nothing between it and this? Look!" he continued almost fiercely. "What if I told you it is the lawyer, it is the doctor, it is the banker that brings me, a gentleman, to this, eh? Ah, bah! What do I say? This is honest, what I do! But the lawyer, the banker, the doctor, what are they?" He shrugged his shoulders, and pacing the apartment with a furtive glance at the half anxious, half frightened girl, suddenly stopped, dragged a small portmanteau from behind the heap of bales and opened it. "Look, Mademoiselle," he said, tremulously lifting a handful of worn and soiled letters and papers. "Look—these are the tools of your banker, your lawyer, your doctor. With this the banker will make you poor, the lawyer will prove you a thief, the doctor will swear you are crazy, eh? What shall you call the work of a gentleman—this"—he dragged the pile of cushions forward—"or this?"

To the young girl's observant eyes some of the papers appeared to be of a legal or official character, and others like bills of lading, with which she was familiar. Their half-theatrical exhibition reminded her of some play she had seen; they might be the clue to some story, or the mere worthless hoardings of a diseased fancy. Whatever they were, de Ferrières did not apparently care to explain further; indeed, the next moment his manner changed to his old absurd extravagance. "But this is stupid for Mademoiselle to hear. What shall we speak of? Ah, what *should* we speak of in Mademoiselle's presence?"

"But are not these papers valuable?" asked Rosey, partly to draw her host's thoughts back to their former channel.

"Perhaps." He paused and regarded the young girl fixedly. "Does Mademoiselle think so?"

"I don't know," said Rosey. "How should I?"

"Ah! if Mademoiselle thought so—if Mademoiselle would deign—" He stopped again and placed his hand upon his forehead. "It might be so!" he muttered.

"I must go now," said Rosey, hurriedly, rising with an awkward sense of constraint. "Father will wonder where I am."

"I shall explain. I will accompany you, Mademoiselle."

"No, no," said Rosey, quickly; "he must not know I have been here!" She stopped. The honest blush flew to her cheek, and then returned again, because she had blushed.

De Ferrières gazed at her with an exalted look. Then drawing himself to his full height, he said, with an exaggerated and indescribable gesture, "Go, my child, go. Tell your father that you have been alone and unprotected in the abode of poverty and suffering, but—that it was in the presence of Armand de Ferrières."

He threw open the door with a bow that nearly swept the ground, but did not again offer to take her hand. At once impressed and embarrassed at this crowning incongruity, her pretty lip trembled between a smile and a cry

as she said, "Good-night," and slipped away into the
darkness.

Erect and grotesque de Ferrières retained the same attitude until the sound of her footsteps was lost, when he
slowly began to close the door. But a strong arm arrested
it from without, and a large carpeted foot appeared at
the bottom of the narrowing opening. The door yielded,
and Mr. Abner Nott entered the room.

IV

With an exclamation and a hurried glance around him,
de Ferrières threw himself before the intruder. But slowly
lifting his large hand, and placing it on his lodger's breast,
he quietly overbore the sick man's feeble resistance with
an impact of power that seemed almost as moral as it was
physical. He did not appear to take any notice of the
room or its miserable surroundings; indeed, scarcely of the
occupant. Still pushing him, with abstracted eyes and im-
mobile face, to the chair that Rosey had just quitted, he
made him sit down, and then took up his own position on
the pile of cushions opposite. His usually underdone complexion was of watery blueness; but his dull, abstracted
glance appeared to exercise a certain dumb, narcotic fascination on his lodger.

"I mout," said Nott, slowly, "hev laid ye out here on
sight, without enny warnin', or dropped ye in yer tracks
in Montgomery Street, wherever ther was room to work a
six-shooter in comf'ably? Johnson, of Petaluny—him, ye
know, ez had a game eye—fetched Flynn comin' outer
meetin' one Sunday, and it was only on account of his wife,
and she a second-hand one, so to speak. There was Walker,
of Contra Costa, plugged that young Sacramento chap,
whose name I disremember, full o' holes just ez *he* was
sayin' 'Good by' to his darter. I mout hev done all this if
it had settled things to please me. For while you and
Flynn and that Sacramento chap ez all about the same
sort o' men, Rosey's a different kind from their sort o'
women."

"Mademoiselle is an angel!" said de Ferrières, suddenly rising, with an excess of extravagance. "A saint! Look! I cram the lie, ha! down his throat who challenges it."

"Ef by mam'selle ye mean my Rosey," said Nott, quietly laying his powerful hands on de Ferrières's shoulders, and slowly pinning him down again upon his chair, "ye're about right, though she ain't mam'selle yet. Ez I was sayin', I might hev killed you off-hand if I hed thought it would hev been a good thing for Rosey."

"For her? Ah, well! Look, I am ready," interrupted de Ferrières, again springing to his feet, and throwing open his coat with both hands. "See! here at my heart—fire!"

"Ez I was sayin'," continued Nott, once more pressing the excited man down in his chair, "I might hev wiped ye out—and mebbee ye wouldn't hev keered—or *you* might hev wiped *me* out, and I mout hev said, 'Thank'ee,' but I reckon this ain't a case for what's comf'able for you and me. It's what's good for *Rosey*. And the thing to kalkilate is, what's to be done."

His small round eyes for the first time rested on de Ferrières's face, and were quickly withdrawn. It was evident that this abstracted look, which had fascinated his lodger, was merely a resolute avoidance of de Ferrières's glance, and it became apparent later that this avoidance was due to a ludicrous appreciation of de Ferrières's attractions.

"And after we've done *that* we must kalkilate what Rosey *is*, and what Rosey wants. P'raps, ye allow, *you* know what Rosey is? P'raps you've seen her prance round in velvet bonnets and white satin slippers, and sich. P'raps you've seen her readin' tracks and v'yages, without waitin' to spell a word, or catch her breath. But that ain't the Rosey ez *I* know. It's a little child ez uster crawl in and out the tail-board of a Mizzouri wagon on the alcali pizoned plains, where there wasn't another bit of God's mercy on yearth to be seen for miles and miles. It's a little gal as uster hunger and thirst ez quiet and mannerly ez she now eats and drinks in plenty; whose voice was ez steady with Injins yelling round her nest in the leaves on Sweetwater ez in her purty cabin up yonder. *That's* the gal ez I know! That's the Rosey ez my ole woman puts into my arms one night arter we left Laramie when the fever was high, and sez, 'Abner,' sez she, 'the chariot is swingin' low for me to-night, but thar ain't room in it for her or you to git in or hitch on. Take her and rare her, so we kin all jine on the other shore,' sez she. And I'd knowed the other shore wasn't no Kaliforny. And that night, p'raps, the chariot swung lower than ever before, and my ole woman stepped into it, and left me and Rosey to creep on in the old wagon alone. It's them kind o' things," added Mr. Nott thoughtfully, "that seem to pint to my killin' you on sight ez the best thing to be done. And yet Rosey mightn't like it."

He had slipped one of his feet out of his huge carpet slippers, and, as he reached down to put it on again, he added calmly: "And ez to yer marrying *her* it ain't to be done."

The utterly bewildered expression which transfigured de Ferrières's face at this announcement was unobserved by Nott's averted eyes, nor did he perceive that his listener the next moment straightened his erect figure and adjusted his cravat.

"Ef Rosey," he continued, "hez read in vy'ges and tracks in Eyetalian and French countries of such chaps ez you and kalkilates you're the right kind to tie to, mebbee it mout hev done if you'd been livin' over thar in a pallis, but somehow it don't jibe in over here and agree with a ship—and that ship lying comf'able ashore in San Francisco. You don't seem to suit the climate, you see, and your general gait is likely to stampede the other cattle. Agin," said Nott, with an ostentation of looking at his companion but really gazing on vacancy, "this fixed up, antique style of yours goes better with them ivy kivered ruins in Rome and Palmyry that Rosey's mixed you up with, than it would yere. I ain't saying," he added as de Ferrières was about to speak, "I ain't sayin' ez that child ain't smitten with ye. It ain't no use to lie and say she don't prefer you to her old father, or young chaps of her own age and kind. I've seed it afor now. I suspicioned it afor I seed her slip out o' this place to-night. Thar! keep your hair on, such ez it is!" he added as de Ferrières attempted a quick deprecatory gesture. "I ain't askin

yer how often she comes here, nor what she sez to you
nor you to her. I ain't asked her and I don't ask you.
I'll allow ez you've settled all the preliminaries and bought
her the ring and sich; I'm only askin' you now, kalkilatin
you've got all the keerds in your own hand, what you'll
take to step out and leave the board?"

The dazed look of de Ferrières might have forced itself
even upon Nott's one-idead fatuity, had it not been a part
of that gentleman's system delicately to look another way
at that moment so as not to embarrass his adversary's
calculation. "Pardon," stammered de Ferrières, "but I do
not comprehend!" He raised his hand to his head. "I am
not well—I am stupid. Ah, mon Dieu!"

"I ain't sayin'," added Nott more gently, "ez you don't
feel bad. It's nat'ral. But it ain't business. I'm asking
you," he continued, taking from his breast-pocket a large
wallet, "how much you'll take in cash now, and the rest
next steamer day, to give up Rosey and leave the ship."

De Ferrières staggered to his feet despite Nott's re-
straining hand. "To leave Mademoiselle and leave the
ship?" he said huskily, "is it not?"

"In course. Yer can leave things yer just ez you
found 'em when you came, you know," continued Nott,
for the first time looking around the miserable apartment.
"It's a business job. I'll take the bales back ag'in, and
you kin reckon up what you're out, countin' Rosey and loss
o' time."

"He wishes me to go—he has said," repeated de Ferrières to himself thickly.

"Ef you mean me when you say him, and ez thar ain't
any other man around, I reckon you do—'yes!'"

"And he asks me—he—this man of the feet and the
daughter—asks me—de Ferrières—what I will take," continued de Ferrières, buttoning his coat. "No! it is a
dream!" He walked stiffly to the corner where his portmanteau lay, lifted it, and going to the outer door, a cut
through the ship's side that communicated with the alley,
unlocked it and flung it open to the night. A thick mist
like the breath of the ocean flowed into the room.

"You ask me what I shall take to go," he said as he

stood on the threshold. "I shall take what *you* cannot give,
Monsieur, but what I would not keep if I stood here another
moment. I take my Honor, Monsieur, and—I take my
leave!"

For a moment his grotesque figure was outlined in the
opening, and then disappeared as if he had dropped into
an invisible ocean below. Stupefied and disconcerted at
this complete success of his overtures, Abner Nott remained
speechless, gazing at the vacant space until a cold influx
of the mist recalled him. Then he rose and shuffled quickly
to the door.

"Hi! Ferrers! Look yer—Say! Wot's your hurry,
pardner?"

But there was no response. The thick mist, which hid
the surrounding objects, seemed to deaden all sound also.
After a moment's pause he closed the door, but did not
lock it, and retreating to the centre of the room remained
blinking at the two candles and plucking some perplexing
problem from his beard. Suddenly an idea seized him.
Rosey! Where was she? Perhaps it had been a pre-
concerted plan, and she had fled with him. Putting out
the lights, he stumbled hurriedly through the passage to
the gangway above. The cabin-door was open; there was
the sound of voices—Renshaw's and Rosey's. Mr. Nott felt
relieved but not unembarrassed. He would have avoided his
daughter's presence that evening. But even while making
this resolution with characteristic infelicity he blundered
into the room. Rosey looked up with a slight start; Renshaw's animated face was changed to its former expression
of inward discontent.

"You came in so like a ghost, father," said Rosey with
a slight peevishness that was new to her. "And I thought
you were in town. Don't go, Mr. Renshaw."

But Mr. Renshaw intimated that he had already tres-
passed upon Miss Nott's time, and that no doubt her
father wanted to talk with her. To his surprise and
annoyance, however, Mr. Nott insisted on accompanying him to his room, and without heeding Renshaw's
cold "Good-night," entered and closed the door behind
him.

"P'rap's," said Mr. Nott with a troubled air, "you disremember that when you first kem here you asked me if you could hev that 'er loft that the Frenchman had down stairs."

"No, I don't remember it," said Renshaw almost rudely. "But," he added, after a pause, with an air of a man obliged to revive a stale and unpleasant memory, "if I did—what about it?"

"Nuthin', only that you kin hev it to-morrow, ez that 'ere Frenchman is movin' out," responded Nott. "I thought you was sorter keen about it when you first kem."

"Umph! we'll talk about it to-morrow." Something in the look of wearied perplexity with which Mr. Nott was beginning to regard his own *mal à propos* presence, arrested the young man's attention. "What's the reason you didn't sell this old ship long ago, take a decent house in the town, and bring up your daughter like a lady?" he asked with a sudden blunt good humor. But even this implied blasphemy against the habitation he worshiped did not prevent Mr. Nott from his usual misconstruction of the question.

"I reckon, now, Rosey's got high-flown ideas of livin' in a castle with ruins, eh?" he said cunningly.

"Haven't heard her say," returned Renshaw abruptly. "Good-night."

Firmly convinced that Rosey had been unable to conceal from Mr. Renshaw the influence of her dreams of a castellated future with de Ferrières, he regained the cabin. Satisfying himself that his daughter had retired, he sought his own couch. But not to sleep. The figure of de Ferrières, standing in the ship side and melting into the outer darkness, haunted him, and compelled him in dreams to rise and follow him through the alleys and by-ways of the crowded city. Again, it was a part of his morbid suspicion that he now invested the absent man with a potential significance and an unknown power. What deep-laid plans might he not form to possess himself of Rosey, of which he, Abner Nott, would be ignorant? Unchecked by the restraint of a father's roof he would now give full license to his power. "Said he'd take his Honor with him," muttered Abner to himself in the dim watches of the night; "lookin' at that sayin' in its right light, it looks bad."

V

The elaborately untruthful account which Mr. Nott gave his daughter of de Ferrières's sudden departure was more fortunate than his usual equivocations. While it disappointed and slightly mortified her, it did not seem to her inconsistent with what she already knew of him. "Said his doctor had ordered him to quit town under an hour, owing to a comin' attack of hay fever, and he had a friend from furrin parts waitin' him at the Springs, Rosey," explained Nott, hesitating between his desire to avoid his daughter's eyes and his wish to observe her countenance.

"Was he worse?—I mean did he look badly, father?" inquired Rosey thoughtfully.

"I reckon not exackly bad. Kinder looked ez if he mout be worse soon ef he didn't hump hisself."

"Did you see him?—in his room?" asked Rosey anxiously. Upon the answer to this simple question depended the future confidential relations of father and daughter. If her father had himself detected the means by which his lodger existed, she felt that her own obligations to secrecy had been removed. But Mr. Nott's answer disposed of this vain hope. It was a response after his usual fashion to the question he *imagined* she artfully wished to ask, *i. e.* if he had discovered their rendezvous of the previous night. This it was part of his peculiar delicacy to ignore. Yet his reply showed that he had been unconscious of the one miserable secret that he might have read easily.

"I was there an hour or so—him and me alone—discussin' trade. I reckon he's got a good thing outer that curled horse hair, for I see he's got in an invoice o' cushions. I've stored 'em all in the forrard bulkhead until he sends for 'em, ez Mr. Renshaw hez taken the loft."

But although Mr. Renshaw had taken the loft, he did not seem in haste to occupy it. He spent part of the morning in uneasily pacing his room, in occasional sallies into the street from which he purposelessly returned, and once or twice in distant and furtive contemplation of Rosey at work in the galley. This last observation was not unnoticed by the astute Nott, who at once conceiving that he was nourishing a secret and hopeless passion for Rosey, began to consider whether it was not his duty to warn the young man of her preoccupied affections. But Mr. Renshaw's final disappearance obliged him to withhold his confidence till morning.

This time Mr. Renshaw left the ship with the evident determination of some settled purpose. He walked rapidly until he reached the counting-house of Mr. Sleight, when he was at once shown into a private office. In a few moments Mr. Sleight, a brusque but passionless man, joined him.

"Well," said Sleight, closing the door carefully. "What news?"

"None," said Renshaw bluntly. "Look here, Sleight," he added, turning to him suddenly. "Let me out of this game. I don't like it."

"Does that mean you've found nothing?" asked Sleight, sarcastically.

"It means that I haven't looked for anything, and that I don't intend to without the full knowledge of that d——d fool who owns the ship."

"You've changed your mind since you wrote that letter," said Sleight coolly, producing from a drawer the note already known to the reader. Renshaw mechanically extended his hand to take it. Mr. Sleight dropped the letter back into the drawer, which he quietly locked. The apparently simple act dyed Mr. Renshaw's cheek with color, but it vanished quickly, and with it any token of his previous embarrassment. He looked at Sleight with the convinced air of a resolute man who had at last taken a disagreeable step but was willing to stand by the consequences.

"I *have* changed my mind," he said coolly. "I found out that it was one thing to go down there as a skilled prospector might go to examine a mine that was to be valued according to his report of the indications, but that it was entirely another thing to go and play the spy in a poor devil's house in order to buy something he didn't know he was selling and wouldn't sell if he did."

"And something that the man *he* bought of didn't think of selling; something *he* himself never paid for, and never expected to buy," sneered Sleight.

"But something that *we* expect to buy from our knowledge of all this, and it is that which makes all the difference."

"But you knew all this before."

"I never saw it in this light before! I never thought of it until I was living there face to face with the old fool I was intending to overreach. I never was *sure* of it until this morning, when he actually turned out one of his lodgers that I might have the very room I required to play off our little game in comfortably. When he did that, I made up my mind to drop the whole thing, and I'm here to do it."

"And let somebody else take the responsibility—with the percentage—unless you've also felt it your duty to warn Nott too," said Sleight with a sneer.

"You only dare say that to me, Sleight," said Renshaw quietly, "because you have in that drawer an equal evidence of my folly and my confidence; but if you are wise you will not presume too far on either. Let us see how we stand. Through the yarn of a drunken captain and a mutinous sailor you became aware of an unclaimed shipment of treasure, concealed in an unknown ship that entered this harbor. You are enabled, through me, to corroborate some facts and identify the ship. You proposed to me, as a speculation, to identify the treasure if possible before you purchased the ship. I accepted the offer without consideration; on consideration I now decline it, but without prejudice or loss to any one but myself. As to your insinuation I need not remind you that my presence here to-day refutes it. I would not require your permission to make a much better bargain with a good natured fool like Nott than I could with you. Or if I did not care for the business I could have warned the girl—"

"The girl—what girl?"

Renshaw bit his lip but answered boldly, "The old man's

daughter—a poor girl—whom this act would rob as well as her father."

Sleight looked at his companion attentively. "You might have said so at first, and let up on this camp-meetin' exhortation. Well then—admitting you've got the old man and the young girl on the same string, and that you've played it pretty low down in the short time you've been there—I suppose, Dick Renshaw, I've got to see your bluff. Well, how much is it! What's the figure you and she have settled on?"

For an instant Mr. Sleight was in physical danger. But before he had finished speaking Renshaw's quick sense of the ludicrous had so far overcome his first indignation as to enable him even to admire the perfect moral insensibility of his companion. As he rose and walked towards the door, he half wondered that he had ever treated the affair seriously. With a smile he replied:

"Far from bluffing, Sleight, I am throwing my cards on the table. Consider that I've passed out. Let some other man take my hand. Rake down the pot if you like, old man, I leave for Sacramento to-night. Adios."

When the door had closed behind him Mr Sleight summoned his clerk.

"Is that petition for grading Pontiac Street ready?"

"I've seen the largest property holders, sir; they're only waiting for you to sign first." Mr. Sleight paused and then affixed his signature to the paper his clerk laid before him. "Get the other names and send it up at once."

"If Mr. Nott doesn't sign, sir?"

"No matter. He will be assessed all the same." Mr. Sleight took up his hat.

"The Lascar seaman that was here the other day has been wanting to see you, sir. I said you were busy."

Mr. Sleight put down his hat. "Send him up."

Nevertheless Mr. Sleight sat down and at once abstracted himself so completely as to be apparently in utter oblivion of the man who entered. He was lithe and Indian-looking; bearing in dress and manner the careless slouch without the easy frankness of a sailor.

"Well!" said Sleight without looking up.

"I was only wantin' to know ef you had any news for me, boss?"

"News?" echoed Sleight as if absently; "news of what?"

"That little matter of the Pontiac we talked about, boss," returned the Lascar with an uneasy servility in the whites of his teeth and eyes.

"Oh," said Sleight, "that's played out. It's a regular fraud. It's an old forecastle yarn, my man, that you can't reel off in the cabin."

The sailor's face darkened.

"The man who was looking into it has thrown the whole thing up. I tell you it's played out!" repeated Sleight, without raising his head.

"It's true, boss—every word," said the Lascar, with an appealing insinuation that seemed to struggle hard with savage earnestness. "You can swear me, boss; I wouldn't lie to a gentleman like you. Your man hasn't half looked, or else—it must be there, or—"

"That's just it," said Sleight slowly; "who's to know that your friends haven't been there already?—that seems to have been your style."

"But no one knew it but me, until I told you, I swear to God. I ain't lying, boss, and I ain't drunk. Say—don't give it up, boss. That man of yours likely don't believe it, because he don't know anything about it. I *do*—I could find it."

A silence followed. Mr. Sleight remained completely absorbed in his papers for some moments. Then glancing at the Lascar, he took his pen, wrote a hurried note, folded it, addressed it, and, holding it between his fingers, leaned back in his chair.

"If you choose to take this note to my man, he may give it another show. Mind, I don't say that he *will*. He's going to Sacramento to-night, but you could go down there and find him before he starts. He's got a room there, I believe. While you're waiting for him, you might keep your eyes open to satisfy yourself."

"Ay, ay, sir," said the sailor, eagerly endeavoring to catch the eye of his employer. But Mr. Sleight looked straight before him, and he turned to go.

"The Sacramento boat goes at nine," said Mr. Sleight quietly.

This time their glances met, and the Lascar's eye glistened with subtle intelligence. The next moment he was gone, and Mr. Sleight again became absorbed in his papers.

Meanwhile Renshaw was making his way back to the Pontiac with that light-hearted optimism that had characterized his parting with Sleight. It was this quality of his nature, fostered perhaps by the easy civilization in which he moved, that had originally drawn him into relations with the man he had just quitted; a quality that had been troubled and darkened by those relations, yet, when they were broken, at once returned. It consequently did not occur to him that he had only selfishly compromised with the difficulty; it seemed to him enough that he had withdrawn from a compact he thought dishonorable; he was not called upon to betray his partner in that compact merely to benefit others. He had been willing to incur suspicion and loss to reinstate himself in his self-respect, more he could not do without justifying that suspicion. The view taken by Sleight was, after all, that which most business men would take—which even the unbusiness-like Nott would take—which the girl herself might be tempted to listen to. Clearly he could do nothing but abandon the Pontiac and her owner to the fate he could not in honor avert. And even that fate was problematical. It did not follow that the treasure was still concealed in the Pontiac, nor that Nott would be willing to sell her. He would make some excuse to Nott—he smiled to think he would probably be classed in the long line of absconding tenants—he would say good-by to Rosey, and leave for Sacramento that night. He ascended the stairs to the gangway with a freer breast than when he first entered the ship.

Mr. Nott was evidently absent, and after a quick glance at the half-open cabin door, Renshaw turned towards the galley. But Miss Rosey was not in her accustomed haunt, and with a feeling of disappointment, which seemed inconsistent with so slight a cause, he crossed the deck impatiently and entered his room. He was about to close the door when the prolonged rustle of a trailing skirt in the passage attracted his attention. The sound was so unlike that made by any garment worn by Rosey that he remained motionless, with his hand on the door. The sound approached nearer, and the next moment a white veiled figure with a trailing skirt slowly swept past the room. Renshaw's pulses halted for an instant in half superstitious awe. As the apparition glided on and vanished in the cabin door he could only see that it was the form of a beautiful and graceful woman—but nothing more. Bewildered and curious, he forgot himself so far as to follow it, and impulsively entered the cabin. The figure turned, uttered a little cry, threw the veil aside, and showed the half troubled, half blushing face of Rosey.

"I—beg—your pardon," stammered Renshaw; "I didn't know it was you."

"I was trying on some things," said Rosey, recovering her composure and pointing to an open trunk that seemed to contain a theatrical wardrobe—"some things father gave me long ago. I wanted to see if there was anything I could use. I thought I was all alone in the ship, but fancying I heard a noise forward I came out to see what it was. I suppose it must have been you."

She raised her clear eyes to his, with a slight touch of womanly reserve that was so incompatible with any vulgar vanity or girlish coquetry that he became the more embarrassed. Her dress, too, of a slightly antique shape, rich but simple, seemed to reveal and accent a certain repose of gentlewomanliness, that he was now wishing to believe he had always noticed. Conscious of a superiority in her that now seemed to change their relations completely, he alone remained silent, awkward, and embarrassed before the girl who had taken care of his room, and who cooked in the galley! What he had thoughtlessly considered a merely vulgar business intrigue against her stupid father, now to his extravagant fancy assumed the proportions of a sacrilege to herself.

"You've had your revenge, Miss Nott, for the fright I once gave you," he said a little uneasily, "for you quite startled me just now as you passed. I began to think the Pontiac was haunted. I thought you were a ghost. I don't know why such a ghost should *frighten* anybody," he went on with a desperate attempt to recover his position by gallantry. "Let me see—that's Donna Elvira's dress—is it not?"

"I don't think that was the poor woman's name," said Rosey simply; "she died of yellow fever at New Orleans as Signora somebody."

Her ignorance seemed to Mr. Renshaw so plainly to partake more of the nun than the provincial that he hesitated to explain to her that he meant the heroine of an opera.

"It seems dreadful to put on the poor thing's clothes, doesn't it?" she added.

Mr. Renshaw's eyes showed so plainly that he thought otherwise, that she drew a little austerely towards the door of her state-room.

"I must change these things before any one comes," she said dryly.

"That means I must go, I suppose. But couldn't you let me wait here or in the gangway until then, Miss Nott? I am going away to-night, and I mayn't see you again." He had not intended to say this, but it slipped from his embarrassed tongue. She stopped with her hand on the door.

"You are going away?"

"I—think—I must leave to-night. I have some important business in Sacramento."

She raised her frank eyes to his. The unmistakable look of disappointment that he saw in them gave his heart a sudden throb and sent the quick blood to his cheeks.

"It's too bad," she said, abstractedly. "Nobody ever seems to stay here long. Captain Bower promised to tell me all about the ship and he went away the second week. The photographer left before he finished the picture of the Pontiac; Monsieur de Ferrières has only just gone, and now *you* are going."

"Perhaps, unlike them, I have finished my season of usefulness here," he replied, with a bitterness he would have recalled the next moment. But Rosey, with a faint sigh, saying, "I won't be long," entered the state-room and closed the door behind her.

Renshaw bit his lip and pulled at the long silken threads of his moustache until they smarted. Why had he not gone at once? Why was it necessary to say he might not see her again—and if he had said it, why should he add anything more? What was he waiting for now? To endeavor to prove to her that he really bore no resemblance to Captain Bower, the photographer, the crazy Frenchman de Ferrières? Or would he be forced to tell her that he was running away from a conspiracy to defraud her father— merely for something to say? Was there ever such folly? Rosey was "not long," as she had said, but he was beginning to pace the narrow cabin impatiently when the door opened and she returned.

She had resumed her ordinary calico gown, but such was the impression left upon Renshaw's fancy that she seemed to wear it with a new grace. At any other time he might have recognized the change as due to a new corset, which strict veracity compels me to record Rosey had adopted for the first time that morning. Howbeit, her slight coquetry seemed to have passed, for she closed the open trunk with a return of her old listless air, and sitting on it rested her elbows on her knees and her oval chin in her hands.

"I wish you would do me a favor," she said after a reflective pause.

"Let me know what it is and it shall be done," replied Renshaw quickly.

"If you should come across Monsieur de Ferrières, or hear of him, I wish you would let me know. He was very poorly when he left here, and I should like to know if he was better. He didn't say where he was going. At least, he didn't tell father; but I fancy he and father don't agree."

"I shall be very glad of having even *that* opportunity of making you remember me, Miss Nott," returned Renshaw with a faint smile; "I don't suppose either that it would be very difficult to get news of your friend—everybody seems to know him."

"But not as I did," said Rosey with an abstracted little sigh.

Mr. Renshaw opened his brown eyes upon her. Was he mistaken? Was this romantic girl only a little coquette playing her provincial airs on him? "You say he and your father didn't agree? That means, I suppose, that *you* and he agreed?—and that was the result."

"I don't think father knew anything about it," said Rosey simply.

Mr. Renshaw rose. And this was what he had been waiting to hear! "Perhaps," he said grimly, "you would also like news of the photographer and Captain Bower, or did your father agree with them better?"

"No," said Rosey quietly. She remained silent for a moment, and lifting her lashes said, "Father always seemed to agree with *you*, and that—" she hesitated.

"That's why *you* don't."

"I didn't say that," said Rosey with an incongruous increase of coldness and color. "I only meant to say it was that which makes it seem so hard you should go now."

Notwithstanding his previous determination Renshaw found himself sitting down again. Confused and pleased, wishing he had said more—or less—he said nothing, and Rosey was forced to continue.

"It's strange, isn't it—but father was urging me this morning to make a visit to some friends at the old Ranch. I didn't want to go. I like it much better here."

"But you cannot bury yourself here forever, Miss Nott," said Renshaw with a sudden burst of honest enthusiasm. "Sooner or later you will be forced to go where you will be properly appreciated, where you will be admired and courted, where your slightest wish will be law. Believe me, without flattery, you don't know your own power."

"It doesn't seem strong enough to keep even the little I like here," said Rosey with a slight glistening of the eyes. "But," she added hastily, "you don't know how much the dear old ship is to me. It's the only home I think I ever had."

"But the Ranch?" said Renshaw.

"The Ranch seemed to be only the old wagon halted in the road. It was a very little improvement on outdoors," said Rosey with a little shiver. "But this is so cozy and snug and yet so strange and foreign. Do you know I think I began to understand why I like it so since you taught me so much about ships and voyages. Before that I only learned from books. Books deceive you, I think, more than people do. Don't you think so?"

She evidently did not notice the quick flush that covered his cheeks and apparently dazzled his troubled eyelid, for she went on confidentially.

"I was thinking of you yesterday. I was sitting by the galley door, looking forward. You remember the first day I saw you when you startled me by coming up out of the hatch?"

"I wish you wouldn't think of that," said Renshaw, with more earnestness than he would have made apparent.

"*I* don't want to either," said Rosey, gravely, "for I've had a strange fancy about it. I saw once when I was younger, a picture in a print shop in Montgomery Street that haunted me. I think it was called 'The Pirate.' There was a number of wicked-looking sailors lying around the deck, and coming out of a hatch was one figure with his hands on the deck and a cutlass in his mouth."

"Thank you," said Renshaw.

"You don't understand. He was horrid-looking, not at all like you. I never thought of *him* when I first saw you; but the other day I thought how dreadful it would have been if some one like him and not like you had come up then. That made me nervous sometimes of being alone. I think father is too. He often goes about stealthily at night, as if he was watching for something."

Renshaw's face grew suddenly dark. Could it be possible that Sleight had always suspected him, and set spies to watch—or was he guilty of some double intrigue?

"He thinks," continued Rosey with a faint smile, "that some one is looking around the ship, and talks of setting bear-traps. I hope you're not mad, Mr. Renshaw," she added, suddenly catching sight of his changed expression, "at my foolishness in saying you reminded me of the pirate. I meant nothing."

"I know you're incapable of meaning anything but good to anybody, Miss Nott, perhaps to me more than I deserve," said Renshaw with a sudden burst of feeling. "I wish—I wish—you would do *me* a favor. *You* asked me one just now." He had taken her hand. It seemed so like a mere illustration of his earnestness, that she did not withdraw it. "Your father tells you everything. If he has any offer to dispose of the ship, will you write to me at once before anything is concluded?" He winced a little —the sentence of Sleight, "What's the figure you and she have settled upon?" flashed across his mind. He scarcely noticed that Rosey had withdrawn her hand coldly.

"Perhaps you had better speak to father, as it is *his* business. Besides, I shall not be here. I shall be at the Ranch."

"But you said you didn't want to go?"

"I've changed my mind," said Rosey listlessly. "I shall go to-night."

She rose as if to indicate that the interview was ended. With an overpowering instinct that his whole future happiness depended upon his next act, he made a step towards her, with eager outstretched hands. But she slightly lifted her own with a warning gesture, "I hear father coming— you will have a chance to talk *business* with him," she said, and vanished into her state-room.

VI

The heavy tread of Abner Nott echoed in the passage. Confused and embarrassed, Renshaw remained standing at the door that had closed upon Rosey as her father entered the cabin. Providence, which always fostered Mr. Nott's characteristic misconceptions, left that perspicacious parent but one interpretation of the situation. Rosey had evidently just informed Mr. Renshaw that she loved another!

"I was just saying 'good-by' to Miss Nott," said Renshaw, hastily regaining his composure with an effort. "I am going to Sacramento to-night, and will not return. I—"

"In course, in course," interrupted Nott, soothingly; "that's wot you say now, and that's what you allow to do. That's wot they allus do."

"I mean," said Renshaw, reddening at what he conceived to be an allusion to the absconding propensities of Nott's previous tenants,—"I mean that you shall keep the advance to cover any loss you might suffer through my giving up the rooms."

"Certingly," said Nott, laying his hand with a large sympathy on Renshaw's shoulder; "but we'll drop that just now. We won't swap hosses in the middle of the river. We'll square up accounts in your room," he added, raising his voice that Rosey might overhear him, after a preliminary wink at the young man. "Yes, sir, we'll just square up and settle in there. Come along, Mr. Renshaw." Pushing him with paternal gentleness from the cabin, with his hand still upon his shoulder, he followed him into the passage. Half annoyed at his familiarity, yet not altogether displeased by this illustration of Rosey's belief of his preference, Renshaw wonderingly accompanied him. Nott closed the door, and pushing the young man into a chair, deliberately seated himself at the table opposite. "It's just as well that Rosey reckons that you and me is settlin' our accounts," he began, cunningly, "and mebbee it's just ez well ez she should reckon you're goin' away."

"But I *am* going," interrupted Renshaw, impatiently. "I leave to-night."

"Surely, surely," said Nott, gently, "that's wot you kalkilate to do; that's just nat'ral in a young feller. That's about what I reckon *I'd* hev done to her mother if anythin' like this hed ever cropped up, which it didn't. Not but what Almiry Jane had young fellers enough round her, but, 'cept ole Judge Peter, ez was lamed in the War of 1812, there ain't no similarity ez I kin see," he added, musingly.

"I am afraid I can't see any similarity either, Mr. Nott," said Renshaw, struggling between a dawning sense of some impending absurdity and his growing passion for Rosey. "For Heaven's sake speak out if you've got anything to say."

Mr. Nott leaned forward, and placed his large hand on the young man's shoulder. "That's it. That's what I sed to myself when I seed how things were pintin'. 'Speak out,' sez I, 'Abner! Speak out if you've got anything to say.

You kin trust this yer Mr. Renshaw. He ain't the kind of man to creep into the bosom of a man's ship for pupposes of his own. He ain't a man that would hunt round until he discovered a poor man's treasure, and then try to rob—' "

"Stop!" said Renshaw, with a set face and darkening eyes. "*What* treasure? *what* man are you speaking of?"

"Why Rosey and Mr. Ferrers," returned Nott, simply.

Renshaw sank into his seat again. But the expression of relief which here passed swiftly over his face gave way to one of uneasy interest as Nott went on.

"P'r'aps it's a little highfalutin talkin' of Rosey ez a treasure. But, considerin', Mr. Renshaw, ez she's the only prop'ty I've kept by me for seventeen years ez hez paid interest and increased in valooe, it ain't sayin' too much to call her so. And ez Ferrers knows this, he oughter been content with gougin' me in that horse-hair spec, without goin' for Rosey. P'r'aps yer surprised at hearing me speak o' my own flesh and blood ez if I was talkin' hoss-trade, but you and me is bus'ness men, Mr. Renshaw, and we discusses ez such. We ain't goin' to slosh round and slop over in po'try and sentiment," continued Nott, with a tremulous voice, and a hand that slightly shook on Renshaw's shoulder. "We ain't goin' to git up and sing, 'Thou'st larned to love another thou'st broken every vow we've parted from each other and my bozom's lonely now oh is it well to sever such hearts as ourn for ever kin I forget thee never farewell farewell farewell.' Ye never happen'd to hear Jim Baker sing that at the moosic hall on Dupont Street, Mr. Renshaw," continued Mr. Nott, enthusiastically, when he had recovered from that complete absence of punctuation which alone suggested verse to his intellect. "He sorter struck water down here," indicating his heart, "every time."

"But what has Miss Nott to do with M. de Ferrières?" asked Renshaw, with a faint smile.

Mr. Nott regarded him with dumb, round, astonished eyes. "Hezn't she told yer?"

"Certainly not."

"And she didn't let on anythin' about him?" he continued, feebly.

"She said she'd liked to know where—" He stopped, with the reflection that he was betraying her confidences.

A dim foreboding of some new form of deceit, to which even the man before him was a consenting party, almost paralyzed Nott's faculties. "Then she didn't tell yer that she and Ferrers was sparkin' and keepin' kimpany together; that she and him was engaged, and was kalkilatin' to run away to furrin parts; that she cottoned to him more than to the ship or her father?"

"She certainly did not, and I shouldn't believe it," said Renshaw, quickly.

Nott smiled. He was amused; he astutely recognized the usual trustfulness of love and youth. There was clearly no deceit here! Renshaw's attentive eyes saw the smile, and his brow darkened.

"I like to hear yer say that, Mr. Renshaw," said Nott, "and it's no more than Rosey deserves, ez it's suthing onnat'ral and spell-like that's come over her through Ferrers. It ain't my Rosey. But it's Gospel truth, whether she's bewitched or not; whether it's them damn fool stories she reads—and it's like ez not he's just the kind o' snipe to write 'em hisself, and sorter advertise hisself, don't yer see—she's allus stuck up for him. They've had clandesent interviews, and when I taxed him with it he ez much ez allowed it was so, and reckoned he must leave, so ez he could run her off, you know—kinder stampede her with 'honor.' Them's his very words."

"But that is all past; he is gone, and Miss Nott does not even know where he is!" said Renshaw, with a laugh, which, however, concealed a vague uneasiness.

Mr. Nott rose and opened the door carefully. When he had satisfied himself that no one was listening, he came back and said in a whisper, "That's a lie. Not ez Rosey means to lie, but it's a trick he's put upon that poor child. That man, Mr. Renshaw, hez been hangin' round the Pontiac ever since. I've seed him twice with my own eyes pass the cabin windys. More than that, I've heard strange noises at night, and seen strange faces in the alley over yer. And only jist now ez I kem in I ketched sight of a furrin lookin' Chinee nigger slinking round the back door of what useter be Ferrers's loft."

"Did he look like a sailor?" asked Renshaw quickly, with a return of his former suspicion.

"Not more than I do," said Nott, glancing complacently at his pea-jacket. "He had rings on his yeers like a wench."

Mr. Renshaw started. But seeing Nott's eyes fixed on him, he said lightly, "But what have these strange faces and this strange man—probably only a Lascar sailor out of a job—to do with Ferrières?"

"Friends o' his—feller furrin citizens—spies on Rosey, don't you see? But they can't play the old man, Mr. Renshaw. I've told Rosey she must make a visit to the old Ranch. Once I've got her ther safe, I reckon I kin manage Mr. Ferrers and any number of Chinee niggers he kin bring along."

Renshaw remained for a few moments lost in thought. Then rising suddenly he grasped Mr. Nott's hand with a frank smile but determined eyes. "I haven't got the hang of this, Mr. Nott—the whole thing gets me! I only know that I've changed my mind. I'm *not* going to Sacramento. I shall stay *here*, old man, until I see you safe through the business, or my name's not Dick Renshaw. There's my hand on it! Don't say a word. Maybe it is no more than I ought to do—perhaps not half enough. Only remember, not a word of this to your daughter. She must believe that I leave to-night. And the sooner you get her out of this cursed ship the better."

"Deacon Flint's girls are goin' up in to-night's boat. I'll send Rosey with them," said Nott with a cunning twinkle. Renshaw nodded. Nott seized his hand with a wink of unutterable significance.

Left to himself Renshaw tried to review more calmly the circumstances in these strange revelations that had impelled him to change his resolution so suddenly. That the ship was under the surveillance of unknown parties, and that the description of them tallied with his own knowledge of a certain Lascar sailor, who was one of Sleight's informants

—seemed to be more than probable. That this seemed to point to Sleight's disloyalty to himself while he was acting as his agent, or a double treachery on the part of Sleight's informants was in either case a reason and an excuse for his own interference. But the connection of the absurd Frenchman with the case, which at first seemed a characteristic imbecility of his landlord, bewildered him the more he thought of it. Rejecting any hypothesis of the girl's affection for the antiquated figure whose sanity was a question of public criticism, he was forced to the equally alarming theory that Ferrières was cognizant of the treasure, and that his attentions to Rosey were to gain possession of it by marrying her. Might she not be dazzled by a picture of this wealth? Was it not possible that she was already in part possession of the secret, and her strange attraction to the ship, and what he had deemed her innocent craving for information concerning it, a consequence? Why had he not thought of this before? Perhaps she had detected his purpose from the first, and had deliberately checkmated him. The thought did not increase his complacency as Nott softly returned.

"It's all right," he began with a certain satisfaction in this rare opportunity for Machiavellian diplomacy, "it's all fixed now. Rosey tumbled to it at once, partiklerly when I said you was bound to go. 'But wot makes Mr. Renshaw go, father,' sez she; 'wot makes everybody run away from the ship?' sez she, rather peart like and sassy for her. 'Mr. Renshaw hez contractin' business,' sez I; 'got a big thing up in Sacramento that'll make his fortun',' sez I—for I wasn't goin' to give yer away, don't ye see. 'He had some business to talk to you about the ship,' sez she, lookin' at me under the corner of her pocket handkerchief. 'Lots o' business,' sez I. 'Then I reckon he don't care to hev me write to him,' sez she. 'Not a bit,' sez I, 'he wouldn't answer ye if ye did. Ye'll never hear from that chap agin.'"

"But what the devil—" interrupted the young man impetuously.

"Keep yer hair on!" remonstrated the old man with dark intelligence. "Ef you'd seen the way she flounced into her stateroom!—she, Rosey, ez allus moves ez softly ez a spirit —you'd hev wished I'd hev unloaded a little more. No sir, gals is gals in some things all the time."

Renshaw rose and paced the room rapidly. "Perhaps I'd better speak to her again before she goes," he said, impulsively.

"P'r'aps you'd better not," replied the imperturbable Nott.

Irritated as he was, Renshaw could not avoid the reflection that the old man was right. What, indeed, could he say to her with his present imperfect knowledge? How could she write to him if that knowledge was correct?

"Ef," said Nott, kindly, with a laying on of large benedictory and paternal hands, "ef yer are willin' to see Rosey agin, without *speakin'* to her, I reckon I ken fix it for yer. I'm goin' to take her down to the boat in half an hour. Ef yer should happen—mind, ef yer should *happen* to be down there, seein' some friends off and sorter promenadin' up and down the wharf like them high-toned chaps on Montgomery Street—ye might ketch her eye unconscious like. Or, ye might do this!" He rose after a moment's cogitation and with a face of profound mystery opened the door and beckoned Renshaw to follow him. Leading the way cautiously, he brought the young man into an open unpartitioned recess beside her stateroom. It seemed to be used as a storeroom, and Renshaw's eye was caught by a trunk the size and shape of the one that had provided Rosey with the materials of her masquerade. Pointing to it Mr. Nott said in a grave whisper: "This yer trunk is the companion trunk to Rosey's. *She's* got the things them opery women wears; this yer contains the *he* things, the duds and fixin's o' the men o' the same stripe." Throwing it open he continued: "Now, Mr. Renshaw, gals is gals; it's nat'ral they should be took by fancy dress and store clothes on young chaps as on theirselves. That man Ferrers hez got the dead wood on all of ye in this sort of thing, and hez been playing, so to speak, a lone hand all along. And ef thar's anythin' in thar," he added, lifting part of a theatrical wardrobe, "that you think you'd fancy —anythin' you'd like to put on when ye promenade the wharf down yonder—it's yours. Don't ye be bashful, but help yourself."

It was fully a minute before Renshaw fairly grasped the old man's meaning. But when he did—when the suggested spectacle of himself arrayed *à la* Ferrières, gravely promenading the wharf as a last gorgeous appeal to the affections of Rosey, rose before his fancy, he gave way to a fit of genuine laughter. The nervous tension of the past few hours relaxed; he laughed until the tears came into his eyes; he was still laughing when the door of the cabin was suddenly opened and Rosey appeared cold and distant on the threshold.

"I—beg your pardon," stammered Renshaw hastily. "I didn't mean—to disturb you—I—"

Without looking at him Rosey turned to her father. "I am ready," she said coldly, and closed the door again.

A glance of artful intelligence came into Nott's eyes, which had remained blankly staring at Renshaw's apparently causeless hilarity. Turning to him he winked solemnly. "That keerless kind o' hoss-laff jist fetched her," he whispered, and vanished before his chagrined companion could reply.

When Mr. Nott and his daughter departed Renshaw was not in the ship, neither did he make a spectacular appearance on the wharf as Mr. Nott had fondly expected, nor did he turn up again until after nine o'clock, when he found the old man in the cabin awaiting his return with some agitation.

"A minit ago," he said, mysteriously closing the door behind Renshaw, "I heard a voice in the passage, and goin' out who should I see agin but that darned furrin nigger ez I told yer 'bout, kinder hidin' in the dark, his eyes shinin' like a catamount. I was jist reachin' for my weppins when he riz up with a grin and handed me this yer letter. I told him I reckoned you'd gone to Sacramento, but he said he wez sure you was in your room, and to prove it I went thar. But when I kem back the d——d skunk had vamoosed—got frightened I reckon—and wasn't nowhar to be seen."

Renshaw took the letter hastily. It contained only a

line in Sleight's hand. "If you change your mind, the bearer may be of service to you."

He turned abruptly to Nott. "You say it was the same Lascar you saw before."

"It was."

"Then all I can say is he is no agent of de Ferrières's," said Renshaw, turning away with a disappointed air. Mr. Nott would have asked another question, but with an abrupt "Good-night" the young man entered his room, locked the door, and threw himself on his bed to reflect without interruption.

But if he was in no mood to stand Nott's fatuous conjectures, he was less inclined to be satisfied with his own. Had he been again carried away through his impulses evoked by the caprices of a pretty coquette and the absurd theories of her half imbecile father? Had he broken faith with Sleight and remained in the ship for nothing, and would not his change of resolution appear to be the result of Sleight's note? But why had the Lascar been haunting the ship before? In the midst of these conjectures he fell asleep.

VII

Between three and four in the morning the clouds broke over the Pontiac, and the moon, riding high, picked out in black and silver the long hulk that lay cradled between the iron shells of warehouses and the wooden frames of tenements on either side. The galley and covered gangway presented a mass of undefined shadow, against which the white deck shone brightly, stretching to the forecastle and bows, where the tiny glass roof of the photographer glistened like a gem in the Pontiac's crest. So peaceful and motionless she lay that she might have been some petrifaction of a past age now first exhumed and laid bare to the cold light of the stars.

Nevertheless this calm security was presently invaded by a sense of stealthy life and motion. What had seemed a fixed shadow suddenly detached itself from the deck, and began to slip stanchion by stanchion along the bulwarks

toward the companion way. At the cabin door it halted
and crouched motionless. Then rising, it glided forward
with the same staccato movement until opposite the slight
elevation of the forehatch. Suddenly it darted to the hatch,
unfastened and lifted it with a swift, familiar dexterity,
and disappeared in the opening. But as the moon shone
upon its vanishing face, it revealed the whitening eyes and
teeth of the Lascar seaman.

Dropping to the lower deck lightly, he felt his way
through the dark passage between the partitions, evidently
less familiar to him, halting before each door to listen.
Returning forward he reached the second hatchway that
had attracted Rosey's attention, and noiselessly unclosed
its fastenings. A penetrating smell of bilge arose from the
opening. Drawing a small bull's-eye lantern from his
breast he lit it, and unhesitatingly let himself down to the
further depth. The moving flash of his light revealed the
recesses of the upper hold, the abyss of the well amid-
ships, and glanced from the shining backs of moving zig-
zags of rats that seemed to outline the shadowy beams and
transoms. Disregarding those curious spectators of his
movements, he turned his attention eagerly to the inner
casings of the hold, that seemed in one spot to have been
strengthened by fresh timbers. Attacking this stealthily
with the aid of some tools hidden in his oil-skin clothing, in
the light of the lantern he bore a fanciful resemblance to
the predatory animals around him. The low continuous
sound of rasping and gnawing of timber which followed
heightened the resemblance. At the end of a few minutes
he had succeeded in removing enough of the outer planking to show that the entire filling of the casing between the
stanchions was composed of small boxes. Dragging out
one of them with feverish eagerness to the light, the Lascar
forced it open. In the rays of the bull's-eye, a wedged
mass of discolored coins showed with a lurid glow. The story
of the Pontiac was true—the treasure was there!

But Mr. Sleight had overlooked the logical effect of this
discovery on the natural villainy of his tool. In the very
moment of his triumphant execution of his patron's suggestions the idea of keeping the treasure to himself flashed

upon his mind. *He* had discovered it—why should he give it up to anybody? *He* had run all the risks; if he were detected at that moment, who would believe that his purpose there at midnight was only to satisfy some one else that the treasure was still intact? No. The circumstances were propitious; he would get the treasure out of the ship at once, drop it over her side, hastily conceal it in the nearest lot adjacent, and take it away at his convenience.—Who would be the wiser for it?

But it was necessary to reconnoitre first. He knew that the loft overhead was empty. He knew that it communicated with the alley, for he had tried the door that morning. He would convey the treasure there, and drop it into the alley. The boxes were heavy. Each one would require a separate journey to the ship's side, but he would at least secure something if he were interrupted. He stripped the casing, and gathered the boxes together in a pile.

Ah, yes, it was funny too that he—the Lascar hound—the d——d nigger—should get what bigger and bullier men than he had died for! The mate's blood was on those boxes, if the salt water had not washed it out. It was a hell of a fight when they dragged the captain—Oh, what was that? Was it the splash of a rat in the bilge, or what?

A superstitious terror had begun to seize him at the thought of blood. The stifling hold seemed again filled with struggling figures he had known; the air thick with cries and blasphemies that he had forgotten. He rose to his feet, and running quickly to the hatchway, leaped to the deck above. All was quiet. The door leading to the empty loft yielded to his touch. He entered, and, gliding through, unbarred and opened the door that gave upon the alley. The cold air and moonlight flowed in silently; the way of escape was clear. Bah! He would go back for the treasure.

He had reached the passage when the door he had just opened was suddenly darkened. Turning rapidly, he was conscious of a gaunt figure, grotesque, silent, and erect, looming on the threshold between him and the sky. Hidden in the shadow, he made a stealthy step towards it, with an iron wrench in his uplifted hand. But the next moment his eyes dilated with superstitious horror; the iron fell from his hand, and with a scream, like a frightened animal, he turned and fled into the passage. In the first access of his blind terror he tried to reach the deck above through the forehatch, but was stopped by the sound of a heavy tread overhead. The immediate fear of detection now overcame his superstition; he would have even faced the apparition again to escape through the loft; but, before he could return there, other footsteps approached rapidly from the end of the passage he would have to traverse. There was but one chance of escape left now—the forehold he had just quitted. He might hide there until the alarm was over. He glided back to the hatch, lifted it, and it closed softly over his head as the upper hatch was simultaneously raised, and the small round eyes of Abner Nott peered down upon it. The other footsteps proved to be Renshaw's but, attracted by the open door of the loft, he turned aside and entered. As soon as he disappeared Mr. Nott cautiously dropped through the opening to the deck below, and, going to the other hatch through which the Lascar had vanished, deliberately refastened it. In a few moments Renshaw returned with a light, and found the old man sitting on the hatch.

"The loft door was open," said Renshaw. "There's little doubt whoever was here escaped that way."

"Surely," said Nott. There was a peculiar look of Machiavellian sagacity in his face which irritated Renshaw.

"Then you're sure it was Ferrières you saw pass by your window before you called me?" he asked.

Nott nodded his head with an expression of infinite profundity.

"But you say he was going *from* the ship. Then it could not have been he who made the noise we heard down here."

"Mebbee no, and mebbee yes," returned Nott, cautiously.

"But if he was already concealed inside the ship, as that open door, which you say you barred from the inside, would indicate, what the devil did he want with this?" said Renshaw, producing the monkey-wrench he had picked up.

Mr. Nott examined the tool carefully, and shook his head

with momentous significance. Nevertheless, his eyes wandered to the hatch on which he was seated.

"Did you find anything disturbed *there?*" said Renshaw, following the direction of his eye. "Was that hatch fastened as it is now?"

"It was," said Nott, calmly. "But ye wouldn't mind fetchin' me a hammer and some o' them big nails from the locker, would yer, while I hang round here just so ez to make sure against another attack."

Renshaw complied with his request; but as Nott proceeded to gravely nail down the fastenings of the hatch, he turned impatiently away to complete his examination of the ship. The doors of the other lofts and their fastenings appeared secure and undisturbed. Yet it was undeniable that a felonious entrance had been made, but by whom or for what purpose still remained uncertain. Even now, Renshaw found it difficult to accept Nott's theory that de Ferrières was the aggressor and Rosey the object, nor could be justify his own suspicion that the Lascar had obtained a surreptitious entrance under Sleight's directions. With a feeling that if Rosey had been present he would have confessed all, and demanded from her an equal confidence, he began to hate his feeble, purposeless, and inefficient alliance with her father, who believed but dare not tax his daughter with complicity in this outrage. What could be done with a man whose only idea of action at such a moment was to nail up an undisturbed entrance in his invaded house! He was so preoccupied with these thoughts that when Nott rejoined him in the cabin he scarcely heeded his presence, and was entirely oblivious of the furtive looks which the old man from time to time cast upon his face.

"I reckon ye wouldn't mind," broke in Nott, suddenly, "ef I asked a favor of ye, Mr. Renshaw. Mebbee ye'll allow it's askin' too much in the matter of expense; mebbee ye'll allow it's askin' too much in the matter o' time. But *I* kalkilate to pay all the expense, and if you'd let me know what yer vally yer time at, I reckon I could stand that. What I'd be askin' is this. Would ye mind takin' a letter from me to Rosey, and bringin' back an answer?"

Renshaw stared speechlessly at this absurd realization of

his wish of a moment before. "I don't think I understand you," he stammered.

"P'r'aps not," returned Nott, with great gravity. "But that's not so much matter to you ez your time and expenses."

"I meant I should be glad to go if I can be of any service to you," said Renshaw, hastily.

"You kin ketch the seven o'clock boat this morning, and you'll reach San Rafael at ten—"

"But I thought Miss Rosey went to Petaluma," interrupted Renshaw quickly.

Nott regarded him with an expression of patronizing superiority. "That's what we ladled out to the public gin'rally, and to Ferrers and his gang in partickler. We *said* Petalumey, but if you go to Madroño Cottage, San Rafael, you'll find Rosey thar."

If Mr. Renshaw required anything more to convince him of the necessity of coming to some understanding with Rosey at once it would have been this last evidence of her father's utterly dark and supremely inscrutable designs. He assented quickly, and Nott handed him a note.

"Ye'll be partickler to give this inter her own hands, and wait for an answer," said Nott gravely.

Resisting the proposition to enter then and there into an elaborate calculation of the value of his time and the expenses of the trip, Renshaw found himself at seven o'clock on the San Rafael boat. Brief as was the journey it gave him time to reflect upon his coming interview with Rosey. He had resolved to begin by confessing all; the attempt of last night had released him from any sense of duty to Sleight. Besides, he did not doubt that Nott's letter contained some reference to this affair only known to Nott's dark and tortuous intelligence.

VIII

Madroño Cottage lay at the entrance of a little *cañada* already green with the early winter rains, and nestled in a thicket of the harlequin painted trees that gave it a name. The young man was a little relieved to find that Rosey had gone to the post-office a mile away, and that he would probably overtake her or meet her returning—alone. The road—little more than a trail—wound along the crest of the hill looking across the *cañada* to the long, dark, heavily-wooded flank of Mount Tamalpais that rose from the valley a dozen miles away. A cessation of the warm rain, a rift in the sky, and the rare spectacle of cloud scenery, combined with a certain sense of freedom, restored that light-hearted gayety that became him most. At a sudden turn of the road he caught sight of Rosey's figure coming towards him, and quickened his step with the impulsiveness of a boy. But she suddenly disappeared, and when he again saw her she was on the other side of the trail apparently picking the leaves of a manzanita. She had already seen him.

Somehow the frankness of his greeting was checked. She looked up at him with cheeks that retained enough of their color to suggest why she had hesitated, and said, *"You* here, Mr. Renshaw? I thought you were in Sacramento."

"And I thought *you* were in Petaluma," he retorted gayly. "I have a letter from your father. The fact is, one of those gentlemen who has been haunting the ship actually made an entry last night. Who he was, and what he came for, nobody knows. Perhaps your father gives you his suspicions." He could not help looking at her narrowly as he handed her the note. Except that her pretty eyebrows were slightly raised in curiosity she seemed undisturbed as she opened the letter. Presently she raised her eyes to his.

"Is this all father gave you?"

"All."

"You're sure you haven't dropped anything?"

"Nothing. I have given you all he gave me."

"And that is all it is." She exhibited the missive, a perfectly blank sheet of paper folded like a note!

Renshaw felt the angry blood glow in his cheeks. "This is unpardonable! I assure you, Miss Nott, there must be some mistake. He himself has probably forgotten the inclosure," he continued, yet with an inward conviction that the act was perfectly premeditated on the part of the old man.

The young girl held out her hand frankly. "Don't think

any more of it, Mr. Renshaw. Father is forgetful at times. But tell me about last night."

In a few words Mr. Renshaw briefly but plainly related the details of the attempt upon the Pontiac, from the moment that he had been awakened by Nott, to his discovery of the unknown trespasser's flight by the open door to the loft. When he had finished, he hesitated, and then taking Rosey's hand, said impulsively, "You will not be angry with me if I tell you all? Your father firmly believes that the attempt was made by the old Frenchman, de Ferrières, with a view of carrying you off."

A dozen reasons other than the one her father would have attributed it to might have called the blood to her face. But only innocence could have brought the look of astonished indignation to her eyes as she answered quickly:

"So *that* was what you were laughing at?"

"Not that, Miss Nott," said the young man eagerly: "though I wish to God I could accuse myself of nothing more disloyal. Do not speak, I beg," he added impatiently, as Rosey was about to reply. "I have no right to hear you; I have no right to even stand in your presence until I have confessed everything. I came to the Pontiac; I made your acquaintance, Miss Nott, through a fraud as wicked as anything your father charges to de Ferrières. I am not a contractor. I never was an honest lodger in the Pontiac. I was simply a spy."

"But you didn't mean to be—it was some mistake, wasn't it?" said Rosey, quite white, but more from sympathy with the offender's emotion than horror at the offense.

"I am afraid I did mean it. But bear with me for a few moments longer and you shall know all. It's a long story. Will you walk on, and—take my arm? You do not shrink from me, Miss Nott. Thank you. I scarcely deserve the kindness."

Indeed so little did Rosey shrink that he was conscious of a slight reassuring pressure on his arm as they moved forward, and for the moment I fear the young man felt like exaggerating his offense for the sake of proportionate sympathy. "Do you remember," he continued, "one evening when I told you some sea tales, you said you always thought there must be some story about the Pontiac? There *was* a story of the Pontiac, Miss Nott—a wicked story—a terrible story—which I might have told you, which I *ought* to have told you—which was the story that brought me there. You were right, too, in saying that you thought I had known the Pontiac before I stepped first on her deck that day. I had."

He laid his disengaged hand across lightly on Rosey's, as if to assure himself that she was listening.

"I was at that time a sailor. I had been fool enough to run away from college, thinking it a fine romantic thing to ship before the mast for a voyage round the world. I was a little disappointed, perhaps, but I made the best of it, and in two years I was second mate of a whaler lying in a little harbor of one of the uncivilized islands of the Pacific. While we were at anchor there a French trading vessel put in, apparently for water. She had the dregs of a mixed crew of Lascars and Portuguese, who said they had lost the rest of their men by desertion, and that the captain and mate had been carried off by fever. There was something so queer in their story that our skipper took the law in his own hands, and put me on board of her with a salvage crew. But that night the French crew mutinied, cut the cables, and would have got to sea if we had not been armed and prepared, and managed to drive them below. When we had got them under hatches for a few hours they parleyed, and offered to go quietly ashore. As we were short of hands and unable to take them with us, and as we had no evidence against them, we let them go, took the ship to Callao, turned her over to the authorities, lodged a claim for salvage, and continued our voyage. When we returned we found the truth of the story was known. She had been a French trader from Marseilles, owned by her captain; her crew had mutinied in the Pacific, killed their officers and the only passenger—the owner of the cargo. They had made away with the cargo and a treasure of nearly half a million of Spanish gold for trading purposes which belonged to the passenger. In course of time the ship was sold for salvage and put into the South American trade until the breaking out of the Californian gold excitement, when she was sent with a cargo to San Francisco. That ship was the Pontiac which your father bought."

A slight shudder ran through the girl's frame. "I wish —I wish you hadn't told me," she said. "I shall never close my eyes again comfortably on board of her, I know."

"I would say that you had purified her of *all* stains of her past—but there may be one that remains. And *that* in most people's eyes would be no detraction. You look puzzled, Miss Nott—but I am coming to the explanation and the end of my story. A ship of war was sent to the island to punish the mutineers and pirates, for such they were, but they could not be found. A private expedition was sent to discover the treasure which they were supposed to have buried, but in vain. About two months ago Mr. Sleight told me one of his shipmates had sent him a Lascar sailor who had to dispose of a valuable secret regarding the Pontiac for a percentage. That secret was that the treasure was never taken by the mutineers out of the Pontiac! They were about to land and bury it when we boarded them. They took advantage of their imprisonment under hatches *to bury it in the ship.* They hid it in the hold so securely and safely that it was never detected by us or the Callao authorities. I was then asked, as one who knew the vessel, to undertake a private examination of her, with a view of purchasing her from your father without awakening his suspicions. I assented. You have my confession now, Miss Nott. You know my crime. I am at your mercy."

Rosey's arm only tightened around his own. Her eyes sought his. "And you didn't find anything?" she said.

The question sounded so oddly like Sleight's, that Renshaw returned a little stiffly—

"I didn't look."

"Why?" asked Rosey simply.

"Because," stammered Renshaw, with an uneasy consciousness of having exaggerated his sentiment, "it didn't seem honorable; it didn't seem fair to you."

"Oh, you silly! you might have looked and told *me.*"

"But," said Renshaw, "do you think that would have been fair to Sleight?"

"As fair to him as to us. For, don't you see, it wouldn't

belong to any of us. It would belong to the friends or the family of the man who lost it."

"But there were no heirs," said Renshaw. "That was proved by some impostor who pretended to be his brother, and libelled the Pontiac at Callao, but the courts decided he was a lunatic."

"Then it belongs to the poor pirates who risked their own lives for it, rather than to Sleight, who did nothing." She was silent for a moment, and then resumed with energy, "I believe he was at the bottom of that attack last night."

"I have thought so too," said Renshaw.

"Then I must go back at once," she continued impulsively. "Father must not be left alone."

"Nor must *you*," said Renshaw, quickly. "Do let me return with you, and share with you and your father the trouble I have brought upon you. Do not," he added in a lower tone, "deprive me of the only chance of expiating my offense, of making myself worthy your forgiveness."

"I am sure," said Rosey, lowering her lids and half withdrawing her arm. "I am sure I have nothing to forgive. You did not believe the treasure belonged to us any more than to anybody else, until you knew *me*—"

"That is true," said the young man, attempting to take her hand.

"I mean," said Rosey, blushing, and showing a distracting row of little teeth in one of her infrequent laughs, "oh, you know what I mean." She withdrew her arm gently, and became interested in the selection of certain wayside bay leaves as they passed along. "All the same, I don't believe in this treasure," she said abruptly, as if to change the subject. "I don't believe it ever was hidden inside the Pontiac."

"That can easily be ascertained now," said Renshaw.

"But it's a pity you didn't find it out while you were about it," said Rosey. "It would have saved so much talk and trouble."

"I have told you why I didn't search the ship," responded Renshaw, with a slight bitterness. "But it seems I could only avoid being a great rascal by becoming a great fool."

"You never intended to be a rascal," said Rosey, earnestly, "and you couldn't be a fool, except in heeding what a silly girl says. I only meant if you had taken me into your confidence it would have been better."

"Might I not say the same to you regarding your friend, the old Frenchman?" returned Renshaw. "What if I were to confess to you that I lately suspected him of knowing the secret, and of trying to gain your assistance?"

Instead of indignantly repudiating the suggestion, to the young man's great discomfiture, Rosey only knit her pretty brows, and remained for some minutes silent. Presently she asked timidly,—

"Do you think it wrong to tell another person's secret for their own good?"

"No," said Renshaw, promptly.

"Then I'll tell you Monsieur de Ferrières's! But only because I believe from what you have just said that he will turn out to have some right to the treasure."

Then with kindling eyes, and a voice eloquent with sympathy, Rosey told the story of her accidental discovery of de Ferrières's miserable existence in the loft. Clothing it with the unconscious poetry of her fresh, young imagination, she lightly passed over his antique gallantry and grotesque weakness, exalting only his lonely sufferings and mysterious wrongs. Renshaw listened, lost between shame for his late suspicions and admiration for her thoughtful delicacy, until she began to speak of de Ferrières's strange allusions to the foreign papers in his portmanteau. "I think some were law papers, and I am alomst certain I saw the word Callao printed on one of them."

"It may be so," said Renshaw, thoughtfully. "The old Frenchman has always passed for a harmless, wandering eccentric. I hardly think public curiosity has ever even sought to know his name, much less his history. But had we not better first try to find if there *is* any property before we examine his claims to it?"

"As you please," said Rosey, with a slight pout; "but you will find it much easier to discover him than his treasure. It's always easier to find the thing you're not looking for."

"Until you want it," said Renshaw, with sudden gravity.

"How pretty it looks over there," said Rosey, turning her conscious eyes to the opposite mountain.

"Very."

They had reached the top of the hill, and in the near distance the chimney of Madroño Cottage was even now visible. At the expected sight they unconsciously stopped —unconsciously disappointed. Rosey broke the embarrassing silence.

"There's another way home, but it's a roundabout way," she said timidly.

"Let us take it," said Renshaw.

She hesitated. "The boat goes at four, and we must return to-night."

"The more reason why we should make the most of our time now," said Renshaw with a faint smile. "To-morrow all things may be changed; to-morrow you may find yourself an heiress, Miss Nott. To-morrow," he added, with a slight tremor in his voice, "I may have earned your forgiveness, only to say farewell.to you forever. Let me keep this sunshine, this picture, this companionship with you long enough to say now what perhaps I must not say to-morrow."

They were silent for a moment, and then by a common instinct turned together into a narrow trail, scarce wide enough for two, that diverged from the straight practical path before them. It was indeed a roundabout way home, so roundabout, in fact, that as they wandered on it seemed even to double on its track, occasionally lingering long and becoming indistinct under the shadow of madroño and willow; at one time stopping blindly before a fallen tree in the hollow, where they had quite lost it, and had to sit down to recall it; a rough way, often requiring the mutual help of each other's hands and eyes to tread together in security; an uncertain way, not to be found without whispered consultation and concession, and yet a way eventually bringing them hand in hand, happy and hopeful, to the gate of Madroño Cottage. And if there was only just time for Rosey to prepare to take the boat, it was due to the deviousness of the way. If a stray curl was lying loose on Rosey's cheek, and a long hair had caught in Renshaw's button, it was owing to the roughness of the way; and if in the tones of their voices and in the glances of their eyes there was a maturer seriousness, it was due to the dim uncertainty of the path they had traveled, and would hereafter tread together.

IX

When Mr. Nott had satisfied himself of Renshaw's departure, he coolly bolted the door at the head of the companion way, thus cutting off any communication with the lower deck. Taking a long rifle from the rack above his berth, he carefully examined the hammer and cap, and then cautiously let himself down through the forehatch to the deck below. After a deliberate survey of the still intact fastenings of the hatch over the forehold, he proceeded quietly to unloose them again with the aid of the tools that still lay there. When the hatch was once more free he lifted it, and, withdrawing a few feet from the opening, sat himself down, rifle in hand. A profound silence reigned throughout the lower deck.

"Ye kin rize up out o' that," said Nott gently.

There was a stealthy rustle below that seemed to approach the hatch, and then with a sudden bound the Lascar leaped on the deck. But at the same instant Nott covered him with his rifle. A slight shade of disappointment and surprise had crossed the old man's face, and clouded his small round eyes at the apparition of the Lascar, but his hand was none the less firm upon the trigger as the frightened prisoner sank on his knees, with his hands clasped in the attitude of supplication for mercy.

"Ef you're thinkin' o' skippin' afore I've done with yer," said Nott with labored gentleness, "I oughter warn ye that it's my style to drop Injins at two hundred yards, and this deck ain't anywhere mor'n fifty. It's an uncomfortable style, a nasty style—but it's *my* style. I thought I'd tell yer, so yer could take it easy where you air. Where's Ferrers?"

Even in the man's insane terror, his utter bewilderment at the question was evident. "Ferrers?" he gasped; "don't know him, I swear to God, boss."

"P'r'aps," said Nott, with infinite cunning, "yer don't know the man ez kem into the loft from the alley last night —p'r'aps yer didn't see an airy Frenchman with a dyed moustache, eh? I thought that would fetch ye!" he continued, as the man started at the evidence that his vision of last night was a living man. "P'r'aps you and him didn't break into this ship last night, jist to run off with my darter Rosey? P'r'aps yer don't know Rosey, eh? P'r'aps yer don't know ez Ferrers wants to marry her, and hez been hangin' round yer ever since he left—eh?"

Scarcely believing the evidence of his senses that the old man whose treasure he had been trying to steal was utterly ignorant of his real offense, and yet uncertain of the penalty of the other crime of which he was accused, the Lascar writhed his body and stammered vaguely, "Mercy! Mercy!"

"Well," said Nott, cautiously, "ez I reckon the hide of a dead Chinee nigger ain't any more vallyble than that of a dead Injin, I don't care ef I let up on yer—seein' the cussedness ain't yours. But ef I let yer off this once, you must take a message to Ferrers from me."

"Let me off this time, boss, and I swear to God I will," said the Lascar eagerly.

"Ye kin say to Ferrers—let me see—" deliberated Nott, leaning on his rifle with cautious reflection. "Ye kin say to Ferrers like this—sez you, 'Ferrers,' sez you, 'the old man sez that afore you went away you sez to him, sez you, "I take my honor with me," sez you'—have you got that?" interrupted Nott suddenly.

"Yes, boss."

"'I take my honor with me,' sez you," repeated Nott slowly. "'Now,' sez you—'the old man sez, sez he—tell Ferrers, sez he, that his honor havin' run away agin, he sends it back to him, and ef he ever ketches it around after this, he'll shoot it on sight.' Hev yer got that?"

"Yes," stammered the bewildered captive.

"Then git!"

The Lascar sprang to his feet with the agility of a panther, leaped through the hatch above him, and disappeared over the bow of the ship with an unhesitating directness that showed that every avenue of escape had been already contemplated by him. Slipping lightly from the cutwater to the ground, he continued his flight, only stopping at the private office of Mr. Sleight.

When Mr. Renshaw and Rosey Nott arrived on board the Pontiac that evening, they were astonished to find the passage before the cabin completely occupied with trunks and boxes, and the bulk of their household goods apparently in the process of removal. Mr. Nott, who was superintending the work of two Chinamen, betrayed not only no surprise at the appearance of the young people, but not the remotest recognition of their own bewilderment at his occupation.

"Kalkilatin'," he remarked casually to his daughter, "you'd rather look arter your fixin's, Rosey, I've left 'em till the last. P'r'aps yer and Mr. Renshaw wouldn't mind sittin' down on that locker until I've strapped this yer box."

"But what does it all mean, father?" said Rosey, taking the old man by the lapels of his sea-jacket, and slightly emphasizing her question. "What in the name of goodness are you doing?"

"Breakin' camp, Rosey dear, breakin' camp, jist ez we uster," replied Nott with cheerful philosophy. "Kinder like old times, ain't it? Lord, Rosey," he continued, stopping and following up the reminiscence, with the end of the rope in his hand as if it were a clue, "don't ye mind that day we started outer Livermore Pass, and seed the hull o' the Californy coast stretchin' yonder—eh? But don't ye be skeered, Rosey dear," he added quickly, as if in recognition of the alarm expressed in her face. "I ain't turning ye outer house and home; I've jist hired that 'ere Madroño Cottage from the Peters ontil we kin look round."

"But you're not leaving the ship, father," continued Rosey, impetuously. "You haven't sold it to that man Sleight?"

Mr. Nott rose and carefully closed the cabin door. Then drawing a large wallet from his pocket, he said, "It's sing'lar ye should hev got the name right the first pop, ain't it, Rosey? but it's Sleight, sure enough, all the time. This yer check," he added, producing a paper from the depths of the wallet, "this yer check for 25,000 dollars is wot he paid for it only two hours ago."

"But," said Renshaw, springing to his feet furiously, "you're duped, swindled—betrayed!"

"Young man," said Nott, throwing a certain dignity into his habitual gesture of placing his hands on Renshaw's shoulders, "I bought this yer ship five years ago jist ez she stood for 8,000 dollars. Kalkilatin' wot she cost me in repairs and taxes, and wot she brought me in since then, accordin' to my figgerin', I don't call a clear profit of 15,000 dollars much of a swindle."

"Tell him all," said Rosey, quickly, more alarmed at Renshaw's despairing face than at the news itself. "Tell him everything, Dick—Mr. Renshaw; it may not be too late."

In a voice half choked with passionate indignation Renshaw hurriedly repeated the story of the hidden treasure, and the plot to rescue it, prompted frequently by Rosey's tenacious memory and assisted by Rosey's deft and tactful explanations. But to their surprise the imperturbable countenance of Abner Nott never altered; a slight moisture of kindly paternal tolerance of their extravagance glistened in his little eyes, but nothing more.

"Ef there was a part o' this ship, a plank or a bolt ez I don't know, ez I hevn't touched with my own hand, and looked into with my own eyes, thar might be suthin' in that story. I don't let on to be a sailor like *you*, but ez I know the ship ez a boy knows his first hoss, as a woman knows her first babby, I reckon thar ain't no treasure yer, onless it was brought into the Pontiac last night by them chaps."

"But are you mad! Sleight would not pay three times the value of the ship to-day if he were not positive! And that positive knowledge was gained last night by the villain who broke into the Pontiac—no doubt the Lascar."

"Surely," said Nott, meditatively. "The Lascar! There's suthin' in that. That Lascar I fastened down in the hold last night unbeknownst to you, Mr. Renshaw, and let him out again this morning ekally unbeknownst."

"And you let him carry his information to Sleight—

without a word!" said Renshaw, with a sickening sense of Nott's utter fatuity.

"I sent him back with a message to the man he kem from," said Nott, winking both his eyes at Renshaw, significantly, and making signs behind his daughter's back.

Rosey, conscious of her lover's irritation, and more eager to soothe his impatience than from any faith in her suggestion, interfered. "Why not examine the place where he was concealed? he may have left some traces of his search."

The two men looked at each other. "Seein' ez I've turned the Pontiac over to Sleight jist ez it stands, I don't know ez it's 'zactly on the square," said Nott doubtfully.

"You've a right to know at least *what* you deliver to him," interrupted Renshaw brusquely: "Bring a lantern."

Followed by Rosey, Renshaw and Nott hurriedly sought the lower deck and the open hatch of the forehold. The two men leaped down first with the lantern, and then assisted Rosey to descend. Renshaw took a step forward and uttered a cry.

The rays of the lantern fell on the ship's side. The Lascar had, during his forced seclusion, put back the boxes of treasure and replaced the planking, yet not so carefully but that the quick eye of Renshaw had discovered it. The next moment he had stripped away the planking again, and the hurriedly-restored box which the Lascar had found fell to the deck, scattering part of its ringing contents. Rosey turned pale; Renshaw's eyes flashed fire; only Abner Nott remained quiet and impassive.

"Are you satisfied you have been duped?" said Renshaw passionately.

To their surprise Mr. Nott stooped down, and picking up one of the coins handed it gravely to Renshaw. "Would ye mind heftin' that 'ere coin in your hand—feelin' it, bitin' it, scrapin' it with a knife, and kinder seein' how it compares with other coins?"

"What do you mean?" said Renshaw.

"I mean that that yer coin—that *all* the coins in this yer box, that all the coins in them other boxes—and ther's forty on 'em—is all and every one of 'em counterfeits!"

The piece dropped unconsciously from Renshaw's hand, and striking another that lay on the deck gave out a dull, suspicious ring.

"They waz counterfeits got up by them Dutch super-cargo sharps for dealin' with the Injins and cannibals and South Sea heathens ez bows down to wood and stone. It satisfied them ez well ez them buttons ye puts in missionary boxes, I reckon, and 'cepting ez freight, don't cost nothin'. I found 'em tucked in the ribs o' the old Pontiac when I bought her, and I nailed 'em up in thar lest they should fall into dishonest hands. It's a lucky thing, Mr. Renshaw, that they comes into the honest fingers of a square man like Sleight—ain't it?"

He turned his small, guileless eyes upon Renshaw with such child-like simplicity that it checked the hysterical laugh that was rising to the young man's lips.

"But did any one know of this but yourself?"

"I reckon not. I once suspicioned that old Cap'en Bowers, who was always foolin' round the hold yer, must hev noticed the bulge in the casin', but when he took to axin' questions I axed others—ye know my style, Rosey? Come."

He led the way grimly back to the cabin, the young people following; but turning suddenly at the companion-way he observed Renshaw's arm around the waist of his daughter.

He said nothing until they had reached the cabin, when he closed the door softly, and looking at them both gently, said with infinite cunning—

"Ef it isn't too late, Rosey, ye kin tell this young man ez how I forgive him for havin' diskivered THE TREASURE of the Pontiac."

.   .   .   .

It was nearly eighteen months afterwards that Mr. Nott one morning entered the room of his son-in-law at Madroño Cottage. Drawing him aside, he said with his old air of mystery, "Now ez Rosey's ailin' and don't seem to be so eager to diskiver what's become of Mr. Ferrers, I don't mind tellin' ye that over a year ago I heard he died suddenly in Sacramento. Thar was suthin' in the paper about his bein' a lunatic and claimin' to be a relation to somebody on the Pontiac; but likes ez not it's only the way those newspaper fellows got hold of the story of his wantin' to marry Rosey."

THANKFUL BLOSSOM

THANKFUL BLOSSOM

I

THE time was the year of grace 1779; the locality, Morristown, New Jersey.

It was bitterly cold. A northeasterly wind had been stiffening the mud of the morning's thaw into a rigid record of that day's wayfaring on the Baskingridge road. The hoof-prints of cavalry, the deep ruts left by baggage-wagons, and the deeper channels worn by artillery, lay stark and cold in the waning light of an April day. There were icicles on the fences, a rime of silver on the windward bark of maples, and occasional bare spots on the rocky protuberances of the road, as if Nature had worn herself out at the knees and elbows through long waiting for the tardy spring. A few leaves disinterred by the thaw became crisp again, and rustled in the wind, making the summer a thing so remote that all human hope and conjecture fled before them.

Here and there the wayside fences and walls were broken down or dismantled; and beyond them fields of snow down-trodden and discolored, and strewn with fragments of leather, camp equipage, harness, and cast-off clothing, showed traces of the recent encampment and congregation of men. On some there were still standing the ruins of rudely constructed cabins, or the semblance of fortification equally rude and incomplete. A fox stealing along a half-filled ditch, a wolf slinking behind an earthwork, typified the human abandonment and desolation.

One by one the faint sunset tints faded from the sky; the far-off crests of the Orange hills grew darker; the nearer files of pines on the Whatnong Mountain became a mere black background; and, with the coming-on of night, came too an icy silence that seemed to stiffen and arrest the very wind itself. The crisp leaves no longer rustled; the waving whips of alder and willow snapped no longer; the icicles no longer dropped a cold fruitage from barren branch and spray; and the roadside trees relapsed into stony quiet, so that the sound of horse's hoofs breaking through the thin, dull, lustreless films of ice that patched the furrowed road, might have been heard by the nearest Continental picket a mile away.

Either a knowledge of this, or the difficulties of the road, evidently irritated the viewless horseman. Long before he became visible, his voice was heard in half-suppressed objurgation of the road, of his beast, of the country folk, and the country generally. "Steady, you jade!" "Jump, you devil, jump!" "Curse the road, and the beggarly farmers that durst not mend it!" And then the moving bulk of horse and rider suddenly arose above the hill, floundered and splashed, and then as suddenly disappeared, and the rattling hoof-beats ceased.

The stranger had turned into a deserted lane still cushioned with untrodden snow. A stone wall on one hand—in better keeping and condition than the boundary monuments of the outlying fields—bespoke protection and exclusiveness. Half-way up the lane the rider checked his speed, and, dismounting, tied his horse to a wayside sapling. This done, he went cautiously forward toward the end of the lane, and a farm-house from whose gable window a light twinkled through the deepening night. Suddenly he stopped, hesitated, and uttered an impatient ejaculation. The light had disappeared. He turned sharply on his heel, and retraced his steps until opposite a farm-shed that stood a few paces from the wall. Hard by, a large elm cast the gaunt shadow of its leafless limbs on the wall and surrounding snow. The stranger stepped into this shadow, and at once seemed to become a part of its trembling intricacies.

At the present moment it was certainly a bleak place for a tryst. There was snow yet clinging to the trunk of the tree, and a film of ice on its bark; the adjacent wall was slippery with frost, and fringed with icicles. Yet in all there was a ludicrous suggestion of some sentiment past and unseasonable: several dislodged stones of the wall were so disposed as to form a bench and seats, and under the elm-tree's film of ice could still be seen carved on its bark the effigy of a heart, divers initials, and the legend, "Thine Forever."

The stranger, however, kept his eyes fixed only on the farm-shed and the open field beside it. Five minutes passed in fruitless expectancy. Ten minutes! And then the rising moon slowly lifted herself over the black range of the Orange hills, and looked at him, blushing a little, as if the appointment were her own.

The face and figure thus illuminated were those of a strongly built, handsome man of thirty, so soldierly in bearing that it needed not the buff epaulets and facings to show his captain's rank in the Continental army. Yet there was something in his facial expression that contradicted the manliness of his presence,—an irritation and querulousness that were inconsistent with his size and strength. This fretfulness increased as the moments went by without sign or motion in the faintly lit field beyond, until, in peevish exasperation, he began to kick the nearer stones against the wall.

"Moo-oo-w!"

The soldier started. Not that he was frightened, nor that he had failed to recognize in these prolonged syllables the deep-chested, half-drowsy low of a cow, but that it was so near him—evidently just beside the wall. If an object so bulky could have approached him so near without his knowledge, might not she—

"Moo-oo!"

He drew nearer the wall cautiously. "So, Cushy! Mooly! Come up, Bossy!" he said persuasively. "Moo"—but here the low unexpectedly broke down, and ended in a very human and rather musical little laugh.

"Thankful!" exclaimed the soldier, echoing the laugh a trifle uneasily and affectedly as a hooded little head arose above the wall.

"Well," replied the figure, supporting a prettily rounded chin on her hands, as she laid her elbows complacently on the wall,—"well, what did you expect? Did you want me to stand here all night, while you skulked moonstruck under a tree? Or did you look for me to call you by name? did you expect me to shout out, 'Capt. Allan Brewster—' "

"Thankful, hush!"

"Capt. Allan Brewster of the Connecticut Contingent," continued the girl, with an affected raising of a low, pathetic voice that was, however, inaudible beyond the tree. "Capt. Brewster, behold me,—your obleeged and humble servant and sweetheart to command."

Capt. Brewster succeeded, after a slight skirmish at the wall, in possessing himself of the girl's hand; at which, although still struggling, she relented slightly.

"It isn't every lad that I'd low for," she said, with an affected pout, "and there may be others that would not take it amiss; though there be fine ladies enough at the assembly balls at Morristown as might think it hoydenish?"

"Nonsense, love," said the captain, who had by this time mounted the wall, and encircled the girl's waist with his arm. "Nonsense! you startled me only. But," he added, suddenly taking her round chin in his hand, and turning her face toward the moon with an uneasy half-suspicion, "why did you take that light from the window? What has happened?"

"We had unexpected guests, sweetheart," said Thankful: "the count just arrived."

"That infernal Hessian!" He stopped, and gazed questioningly into her face. The moon looked upon her at the same time: the face was as sweet, as placid, as truthful, as her own. Possibly these two inconstants understood each other.

"Nay, Allan, he is not a Hessian, but an exiled gentleman from abroad,—a nobleman—"

"There are no noblemen now," sniffed the trooper contemptuously. "Congress has so decreed it. All men are born free and equal."

"But they are not, Allan," said Thankful, with a pretty trouble in her brows: "even cows are not born equal. Is yon calf that was dropped last night by Brindle the equal of my red heifer whose mother come by herself in a ship from Surrey? Do they look equal?"

"Titles are but breath," said Capt. Brewster doggedly. There was an ominous pause.

"Nay, there is one nobleman left," said Thankful; "and he is my own,—my nature's nobleman!"

Capt. Brewster did not reply. From certain arch gestures and wreathed smiles with which this forward young woman accompanied her statement, it would seem to be implied that the gentleman who stood before her was the nobleman alluded to. At least, he so accepted it, and embraced her closely, her arms and part of her mantle clinging around his neck. In this attitude they remained quiet for some moments, slightly rocking from side to side like a metronome; a movement, I fancy, peculiarly bucolic, pastoral, and idyllic, and as such, I wot, observed by Theocritus and Virgil.

At these supreme moments weak woman usually keeps her wits about her much better than your superior reasoning masculine animal; and, while the gallant captain was losing himself upon her perfect lips, Miss Thankful distinctly heard the farm-gate click, and otherwise noticed that the moon was getting high and obtrusive. She half released herself from the captain's arms, thoughtfully and tenderly —but firmly. "Tell me all about yourself, Allan dear," she said quietly, making room for him on the wall,—"all, everything."

She turned upon him her beautiful eyes,—eyes habitually earnest and even grave in expression, yet holding in their brave brown depths a sweet, childlike reliance and dependency; eyes with a certain tender, deprecating droop in the brown-fringed lids, and yet eyes that seemed to say to every man who looked upon them, "I am truthful: be frank with me." Indeed, I am convinced there is not one of my impressible sex, who, looking in those pleading eyes, would not have perjured himself on the spot rather than have disappointed their fair owner.

Capt. Brewster's mouth resumed its old expression of discontent.

"Everything is growing worse, Thankful, and the cause is lost. Congress does nothing, and Washington is not the man for the crisis. Instead of marching to Philadelphia, and forcing that wretched rabble of Hancock and Adams at the point of the bayonet, he writes letters."

"A dignified, formal old fool," interrupted Mistress Thankful indignantly; "and look at his wife! Didn't Mistress Ford and Mistress Baily, ay, and the best blood of Morris County, go down to his Excellency's in their finest bibs and tuckers, and didn't they find my lady in a pinafore doing chores? Vastly polite treatment, indeed! As if the whole world didn't know that the general was taken by surprise when my lady came riding up from Virginia with all those fine cavaliers, just to see what his Excellency was doing at these assembly balls. And fine doings, I dare say."

"This is but idle gossip, Thankful," said Capt. Brewster with the faintest appearance of self-consciousness; "the assembly balls are conceived by the general to strengthen the confidence of the townsfolk, and mitigate the rigors of the winter encampment. I go there myself rarely: I have but little taste for junketing and gavotting, with my country in such need. No, Thankful! What we want is a leader; and the men of Connecticut feel it keenly. If I have been spoken of in that regard," added the captain with a slight inflation of his manly breast, "it is because they know of my sacrifices,—because as New England yeomen they know my devotion to the cause. They know of my suffering—"

The bright face that looked into his was suddenly afire with womanly sympathy, the pretty brow was knit, the sweet eyes overflowed with tenderness. "Forgive me, Allan. I forgot—perhaps, love—perhaps, dearest, you are hungry now."

"No, not now," replied Captain Brewster, with gloomy stoicism; "yet," he added, "it is nearly a week since I have tasted meat."

"I—I—brought a few things with me," continued the girl, with a certain hesitating timidity. She reached down, and produced a basket from the shadow of the wall. "These chickens"—she held up a pair of pullets—"the commander-in-chief himself could not buy: I kept them for *my* commander! And this pot of marmalade, which I know my Allan loves, is the same I put up last summer. I thought [very tenderly] you might like a piece of that bacon you liked so once, dear. Ah, sweetheart, shall we ever sit down to our little board? Shall we ever see the end of this awful war? Don't you think, dear [very pleadingly], it would be best to give it up? King George is not such a very bad man, is he? I've thought, sweetheart [very confidently], that mayhap you and he might make it all up without the aid of those Washingtons, who do nothing but starve one to death. And if the king only knew you, Allan, —should see you as I do, sweetheart,—he'd do just as you say."

During this speech she handed him the several articles alluded to; and he received them, storing them away in such receptacles of his clothing as were convenient—with this notable difference, that with *her* the act was graceful and picturesque: with him there was a ludicrousness of suggestion that his broad shoulders and uniform only heightened.

"I think not of myself, lass," he said, putting the eggs in his pocket, and buttoning the chickens within his martial breast. "I think not of myself, and perhaps I often spare that counsel which is but little heeded. But I have a duty to my men—to Connecticut. [He here tied the marmalade up in his handkerchief.] I confess I have sometimes thought I might, under provocation, be driven to extreme measures for the good of the cause. I make no pretence to leadership, but—"

"With you at the head of the army," broke in Thankful enthusiastically, "peace would be declared within a fortnight."

There is no flattery, however outrageous, that a man will not accept from the woman whom he believes loves him. He will perhaps doubt its influence in the colder judgment of mankind; but he will consider that this poor creature, at least, understands him, and in some vague way represents the eternal but unrecognized verities. And when this is voiced by lips that are young and warm and red, it is somehow quite as convincing as the bloodless, remoter utterance of posterity.

Wherefore the trooper complacently buttoned the compliment over his chest with the pullets.

"I think you must go now, Allan," she said, looking at him with that pseudo-maternal air which the youngest of women sometimes assume to their lovers, as if the doll had suddenly changed sex, and grown to man's estate. "You must go now, dear; for it may so chance that father is considering my absence overmuch. You will come again a' Wednesday, sweetheart; and you will not go to the assemblies, nor visit Mistress Judith, nor take any girl pick-a-back again on your black horse; and you will let me know when you are hungry?"

She turned her brown eyes lovingly, yet with a certain pretty trouble in the brow, and such a searching, pleading inquiry in her glance, that the captain kissed her at once. Then came the final embrace, performed by the captain in a half-perfunctory, quiet manner, with a due regard for the friable nature of part of his provisions. Satisfying himself of the integrity of the eggs by feeling for them in his pocket, he waved a military salute with the other hand to Miss Thankful, and was gone. A few minutes later the sound of his horse's hoofs rang sharply from the icy hillside.

But, as he reached the summit, two horsemen wheeled suddenly from the shadow of the roadside, and bade him halt.

"Capt. Brewster, if this moon does not deceive me?" queried the foremost stranger with grave civility.

"The same. Major Van Zandt, I calculate?" returned Brewster querulously.

"Your calculation is quite right. I regret Capt. Brewster, that it is my duty to inform you that you are under arrest."

"By whose orders?"

"The commander-in-chief's."

"For what?"

"Mutinous conduct, and disrespect of your superior officers."

The sword that Capt. Brewster had drawn at the sudden appearance of the strangers quivered for a moment in his strong hand. Then, sharply striking it across the pommel of his saddle, he snapped it in twain, and cast the pieces at the feet of the speaker.

"Go on," he said doggedly.

"Capt. Brewster," said Major Van Zandt, with infinite gravity, "it is not for me to point out the danger to you of this outspoken emotion, except practically in its effect upon the rations you have in your pocket. If I mistake not, they have suffered equally with your steel. Forward, march!"

Capt. Brewster looked down, and then dropped to the rear, as the diseased yolks of Mistress Thankful's most precious gift slid slowly and pensively over his horse's flanks to the ground.

II

Mistress Thankful remained at the wall until her lover had disappeared. Then she turned, a mere lissom shadow in that uncertain light, and glided under the eaves of the shed, and thence from tree to tree of the orchard, lingering a moment under each as a trout lingers in the shadow of the bank in passing a shallow, and so reached the farmhouse and the kitchen door, where she entered. Thence by a back staircase she slipped to her own bower, from whose window half an hour before she had taken the signalling light. This she lit again and placed upon a chest of drawers; and, taking off her hood and a shapeless sleeveless mantle she had worn, went to the mirror, and proceeded to re-adjust a high horn comb that had been somewhat displaced by the captain's arm, and otherwise after the fashion of her sex to remove all traces of a previous lover. It may be here observed that a man is very apt to come from the smallest encounter with his dulcinea *distrait,* bored, or shame-faced; to forget that his cravat is awry, or that a long blond hair is adhering to his button. But as to *Mademoiselle*—well, looking at Miss Pussy's sleek paws and spotless face, would you ever know that she had been at the cream-jug?

Thankful was, I think, satisfied with her appearance. Small doubt but she had reason for it. And yet her gown was a mere slip of flowered chintz, gathered at the neck, and falling at an angle of fifteen degrees to within an inch

of a short petticoat of gray flannel. But so surely is the
complete mould of symmetry indicated in the poise or line
of any single member, that looking at the erect carriage of
her graceful brown head, or below to the curves that were
lost in her shapely ankles, or the little feet that hid themselves in the broad-buckled shoes, you knew that the rest
was as genuine and beautiful.

Mistress Thankful, after a pause, opened the door, and
listened. Then she softly slipped down the back staircase
to the front hall. It was dark; but the door of the "company-room," or parlor, was faintly indicated by the light
that streamed beneath it. She stood still for a moment
hesitatingly, when suddenly a hand grasped her own, and
half led, half dragged her, into the sitting-room opposite.
It was dark. There was a momentary fumbling for the
tinder-box and flint, a muttered oath over one or two impeding articles of furniture, and Thankful laughed. And
then the light was lit; and her father, a gray wrinkled man
of sixty, still holding her hand, stood before her.

"You have been out, mistress!"

"I have," said Thankful.

"And not alone," growled the old man angrily.

"No," said Mistress Thankful, with a smile that began
in the corners of her brown eyes, ran down into the dimpled
curves of her mouth, and finally ended in the sudden revelation of her white teeth,—"no, not alone."

"With whom?" asked the old man, gradually weakening
under her strong, saucy presence.

"Well, father," said Thankful, taking a seat on a table,
and swinging her little feet somewhat ostentatiously toward
him, "I was with Capt. Allan Brewster of the Connecticut
Contingent."

"That man?"

"That man!"

"I forbid you seeing him again."

Thankful gripped the table with a hand on each side of
her, to emphasize the statement, and swinging her feet
replied,—

"I shall see him as often as I like, father."

"Thankful Blossom!"

"Abner Blossom!"

"I see you know not," said Mr. Blossom, abandoning the severely paternal mandatory air for one of confidential disclosure, "I see you know not his reputation. He is accused of inciting his regiment to revolt,—of being a traitor to the cause."

"And since when, Abner Blossom, have *you* felt such concern for the cause? Since you refused to sell supplies to the Continental commissary, except at double profits? since you told me you were glad I had not politics like Mistress Ford—"

"Hush!" said the father, motioning to the parlor.

"Hush," echoed Thankful indignantly. "I won't be hushed! Everybody says 'Hush' to me. The count says 'Hush!' Allan says 'Hush!' You say 'Hush!' I'm a-weary of this hushing. Ah, if there was a man who didn't say it to me!" and Mistress Thankful lifted her fine eyes to the ceiling.

"You are unwise, Thankful,—foolish, indiscreet. That is why you require much monition."

Thankful swung her feet in silence for a few moments, then suddenly leaped from the table, and, seizing the old man by the lapels of his coat, fixed her eyes upon him, and said suspiciously. "Why did you keep me from going in the company-room? Why did you bring me in here?"

Blossom senior was staggered for a moment. "Because, you know, the count—"

"And you were afraid the count should know I had a sweetheart? Well, I'll go in and tell him now," she said, marching toward the door.

"Then, why did you not tell him when you slipped out an hour ago? eh, lass?" queried the old man, grasping her hand. "But 'tis all one, Thankful: 'twas not for him I stopped you. There is a young spark with him,—ay, came even as you left, lass,—a likely young gallant; and he and the count are jabbering away in their own lingo, a kind of Italian, belike; eh, Thankful?"

"I know not," she said thoughtfully. "Which way came the other?" In fact, a fear that this young stranger might have witnessed the captain's embrace began to creep over her.

"From town, my lass."

Thankful turned to her father as if she had been waiting a reply to a long-asked question: "Well?"

"Were it not well to put on a few furbelows and a tucker?" queried the old man. " 'Tis a gallant young spark; none of your country folk."

"No," said Thankful, with the promptness of a woman who was looking her best, and knew it. And the old man, looking at her, accepted her judgment, and without another word led her to the parlor door, and, opening it, said briefly, "My daughter, Mistress Thankful Blossom."

With the opening of the door came the sound of earnest voices that instantly ceased upon the appearance of Mistress Thankful. Two gentlemen lolling before the fire arose instantly, and one came forward with an air of familiar yet respectful recognition.

"Nay, this is far too great happiness, Mistress Thankful," he said, with a strongly marked foreign accent, and a still more strongly marked foreign manner. "I have been in despair, and my friend here, the Baron Pomposo, likewise."

The slightest trace of a smile, and the swiftest of reproachful glances, lit up the dark face of the baron as he bowed low in the introduction. Thankful dropped the courtesy of the period,—i. e., a duck, with semicircular sweep of the right foot forward. But the right foot was so pretty, and the grace of the little figure so perfect, that the baron raised his eyes from the foot to the face in serious admiration. In the one rapid feminine glance she had given him, she had seen that he was handsome; in the second, which she could not help from his protracted silence, she saw that his beauty centred in his girlish, half fawn-like dark eyes.

"The baron," explained Mr. Blossom, rubbing his hands together as if through mere friction he was trying to impart a warmth to the reception which his hard face discountenanced,—"the baron visits us under discouragement. He comes from far countries. It is the custom of gentlefolk of—of foreign extraction to wander through strange lands, commenting upon the habits and doings of the peoples. He will find in Jersey," continued Mr. Blossom, apparently appealing to Thankful, yet really evading her contemptuous glance, "a hard-working yeomanry, ever ready to welcome the stranger, and account to him, penny for penny, for all his necessary expenditure; for which purpose, in these troublous times, he will provide for himself gold or other moneys not affected by these local disturbances."

"He will find, good friend Blossom," said the baron in a rapid, voluble way, utterly at variance with the soft, quiet gravity of his eyes, "Beauty, Grace, Accom-plishment, and —eh—Santa Maria, what shall I say?" He turned appealingly to the count.

"Virtue," nodded the count.

"Truly, Birtoo! all in the fair lady of thees countries. Ah, believe me, honest friend Blossom, there is mooch more in thees than in thoss!"

So much of this speech was addressed to Mistress Thankful, that she had to show at least one dimple in reply, albeit her brows were slightly knit, and she had turned upon the speaker her honest, questioning eyes.

"And then the General Washington has been kind enough to offer his protection," added the count.

"Any fool—any one," supplemented Thankful hastily, with a slight blush—"may have the general's pass, ay, and his good word. But what of Mistress Prudence Bookstaver? —she that has a sweetheart in Knyphausen's brigade, ay,— I warrant a Hessian, but of gentle blood, as Mistress Prudence has often told me,—and, look you, all her letters stopped by the general, ay, I warrant, read by my Lady Washington too, as if 'twere *her* fault that her lad was in arms against Congress. Riddle me that, now!"

" 'Tis but prudence, lass," said Blossom, frowning on the girl. " 'Tis that she might disclose some movement of the army, tending to defeat the enemy."

"And why should she not try to save her lad from capture or ambuscade such as befell the Hessian commissary with the provisions that you—"

Mr. Blossom, in an ostensible fatherly embrace, managed to pinch Mistress Thankful sharply. "Hush, lass," he said with simulated playfulness; "your tongue clacks like

the Whippany mill.—My daughter has small concern—'tis
the manner of womenfolk—in politics," he explained to his
guests. "These dangersome days have given her sore affliction by way of parting comrades of her childhood, and
others whom she has much affected. It has in some sort
soured her."

Mr. Blossom would have recalled this speech as soon as
it escaped him, lest it should lead to a revelation from the
truthful Mistress Thankful of her relations with the Continental captain. But to his astonishment, and, I may add,
to my own, she showed nothing of that disposition she had
exhibited a few moments before. On the contrary, she
blushed slightly, and said nothing.

And then the conversation changed,—upon the weather,
the hard winter, the prospects of the Cause, a criticism
upon the commander-in-chief's management of affairs, the
attitude of Congress, etc., between Mr. Blossom and the
count; characterized, I hardly need say, by that positiveness
of opinion that distinguishes the unprofessional. In
another part of the room, it so chanced that Mistress Thankful and the baron were talking about themselves; the assembly balls; who was the prettiest woman in Morristown;
and whether Gen. Washington's attentions to Mistress Pyne
were only perfunctory gallantry, or what; and if Lady
Washington's hair was really gray; and if that young aide-
de-camp, Major Van Zandt were really in love with Lady
W., or whether his attentions were only the zeal of a subaltern,—in the midst of which a sudden gust of wind
shook the house; and Mr. Blossom, going to the front door,
came back with the announcement that it was snowing
heavily.

And indeed, within that past hour, to their astonished
eyes the whole face of nature had changed. The moon was
gone, the sky hidden in a blinding, whirling swarm of
stinging flakes. The wind, bitter and strong, had already
fashioned white feathery drifts upon the threshold, over the
painted benches on the porch, and against the door-posts.

Mistress Thankful and the baron had walked to the rear
door—the baron with a slight tropical shudder—to view
this meteorological change. As Mistress Thankful looked

over the snowy landscape, it seemed to her that all record
of her past experience had been effaced: her very footprints of an hour before were lost; the gray wall on which
she leaned was white and spotless now; even the familiar
farm-shed looked dim and strange and ghostly. Had she
been there? had she seen the captain? was it all a fancy?
She scarcely knew.

A sudden gust of wind closed the door behind them with
a crash, and sent Mistress Thankful, with a slight feminine
scream, forward into the outer darkness. But the baron
caught her by the waist, and saved her from Heaven knows
what imaginable disaster; and the scene ended in a half-
hysterical laugh. But the wind then set upon them both
with a malevolent fury; and the baron was, I presume,
obliged to draw her closer to his side.

They were alone, save for the presence of those mischievous confederates, Nature and Opportunity. In the
half-obscurity of the storm she could not help turning her
mischievous eyes on his. But she was perhaps surprised to
find them luminous, soft, and, as it seemed to her at that
moment, grave beyond the occasion. An embarrassment
utterly new and singular seized upon her; and when, as
she half feared yet half expected, he bent down and pressed
his lips to hers, she was for a moment powerless. But in
the next instant she boxed his ears sharply, and vanished
in the darkness. When Mr. Blossom opened the door to
the baron he was surprised to find that gentleman alone,
and still more surprised to find, when they re-entered the
house, to see Mistress Thankful enter at the same moment,
demurely, from the front door.

When Mr. Blossom knocked at his daughter's door the
next morning it opened upon her completely dressed, but
withal somewhat pale, and, if the truth must be told, a
little surly.

"And you were stirring so early, Thankful," he said:
" 'twould have been but decent to have bidden God-speed to
the guests, especially the baron, who seemed much concerned
at your absence."

Miss Thankful blushed slightly, but answered with savage
celerity, "And since when is it necessary that I should

dance attendance upon every foreign jack-in-the-box that may lie at the house?"

"He has shown great courtesy to you, mistress, and is a gentleman."

"Courtesy, indeed!" said Mistress Thankful.

"He has not presumed?" said Mr. Blossom suddenly, bringing his cold gray eyes to bear upon his daughter's.

"No, no," said Thankful hurriedly, flaming a bright scarlet; "but—nothing. But what have you there? a letter?"

"Ay,—from the captain, I warrant," said Mr. Blossom, handing her a three-cornered bit of paper: " 'twas left here by a camp-follower. Thankful," he continued, with a meaning glance, "you will heed my counsel in season. The captain is not meet for such as you."

Thankful suddenly grew pale and contemptuous again as she snatched the letter from his hand. When his retiring footsteps were lost on the stairs she regained her color, and opened the letter. It was slovenly written, grievously misspelled, and read as follows:—

"SWEETHEART: A tyranous Act, begotten in Envy and Jealousie, keeps me here a prisoner. Last night I was Basely arrested by Servile Hands for that Freedom of Thought and Expression for which I have already Sacrifized so much—aye all that Man hath but Love and Honour. But the End is Near. When for the Maintenance of Power, the Liberties of the Peoples are subdued by Martial Supremacy and the Dictates of Ambition the State is Lost. I lie in Vile Bondage here in Morristown under charge of Disrespeck—me that a twelvemonth past left a home and Respectable Connexions to serve my Country. Believe me still your own Love, albeit in the Power of Tyrants and condemned it may be to the scaffold.

"The Messenger is Trustworthy and will speed safely to me such as you may deliver unto him. The Provender sanktified by your Hands and made precious by yr. Love was wrested from me by Servil Hands and the Eggs, Sweetheart, were somewhat Addled. The Bacon is, methinks by this time on the Table of the Com'r-in-Chief. Such is Tyranny and Ambition. Sweetheart, farewell, for the present. ALLAN."

Mistress Thankful read this composition once, twice, and then tore it up. Then, reflecting that it was the first letter of her lover's that she had not kept, she tried to put together again the torn fragments, but vainly, and then in a pet, new to her, cast them from the window. During the rest of the day she was considerably *distraite,* and even manifested more temper than she was wont to do; and later, when her father rode away on his daily visit to Morristown, she felt strangely relieved. By noon the snow ceased, or rather turned into a driving sleet that again in turn gave way to rain. By this time she became absorbed in her household duties,—in which she was usually skilful, —and in her own thoughts that to-day had a novelty in their meaning. In the midst of this, at about dark, her room being in the rear of the house, she was perhaps unmindful of the trampling of horse without, or the sound of voices in the hall below. Neither was uncommon at that time. Although protected by the Continental army from forage or the rudeness of soldiery, the Blossom farm had always been a halting-place for passing troopers, commissary teamsters, and reconnoitring officers. Gen. Sullivan and Col. Hamilton had watered their horses at its broad, substantial wayside trough, and sat in the shade of its porch. Miss Thankful was only awakened from her daydream by the entrance of the negro farm-hand, Cæsar.

"Fo' God, Missy Thankful, them sogers is g'wine into camp in the road, I reckon, for they's jest makin' theysevs free afo' the house, and they's an officer in the company-room with his spurs cocked on the table, readin' a book."

A quick flame leaped into Thankful's cheek, and her pretty brows knit themselves over darkening eyes. She arose from her work no longer the moody girl, but an indignant goddess, and, pushing the servant aside, swept down the stairs, and threw open the door.

An officer sitting by the fire in an easy, lounging attitude that justified the servant's criticism, arose instantly with an air of evident embarrassment and surprise that was, however, as quickly dominated and controlled by a gentleman's breeding.

"I beg your pardon," he said, with a deep inclination of his handsome head, "but I had no idea that there was any member of this household at home—at least, a lady." He

14   v. 1

hesitated a moment, catching in the raising of her brown-fringed lids a sudden revelation of her beauty, and partly losing his composure. "I am Major Van Zandt: I have the honor of addressing—"

"Thankful Blossom," said Thankful a little proudly, divining with a woman's swift instinct the cause of the major's hesitation. But her triumph was checked by a new embarrassment visible in the face of the officer at the mention of her name.

"Thankful Blossom," repeated the officer quickly. "You are, then, the daughter of Abner Blossom?"

"Certainly," said Thankful, turning her inquiring eyes upon him. "He will be here betimes. He has gone only to Morristown." In a new fear that had taken possession of her, her questioning eyes asked, "Has he not?"

The officer, answering her eyes rather than her lips, came toward her gravely. "He will not return to-day, Mistress Thankful, nor perhaps even to-morrow. He is—a prisoner."

Thankful opened her brown eyes aggressively on the major. "A prisoner—for what?"

"For aiding and giving comfort to the enemy, and for harboring spies," replied the major with military curtness.

Mistress Thankful's cheek flushed slightly at the last sentence: a recollection of the scene on the porch and the baron's stolen kiss flashed across her, and for a moment she looked as guilty as if the man before her had been a witness to the deed. He saw it, and misinterpreted her confusion.

"Belike, then," said Mistress Thankful, slightly raising her voice, and standing squarely before the major, "belike, then, *I* should be a prisoner too; for the guests of this house, if they be spies, were *my* guests, and, as my father's daughter, I was their hostess; ay, man, and right glad to be the hostess of such gallant gentlemen,—gentlemen, I warrant, too fine to insult a defenceless girl; gentlemen spies that did not cock their boots on the table, or turn an honest farmer's house into a tap-room."

An expression of half pain, half amusement, covered the face of the major, but he made no other reply than by a profound and graceful bow. Courteous and deprecatory as it was, it apparently exasperated Mistress Thankful only the more.

"And pray who are these spies, and who is the informer?" said Mistress Thankful, facing the soldier, with one hand truculently placed on her flexible hip, and the other slipped behind her. "Methinks 'tis only honest we should know when and how we have entertained both."

"Your father, Mistress Thankful," said Major Van Zandt gravely, "has long been suspected of favoring the enemy; but it has been the policy of the commander-in-chief to overlook the political preferences of non-combatants, and to strive to win their allegiance to the good cause by liberal privileges. But when it was lately discovered that two strangers, although bearing a pass from him, have been frequenters of this house under fictitious names—"

"You mean Count Ferdinand and the Baron Pomposo," said Thankful quickly,—"two honest gentlefolk; and if they choose to pay their devoirs to a lass—although, perhaps, not a quality lady, yet an honest girl—"

"Dear Mistress Thankful," said the major with a profound bow and smile, that, spite of its courtesy, drove Thankful to the verge of wrathful hysterics, "if you establish that fact,—and, from this slight acquaintance with your charms, I doubt not you will,—your father is safe from further inquiry or detention. The commander-in-chief is a gentleman who has never underrated the influence of your sex, nor held himself averse to its fascinations."

"What is the name of this informer?" broke in Mistress Thankful angrily. "Who is it that has dared—"

"It is but king's evidence, mayhap, Mistress Thankful; for the informer is himself under arrest. It is on the information of Capt. Allan Brewster of the Connecticut Contingent."

Mistress Thankful whitened, then flushed, and then whitened again. Then she stood up to the major.

"It's a lie,—a cowardly lie!"

Major Van Zandt bowed. Mistress Thankful flew up stairs, and in another moment swept back again into the room in riding hat and habit.

"I suppose I can go and see—my father," she said, without lifting her eyes to the officer.

"You are free as air, Mistress Thankful. My orders and instructions, far from implicating you in your father's offences, do not even suggest your existence. Let me help you to your horse."

The girl did not reply. During that brief interval, however, Cæsar had saddled her white mare, and brought it to the door. Mistress Thankful, disdaining the offered hand of the major, sprang to the saddle.

The major still held the reins. "One moment, Mistress Thankful."

"Let me go!" she said, with suppressed passion.

"One moment, I beg."

His hand still held her bridle-rein. The mare reared, nearly upsetting her. Crimson with rage and mortification, she raised her riding-whip, and laid it smartly over the face of the man before her.

He dropped the rein instantly. Then he raised to her a face calm and colorless, but for a red line extending from his eyebrow to his chin, and said quietly,—

"I had no desire to detain you. I only wished to say that when you see Gen. Washington I know you will be just enough to tell him that Major Van Zandt knew nothing of your wrongs, or even your presence here, until you presented them, and that since then he has treated you as became an officer and a gentleman."

Yet even as he spoke she was gone. At the moment that her fluttering skirt swept in a furious gallop down the hillside, the major turned, and re-entered the house. The few lounging troopers who were witnesses of the scene prudently turned their eyes from the white face and blazing eyes of their officer as he strode by them. Nevertheless, when the door closed behind him, contemporary criticism broke out:—

" 'Tis a Tory jade, vexed that she cannot befool the major as she has the captain," muttered Sergeant Tibbitts.

"And going to try her tricks on the general," added Private Hicks.

Howbeit both these critics may have been wrong. For

as Mistress Thankful thundered down the Morristown road she thought of many things. She thought of her sweetheart Allan, a prisoner, and pining for *her* help and *her* solicitude; and yet—how dared he—if he *had* really betrayed or misjudged her! And then she thought bitterly of the count and the baron, and burned to face the latter, and in some vague way charge the stolen kiss upon him as the cause of all her shame and mortification. And lastly she thought of her father, and began to hate everybody. But above all and through all, in her vague fears for her father, in her passionate indignation against the baron, in her fretful impatience of Allan, one thing was ever dominant and obtrusive; one thing she tried to put away, but could not,—the handsome, colorless face of Major Van Zandt, with the red welt of her riding-whip overlying its cold outlines.

III

THE rising wind, which had ridden much faster than Mistress Thankful, had increased to a gale by the time it reached Morristown. It swept through the leafless maples, and rattled the dry bones of the elms. It whistled through the quiet Presbyterian churchyard, as if trying to arouse the sleepers it had known in days gone by. It shook the blank, lustreless windows of the Assembly Rooms over the Freemasons' Tavern, and wrought in their gusty curtains moving shadows of those amply petticoated dames and tightly hosed cavaliers who had swung in "Sir Roger," or jigged in "Money Musk," the night before.

But I fancy it was around the isolated "Ford Mansion," better known as the "Headquarters," that the wind wreaked its grotesque rage. It howled under its scant eaves, it sang under its bleak porch, it tweaked the peak of its front gable, it whistled through every chink and cranny of its square, solid, unpicturesque structure. Situated on a hillside that descended rapidly to the Whippany River, every summer zephyr that whispered through the porches of the Morristown farm-houses charged as a stiff breeze upon the swinging half doors and windows of the "Ford Mansion";

every wintry wind became a gale that threatened its security. The sentry who paced before its front porch knew from experience when to linger under its lee, and adjust his threadbare outer coat to the bitter north wind.

Within the house something of this cheerlessness prevailed. It had an ascetic gloom, which the scant firelight of the reception-room, and the dying embers on the dining-room hearth, failed to dissipate. The central hall was broad, and furnished plainly with a few rush-bottomed chairs, on one of which half dozed a black body-servant of the commander-in-chief. Two officers in the dining-room, drawn close by the chimney-corner, chatted in undertones, as if mindful that the door of the drawing-room was open, and their voices might break in upon its sacred privacy. The swinging light in the hall partly illuminated it, or rather glanced gloomily from the black polished furniture, the lustreless chairs, the quaint cabinet, the silent spinet, the skeleton-legged centre-table, and finally upon the motionless figure of a man seated by the fire.

It was a figure since so well known to the civilized world, since so celebrated in print and painting, as to need no description here. Its rare combination of gentle dignity with profound force, of a set resoluteness of purpose with a philosophical patience, have been so frequently delivered to a people not particularly remarkable for these qualities, that I fear it has too often provoked a spirit of playful aggression, in which the deeper underlying meaning was forgotten. So let me add that in manner, physical equipoise, and even in the mere details of dress, this figure indicated a certain aristocratic exclusiveness. It was the presentment of a king,—a king who by the irony of circumstances was just then waging war against all kingship; a ruler of men, who just then was fighting for the right of these men to govern themselves, but whom by his own inherent right he dominated. From the crown of his powdered head to the silver buckle of his shoe he was so royal that it was not strange that his brother George of England and Hanover —ruling by accident, otherwise impiously known as the "grace of God"—could find no better way of resisting his power than by calling him "Mr. Washington."

The sound of horses' hoofs, the formal challenge of sentry, the grave questioning of the officer of the guard, followed by footsteps upon the porch, did not apparently disturb his meditation. Nor did the opening of the outer door, and a charge of cold air into the hall that invaded even the privacy of the reception-room, and brightened the dying embers on the hearth, stir his calm pre-occupation. But an instant later there was the distinct rustle of a feminine skirt in the hall, a hurried whispering of men's voices, and then the sudden apparition of a smooth, fresh-faced young officer over the shoulder of the unconscious figure.

"I beg your pardon, general," said the officer doubtingly, "but—"

"You are not intruding, Col. Hamilton," said the general quietly.

"There is a young lady without who wishes an audience of your Excellency. 'Tis Mistress Thankful Blossom,—the daughter of Abner Blossom, charged with treasonous practice and favoring the enemy, now in the guard-house at Morristown."

"Thankful Blossom?" repeated the general interrogatively.

"Your Excellency doubtless remembers a little provincial beauty and a famous toast of the country-side,—the Cressida of our Morristown epic, who led our gallant Connecticut captain astray—"

"You have the advantages, besides the better memory of a younger man, colonel," said Washington, with a playful smile that slightly reddened the cheek of his aide-de-camp. "Yet I think I *have* heard of this phenomenon. By all means, admit her—and her escort."

"She is alone, general," responded the subordinate.

"Then the more reason why we should be polite," returned Washington, for the first time altering his easy posture, rising to his feet, and lightly clasping his ruffled hands before him. "We must not keep her waiting. Give her access, my dear colonel, at once; and even as she came, —*alone*."

The aide-de-camp bowed and withdrew. In another mo-

ment the half-opened door swung wide to Mistress Thankful Blossom.

She was so beautiful in her simple riding-dress, so quaint
and original in that very beauty, and, above all, so teem-
ing with a certain vital earnestness of purpose just positive
and audacious enough to set off that beauty, that the grave
gentleman before her did not content himself with the
usual formal inclination of courtesy, but actually advanced,
and, taking her cold little hand in his, graciously led her to
the chair he had just vacated.

"Even if your name were not known to me, Mistress
Thankful," said the commander-in-chief, looking down upon
her with grave politeness, "nature has, methinks, spared
you the necessity of any introduction to the courtesy of a
gentleman. But how can I especially serve you?"

Alack! the blaze of Mistress Thankful's brown eyes had
become somewhat dimmed in the grave half-lights of the
room, in the graver, deeper dignity of the erect, soldier-
like figure before her. The bright color born of the tempest
within and without had somehow faded from her cheek;
the sauciness begotten from bullying her horse in the last
half-hour's rapid ride was so subdued by the actual presence
of the man she had come to bully, that I fear she had to
use all her self-control to keep down her inclination to
whimper, and to keep back the tears, that, oddly enough,
rose to her sweet eyes as she lifted them to the quietly
critical yet placid glance of her interlocutor.

"I can readily conceive the motive of this visit, Miss
Thankful," continued Washington, with a certain dignified
kindliness that was more reassuring than the formal gallantry of the period; "and it is, I protest, to your credit.
A father's welfare, however erring and weak that father
may be, is most seemly in a maiden—"

Thankful's eyes flashed again as she rose to her feet.
Her upper lip, that had a moment before trembled in a
pretty infantine distress, now stiffened and curled as she
confronted the dignified figure before her. "It is not of
my father I would speak," she said saucily: "I did not
ride here alone to-night, in this weather, to talk of *him;*
I warrant *he* can speak for himself. I came here to speak

of myself, of lies—ay, *lies* told of me, a poor girl; ay, of cowardly gossip about me and my sweetheart, Capt. Brewster, now confined in prison because he hath loved me, a lass without politics or adherence to the cause—as if 'twere necessary every lad should ask the confidence or permission of yourself or, belike, my Lady Washington, in his preferences."

She paused a moment, out of breath. With a woman's quickness of intuition she saw the change in Washington's face,—saw a certain cold severity overshadowing it. With a woman's fateful persistency—a persistency which I humbly suggest might, on occasion, be honorably copied by our more politic sex—she went on to say what was in her, even if she were obliged, with a woman's honorable inconsistency, to unsay it an hour or two later; an inconsistency which I also humbly protest might be as honorably imitated by us—on occasion.

"It has been said," said Thankful Blossom quickly, "that my father has given entertainment knowingly to two spies, —two spies that, begging your Excellency's pardon, and the pardon of Congress, I know only as two honorable gentlemen who have as honorably tendered me their affections. It is said, and basely and most falsely too, that my sweetheart, Capt. Allan Brewster, has lodged this information. I have ridden here to deny it. I have ridden here to demand of you that an honest woman's reputation shall not be sacrificed to the interests of politics; that a prying mob of ragamuffins shall not be sent to an honest farmer's house to spy and spy—and turn a poor girl out of doors that they might do it. 'Tis shameful, so it is; there! 'tis most scandalous, so it is: there, now! Spies, indeed! what are *they*, pray?"

In the indignation which the recollection of her wrongs had slowly gathered in her, from the beginning of this speech, she had advanced her face, rosy with courage, and beautiful in its impertinence, within a few inches of the dignified features and quiet gray eyes of the great commander. To her utter stupefaction, he bent his head and kissed her, with a grave benignity, full on the centre of her audacious forehead.

"Be seated, I beg, Mistress Blossom," he said, taking her cold hand in his, and quietly replacing her in the unoccupied chair. "Be seated, I beg, and give me, if you can, your attention for a moment. The officer intrusted with the ungracious task of occupying your father's house is a member of my military family, and a gentleman. If he has so far forgotten himself—if he has so far disgraced himself and me as—"

"No! no!" uttered Thankful, with feverish alacrity, "the gentleman was most considerate. On the contrary—mayhap—I"—she hesitated, and then came to a full stop, with a heightened color, as a vivid recollection of that gentleman's face, with the mark of her riding-whip lying across it, rose before her.

"I was about to say that Major Van Zandt, as a gentleman, has known how to fully excuse the natural impulses of a daughter," continued Washington, with a look of perfect understanding; "but let me now satisfy you on another point, where it would seem we greatly differ."

He walked to the door, and summoned his servant, to whom he gave an order. In another moment the fresh-faced young officer who had at first admitted her re-appeared with a file of official papers. He glanced slyly at Thankful Blossom's face with an amused look, as if he had already heard the colloquy between her and his superior officer, and had appreciated that which neither of the earnest actors in the scene had themselves felt,—a certain sense of humor in the situation.

Howbeit, standing before them, Col. Hamilton gravely turned over the file of papers. Thankful bit her lips in embarrassment. A slight feeling of awe, and a presentiment of some fast-coming shame; a new and strange consciousness of herself, her surroundings, of the dignity of the two men before her; an uneasy feeling of the presence of two ladies who had in some mysterious way entered the room from another door, and who seemed to be intently regarding her from afar with a curiosity as if she were some strange animal; and a wild premonition that her whole future life and happiness depended upon the events of the next few moments,—so took possession of her, that the brave girl trembled for a moment in her isolation and loneliness. In another instant Col. Hamilton, speaking to his superior, but looking obviously at one of the ladies who had entered, handed a paper to Washington, and said, "Here are the charges."

"Read them," said the general coldly.

Col. Hamilton, with a manifest consciousness of another hearer than Mistress Blossom and his general, read the paper. It was couched in phrases of military and legal precision, and related briefly, that upon the certain and personal knowledge of the writer, Abner Blossom of the "Blossom Farm" was in the habit of entertaining two gentlemen, namely, the "Count Ferdinand" and the "Baron Pomposo," suspected enemies of the cause, and possible traitors to the Continental army. It was signed by Allan Brewster, late captain in the Connecticut Contingent.

As Col. Hamilton exhibited the signature, Thankful Blossom had no difficulty in recognizing the familiar bad hand and equally familiar mis-spelling of her lover.

She rose to her feet. With eyes that showed her present trouble and perplexity as frankly as they had a moment before blazed with her indignation, she met, one by one, the glances of the group who now seemed to be closing round her. Yet with a woman's instinct she felt, I am constrained to say, more unfriendliness in the silent presence of the two women than in the possible outspoken criticism of our much-abused sex.

"Of course," said a voice which Thankful at once, by a woman's unerring instinct, recognized as the elder of the two ladies, and the legitimate keeper of the conscience of some one of the men who were present,—"of course Mistress Thankful will be able to elect which of her lovers among her country's enemies she will be able to cling to for support in her present emergency. She does not seem to have been so special in her favors as to have positively excluded any one."

"At least, dear Lady Washington, she will not give it to the man who has proven a traitor to *her*," said the younger woman impulsively. "That is—I beg your ladyship's pardon"—she hesitated, observing in the dead silence that ensued that the two superior male beings present looked at each other in lofty astonishment.

"He that is trait'rous to his country," said Lady Washington coldly, "is apt to be trait'rous elsewhere."

"'Twere as honest to say that he that was trait'rous to his king was trait'rous to his country," said Mistress Thankful with sudden audacity, bending her knit brows on Lady Washington. But that lady turned dignifiedly away, and Mistress Thankful again faced the general.

"I ask your pardon," she said proudly, "for troubling you with my wrongs. But it seems to me that even if another and a greater wrong were done me by my sweetheart, through jealousy, it would not justify this accusation against me, even though," she added, darting a wicked glance at the placid brocaded back of Lady Washington, "even though that accusation came from one who knows that jealousy may belong to the wife of a patriot as well as a traitor." She was herself again after this speech, although her face was white with the blow she had taken and returned.

Col. Hamilton passed his hand across his mouth, and coughed slightly. Gen. Washington, standing by the fire with an impassive face, turned to Thankful gravely:—

"You are forgetting, Mistress Thankful, that you have not told me how I can serve you. It cannot be that you are still concerned in Capt. Brewster, who has given evidence against your other—*friends,* and tacitly against *you.* Nor can it be on their account, for I regret to say they are still free and unknown. If you come with any information exculpating them, and showing they are not spies or hostile to the cause, your father's release shall be certain and speedy. Let me ask you a single question: Why do you believe them honest?"

"Because," said Mistress Thankful, "they were—were—gentlemen."

"Many spies have been of excellent family, good address, and fair talents," said Washington gravely; "but you have, mayhap, some other reason."

"Because they talked only to ME," said Mistress Thankful, blushing mightily; "because they preferred my com-

pany to father's; because"—she hesitated a moment—
"because they spoke not of politics, but—of—that which
lads mainly talk of—and—and,"—here she broke down a
little,—"and the baron I only saw once, but he"—here she
broke down utterly—"I know they weren't spies: there,
now!'

"I must ask you something more," said Washington, with
grave kindness: "whether you give me the information or
not, you will consider, that, if what you believe is true, it
cannot in any way injure the gentlemen you speak of;
while, on the other hand, it may relieve your father of suspicion. Will you give to Col. Hamilton, my secretary, a
full description of them,—that fuller description which
Capt. Brewster, for reasons best known to yourself, was
unable to give?"

Mistress Thankful hesitated for a moment, and then,
with one of her truthful glances at the commander-in-chief,
began a detailed account of the outward semblance of the
count. Why she began with him, I am unable to say; but
possibly it was because it was easier, for when she came to
describe the baron, she was, I regret to say, somewhat vague
and figurative. Not so vague, however, but that Col. Hamilton suddenly started up with a look at his chief, who
instantly checked it with a gesture of his ruffled hand.

"I thank you, Mistress Thankful," he said quite impassively, "but did this other gentleman, this baron—"

"Pomposo," said Thankful proudly. A titter originated
in the group of ladies by the window, and became visible
on the fresh face of Col. Hamilton; but the dignified color
of Washington's countenance was unmoved.

"May I ask if the baron made an honorable tender of
his affections to you," he continued, with respectful gravity,
—"if his attentions were known to your father, and were
such as honest Mistress Blossom could receive?"

"Father introduced him to me, and wanted me to be kind
to him. He—he kissed me, and I slapped his face," said
Thankful quickly, with cheeks as red, I warrant, as the
baron's might have been.

The moment the words had escaped her truthful lips, she
would have given her life to recall them. To her astonish-

ment, however, Col. Hamilton laughed outright, and the ladies turned and approached her, but were checked by a slight gesture from the otherwise impassive figure of the general.

"It is possible, Mistress Thankful," he resumed, with undisturbed composure, "that one at least of these gentlemen may be known to us, and that your instincts may be correct. At least rest assured that we shall fully inquire into it, and that your father shall have the benefit of that inquiry."

"I thank your Excellency," said Thankful, still reddening under the contemplation of her own late frankness, and retreating toward the door. "I—think—I—must—go—now. It is late, and I have far to ride."

To her surprise, however, Washington stepped forward, and, again taking her hands in his, said with a grave smile, "For that very reason, if for none other, you must be our guest to-night, Mistress Thankful Blossom. We still retain our Virginian ideas of hospitality, and are tyrannous enough to make strangers conform to them, even though we have but perchance the poorest of entertainment to offer them. Lady Washington will not permit Mistress Thankful Blossom to leave her roof to-night until she has partaken of her courtesy as well as her counsel."

"Mistress Thankful Blossom will make us believe that she has at least in so far trusted our desire to serve her justly, by accepting our poor hospitality for a single night," said Lady Washington, with a stately courtesy.

Thankful Blossom still stood irresolutely at the door. But the next moment a pair of youthful arms encircled her; and the younger gentlewoman, looking into her brown eyes with an honest frankness equal to her own, said caressingly, "Dear Mistress Thankful, though I am but a guest in her ladyship's house, let me, I pray you, add my voice to hers. I am Mistress Schuyler of Albany, at your service, Mistress Thankful, as Col. Hamilton here will bear me witness, did I need any interpreter to your honest heart. Believe me, dear Mistress Thankful, I sympathize with you, and only beg you to give me an opportunity to-night to serve you. You will stay, I know, and you will stay with me; and we shall talk over the faithlessness of that over-jealous

Yankee captain who has proved himself, I doubt not, as unworthy of *you* as he is of his country."

Hateful to Thankful as was the idea of being commiserated, she nevertheless could not resist the gentle courtesy and gracious sympathy of Miss Schuyler. Besides, it must be confessed that for the first time in her life she felt a doubt of the power of her own independence, and a strange fascination for this young gentlewoman whose arms were around her, who could so thoroughly sympathize with her, and yet allow herself to be snubbed by Lady Washington.

"You have a mother, I doubt not?" said Thankful, raising her questioning eyes to Miss Schuyler.

Irrelevant as this question seemed to the two gentlemen, Miss Schuyler answered it with feminine intuition: "And you, dear Mistress Thankful—"

"Have none," said Thankful; and here, I regret to say, she whimpered slightly, at which Miss Schuyler, with tears in her own fine eyes, bent her head suddenly to Thankful's ear, put her arm about the waist of the pretty stranger, and then, to the astonishment of Col. Hamilton, quietly swept her out of the august presence.

When the door had closed upon them, Col. Hamilton turned half-smilingly, half-inquiringly, to his chief. Washington returned his glance kindly but gravely, and then said quietly,—

"If your suspicions jump with mine, colonel, I need not remind you that it is a matter so delicate that it would be as well if you locked it in your own breast for the present; at least, that you should not intimate to the gentleman whom you may have suspected, aught that has passed this evening."

"As you will, general," said the subaltern respectfully; "but may I ask"—he hesitated—"if you believe that anything more than a passing fancy for a pretty girl—"

"When I asked your silence, colonel," interrupted Washington kindly, laying his hand upon the shoulder of the younger man, "it was because I thought the matter sufficiently momentous to claim my own private and especial attention."

"I ask your Excellency's pardon," said the young man, reddening through his fresh complexion like a girl; "I only meant—"

"That you would ask to be relieved to-night," interrupted Washington, with a benign smile, "forasmuch as you wished the more to show entertainment to our dear friend Miss Schuyler, and her guest; a wayward girl, colonel, but, methinks, an honest one. Treat her of your own quality, colonel, but discreetly, and not too kindly, lest we have Mistress Schuyler, another injured damsel, on our hands;" and with a half playful gesture peculiar to the man, and yet not inconsistent with his dignity, he half led, half pushed his youthful secretary from the room.

When the door had closed upon the colonel, Lady Washington rustled toward her husband, who stood still, quiet and passive, on the hearthstone.

"You surely see in this escapade nothing of political intrigue—no treachery?" she said hastily.

"No," said Washington quietly.

"Nothing more than an idle, wanton intrigue with a foolish, vain country girl?"

"Pardon me, my lady," said Washington gravely. "I doubt not we may misjudge her. 'Tis no common rustic lass that can thus stir the country side. 'Twere an insult to your sex to believe it. It is not yet sure that she has not captured even so high game as she has named. If she has, it would add another interest to a treaty of comity and alliance."

"That creature!" said Lady Washington,—"that light-o'-love with her Connecticut captain lover! Pardon me, but this is preposterous;" and with a stiff courtesy she swept from the room, leaving the central figure of history—as such central figures are apt to be left—alone.

Later in the evening Mistress Schuyler so far subdued the tears and emotions of Thankful, that she was enabled to dry her eyes, and re-arrange her brown hair in the quaint little mirror in Mistress Schuyler's chamber; Mistress Schuyler herself lending a touch and suggestion here and there, after the secret freemasonry of her sex. "You are well rid of this forsworn captain, dear Mistress Thankful; and methinks that with hair as beautiful as yours, the new style of wearing it, though a modish frivolity, is most becoming. I assure you 'tis much affected in New York and Philadelphia,—drawn straight back from the forehead, after this manner, as you see."

The result was, that an hour later Mistress Schuyler and Mistress Blossom presented themselves to Col. Hamilton in the reception-room, with a certain freshness and elaboration of toilet that not only quite shamed the young officer's *affairé* negligence, but caused him to open his eyes in astonishment. "Perhaps she would rather be alone, that she might indulge her grief," he said doubtingly, in an aside to Miss Schuyler, "rather than appear in company."

"Nonsense," quoth Mistress Schuyler. "Is a young woman to mope and sigh because her lover proves false?"

"But her father is a prisoner," said Hamilton in amazement.

"Can you look me in the face," said Mistress Schuyler mischievously, "and tell me that you don't know that in twenty-four hours her father will be cleared of these charges? Nonsense! Do you think I have no eyes in my head? Do you think I misread the general's face and your own?"

"But, my dear girl," said the officer in alarm.

"Oh! I told her so, but not *why*," responded Miss Schuyler with a wicked look in her dark eyes, "though I had warrant enough to do so, to serve you for keeping a secret from *me!*"

And with this Parthian shot she returned to Mistress Thankful, who, with her face pressed against the window, was looking out on the moonlit slope beside the Whippany River.

For, by one of those freaks peculiar to the American springtide, the weather had again marvellously changed. The rain had ceased, and the ground was covered with an icing of sleet and snow, that now glittered under a clear sky and a brilliant moon. The northeast wind that shook the loose sashes of the windows had transformed each dripping tree and shrub to icy stalactites that silvered under the moon's cold touch.

" 'Tis a beautiful sight, ladies," said a bluff, hearty, middle-aged man, joining the group by the window. "But God send the spring to us quickly, and spare us any more such cruel changes! My lady moon looks fine enough, glittering in yonder treetops; but I doubt not she looks down upon many a poor fellow shivering under his tattered blankets in the camp beyond. Had ye seen the Connecticut tatterdemalions file by last night, with arms reversed, showing their teeth at his Excellency, and yet not daring to bite; had ye watched these faint-hearts, these doubting Thomases, ripe for rebellion against his Excellency, against the cause, but chiefly against the weather,—ye would pray for a thaw that would melt the hearts of these men as it would these stubborn fields around us. Two weeks more of such weather would raise up not one Allan Brewster, but a dozen such malcontent puppies ripe for a drum-head court-martial."

"Yet 'tis a fine night, Gen. Sullivan," said Col. Hamilton, sharply nudging the ribs of his superior officer with his elbow. "There would be little trouble on such a night, I fancy, to track our ghostly visitant." Both of the ladies becoming interested, and Col. Hamilton having thus adroitly turned the flank of his superior officer, he went on, "You should know that the camp, and indeed the whole locality here, is said to be haunted by the apparition of a gray-coated figure, whose face is muffled and hidden in his collar, but who has the password pat to his lips, and whose identity hath baffled the sentries. This figure, it is said, forasmuch as it has been seen just before an assault, an attack, or some tribulation of the army, is believed by many to be the genius or guardian spirit of the cause, and, as such, has incited sentries and guards to greater vigilance, and has to some seemed a premonition of disaster. Before the last outbreak of the Connecticut militia, Master Graycoat haunted the outskirts of the weather-beaten and bedraggled camp, and, I doubt not, saw much of that preparation that sent that regiment of faint-hearted onion-gatherers to flaunt their woes and their wrongs in the face of the general himself."

Here Col. Hamilton, in turn, received a slight nudge

from Mistress Schuyler, and ended his speech somewhat
abruptly.

Mistress Thankful was not unmindful of both these allusions to her faithless lover, but only a consciousness of
mortification and wounded pride was awakened by them. In
fact, during the first tempest of her indignation at his
arrest, still later at the arrest of her father, and finally at
the discovery of his perfidy to her, she had forgotten that
he was her lover; she had forgotten her previous tenderness toward him; and, now that her fire and indignation
were spent, only a sense of numbness and vacancy remained.
All that had gone before seemed not something to be regretted as her own act, but rather as the act of another
Thankful Blossom, who had been lost that night in the
snow-storm: she felt she had become, within the last twenty-
four hours, not perhaps *another* woman, but for the first
time a *woman*.

Yet it was singular that she felt more confused when, a
few moments later, the conversation turned upon Major Van
Zandt: it was still more singular that she even felt considerably frightened at that confusion. Finally she found
herself listening with alternate irritability, shame, and
curiosity, to praises of that gentleman, of his courage, his
devotion, and his personal graces. For one wild moment
Thankful felt like throwing herself on the breast of Mistress Schuyler, and confessing her rudeness to the major;
but a conviction that Mistress Schuyler would share that
secret with Col. Hamilton, that Major Van Zandt might
not like that revelation, and, oddly enough associated with
this, a feeling of unconquerable irritability toward that
handsome and gentle young officer, kept her mouth closed.
"Besides," she said to herself, "he ought to know, if he's
such a fine gentleman as they say, just how I was feeling,
and that I don't mean any rudeness to him;" and with this
unanswerable feminine logic poor Thankful to some extent
stilled her own honest little heart.

But not, I fear, entirely. The night was a restless one
to her: like all impulsive natures, the season of reflection,
and perhaps distrust, came to her upon acts that were already committed, and when reason seemed to light the

way only to despair. She saw the folly of her intrusion at the headquarters, as she thought, only when it was too late to remedy it; she saw the gracelessness and discourtesy of her conduct to Major Van Zandt, only when distance and time rendered an apology weak and ineffectual. I think she cried a little to herself, lying in the strange gloomy chamber of the healthfully sleeping Mistress Schuyler, the sweet security of whose manifest goodness and kindness she alternately hated and envied; and at last, unable to stand it longer, slipped noiselessly from her bed, and stood very wretched and disconsolate before the window that looked out upon the slope toward the Whippany River. The moon on the new-fallen, frigid, and untrodden snow shone brightly. Far to the left it glittered on the bayonet of a sentry pacing beside the river-bank, and gave a sense of security to the girl that perhaps strengthened another idea that had grown up in her mind. Since she could not sleep, why should she not ramble about until she could? She had been accustomed to roam about the farm in all weathers and at all times and seasons. She recalled to herself the night—a tempestuous one—when she had risen in serious concern as to the lying-in of her favorite Alderney heifer, and how she had saved the life of the calf, a weakling, dropped apparently from the clouds in the tempest, as it lay beside the barn. With this in her mind, she donned her dress again, and, with Mistress Schuyler's mantle over her shoulders, noiselessly crept down the narrow staircase, passed the sleeping servant on the settee, and, opening the rear door, in another moment was inhaling the crisp air, and tripping down the crisp snow of the hillside.

But Mistress Thankful had overlooked one difference between her own farm and a military encampment. She had not proceeded a dozen yards before a figure apparently started out of the ground beneath her, and, levelling a bayoneted musket across her path, called, "Halt!"

The hot blood mounted to the girl's cheek at the first imperative command she had ever received in her life: nevertheless she halted unconsciously, and without a word confronted the challenger with her old audacity.

"Who comes there?" reiterated the sentry, still keeping his bayonet level with her breast.

"Thankful Blossom," she responded promptly.

The sentry brought his musket to a "present." "Pass, Thankful Blossom, and God send it soon and the spring with it, .and good-night," he said, with a strong Milesian accent. And before the still-amazed girl could comprehend the meaning of his abrupt challenge, or his equally abrupt departure, he had resumed his monotonous pace in the moon-light. Indeed, as she stood looking after him, the whole episode, the odd unreality of the moonlit landscape, the novelty of her position, the morbid play of her thoughts, seemed to make it part of a dream which the morning light might dissipate, but could never fully explain.

With something of this feeling still upon her, she kept her way to the river. Its banks were still fringed with ice, through which its dark current flowed noiselessly. She knew it flowed through the camp where lay her faithless lover, and for an instant indulged the thought of following it, and facing him with the proof of his guilt; but even at the thought she recoiled with a new and sudden doubt in her-self, and stood dreamily watching the shimmer of the moon on the icy banks, until another, and, it seemed to her, equally unreal vision suddenly stayed her feet, and drove the blood from her feverish cheeks.

A figure was slowly aproaching from the direction of the sleeping encampment. Tall, erect, and habited in a gray surtout, with a hood partially concealing its face, it was the counterfeit presentment of the ghostly visitant she had heard described. Thankful scarcely breathed. The brave little heart that had not quailed before the sentry's levelled musket a moment before now faltered and stood still, as the phantom with a slow and majestic tread moved toward her. She had only time to gain the shelter of a tree before the figure, majestically unconscious of her presence, passed slowly by. Through all her terror Thankful was still true to a certain rustic habit of practical perception to observe that the tread of the phantom was quite audible over the crust of snow, and was visible and palpable as the imprint of a military boot.

The blood came back to Thankful's cheek, and with it
her old audacity. In another instant she was out from the
tree, and tracking with a light feline tread the apparition
that now loomed up the hill before her. Slipping from
tree to tree, she followed until it passed before the door of
a low hut or farm-shed that stood midway up the hill.
Here it entered, and the door closed behind it. With every
sense feverishly alert, Thankful, from the secure advantage
of a large maple, watched the door of the hut. In a few
moments it re-opened to the same figure free of its gray
enwrappings. Forgetful of every thing now, but detecting
the face of the impostor, the fearless girl left the tree,
and placed herself directly in the path of the figure. At
the same moment it turned toward her inquiringly, and the
moonlight fell full upon the calm, composed features of
Gen. Washington.

In her consternation Thankful could only drop an embarrassed courtesy, and hang out two lovely signals of distress in her cheeks. The face of the pseudo ghost alone
remained unmoved.

"You are wandering late, Mistress Thankful," he said
at last, with a paternal gravity; "and I fear that the formal
restraint of a military household has already given you
some embarrassment. Yonder sentry, for instance, might
have stoped you."

"Oh, he did!" said Thankful quickly; "but it's all right,
please your Excellency. "He asked me 'Who went there,'
and I told him; and he was vastly polite, I assure you."

The grave features of the commander-in-chief relaxed in
a smile. "You are more happy than most of your sex in
turning a verbal compliment to practical account. For
know then, dear young lady, that in honor of your visit
to the headquarters, the password to-night through this
encampment was none other than your own pretty pat-
ronymic,—'Thankful Blossom.'"

The tears glittered in the girl's eyes, and her lip trembled;
but, with all her readiness of speech, she could only say,
"Oh, your Excellency."

"Then you *did* pass the sentry?" continued Washington,
looking at her intently with a certain grave watchfulness

in his gray eyes. "And doubtless you wandered at the
river-bank. Although I myself, tempted by the night,
sometimes extend my walk as far as yonder shed, it were
a hazardous act for a young lady to pass beyond the protection of the line."

"Oh! I met no one, your Excellency," said the usually
truthful Thankful hastily, rushing to her first lie with
grateful impetuosity.

"And saw no one?" asked Washington quietly.

"No one," said Thankful, raising her brown eyes to the
general's.

They both looked at each other,—the naturally most
veracious young woman in the colonies, and the subsequent
allegorical impersonation of truth in America,—and knew
each other lied, and, I imagine, respected each other for it.

"I am glad to hear you say so, Mistress Thankful," said
Washington quietly; "for 'twould have been natural for
you to have sought an interview with your recreant lover
in yonder camp, though the attempt would have been unwise and impossible."

"I had no such thought, your Excellency," said Thankful, who had really quite forgotten her late intention; "yet,
if with your permission I could hold a few moments' con-
verse with Capt. Brewster, it would greatly ease my mind."

" 'Twould not be well for the present," said Washington thoughtfully. "But in a day or two Capt. Brewster
will be tried by court-martial at Morristown. It shall be
so ordered that when he is conveyed thither his guard shall
halt at the Blossom Farm. I will see that the officer in
command gives you an opportunity to see him. And I
think I can promise also, Mistress Thankful, that your
father shall be also present under his own roof, a free
man."

They had reached the entrance to the mansion, and entered the hall. Thankful turned impulsively, and kissed
the extended hand of the commander. "You are so good!
I have been so foolish—so very, very wrong," she said,
with a slight trembling of her lip. "And your Excellency
believes my story; and those gentlemen were *not* spies, but
even as they gave themselves to be."

"I said not that much," replied Washington with a kindly smile, "but no matter. Tell me rather, Mistress Thankful, how far your acquaintance with these gentlemen has gone; or did it end with the box on the ear that you gave the baron?"

"He had asked me to ride with him to the Baskingridge, and I—had said—yes," faltered Mistress Thankful.

"Unless I misjudge you, Mistress Thankful, you can without great sacrifice promise me that you will not see him until I give you my permission," said Washington, with grave playfulness.

The swinging light shone full in Thankful's truthful eyes as she lifted them to his.

"I do," she said quietly.

"Good-night," said the commander, with a formal bow.

"Good-night, your Excellency."

IV

THE sun was high over the Short Hills when Mistress Thankful, the next day, drew up her sweating mare beside the Blossom Farm gate. She had never looked prettier, she had never felt more embarrassed, as she entered her own house. During her rapid ride she had already framed a speech of apology to Major Van Zandt, which, however, utterly fled from her lips as that officer showed himself respectfully on the threshold. Yet she permitted him to usurp the functions of the grinning Cæsar, and help her from her horse; albeit she was conscious of exhibiting the awkward timidity of a bashful rustic, until at last, with a stammering, "Thank ye," she actually ran up stairs to hide her glowing face and far too conscious eyelids.

During the rest of that day Major Van Zandt quietly kept out of the way, without obtrusively seeming to avoid her. Yet, when they met casually in the performance of her household duties, the innocent Mistress Thankful noticed, under her downcast penitential eyelids, that the eyes of the officer followed her intently. And thereat she fell unconsciously to imitating him; and so they eyed each other

furtively like cats, and rubbed themselves along the walls
of rooms and passages when they met, lest they should
seem designedly to come near each other, and enacted the
gravest and most formal of genuflexions, courtesies, and
bows, when they accidentally *did* meet. And just at the
close of the second day, as the elegant Major Van Zandt
was feeling himself fast becoming a drivelling idiot and an
awkward country booby, the arrival of a courier from headquarters saved that gentleman his self-respect forever.

Mistress Thankful was in her sitting-room when he
knocked at her door. She opened it in sudden, conscious
trepidation.

"I ask pardon for intruding, Mistress Thankful Blossom," he said gravely; "but I have here"—he held out a
pretentious document—"a letter for you from headquarters.
May I hope that it contains good news,—the release of your
father,—and that it relieves you from my presence, and an
espionage which I assure you cannot be more unpleasant to
you than it has been to myself."

As he entered the room, Thankful had risen to her feet
with the full intention of delivering to him her little set
apology; but, as he ended his speech, she looked at him
blankly, and burst out crying.

Of course he was in an instant at her side, and holding
her cold little hand. Then she managed to say, between
her tears, that she had been wanting to make an apology
to him; that she had wanted to say ever since she arrived
that she had been rude, very rude, and that she knew he
never could forgive her; that she had been trying to say
that she never could forget his gentle forbearance: "only,"
she added, suddenly raising her tear-fringed brown lids to
the astonished man, *"you wouldn't ever let me!"*

"Dear Mistress Thankful," said the major, in conscience-
stricken horror, "if I have made myself distant to you, believe me it was only because I feared to intrude upon your
sorrow. I really—dear Mistress Thankful—I—"

"When you took all the pains to go round the hall instead of through the dining-room, lest I should ask you to
forgive me," sobbed Mistress Thankful, "I thought—you—
must—hate me, and preferred to—"

"Perhaps this letter may mitigate your sorrow, Mistress Thankful," said the officer, pointing to the letter she still held unconsciously in her hand.

With a blush at her pre-occupation, Thankful opened the letter. It was a half-official document, and ran as follows:—

"The Commander-in-Chief is glad to inform Mistress Thankful Blossom that the charges preferred against her father have, upon fair examination, been found groundless and trivial. The Commander-in-Chief further begs to inform Mistress Blossom that the gentleman known to her under the name of the 'Baron Pomposo' was his Excellency Don Juan Morales, Ambassador and Envoy Extraordinary of the Court of Spain, and that the gentleman known to her as the 'Count Ferdinand' was Señor Godoy, Secretary to the Embassy. The Commander-in-Chief wishes to add that Mistress Thankful Blossom is relieved of any further obligation of hospitality toward these honorable gentlemen, as the Commander-in-Chief regrets to record the sudden and deeply-to-be-deplored death of his Excellency this morning by typhoid fever, and the possible speedy return of the Embassy.

"In conclusion, the Commander-in-Chief wishes to bear testimony to the Truthfulness, Intuition, and Discretion of Mistress Thankful Blossom.

"By order of his Excellency,
"Gen. GEORGE WASHINGTON.
"ALEX. HAMILTON, Secretary.

"To Mistress THANKFUL BLOSSOM, of Blossom Farm."

Thankful Blossom was silent for a few moments, and then raised her abashed eyes to Major Van Zandt. A single glance satisfied her that he knew nothing of the imposture that had been practised upon her,—knew nothing of the trap into which her vanity and self-will had led her.

"Dear Mistress Thankful," said the major, seeing the distress in her face, "I trust the news is not ill. Surely I gathered from the sergeant that—"

"What?" said Thankful, looking at him intently.

"That in twenty-four hours at furthest your father would be free, and that I should be relieved—"

"I know that you are a-weary of your task, major," said Thankful bitterly: "rejoice, then, to know your information is correct, and that my father is exonerated—unless—un-

less this is a forgery, and Gen. Washington should turn
out to be somebody else, and *you* should turn out to be
somebody else—" And she stopped short, and hid her wet
eyes in the window-curtains.

"Poor girl!" said Major Van Zandt to himself. "This
trouble has undoubtedly frenzied her. Fool that I was to
lay up the insult of one that sorrow and excitement had
bereft of reason and responsibility! 'Twere better I should
retire at once, and leave her to herself," and the young
man slowly retreated toward the door.

But at this moment there were alarming symptoms of
distress in the window-curtain; and the major paused as a
voice from its dimity depths said plaintively, "And *you* are
going without forgiving me!"

"Forgive *you*, Mistress Thankful," said the major, strid-
ing to the curtain, and seizing a little hand that was obtruded from its folds,—"forgive you? rather can you
forgive me for the folly—the cruelty of mistaking—of
—of"—and here the major, hitherto famous for facile compliments, utterly broke down. But the hand he held was
no longer cold, but warm and intelligent; and in default
of coherent speech he held fast by that as the thread of
his discourse, until Mistress Thankful quietly withdrew it,
thanked him for his forgiveness, and retired deeper behind
the curtain.

When he had gone, she threw herself in a chair, and
again gave way to a passionate flood of tears. In the last
twenty-four hours her pride had been utterly humbled: the
independent spirit of this self-willed little beauty had met
for the first time with defeat. When she had got over
her womanly shock at the news of the sham baron's death,
she had, I fear, only a selfish regard at his taking off;
believing that if living he would in some way show the world
—which just then consisted of the headquarters and Major
Van Zandt—that he had really made love to her, and possibly did honorably love her still, and might yet give her
an opportunity to reject him. And now he was dead, and
she was held up to the world as the conceited plaything of
a fine gentleman's masquerading sport. That her father's
cupidity and ambition made him sanction the imposture,

in her bitterness she never doubted. No! Lover, friend, father—all had been false to her, and the only kindness she had received was from the men she had wantonly insulted. Poor little Blossom! indeed, a most premature Blossom; I fear a most unthankful Blossom, sitting there shivering in the first chill wind of adversity, rocking backward and forward, with the skirt of her dimity short-gown over her shoulders, and her little buckled shoes and clocked stockings pathetically crossed before her.

But healthy youth is re-active; and in an hour or two Thankful was down at the cow-shed, with her arms around the neck of her favorite heifer, to whom she poured out much of her woes, and from whom she won an intelligent sort of slobbering sympathy. And then she sharply scolded Cæsar for nothing at all, and a moment after returned to the house with the air and face of a deeply injured angel, who had been disappointed in some celestial idea of setting this world right, but was still not above forgiveness,—a spectacle that sunk Major Van Zandt into the dark depths of remorse, and eventually sent him to smoke a pipe of Virginia with his men in the roadside camp; seeing which, Thankful went early to bed, and cried herself to sleep. And Nature possibly followed her example; for at sunset a great thaw set in, and by midnight the freed rivers and brooks were gurgling melodiously, and tree and shrub and fence were moist and dripping.

The red dawn at last struggled through the vaporous veil that hid the landscape. Then occurred one of those magical changes peculiar to the climate, yet perhaps pre-eminently notable during that historic winter and spring. By ten o'clock on that 3d of May, 1780, a fervent June-like sun had rent that vaporous veil, and poured its direct rays upon the gaunt and haggard profile of the Jersey hills. The chilled soil responded but feebly to that kiss; perhaps a few of the willows that yellowed the river-banks took on a deeper color. But the country folk were certain that spring had come at last; and even the correct and self-sustained Major Van Zandt came running in to announce to Mistress Thankful that one of his men had seen a violet in the meadow. In another moment Mistress Thankful had donned her cloak and pattens to view this firstling of the laggard summer. It was quite natural that Major Van Zandt should accompany her as she tripped on; and so, without a thought of their past differences, they ran like very children down the moist and rocky slope that led to the quaggy meadow. Such was the influence of the vernal season.

But the violets were hidden. Mistress Thankful, regardless of the wet leaves and her new gown, groped with her fingers among the withered grasses. Major Van Zandt leaned against a bowlder, and watched her with admiring eyes.

"You'll never find flowers that way," she said at last, looking up to him impatiently. "Go down on your knees like an honest man. There are some things in this world worth stooping for."

The major instantly dropped on his knees beside her. But at that moment Mistress Thankful found her posies, and rose to her feet. "Stay where you are," she said mischievously, as she stooped down, and placed a flower in the lapel of his coat. "That is to make amends for my rudeness. Now get up."

But the major did not rise. He caught the two little hands that had seemed to flutter like birds against his breast, and, looking up into the laughing face above him, said, "Dear Mistress Thankful, dare I remind you of your own words, that 'there be some things worth stooping for'? Think of my love, Mistress Thankful, as a flower,—mayhap not as gracious to you as your violets, but as honest and —and—and—as—"

"Ready to spring up in a single night," laughed Thankful. "But no; get up, major! What would the fine ladies of Morristown say of your kneeling at the feet of a country girl,—the play and sport of every fine gentleman? What if Mistress Bolton should see her own cavalier, the modish Major Van Zandt, proffering his affections to the disgraced sweetheart of a perjured traitor? Leave go my hand, I pray you, major,—if you respect—"

She was free, yet she faltered a moment beside him, with tears quivering on her long brown lashes. Then she said tremulously, "Rise up, major. Let us think no more of this. I pray you forgive me, if I have again been rude."

The major struggled to rise to his feet. But he could not. And then I regret to have to record that the fact became obvious that one of his shapely legs was in a bog-hole, and that he was perceptibly sinking out of sight. Whereat Mistress Thankful trilled out a three-syllabled laugh, looked demure and painfully concerned at his condition, and then laughed again. The major joined in her mirth, albeit his face was crimson. And then, with a little cry of alarm, she flew to his side, and put her arms around him.

"Keep away, keep away, for Heaven's sake, Mistress Blossom," he said quickly, "or I shall plunge you into my mishap, and make you as ridiculous as myself."

But the quick-witted girl had already leaped to an adjacent bowlder. "Take off your sash," she said quickly; "fasten it to your belt, and throw it to me." He did so. She straightened herself back on the rock. "Now, all together," she cried, with a preliminary strain on the sash; and then the cords of her well-trained muscles stood out on her rounded arms, and, with a long pull and a strong pull and a pull all together, she landed the major upon the rock. And then she laughed; and then, inconsistent as it may appear, she became grave, and at once proceeded to scrape him off, and rub him down with dried leaves, with fern-twigs, with her handkerchief, with the border of her mantle, as if he were a child, until he blushed with alternate shame and secret satisfaction.

They spoke but little on their return to the farm-house, for Mistress Thankful had again become grave. And yet the sun shone cheerily above them; the landscape was filled with the joy of resurrection and new and awakened life; the breeze whispered gentle promises of hope, and the fruition of their hopes in the summer to come. And these two fared on until they reached the porch, with a half-pleased, half-frightened consciousness that they were not the same beings who had left it a half-hour before.

Nevertheless at the porch Mistress Thankful regained something of her old audacity. As they stood together in the hall, she handed him back the sash she had kept with her. As she did so, she could not help saying, "There are some things worth stooping for, Major Van Zandt."

But she had not calculated upon the audacity of the man; and as she turned to fly she was caught by his strong arm, and pinioned to his side. She struggled, honestly I think, and perhaps more frightened at her own feelings than at his strength; but it is to be recorded that he kissed her in a moment of comparative yielding, and then, frightened himself, released her quickly, whereat she fled to her room, and threw herself panting and troubled upon her bed. For an hour or two she lay there, with flushed cheeks and conflicting thoughts. "He must never kiss me again," she said softly to herself, "unless"—but the interrupting thought said, "I shall die if he kiss me not again; and I never can kiss another." And then she was roused by a footstep upon the stair, which in that brief time she had learned to know and look for, and a knock at the door. She opened it to Major Van Zandt, white and so colorless as to bring out once more the faint red line made by her riding-whip two days before, as if it had risen again in accusation. The blood dropped out of her cheeks as she gazed at him in silence.

"An escort of dragoons," said Major Van Zandt slowly, and with military precision, "has just arrived, bringing with them one Capt. Allan Brewster, of the Connecticut Contingent, on his way to Morristown to be tried for mutiny and treason. A private note from Col. Hamilton instructs me to allow him to have a private audience with you—if *you* so wish it."

With a woman's swift and too often hopeless intuition, Thankful knew that this was not the sole contents of the letter, and that her relations with Capt. Brewster were known to the man before her. But she drew herslf up a little proudly, and, turning her truthful eyes upon the major, said, "I *do* so wish it."

"It shall be done as you desire, Mistress Blossom," returned the officer with cold politeness, as he turned upon his heel.

"One moment, Major Van Zandt," said Thankful swiftly.

The major turned quickly; but Thankful's eyes were gazing thoughtfully forward, and scarcely glanced at him. "I would prefer," she said timidly and hesitatingly, "that this interview should not take place under the roof where—where—where—my father lives. Half-way down the meadow there is a barn, and before it a broken part of the wall, fronting on a sycamore-tree. *He* will know where it is. Tell him I will see him there in half an hour."

A smile, which the major had tried to make a careless one, curled his lip satirically as he bowed in reply. "It is the first time," he said dryly, "that I believe I have been honored with arranging a tryst for two lovers; but believe me, Mistress Thankful, I will do my best. In half an hour I will turn my prisoner over to you."

In half an hour the punctual Mistress Thankful, with a hood hiding her pale face, passed the officer in the hall, on the way to her rendezvous. An hour later Cæsar came with a message that Mistress Thankful would like to see him. When the major entered the sitting-room, he was shocked to find her lying pale and motionless on the sofa; but as the door closed she rose to her feet, and confronted him.

"I do not know," she said slowly, "whether you are aware that the man I just now parted from was for a twelve-month past my sweetheart, and that I believed I loved him, and *knew* I was true to him. If you have not heard it, I tell you now, for the time will come when you will hear part of it from the lips of others, and I would rather you should take the whole truth from mine. This man was false to me. He betrayed two friends of mine as spies. I could have forgiven it, had it been only foolish jealousy; but it was, I have since learned from his own lips, only that he might gratify his spite against the commander-in-chief by procuring their arrest, and making a serious difficulty in the American camp, by means of which he hoped to serve his own ends. He told me this, believing that I sympathized with him in his hatred of the commander-in-chief, and in his own wrongs and sufferings. I confess to my shame, Major Van Zandt, that two days ago I did believe him, and that I looked upon you as a mere catch-poll or bailiff of the tyrant. That I found out how I was deceived when I saw the commander-in-chief, you, major, who know him so well, need not be told. Nor was it necessary for me to tell this man that he had deceived me: for I felt that—that—was—not—the—only reason—why I could no longer return—his love."

She paused, as the major approached her earnestly, and waved him back with her hand. "He reproached me bitterly with my want of feeling for his misfortunes," she went on again: "he recalled my past protestations; he showed me my love-letters; and he told me that if I were still his true sweetheart I ought to help him. I told him if he would never call me by that name again; if he would give up all claim to me; if he would never speak, write to me, nor see me again; if he would hand me back my letters,—I would help him." She stopped: the blood rushed into her pale face. "You will remember, major, that I accepted this man's love as a young, foolish, trustful girl; but when I made him this offer—he—he accepted it."

"The dog!" said Major Van Zandt. "But in what way could you help this double traitor?"

"I *have* helped him," said Thankful quietly.

"But how?" said Major Van Zandt.

"By becoming a traitor myself," she said, turning upon him almost fiercely. "Hear me! While you were quietly pacing these halls, while your men were laughing and talking in the road, Cæsar was saddling my white mare, the fleetest in the country. He led her to the lane below. That mare is now two miles away, with Capt. Brewster on her back. Why do you not start, major? Look at me. *I* am a traitor, and this is my bribe;" and she drew a package of letters from her bosom, and flung them on the table.

She had been prepared for an outbreak or exclamation from the man before her, but not for his cold silence. "Speak," she cried at last, passionately. "Speak! Open your lips, if only to curse me! Order in your men to arrest me. I will proclaim myself guilty, and save your honor. But only speak!"

"May I ask," said Major Van Zandt coldly, "why you have twice honored me with a blow?"

"Because I loved you; because, when I first saw you I

saw the only man that was my master, and I rebelled; because, when I found I could not help but love you, I knew I never had loved before, and I would wipe out with one stroke all the past that rose in judgment against me; because I would not have you ever confronted with one endearing word of mine that was not meant for you."

Major Van Zandt turned from the window where he had stood, and faced the girl with sad resignation. "If I have in my foolishness, Mistress Thankful, shown you how great was your power over me, when you descended to this artifice to spare my feelings by confessing your own love for me, you should have remembered that you were doing that which forever kept me from wooing or winning you. If you had really loved me your heart, as a woman's, would have warned you against that which my heart, as a gentleman's, has made a law of honor; when I tell you, as much for the sake of relieving your own conscience as for the sake of justifying mine, that if this man, a traitor, my prisoner, and your recognized lover, had escaped from my custody without your assistance, connivance, or even knowledge, I should have deemed it my duty to forsake you until I caught him, even if we had been standing before the altar."

Thankful heard him, but only as a strange voice in the distance, as she stood with fixed eyes, and breathless, parted lips before him. Yet even then I fear that, womanlike, she did not comprehend his rhetoric of honor, but only caught here and there a dull, benumbing idea that he despised her, and that in her effort to win his love she had killed it, and ruined him forever.

"If you think it strange," continued the major, "that, believing as I do, I stand here only to utter moral axioms when my duty calls me to pursue your lover, I beg you to believe that it is only for your sake. I wish to allow a reasonable time between your interview with him, and his escape, that shall save you from any suspicion of complicity. Do not think," he added with a sad smile, as the girl made an impatient step toward him, "do not think I am running any risk. The man cannot escape. A cordon of pickets surrounds the camp for many miles. He has not the countersign, and his face and crime are known."

"Yes," said Thankful eagerly, "but a part of his own regiment guards the Baskingridge road."

"How know you this?" said the major, seizing her hand.

"He told me."

Before she could fall on her knees, and beg his forgiveness, he had darted from the room, given an order, and returned with cheeks and eyes blazing.

"Hear me," he said rapidly, taking the girl's two hands, "you know not what you've done. I forgive you. But this is no longer a matter of duty, but my personal honor. I shall pursue this man alone. I shall return with him, or not at all. Farewell. God bless you!"

But before he reached the door she caught him again. "Only say you have forgiven me once more."

"I do."

"Guert!"

There was something in the girl's voice more than this first utterance of his Christian name, that made him pause.

"I told—a—lie—just—now. There is a fleeter horse in the stable than my mare; 'tis the roan filly in the second stall."

"God bless you!"

He was gone. She waited to hear the clatter of his horse's hoofs in the roadway. When Cæsar came in a few moments later, to tell the news of Capt. Brewster's escape, the room was empty; but it was soon filled again by a dozen turbulent troopers.

"Of course she's gone," said Sergeant Tibbitts: "the jade flew with the captain."

"Ay, 'tis plain enough. Two horses are gone from the stable besides the major's," said Private Hicks.

Nor was this military criticism entirely a private one. When the courier arrived at headquarters the next morning, it was to bring the report that Mistress Thankful Blossom, after assisting her lover to escape had fled with him. "The renegade is well off our hands," said Gen. Sullivan gruffly: "he has saved us the public disgrace of a trial. But this is bad news of Major Van Zandt."

"What news of the major?" asked Washington quickly.

"He pursued the vagabond as far as Springfield, killing

his horse, and falling himself insensible before Major
Merton's quarters. Here he became speedily delirious,
fever supervened, and the regimental surgeon, after a careful examination, pronounced his case one of small-pox."

A whisper of horror and pity went around the room.
"Another gallant soldier, who should have died leading a
charge, laid by the heels by a beggar's filthy distemper,"
growled Sullivan. "Where will it end?"

"God knows," said Hamilton. "Poor Van Zandt! But
whither was he sent,—to the hospital?"

"No: a special permit was granted in his case; and 'tis
said he was removed to the Blossom Farm,—it being remote
from neighbors,—and the house placed under quarantine.
Abner Blossom has prudently absented himself from the
chances of infection, and the daughter has fled. The sick
man is attended only by a black servant and an ancient
crone; so that, if the poor major escapes with his life or
without disfigurement, pretty Mistress Bolton of Morristown need not be scandalized or jealous."

V

THE ancient crone alluded to in the last chapter had
been standing behind the window-curtains of that bedroom
which had been Thankful Blossom's in the weeks gone by.
She did not move her head, but stood looking demurely,
after the manner of ancient crones, over the summer landscape. For the summer had come before the tardy spring
was scarce gone, and the elms before the window no longer
lisped, but were eloquent in the softest zephyrs. There was
the flash of birds in among the bushes, the occasional droning
of bees in and out the open window, and a perpetually
swinging censer of flower incense rising from below. The
farm had put on its gayest bridal raiment; and looking at
the old farm-house shadowed with foliage and green with
creeping vines, it was difficult to conceive that snow had
ever lain on its porches, or icicles swung from its mossy
eaves.

"Thankful!" said a voice still tremulous with weakness.

The ancient crone turned, drew aside the curtains, and showed the sweet face of Thankful Blossom, more beautiful even in its paleness.

"Come here, darling," repeated the voice.

Thankful stepped to the sofa whereon lay the convalescent Major Van Zandt.

"Tell me, sweetheart," said the major, taking her hand in his, "when you married me, as you told the chaplain, that you might have the right to nurse me, did you never think that if death spared me I might be so disfigured that even you, dear love, would have turned from me with loathing?"

"That was why I did it, dear," said Thankful mischievously. "I knew that the pride, and the sense of honor, and self-devotion of some people, would have kept them from keeping their promises to a poor girl."

"But, darling," continued the major, raising her hand to his lips, "suppose the case had been reversed: suppose you had taken the disease, that I had recovered without disfigurement, but that this sweet face—"

"I thought of that too," interrupted Thankful.

"Well, what would you have done, dear?" said the major, with his old mischievous smile.

"I should have died," said Thankful gravely.

"But how?"

"Somehow. But you are to go to sleep, and not ask impertinent and frivolous questions; for father is coming to-morrow."

"Thankful, dear, do you know what the trees and the birds said to me as I lay there tossing with fever?"

"No, dear."

"Thankful Blossom! Thankful Blossom! Thankful Blossom is coming!"

"Do you know what I said, sweetheart, as I lifted your dear head from the ground when you reeled from your horse just as I overtook you at Springfield?"

"No, dear."

"There are some things in life worth stooping for."

And she winged this Parthian arrow home with a kiss.